Kate Solly is a writer, mother of six and really quite good at getting the bubbles out of plastic book wrap. While most of her time is spent finding lost shoes and investigating what's making the car smell bad, Kate frequently escapes to write entertaining things. She has penned many articles, columns and reviews for various publications and is the author of *Tuesday Evenings with the Copeton Craft Resistance*. When she is not writing, she enjoys starting crochet projects and never finishing them.

PRAISE FOR KATE SOLLY'S
THE PARADISE HEIGHTS CRAFT STORE STITCH-UP

'A cosy detective story about craft and craftiness, told with heart and humour – the perfect pick-me-up and beach read all in one.' – Sophie Green

'Warm, witty and wise – Kate Solly is the balm for a bruised world.' – Josephine Moon

'Move over, Miss Marple. Fleck Parker is here! Be prepared to snort-laugh your way through this funny and unpredictable mystery by the charming Kate Solly.' – Kerryn Mayne

'Kate Solly has penned a delightful cosy crime for those who want mystery and intrigue in a feel-good package. Her main character is so relatable you'll feel like you're reading about your best friend.' – Rachael Johns

'Kate Solly's effervescent storytelling and cast of eclectic characters kept me delighted and intrigued from the first word to the very last.' – Rhianna King

'Another gloriously tangled yarn from Kate Solly, who's fast establishing herself as Australia's champion author of craft-centric fiction! Solly mashes up the invisible load of motherhood with a cosy crime as impossible to put down as a baby smeared with squashed banana. Solly brings a light touch and warm heart to some complex and dark themes.' – Clare Fletcher

'A delightfully modern mystery for anyone who knows what it's like to feel invisible. Once again, Kate Solly weaves serious themes into an astute tapestry of heart, humour and a cast of gloriously unique characters … A beautifully crafted cosy crime that will charm, delight and keep you guessing. I'll be first in line for a sequel.' – Jane Tara

'Kate Solly is back with a warm, funny and deliciously tangled cosy crime. I loved it to pieces!' – Emma Grey

PRAISE FOR KATE SOLLY'S *TUESDAY EVENINGS WITH THE COPETON CRAFT RESISTANCE*

'Joyous, warm and utterly charming – I smiled for days.' – Toni Jordan

'Warm, funny and big-hearted, Kate Solly stitches together a cast of characters here who will restore your faith in people power.' – Cate Kennedy

'Kate Solly's debut novel is certainly big-hearted feel-good fiction with larger-than-life characters.' – *The Age* and *The Sydney Morning Herald*

'This charming story is a fun read with a deeper message. Resistance has to start somewhere and small gestures can have a big impact. With engaging characters and some sharp observations about modern Australia, it's both entertaining and enlightening.' – *Good Reading*

'A sharp, witty, clever but kind observation of our society, told via the multiple points of view of an irresistibly interesting and diverse collection of characters.' – Living Arts Canberra

'If you feel in the mood for a fun bit of escapism, I highly recommend Kate Solly's debut, *Tuesday Evenings with the Copeton Craft Resistance*.' – Meredith Jaffé

'*Tuesday Evenings with the Copeton Craft Resistance* is funny, charming and will keep you turning the pages. Heck, it might even have you reaching for your crochet hook.' – *The AU Review*

'A fantastic debut novel from Kate Solly. She brings these characters together, with their intentions, flaws and insecurities, in what had me turning page after page, unable to put it down.' – Tara Marlow

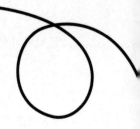

To Mum and Dad
For always listening to my stories

affirm
press

First published by Affirm Press in 2025
Bunurong/Boon Wurrung Country
28 Thistlethwaite Street
South Melbourne VIC 3205
affirmpress.com.au

10 9 8 7 6 5 4 3 2 1

Affirm Press is located on the unceded land of the Bunurong/Boon Wurrung
peoples of the Kulin Nation. Affirm Press pays respect to their Elders past and
present.

 A catalogue record for this
book is available from the
National Library of Australia

ISBN: 9781923022249 (paperback)

Cover design by Karen Wallis © Affirm Press
Author photograph by Darren James
Typeset in Adobe Garamond Pro by J&M Typesetting
Proudly printed and bound in Australia by the Opus Group

The
Paradise Heights
CRAFT STORE
STITCH-UP

KATE SOLLY

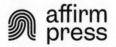
affirm
press

CHAPTER ONE

They were going to be on time today. Fleck just knew it. She finally had a system. Sam's school uniform and Norah's kinder clothes had been laid out the night before. They were both awake and eating breakfast. Sam's hair was brushed. Alice was also awake and painting herself with toast fingers in her highchair. Library bags were packed and she had even remembered to clean both the lunch boxes.

It was when she was tying Norah's hair into two neat plaits that things started to go wrong.

'I can't find my other shoe,' said Sam.

'I'm sure it's there. We laid it out, remember?'

'It's not here.'

'It's not a shoe.' This was Norah chiming in.

'Check under the couch.'

'Nope.'

'Are you sure it's not there? Did you check all around?'

'Yep.'

'It's not a shoe.' Norah again.

'Well, did you move it?'

'Nope.'

'Well, where can it be?'

'Are you cross, Mummy?'

'No. No, I'm not cross. I'm just confused. Why did the shoe decide to go off on a holiday by itself?'

'You're funny, Mummy.'

'Okay, Norah, that's your hair done. I'm going to put the lunches together. Sam, you keep looking for your shoe.'

'*It's not a shoe!*'

Fleck began loading the two lunch boxes with sandwiches and snacks. The fruit bowl was bare, despite having been full yesterday, but Fleck had a backup plan: she reached into the pantry, took out a Vita-Weat box and shook out two mandarins.

Norah's eyes lit up at the sight of the two pieces of fruit. 'I want a mandy!'

'No, Norah. We need these for kinder and school. You can have one for your fruit break.'

'I want a mandy NOW!'

'These are the only ones left. They need to go in the lunch boxes.'

'You go to the fruit shop.'

'There's no time. I'll get some more later, but we have to go to school soon.' Why was she having this conversation? Why was she negotiating fruit shortages with a three-year-old?

Alice, sitting happily in the highchair, made a noise that could only mean one thing.

'Sounds like it's nappy-change time for you, young lady!'

Fleck had just finished applying the nappy cream when she heard a colossal crash from the family room. She quickly placed Alice in the cot for safekeeping and rushed to the scene of the crime. It wasn't as bad as it had sounded. Sam, while vigorously searching for his lost shoe, had toppled a basket of clean washing over the floor. Matthew's business shirts and Alice's bunny-rugs lay unfurled across the floorboards. It was a mess, but that wasn't the main problem.

'*Norah!*'

A picture of innocence, the small child sat primly at the table in her favourite Batman t-shirt. She gazed back at her mother with her enormous brown eyes, blinked her impossibly long lashes and continued to clumsily peel one of the mandarins. 'I'm hungry,' she said, stone-faced.

'No.' Fleck lifted Norah out of her chair and placed her at her original place at the table in front of her half-finished breakfast. 'If you're hungry, you can finish your toast.'

'NOOOOOOO!' Norah stormed out of the room.

Fleck gazed forlornly at the half-peeled mandarin. There was already a small bite mark in one of the segments. Now what was she going to pack for fruit break? Did she have time to cut carrot sticks? Norah wouldn't eat them, but at least Fleck would look like she'd made an effort.

'Mummy!' Sam said. 'I still can't find my shoe! It isn't anywhere!'

Fleck opened the fridge and peered into the veggie drawer. 'Just keep looking.'

The carrots in the fridge were pretty sad. But what if she finished peeling the mandarin and broke it up? She could put the unbitten segments in one of those little containers from the plastics cupboard. Done!

She was on her hands and knees digging into the back of the cupboard when it struck her: things were a little too quiet. All she could hear was Alice babbling and giggling in the next room. Where was Norah?

'I can't go to school with no shoes on!' Sam stood in her path, bouncing from foot to foot.

Fleck stepped quickly around him. 'Hold on a minute.'

Norah and Alice were sitting side by side in Alice's cot. Alice's skin was white as snow. She gazed haughtily up at her mother like some tiny French aristocrat while Norah *continued to apply zinc cream to her chubby arms and legs*. Norah, meanwhile, had at some point liberated her plaits from their restraints. She doggedly persisted in her costume design pursuits beneath a frenzied halo of red hair.

'*Norah!*'

Norah shot her a defiant glare. 'Alice is Mr Freeze.'

Fleck cocked an eyebrow. 'Naughty step.'

They were already running behind. Three minutes on the naughty step for Norah would throw them out even more, but it had to be done.

Alice, who had been enjoying her stint as the Crown Prince of Chilblains, did not take kindly to the warm face washer. Fleck soon discovered that lotions designed to repel moisture were near impossible to wash off. It was 8.49am. Fleck hunted for a long-sleeved onesie in the laundry, the nappy bag and the upstairs chest of drawers, then zipped Alice's still mostly white limbs into it. Nobody needed to know.

Sam stood at the door, looking to be near tears. 'I don't have any more places to look. I can't find my shoe!'

Fleck looked at her son. Something clicked into place. 'It's not a shoe,' she murmured under her breath.

'What?'

'Hang on a minute, Sam.' With Alice on her hip, Fleck strode across to the step where Norah was perched. She crouched down to look her in the eye, ignoring the loud popping sound her left knee made.

'Norah, where is Sam's shoe?'

'You can't talk to me. I'm on the naughty step.'

'Is it not a shoe?'

'Not. A. Shoe,' Norah repeated emphatically.

'Then what is it?'

'Batmobile.'

'Batmobile?'

Norah gave a firm nod. Fleck stood up and walked to the toy box. Inside it was Sam's shoe. Inside Sam's shoe was Batman, looking coolly impressed with himself in his new black leather vehicle.

It was 8.58am – well past time to go.

Technically, having a coffee at George's Kitchen was supposed to be her reward for a successfully executed school run. Fleck often set up systems of reminders and rewards to coax her brain to focus on boring things. But it didn't always work. On mornings like today, when they'd stumbled in after the bell with Sam before dropping Norah off late at kinder, her hair in a messy bun, Fleck still went to the cafe. The thing was, she *needed* the coffee more on the mornings when she'd failed. And it all came down to how she defined success, really. Were all three children alive? Yes? Were they naked? No? Job done. Strong latte, please.

George was busy with some takeaway orders as Fleck slipped into the cafe and set Alice's capsule down at her favourite corner table. While she waited, she got out her exercise book, in which she'd been nutting out her morning routine. Fleck carried an exercise book around with her for to-do lists and meal plans and drafts of notes and random thoughts. She called it her 'everything book'. She examined her nightly to-do list now. Having clothes laid out the night before had worked well, but next time she should put the shoes out of reach. And the zinc cream out of reach. And the rare lunch-box items out of reach.

George placed Fleck's coffee on the table. 'I've got one for you.'

'Ooh! What is it?'

'There are four countries in the world that have only one vowel. Can you name them all?'

'Ooh, that's a tough one,' Fleck said. Then, 'Chad!'

'Chad is one. Can you name the rest?'

'Give me a minute.'

She flipped the page over and started scratching out answers to the riddle. This was far more interesting than the morning routine. As she scoured her memory, made lists and turned the problem around in her head, she felt her brain slip into that sweet spot. This was a good puzzle.

If there was one thing that Fleck Parker loved, it was a puzzle to solve. She wasn't fussy. Sometimes it was the codebreaker in the Sunday paper. Sometimes it was the Friday cryptic. Sometimes she even pulled out a maths textbook and brushed up on logarithmic functions. But it was never the word finds or sudokus, or the one where you had to guess the song from all the little sound bites. Okay, maybe she *was* fussy.

'This is hard,' Fleck announced. George had returned to the counter and was making his own morning coffee. 'Niue has only four letters but three of them are vowels!'

'Niue's not a country!'

A new knot of patrons arrived. George always maintained that making himself a coffee was like a rain dance for attracting customers. As he took their orders, Fleck continued to play with the problem. She stayed away from South America. They all seemed to have vowel-heavy names. Was it some obscure Caribbean country like Saint Kitts and Nevis? She'd be in trouble if it was.

'Egypt!' Fleck exclaimed.

'Egypt is another,' George said as he passed a tray of takeaway cups to a portly man in a suit.

Alice stirred in her capsule but slept on. Fleck continued to scribble in the margin of the page. 'Does "Czech" count? As in "Czech Republic"?'

'Have you ever heard anyone call that country "Czech" by itself? No. Czech Republic does not count. I think it's Czechia now anyway.'

'Ugh.' This was hard. It was delicious, but it was hard. Of course, her phone was right there. She could easily just google a list of the world's countries. But she didn't want to. She knew she could solve this herself, even if it took some time. But she would take a break from it for now. She stored it carefully away in her mind to play with later. Then she grabbed the newspaper from another table.

This was definitely the best table in the small cafe. In this seat, with her back to the wall, Fleck could chat to George and easily look out both windows. On her right was busy Highett Road, with its trucks, buses and occasional tram, and straight ahead was the smaller Peppercorn Street – with its collection of shops, their racks out on the footpath – which real estate agents loved to describe as having a 'village feel'.

Fleck flipped forward to the puzzles page of the paper. She snapped a photo of the crosswords and brainteasers to look at later. They weren't the supreme Friday crossword, but they were still worth a look. Sometimes she would get obsessed with a particular type – acrostics or nonograms, say – and spend every spare moment on it until she had completely mastered the form, after which it was too easy and she became sick of it. Then she would abandon it entirely for a new obsession.

It was like her brain was constantly itching for the perfect problem to solve, when her brain clicked into rhythm. She became completely absorbed, investigating, turning things over. The perfect problem was rare, but it was *wonderful*.

She flipped back to the front of the paper and started reading the news. The second wave of takeaway orders dwindled away. Fleck was now the only customer in the cafe.

'Quiz?' George called.

'Quiz!' Fleck rifled through the pages to find today's twenty-five questions.

Doing the quiz was another rain dance for making customers arrive, but today they managed to make it through the one-point and two-point sections without interruption. Fleck was preparing to read out the first of the three-point questions ('Which Australian capital city was once known as Palmerston?') when George narrowed his eyes and squinted across the road – the big road, that was – at the new cafe.

'What is their story?' he muttered. He strode out from behind the counter to get a better look through the window. Fleck followed his gaze.

'Five staff on and zero customers. Look: there are five! And they've had a full roster since seven! Who puts all their staff on that early? I do not understand their logic.'

It was true. The cafe across Highett Road was bustling, but not with customers. Staff in aprons straightened signs, dusted counters and paced around empty tables. Meanwhile, Fleck knew the answer to the question. It was Darwin.

George shook his head slowly. 'They are a textbook case on how not to run a cafe. I really feel like I should go over and give them some advice. And they should have gone with a different name. "Espresso 312"? Not very creative!'

'Well, the other cafe is *too* creative.' Fleck gestured at the large cafe on the other side of Peppercorn Street. 'It's like they went through a multi-step process to arrive at "dangermouse". Step one – find an obscure nostalgic reference. Step two – make it all one word. Step three – remove any capital letters. Step four – open your brand-new edgy cafe.'

George chuckled and shook his head. 'Yes, because opening a cafe is definitely that simple. I'm going to think up some new names for them. Stay tuned.' He walked back to take a tray of croissants off the counter and slotted them into the display fridge. He shot another look at the cafe across the road as he straightened. 'But look at them! I definitely want to give those new guys some advice. It's driving me crazy watching them make such simple mistakes.'

Fleck laughed. 'Don't give them advice! They're the competition! You're too nice, George.' Palmerston changed its name to Darwin in – when was it? 1911? 1912? – after Federation, anyway. It was when the Northern Territory was transferred to the Commonwealth. Before that, it was all part of South Australia. They needed to get back to the quiz so that she could show off.

George smiled. 'I'm not stressed about their competition just yet. Yesterday they didn't open until ten. And they left their deliveries just sitting there on the doorstep for almost an hour! That's very unprofessional.'

George put his hands on his hips. He was a large man with a neatly trimmed beard. His black hair was not yet turning grey, even though he must have been in his fifties. 'You'd think, with that many people on, they could get someone to fix that graffiti. That's been there all week!' He gestured to the side of the cafe where a large tag in a dull purple scrawl defaced the bricks. 'I'm going to call the council on them. You can't leave graffiti up. You have to nip it in the butt.'

Bud, Fleck thought. *You nip things in the bud. Like flowers on a basil plant.* Fleck only ever corrected people's grammar in her mind. This was the best policy for maintaining friendships. Anyway, 'nip in the butt' was funnier. She pictured George in his apron, with massive lobster claws instead of arms, chasing a hapless graffiti artist who was covering his backside in fear.

The bell jangled. More customers! Fleck sighed. No more quiz today. At least they'd made it through most of the questions. Plus, it was time she got going. She packed up her things and carried her cup over to the counter. George rang up her purchase.

Fleck tapped her card on the side of the reader. It beeped. 'Cyprus!' she exclaimed.

George beamed. 'Cyprus,' he confirmed. 'I'll see you soon.'

CHAPTER TWO

Fleck had become used to the facial expression people made when she told them her job was being a stay-at-home mum: a benign smile, a blink and then an almost imperceptible withdrawal from the conversation. Even as the other person delivered platitudes like 'it's the hardest job in the world' and 'my hat goes off to you', their eyes were surreptitiously scanning the room for somebody more important to talk to.

She was hoping things might be different now that Sam had started school. School would provide new friends, new social activities. Perhaps now Fleck would no longer feel so adrift as a mother, like she was making it up as she went along. Perhaps this was what she needed for things to click into place. It had only been a couple of weeks so far, but Fleck looked forward to the effects kicking in.

Tuesday's morning routine was easier. The mornings when she didn't have to get Norah ready for kinder were always easier. They were on time. Fleck needed to make the most of it. She was going to Connect With The Other Parents. Today she would make an effort. After all, Fleck was much more likely to remember what day Casual Clothes Day was or what brand of art smock she was expected to buy if she had some school parents she could exchange friendly texts with.

Sam and the other preps still looked so tiny compared to the other kids at school as they all filed in through the gates. Dwarfed by his schoolbag, he walked down the hill to his classroom ahead of Fleck. Most of the children at Our Holy Redeemer Primary, Paradise Heights, had come from the two larger kindergartens, so Sam – who had gone to the small community kinder on the other side of Musbrooke Highway – was on his own. Within days of starting school, however, he had befriended a little boy named Joseph.

Fleck hadn't met Joseph's mum yet, so she kept an eye out for her. She imagined a tall African lady with braided hair. Somebody effortlessly stylish. Perhaps she should have Joseph over for a play. Or were playdates just a kinder thing?

Fleck had been trying her best, but she wasn't great at keeping track of all the school parents so far. She had only just worked out that the woman with chin-length blonde hair and sunglasses was in fact *three* different women. They just looked very similar to each other. Now, whenever one of them approached, Fleck scrabbled desperately around for distinguishing features. *Which child is she with? What dog is that?* And there were two dads who she'd thought were the same person too, except one was tall and the other was short. But they were both called 'Paul' anyway, so she could get away with confusing them.

A cluster of mums, dads, grandparents and other carers stood chatting around the bag hooks outside the classroom door. Sam ran past them to join a group of older boys who were playing with a basketball. Fleck drew a deep breath and sidled in as casually as she could. They were discussing a TV show.

'Cynthia's going to get voted out soon, I just know it.'

'I don't know. She's pretty sneaky. She's playing the long game. I don't trust her.'

'But did you see what Lachlan did in the immunity challenge?'

'I could not believe that. Ugh. I hate Lachlan.'

'Lachlan? I love Lachlan! He's my favourite!'

Fleck smiled brightly and nodded along. She had never seen an episode of the TV show in question. A man with a scruffy beard responded to this. Milo's dad.

'Yeah, I like Lachlan too. But he's gone and aligned himself with Fiona, which is a mistake, I think. He's going to regret that.'

'Do you think he has the hots for her?'

'Nah. He's just being strategic. But it's a mistake.'

Fleck would probably have to watch a few episodes of this show before her next on-time school run. She should put it on her to-do list. And also find out what the show is called. For now, she could bluff.

'Definitely a mistake,' she piped in.

The tall brunette, Will's mum, pursed her lips and frowned. 'Why do you think it's a mistake?' she demanded.

Fleck hesitated. 'Because, well, *Fiona*,' she said, with what she hoped was a significant nod.

Will's mum narrowed her eyes. Then she nodded. 'Exactly. *Exactly.*'

Fleck grinned. Then she got cocky. 'And how about that immunisation challenge?'

Milo's dad looked confused. 'Immunity challenge?'

'Oh. Um. Yeah. Immunity. Immunity challenge. Yeah. Except I think they should do an immunisation challenge for their immunity challenge. Everybody gets assigned a cranky baby and an angry toddler and they have to queue up at the Maternal and Child Health nurse for measles shots. *Lachlan* wouldn't last five minutes.'

This didn't garner much reaction from the parents. Milo's dad seemed to shrug, but not with his shoulders. He shrugged with one corner of his mouth. Was that a good thing? Was she in? Sam, meanwhile, was running around the group of Grade Two boys with their ball. He thought he was playing with them. They seemed unaware of this fact.

One of the prep mums emerged from the classroom. She was tall and slim, with vivid turquoise hair piled on her head. Her eyes were also a vivid blue-green. She wore a long, classic trench coat over what looked like a 1940s silk nightgown. She paused at the display of cellophane jellyfish, pulled out her phone and jabbed at it. Then she reached into one of her large coat pockets, pulled out a piece of crochet work and started hooking. There would be no danger of Fleck ever confusing this woman with anybody else.

'Anyway, I just think Cynthia's days are numbered.' Will's mum spoke with authority. She knew Cynthia. She was across everything.

Fleck was fairly certain Green-Haired Crochet Lady's name was Trixie. She wasn't sure how she knew that, but she did. Trixie yanked at the yarn that seemed to be coming out of her coat pocket and continued working, her brow furrowed.

'I dunno. I think Cynthia's planning something. It's the quiet ones you have to watch.'

A grandmother had stopped to talk to Trixie. They made an odd pair. Trixie was tall and whimsical. The grandmother wasn't as tall but had the grave dignity of a Shakespearean actor.

'It's going to get ugly when the alliances break down. It always does.'

'Oh yeah. *Alliances.*' Fleck nodded and tried to look like she had some idea of what they were talking about. She had no clue.

After Sam had been safely deposited in his classroom, Fleck steered Norah and the pusher to the school office.

There were already two people waiting at the counter when she got there: Trixie with the Turquoise Hair and the grandmother from earlier. At least, Fleck assumed the other lady was a grandmother, but that was the tricky thing. There were parents who had children later in life, who were older and sleep-deprived, and there were young grandparents who had access to all manner of age-defying treatments. You couldn't always tell which was which. And you didn't want to get it wrong. Still, Fleck was almost certain that this lady was the grandmother of Asher, a boy in the other prep class. Fleck smiled at the two women. 'Are you here to show your Working with Children cards so you can volunteer in the classrooms?'

Trixie smiled and shook her head. 'No, we're both here to get things sorted for the Button Line.'

Fleck felt cold all of a sudden. 'The Button Line? Oh, I remember getting a notice about that. Was I supposed to bring something? I completely forgot!'

'Relax! It's not till Friday. You bring money in an envelope.' Trixie looked at her appraisingly. 'That's hard work, though, isn't it? Finding cash and remembering to send it along with your kid?'

Asher's grandmother shot her a warning look. 'Trixie …'

'No, but I'm just saying. It's true, isn't it? Finding cash is a pain. Wouldn't it be easier if you could pay with a card? You would probably even pay more if you could pay with a card.'

The older woman crossed her arms. She seemed to be making a stand. 'It's no great imposition to put money in an envelope. It's how we have always done it.'

Trixie ignored this and continued to address Fleck. 'You would, though. Getting cash out is a pain in the butt. Most people would rather just pay with a card.'

'Leave the poor woman alone. You're confusing her. It is cash only. It has always been cash only.'

Trixie pursed her lips. 'We live in a cashless society, Helen. I bet parents would pay heaps more if they could just *tapitty-tap-tap*.'

Asher's grandmother – Helen – crossed her arms. 'Well, it's a moot point anyway. We don't have the means for them to tap.'

'Yeah, but we could *get* the means.'

Helen frowned. 'That's enough, Trixie.'

Fleck considered their arguments. 'I never have enough cash when I need it,' she said. 'If I were more organised, I'd keep a little jar of cash I could raid for this sort of thing.'

'That's a very good idea.' Helen gave an approving nod. 'They're not hard to set up.'

Fleck shook her head. 'They're not hard to set up. Setting them up isn't the problem. I have set up so many little jars of cash. But I keep losing them or spending them or Norah gets her hand on one and uses it to play shops and the money ends up scattered under the couch.'

Trixie smiled broadly in recognition. 'Yes! Or they think the vent in the wall is a vending machine and feed all of the coins into it. My boy did that to me once.'

Fleck laughed. 'Yes! This is why we can't have nice things!'

Trixie peered at Fleck. 'So, let's assume your last jar of cash has been absorbed into the household chaos. Would you take us through the steps you would have to take to have cash on Friday?'

Fleck shot Helen a semi-apologetic look. In this point-scoring exercise, she had chosen a side. She was not Team Helen. She was Team Trixie. 'First, I would need to go to the ATM and get some money out.'

'The one ATM left in town,' Trixie interjected.

'The one ATM left in town,' Fleck confirmed. 'And it's in that really awkward spot on the main road which is the worst when you have kids. You don't want to leave them in the car, but it's hard having them there with you when there are cars zooming past and you're trying to hold

16

their hand but also get your money. It's the worst.'

Helen smiled politely. 'True, but you'd just be getting a bit extra out. You'd be going to the ATM anyway, wouldn't you?'

Fleck and Trixie looked at each other, then shook their heads and giggled. 'Nobody gets cash out anymore, Helen. What's the next step?' Trixie asked.

Fleck considered. 'Next, I would need to find a way to break the note. Some place where they don't mind you paying with cash. After that, I would need to find an envelope and a pen that works.'

'I filled a school form out with a green crayon once,' Trixie announced. 'My pens had all staged a mass walk-out from my house.'

Fleck nodded. 'After all of that, I would need to consolidate cash, envelope and working pen to form a little package for Sam to take to school. And then I would need to remember not to leave the little package on the kitchen table on Friday morning.'

'That is a lot of steps.' said Trixie.

'It is, altogether, too many steps!' confirmed Fleck.

Trixie turned to address Helen. 'I'm telling you, Helen, we need to start getting some machines that can take cards. It will make everything so much better.'

Helen shook her head firmly. 'And I'm telling you: we are doing just fine. We have been running this fundraising drive for thirty-five years and I won't have—'

Helen paused. Julie, the school secretary, had appeared with another woman. 'Here we are, ladies. Chelle Griffin is our acting Outreach Coordinator. Chelle, this is Helen Greythorn and Trixie McAuley. And you're Felicity, right? Felicity … Flanagan?'

'Felicity Parker, but my son's last name is Flanagan. I didn't change my name when I married.'

Fleck stepped forward and gave Julie her Working with Children card to photocopy while the younger woman, Chelle, smiled at Helen and Trixie.

'Hi there,' she said. 'I'm still finding my feet in this role, I'm afraid. I'm still not fully across what happens at the Button Line. I know that it's a house competition and it raises money for a charity. Are the buttons actual buttons?'

'Yes. Don't worry about the buttons. We provide those.' This was Trixie.

Helen shot Trixie a look. If this look had a name, it would be called 'Children Should Be Seen and Not Heard'. Then she cleared her throat. 'It is a fundraising exercise. The children collect donations for the Society. Each dollar raised buys them one button.'

Chelle nodded. 'And what do they do with the buttons?'

'Well, Friday is the competition. It is set up in the gymnasium. There are four lines, one for each house, and they compete for the longest button line. Last year, Mackillop house won.'

'Okay. And the money raised goes to the Many Hands Society. That's the craft shop on Peppercorn Street, is that right?'

'Well, yes and no,' Helen said. 'We run the craft shop in order to raise money for the Society. The Society itself is an organisation that provides assistance to women from low-income and crisis situations. We have had a relationship with the school since the Society was first founded in the 1980s.'

'Back when Helen was a school mum!' Julie chimed in as she came back to the counter.

When Fleck was putting the card back in her wallet and preparing to leave, Trixie pulled away from the group and spoke to her. 'If you're around on Friday morning, we could definitely use some more parent helpers. Babies welcome.'

Fleck smiled broadly and nodded. 'Sounds like fun!'

18

CHAPTER THREE

The best part of Fleck's day was the Wordle line-up. On a good day, she played it while drinking her morning coffee. Fleck would sit and frown at the grid as the mystery word slowly revealed itself. She usually got it in three or four guesses.

There wasn't always time for puzzles in her day. Some days were relentless onslaughts of spills, tantrums, nap-dodging, mischief discovery, face-wiping and general-purpose disaster management – Fleck was a stay-at-home mum to three small children, after all.

Of course, 'stay-at-home mother' wasn't really an accurate description. She never stayed at home if she could help it. 'Full-time mother' sounded strange as well. It wasn't as if mothers who had jobs were 'part-time mothers'. Using terms like 'CEO of the Home' and 'Principal Domestic Engineer' sounded at once twee and oddly defensive. She was a mother. That was what she was and that was what she did. And she didn't have any other job outside the home. Unlike her husband, Matthew, who went into the office most days, Fleck's days were spent feeding, wiping, changing, washing, scraping, folding, stirring, pegging, sweeping, singing, bouncing, spooning and saying

'Put that down' in a nice voice. Sometimes her job meant working tirelessly without a break, only to get to the end of the day and feel like she had accomplished nothing at all. Most days, the only puzzle she got to solve was the mystery of what was making the car smell bad.

But Wordle was a game perfectly suited to Fleck's stage of life. You could play it between multiple interruptions. You could keep visiting it throughout the day. It would just wait patiently for you to be ready. Or sometimes, you could solve the whole thing before your second sip of coffee.

She had tried, once, to download an app that promised free and unlimited Wordle-style puzzles. She wouldn't have to wait for a new one every day. But 'Word Tile Plus' just wasn't the same somehow. Nothing was the same as that fresh, unsolved puzzle delivered to her phone each morning, like virtual warm bread.

Fleck knew how it could be when something was a craze, and she could already see how this little word game was becoming more niche, less mainstream. Not everyone played Wordle these days. But then, Matthew was still an avid Pokémon Go player, even though the world seemed to have left that behind long ago. Fleck was sure she would be the same with Wordle. She would never give it up. Wordle was life.

Getting it in two moves was at once exciting and a bit of a let-down. This was exactly why you needed the Wordle line-up. Fleck was always trying out other -ordle games that other people recommended to her. Some of them would become a permanent fixture on the line-up; others would stay a few weeks but not last the distance. There was one of these games that she had come to love *even more* than Wordle. It was called Waffle.

Waffle was a bit like Wordle, with its use of five-letter words and green and yellow tiles, but the premise was quite different. The waffle was like a knot to be gently untangled, swapping letters until a grid of six intersecting words was revealed. So much of solving a Wordle came down to luck, but it was possible to get a perfect score every time in Waffle using nothing but skill and logic. Of course, you needed to think several moves ahead, holding several possibilities in your mind at the same time before shifting a single tile, but this was part of the challenge. A perfect score gave you five stars. Fleck got five stars on most days. It was her special skill. It was also possible to go back to the archives to replay any games that you'd missed, or to improve a score. Fleck's Waffle archives were now at 100 per cent played, 100 per cent five stars. Her streak was 398: Waffle Master.

What would happen when she hit 400? In the past, as her streak climbed ever higher, Fleck had progressed from bronze, to silver, to gold. At one point she'd been on the diamond team. Later, she became a Waffle Wizard. Would she get a new emoji at 400? Or would she have to wait till she hit 500? She could not wait to find out.

On some days Fleck tore through her puzzle line-up on a single cup of coffee and itched for more, but there were also days filled with so many interruptions and small disasters that the puzzles remained untouched until just before bed. That was when they became a little consolation prize for a hard-fought day.

Today, though, Fleck sat in the school reflection garden after her business in the office. The bench here was perfect for breastfeeding: the exact depth and width required, and with good back support. Norah was happily playing on the play equipment. Alice had settled in for her feed. Fleck had a Moment.

Wordle wasn't loading. Why was Wordle not loading? Her moment would be over soon. She needed her daily fix of puzzley goodness. A quick Google search told her what she needed to do: go to settings and clear cookies. Fleck followed the steps, then tried Wordle again. Success! Today's answer was JELLY. Fleck got it in five.

Alice was still feeding and Norah was happily twirling on the spot. Fleck had time for another puzzle. Waffle was nice and difficult today. She frowned at it for ages before she made her first move. She made one misstep when she mistakenly thought the down word on the left-hand side was TONIC. It was, in fact, TUNIC. Still, somehow she managed to make up the lost ground and finished with five stars. A perfect score. Fleck smiled to herself in satisfaction, then she stopped and gasped in horror.

There, in the results, her streak was not 399. There, in the results, her streak was one. Her streak was *one*. How was this happening? She hadn't lost. She hadn't lost yesterday either. Her score yesterday was five stars. Her streak yesterday was 398. How had she lost her streak? How?

Of course. The cookies. The stupid cookies. Fleck hadn't realised when she had cleared the cookies and cache that she would also be wiping all evidence of her Waffle success. It was all gone. It was completely lost.

Later, she would blame breastfeeding hormones, but it wasn't that. She couldn't help it. She tried to hold it back, but it was definitely happening. She could feel it coming. Fleck started crying. And not delicate silent tears escaping out the sides of her eyes. Fleck was sobbing. Proper snorting, shuddering sobs. She might have actually said 'Wahh' at some point. It was an ugly cry.

There wasn't anyone else around. At least, she didn't think there was. She didn't realise there was somebody else until the somebody else plonked down right beside her. It was one of the mums. Had she noticed Fleck was crying? She must know. It was obvious. Fleck wanted to disappear. To dissolve completely into water and run off down the drain.

It was Trixie, the woman she'd met in the office before. Up close, Fleck noticed that Trixie was very pretty and slightly odd. She had thick, curling eyelashes and large earrings shaped like dangling fried eggs. 'Hey,' she said. 'What's up?'

No. No, this was the worst. She couldn't admit to what she'd been crying about. But what could she say instead? Her mind was blank. Should she invent a sick aunt? Or a dead pet? Or a pet aunt? Wait: scratch that last one. Should she pretend she hadn't even been crying at all? That she was just washing her face in an unconventional way? Some TikTok beauty cleanse trend? Trixie was looking at her.

Fleck sniffed and used her free hand to brush her face dry. 'It's nothing. It's silly.'

Trixie shrugged and adjusted the large claw clip behind her head. Her hair really was a vivid colour. 'You can still tell me, if you like. I mean, if it's not confidential.'

Fleck barked a little laugh. 'It's definitely not confidential. It's just something so small I shouldn't be crying about it.'

'Yeah, but you are crying about it, so it must be a bit important.'

Fleck shook her head. 'It is so not important. I can't believe I even got upset about it. It's nothing.'

Trixie nodded and waited. After a moment, she pulled a ball of yarn and some crochet on a hook out of her coat pocket. She began to stitch. She was working on something that looked like a little blue cup.

Fleck swallowed. 'I mean. It's so silly. I like doing these Wordle puzzles every day, and it wasn't working today, so I tried to fix it, but as a result I lost my streak. I mean, that's it. I'm crying because I lost my streak on some game.'

She was aiming for a lighthearted, self-effacing laugh. Instead, to her horror, fresh tears sprang to her eyes. What was wrong with her? She shook her head. 'I don't know why it's upsetting me so much.' She paused and drew a ragged breath. 'It's just that it's my one thing that I like. The one thing I'm good at. It's the only thing I do for me all day.

Everything else is for other people.' She gave a little hiccuppy gasp, then her tears subsided.

Trixie made a sympathetic grimace. She continued stitching for a while and then paused to rest her hands. 'I don't think the problem is that you were getting upset about something silly. I think the problem is that you don't do enough things for yourself. Do you have any hobbies? And you're not allowed to say that you think hobbies are stupid.'

Fleck paused. In her mind, a small voice said, *But hobbies are definitely stupid.* She chose not to say this out loud. Instead, she said, 'I don't have time for hobbies.'

'Nobody has time for hobbies unless they're intentional about it.' Trixie tugged more yarn from the ball. 'And that's the thing: as women, we are conditioned to eschew the things that give us joy and pleasure. You should definitely get yourself a hobby. Otherwise, the patriarchy wins.'

'I've never heard anyone say "eschew" in real life before,' Fleck said. She gave Alice's ear a stroke with her thumb to wake her up. Alice gave a little start, then continued to feed. 'I don't know what I would do for a hobby. I don't even know what I like anymore. I feel like I've stopped being a person. I don't know. It's like motherhood came at the cost of my personality.'

Trixie counted the stitches around the rim of her blue crocheted cup. 'I don't think a person with no personality would be having a good old teary about their Wordle streak status.'

Fleck sighed. 'Actually, it was my Waffle streak, but same-same.'

Alice finished feeding on the left side. Fleck eased her upright. Though floppy with sleep, Alice immediately emitted an enormous belch, then looked startled. Both women laughed.

'Joseph used to do that,' Trixie said. 'He was such a tiny baby, but he did the most enormous burps.'

Fleck gasped and smiled. 'Oh, are you *Joseph*'s mum? Sam has been talking about Joseph every day of the week.' It was funny. She hadn't expected Joseph's mum would be white. Joseph looked African, but she supposed he must be multiracial.

'Are you Sam's mum? Joseph *loves* Sam! I know we met in the office, but I've forgotten your name already. My name is Trixie, though I suppose I'll be known as "Joseph's Mum" till the end of my days.'

Fleck eased Alice into her baby capsule and strapped her in. 'I'm Felicity, but everyone calls me Fleck.'

'Fleck? Not Flick?'

'I did get called Flick a little bit when I was younger. I got lots of nicknames. My school friends used to call me Facility and Faculty. My mum called me Felicity June. My dad sometimes called me Velocity and Ferocity. My brothers called me Nosy. Actually, they still do call me Nosy. Nosy Parker.

'I can't remember who first called me Fleck, but it has stuck. I don't know why. My husband, Matthew, thinks it's because I'm small and vivid,' she gestured to her masses of red curls, 'like a fleck of paint.'

Trixie nodded. She sang a song Fleck didn't recognise under her breath and continued adding rows to her cup. Fleck watched her for a minute. 'What are you making?'

Trixie grinned. 'It's a budgerigar, of course. Can't you tell? I just need to do the grey bit here, and the eyes and beak, and the wings down here ...'

Fleck frowned. 'I can't see it.'

'I don't have any with me to show you what they look like when they're done. I need to carry about one of those "see what I prepared earlier" models. Maybe you can come to the shop sometime when you're free to see some finished ones.'

'What shop?'

'I sell these at Many Hands. You know, the little shop on Peppercorn Street?'

Fleck had seen the shop; it was on the same street as George's Kitchen. But, she told Trixie, she had never actually ventured inside.

'It'll be open soon. Do you want to come see my budgies now? Come on. An excursion will do us both good.'

Fleck paused and thought. At home was a sink full of dishes and three baskets of washing to fold. Her cutlery drawer never stayed closed – it just floated open again whenever you tried to shut it. There was something wrong with it. And then food dropped into it off the bench and it got all grotty. She couldn't face the housework and the gaping cutlery drawer just yet. 'Okay,' she said. 'Let's go see your budgies.'

CHAPTER FOUR

'This place is a bit of a crafter's paradise.' Trixie opened the front door of Many Hands, setting the shop bell off with a jaunty tinkle. 'I mean, some of the stuff they have is a bit old-fashioned and fussy, and they definitely overdo it on the lace sometimes, but all the pieces are handmade, plus they sell supplies as well.'

Although Fleck had often looked in the window of Many Hands as she walked up Peppercorn Street to George's Kitchen, she'd never been inside. The little shop was beautiful, but it was *not* pram-friendly and, while the shelves were filled with children's clothes and toys, the intended market was clearly wealthy grandparents and not Fleck.

Fleck paused and crouched down to Norah's level. 'Okay, Norah, what's the rule?'

'You can point but don't touch,' Norah parroted obediently.

'That's right. And what's the other rule?'

'Stick to Mummy like glue.'

'Stick to Mummy like glue. Let's go.'

Trixie held the door open as Fleck backed the pusher up the steps and into the shop. Norah immediately raced to the other side of the shop, picked up a knitted gnome that was almost as big as her and carried it back to Fleck, jostling a stand of glass earrings in the process. 'Look, Mummy! Santa!'

Fleck parked the pusher in the corner and scooped Norah up, stuffed gnome and all. She put the blue character with its traffic-cone hat back on the shelf with its bearded brothers. She cast a guilty look at the lady behind the counter, a silver-haired woman in her seventies, but she was busy sewing patches and did not look up.

Trixie, meanwhile, was striding around the shop in search of something. When she found it, she stopped. 'Hey, Bev,' she barked.

Bev continued to stitch and did not look up. 'Hay is what horses eat,' she said tartly.

Trixie rolled her eyes. 'Do *pardon* me, Miss Beverley. I wish to enquire after a matter of some urgency.'

Bev raised an eyebrow at Trixie, folded her work together and zipped it into a binder. She lumbered over to the shelves in question. 'We've had to make some changes,' she said.

'You mean *Helen* wanted to move my work into the darkest corner of the shop!' Trixie's lips were pressed into a tight line. Her nostrils flared.

Bev rested her hand on the back of one of her substantial hips and tilted her stance. She peered up at Trixie. 'This is Helen's shop, Trixie. She's allowed to move the stock around.'

Trixie's dark eyes flashed. 'This is *the Society's* shop,' she said. 'Helen is just another worker here, despite what she's managed to convince everybody. And this isn't even all my stock. Where are my embroideries? Surely you didn't sell all five of them this afternoon. Where did they go?'

Bev drew herself to her full height, which really wasn't all that tall. Despite her newfound allegiance to Team Trixie, Fleck couldn't help but feel a passing twinge of short-girl solidarity. 'Your cross-stitch displays have been moved behind the counter.'

Trixie's mouth dropped open. 'What? Why? I *got rid* of the sweary ones! These ones all had clean language. They were fine!' She stormed towards the shop counter and disappeared behind it. Moments later, she appeared with her arms full of small embroidery hoops. She began setting them back on the shelves. Each cross-stitch design had words embroidered in flowing script, in a 'home sweet home' style. Alongside rosebuds on vines and daffodil sprays were phrases like, *Please leave by nine*, or *Carry yourself with the confidence of a mediocre white man*, or *Bite me*.

Trixie straightened a display hoop that proclaimed, *A woman's place is in the Revolution*. 'FYI, I sold the sweary ones off my website and made an absolute mint. The patterns too. You guys are missing out.'

'I really don't think you should be putting those hoops back, Trixie. Helen said—'

'Just because Helen is the boss of *you*, doesn't mean we are all required to bow down to the Cult of Helen. I refuse to convert! I refuse!'

'What on earth is going on?' Helen, in a stylishly cut silk blouse and tailored trousers, appeared in the doorway of the back room. Trixie wheeled around to face her patrician rival. 'Helen. Explain to me why my stock is hiding back here when yesterday I had it on the shelves near the register.'

'I don't think I need to explain anything. That stock belongs to the shop. You donated it. It no longer belongs to you. I have the right to move stock around to where it will best sell.'

'How on earth is *this* the place where it will best sell?' Trixie exclaimed. 'You can barely see it here. You could easily walk past and not even notice. And why were my embroidery hoops behind the counter?'

'They are inappropriate—'

'I took *out* the ones with swearwords. See?'

'They are *still* inappropriate. They do not fit with the tone of this shop.'

'Why do you get to say what the *tone* of this shop is? What if I disagree?'

'I find it curious that after a mere three months of volunteering here, you consider yourself an expert on the matter.'

'It has been five months, and you know it,' Trixie hissed.

'Yes, well for me it has been thirty-seven years,' Helen said (Trixie: 'Oh, *here* we go!'). 'And that amount of time has given me a *bit* more perspective on this shop's culture – on what our customers want.'

'But the stuff is selling. So customers must want it.'

'It cheapens our brand. We are not some novelty shop selling hens' party gimmicks. And I do not believe that actively insulting our customers is ever a wise business move.'

Fleck cleared her throat. 'I really like—'

Helen continued talking loudly as if Fleck hadn't said a word. 'The cartoon characters are fine, I suppose, but they are not really our style.' Fleck looked to where Helen had indicated with a dismissive wave of her hand, and she could see that they were crocheted in Trixie's more modern style – there were figurines from various fandoms including Yoda, Captain Picard, Luna Lovegood and assorted Doctors Who. 'We don't need to confuse people. They can be in the shop, but they don't need to be front and centre.'

'Oh, *thank you*. Thank you *so much*. You will *let* me donate my work to the shop, will you? You are generosity itself.'

Fleck tried again. 'If you ask me—'

'Do you see, Beverley? This is what I was talking about when we were discussing attitude problems.' Helen spoke to Bev, but she looked straight at Trixie.

'And my budgies?' Trixie demanded. 'What have you done with my budgies? I brought my friend here specifically to show her my budgies.'

Fleck swallowed. If she'd known that budgie-viewing was going to be such a contentious event, she wouldn't have insisted on seeing them. She began to say something placatory, but Helen cut in over the top of her.

'There is a lot of stock in this shop. You are far from the only maker who donates. I cannot be expected to keep track of every piece that comes through these doors. I'm sure your *budgies* will turn up. Now *if* you will excuse me, I have work to do.' Helen turned on her heel.

Trixie groaned out an elaborate sigh. Then she turned to Fleck. 'Would you like a cup of tea in the back room?'

'Tea and coffee facilities are for staff use only.' Helen delivered this parting shot over her shoulder.

'I thought you had work to do, Helen.'

Helen chose not to respond to Trixie's comment.

Bev sighed. 'You two really bring out the worst in each other, you know,' she said to Trixie. She adjusted a small orange coat on its hanger. It was made from an upcycled woollen blanket. Then she turned to Fleck: 'You really are welcome to stay for a cup of tea. Helen has just been dealing with some difficult people on the phone all morning. She didn't mean to be short with you.'

Fleck smiled apologetically. 'It's fine, really. I don't need tea.'

Bev winked. 'Everyone needs tea. They just don't always know it.'

Trixie's face softened. 'Thanks, Bev. I didn't mean to go off at you before.'

Bev shrugged. 'Go have a cup of tea. Dima's back there. She brought cake.'

Trixie pulled the curtain to the back room open and ushered Fleck and the children inside. 'Dima! Bev said you brought cake!'

A young woman with olive skin and a purple headscarf looked up from her knitting and grinned broadly. 'It's nice to see you too, Trixie! How *are* you, Trixie? Tell me about your *day*, Trixie!'

Trixie rolled her eyes. 'No time for any of that. Cake? Cake? Yes or no?' She turned to Fleck. 'You don't understand. Dima makes the most amazing cakes. I can't even describe it. And sometimes we get to eat the offcuts. Dima: show Fleck pictures of your cakes.'

Dima grinned. 'It's nice to meet you, Fleck. I'm so glad Trixie introduced us so properly!' She spoke in a teasing tone with a light accent.

Fleck grinned. 'Personally, I think all introductions should involve an exchange of cake photos. You could find out so much about a person if you could just see the last thing they baked.'

They were standing in a small room filled with boxes and bags. It was little more than a nook behind a curtain at the back of the shop and beside the foot of the stairs. There was a kitchenette with a sink, microwave and urn. A large wooden table dominated the space, and there was a spinning wheel in the corner.

'Here. Here's Dima's Instagram.' Trixie shoved her phone into Fleck's face. 'Swipe across so you can see more.'

Fleck looked at the pictures on Trixie's phone. Some cakes were smooth domes with delicate gold flakes clinging to the surface like frost. Some were cylindrical stacks with hardly any icing scraped on the sides, showing off the different colours of sponge. Many had delicate flower blooms as decorations: cherry blossoms or magnolias or California poppies. Fleck looked at Dima, shaking her head. 'These are works of art!'

Dima smiled. 'It's what I love to do. And yes, Trixie: I delivered a very special cake for a fiftieth birthday yesterday. There are scraps in the fridge.'

Trixie dashed to the fridge and pulled out a plate covered in odd-shaped pieces of cake. Dima pointed. 'That bit is lemon and pistachio, that is matcha and those bits are brown sugar, rosemary and fig.'

'I'm going to make us some tea so we can properly enjoy it,' said Trixie.

'Nothing for me. I've already had too much cake. That's why I brought it here. I need to get it out of the house!'

'What about Bev? Does she want any?'

'I already made her up a plate. She's got it hiding under the counter.'

Trixie busied herself with the urn. Fleck gestured to Dima's knitting work. 'What are you making?'

'Another beanie.' She pointed to a washing hamper in the corner of the room. It was labelled *Beanies for Syrian Refugees*. 'I arrived here as a refugee nine years ago and Many Hands did so much to help me get settled. I do what I can to give back.'

There was a row of other laundry hampers along the back wall, on either side of the door that led into the rear lane. As well as the beanies basket, there were hampers labelled *Blanket Squares*, *Trauma Teddies* and *Premmie Octopuses*. Fleck lifted the lid of the *Premmie Octopuses* basket and peered inside. 'What are all these for?' She held up a crocheted toy octopus that had extra-long, curly tentacles.

'We crochet those octopuses and jellyfish for premature babies. The long tentacles are good for them. They grasp them and find it soothing. It mimics the umbilical cord, I think. And it stops the babies from pulling on cords and air tubes and unplugging things. The trauma teddies are for the Red Cross. They distribute them to hospitals and police stations to give out to kids who might be having a hard time. We knit or crochet them using the patterns the Red Cross provides.'

'And the blanket squares?'

'Exactly what it sounds like. Knitted and crocheted squares that will get sewn together into blankets and donated to local women's shelters. By the way, Trixie, we've got some new yarn in!'

'Yarn? What? Where?' Trixie spun around, her face alight.

'A whole bunch of mill ends from Fibrelicious. Plus, we had a donation from Mullaney's company last week, did you see? They're beanie kits, but you could use the wool for anything.'

'Hello, my pretties!' Trixie dug through the box on the end of the table. 'So many colours!'

'Bev said Dima brought cake?' A stylishly dressed woman appeared in the curtained doorway to the shop.

'Does nobody say hello? Hello, Jo. Good to see you, Jo!' Dima grinned broadly and gestured to the plate of cake pieces on the table. 'Plenty of cake. I'll probably have some more in on Monday. I'm doing a yuzu cake with calamansi curd for a wedding. I'm going to decorate it with little orange blossoms.'

'I don't want to hear about Future Cake,' Jo said. 'I need Today Cake. It's performance appraisals at work this week. It doesn't matter that I quit smoking thirteen years ago – I'm always desperate for a cigarette in performance appraisals.'

'Is that why you've been knitting so many gnomes?' Trixie was back at the kitchenette bench, opening a box of teabags. 'Does anyone else want tea, by the way?'

'When Jo gets stressed, she knits,' Dima told Fleck, as she waved a dismissive hand at Trixie's offer of tea.

'And when I knit, I knit gnomes,' Jo said, squeezing in next to Trixie at the bench to scoop some instant coffee into a mug. 'Just gnome after gnome after gnome. It's lucky the store can sell them, otherwise I'd be lost in gnome land!'

Trixie brought two steaming mugs across to the table and handed one to Fleck. Norah had climbed into one of the chairs and was eyeing the cake suspiciously. Trixie put a Scotch Finger biscuit into her hand.

As Fleck expected, the cake was transcendental. Dima knitted and accepted compliments as Trixie, Fleck and Jo flopped around their chairs in ecstasy. Norah happily nibbled on her safe and predictable biscuit.

'Is this what you do for a job?' Fleck asked, as she sank her teeth into an odd-shaped wedge of lemon and pistachio cake.

'Sort of. Not really.' Dima laughed. 'I do have a business that I run from home, but I only do it part-time. I work a normal, boring job part-time as well. But I think that's what suits me. If I tried to do the cake thing full-time, it would be too stressful.'

'I get that,' said Trixie, poking at the crumbs on her plate to pick them up. 'Do you get people trying to convince you that you need to go full-time? Like it's only a valid pursuit if it earns you a living wage?'

'Urgh! All the time. Usually it's a man.'

'Yes. Named Kevin.'

'*Yes*. What is it with all the Kevins? Let us get on with it, Kevin! It's enough to do what you love. It doesn't have to make money.'

'I'm a bit like Dima,' Trixie told Fleck. 'I have a few different jobs. I create crochet patterns and tutorials and sell them online. I also freelance for a few craft magazines, writing patterns and articles. I run stalls at craft markets. Sometimes I copywrite ads as well. Plus, I do a few shifts at Bakers Delight when the work dries up. Which happens sometimes.'

'Don't tell Kevin,' said Dima.

'Oh, Kevin doesn't need to know.' Trixie grinned.

'What are you two on about?' Jo was pulling her knitting from her bag. 'I swear you don't make sense half the time. Who is Kevin?'

Dima smiled and shook her head. She packed away her own knitting work and stood up. 'I've got to go. Make sure Helen gets a bit of cake. I think she's on a phone call upstairs.'

'Complaining to Telstra?' Jo quirked an eyebrow.

'Sitting on hold, more like. She might need cake once she's finished doing battle with them.' Dima waved as she exited through the back door.

'There they are!' Trixie said, and she leaped out of her seat towards the collection of shopping bags and boxes by the door.

Fleck watched as Trixie grabbed a green shopping bag from the pile and brought it back to the table. She pulled crocheted budgerigars out of the bag and lined them up along the table: blue and grey, green and yellow, purple and white.

'These are gorgeous!' Fleck exclaimed, examining the green one. 'Do you sell these online?'

'Sometimes, but mostly I sell the patterns. These here are my prototypes. I make them up while I'm working out the pattern, and for the tutorial photos, then donate them to the shop. It makes more sense, business-wise, to write a decent pattern and make it into a PDF download that people can purchase, than to spend all your time constructing one-off pieces and posting them out. And I love seeing photos when people have made their own ones.'

'I didn't know you could sell crochet patterns.'

'Oh, yeah. People do it all the time. I say I sell patterns, but really it's tutorials with photos of each stage. It helps if you can see clearly where you need to put the hook. And sometimes I do videos, but they're harder to monetise. I have two versions of this pattern tutorial. One is called "plush budgie" and the other is called "plush parakeet". I have a lot of customers in the US and I've only just discovered that budgies and parakeets are basically the same bird. I changed one word and tripled my sales!'

Fleck turned the budgie over in her hands. 'This looks so cool. I can't believe you can just make something like this out of a ball of yarn.'

The sound of Helen's voice floated down the stairs.

'No. No, that is really not good enough, Daniel. I have been on hold for fifteen minutes and I expect a better level of service than this. No. We've already gone over this, Daniel. I am looking at the bill dated twenty-first of January. Yes. That one. Now, what you need to understand …'

Trixie had picked up a box of tea bags and was holding it against her head like a phone. She mimed Helen's conversation with exaggerated facial expressions. Jo smiled and rolled her eyes. Norah squealed with giggles.

'… No. This is unacceptable. Please direct your attention to the third …'

Trixie paused in her mimicry to lean forward and whisper. 'Okay, what's the bet she asks to speak to the manager?'

Fleck grinned. 'Oh, one hundred per cent. Any minute now.'

'… No, Daniel. I'm afraid I will need to escalate this. Please put me on to your supervisor.'

Fleck and Trixie made little cheering noises and collapsed into giggles.

There was mail in the letterbox when Fleck got home from the shop. There was a magazine for Matthew, two bills and a piece of paper in a clear zip-lock bag. It was the kind of bag you might put a sandwich in – that is, if your school didn't enforce 'nude food' policies.

Fleck immediately recognised the letter in the bag as one from her next-door neighbour. Fleck had never met the man. She probably should make more of an effort. Their interactions were limited to notes in the letterbox. He had written to them before, using the same thick cream-coloured notepaper, using the same neat, inky handwriting and sealed in the same Hercules Sustain Compostable zip-lock bags. His letters were always polite. Always oddly formal. The last letter had been a few months ago. Fleck had taken a while to throw it out because the paper had been so nice.

When they got inside, she dropped the bills on the side table, unsealed the zip-lock bag and unfolded the letter.

Esteemed neighbour,

I have booked a hard rubbish collection on Thursday February 23 (the week after next). I will require no more than two cubic metres for my anticipated waste. If you wish to avail yourself of the remaining cubic metre, as per the council quota, you are invited to place items on my nature strip from February 21 onwards.

I remain,

Yours respectfully,

Ranveer D Singh, PhD, CPA

So now her mysterious neighbour was having a hard-rubbish collection. Fleck loved hard-rubbish collections. It was like a sneak peek into a stranger's secret inner world. Her neighbour was a private man, alone with his tidy garden. His house did not have any windows you could see from the street, which was a pity. Fleck loved the way some houses had windows lit up with the curtains left open on her twilit walks after dinner. They were golden rectangles that provided glowing tableaus to passers-by. Sneaking looks into people's houses was one of Fleck's guilty pleasures. The lady in a suit cooking dinner. The old man patting his dog. The young students draped over couches. These half-second glimpses into worlds and lives she knew nothing about were addictive shots of voyeuristic pleasure. But Mr Singh had no such windows. His house was quiet and dark.

Hard-rubbish collections were another way to see inside a person's house. Sometimes they were a source of surprise freebies. But even when they didn't provide a backyard mud kitchen or a pink tricycle with a push bar attached or a perfectly good desk, they provided entertainment on a neighbourhood walk. They provided insight into an otherwise impassive house. Fleck wondered what sorts of items the neat man next door would put out for collection.

Fleck used the empty zip-lock bag to corral the Uno cards that no longer fit in their tattered box and were scattered all over the living room. Then she flipped the letter over. If she were to paint with watercolours, this paper would be perfect. Of course, she never painted with watercolours. She didn't own any watercolour paints. But that didn't mean she never would. Maybe watercolour painting would become her Thing. She placed the note carefully on the sideboard. Where did you buy watercolour paints from, anyway?

CHAPTER FIVE

Why had Fleck chosen a shopping centre? If she were cooler, if she were more sophisticated, she would have gone to an underground play or a farmers' market or a music festival or – what? She didn't even know what a sophisticated person would do, but it would not be wandering through this glossy, climate-controlled monument to consumerism in search of a Thing.

Shoes? Was her Thing shoes? Cute stationery? Tea? Scented candles? They were all nice, she supposed. They were okay.

Being out by herself was a new development for Fleck. Her mother-in-law, Marian, had retired two months ago, and she'd announced that she wanted to support the mothers of her grandchildren. 'I'm happy to babysit another time if you want to run errands or make doctors' appointments or do the shopping,' she had said to Fleck. 'But every second Thursday? I want that to be time just for you. Fill up your cup.' The arrangement was that Fleck would feed Alice just before Marian arrived, giving her four hours all to herself before she came back for her next feed.

The first few times Marian had come, Fleck had used the

opportunity to sleep. It had been pretty wonderful. Today, though, Alice had slept through the night. Lately, Fleck had the uncomfortable feeling that sleep did not count as a hobby or an interest, as passionate as she was about the activity. Other people had favourite pastimes. Why didn't Fleck have a Thing? She didn't even know what it was she liked to do anymore. Apart from her puzzles, was there anything she liked to do that she didn't *have* to do?

Fleck wandered past chain stores and through TK Maxx. It was strange to be out without any children. She kept instinctively checking for them. She could go right inside the shops with tight shelves and breakable things. She had no pusher to manoeuvre. There was nobody pulling at her. She could take her time. She didn't have to watch for tiny hands darting out to grab things off the shelves.

'Go get a massage,' Marian had suggested that morning. It sounded nice. Fleck liked the idea of doing something special and indulgent just for her. But when it came down to it, a massage wasn't what she really wanted. Staying still for an extended amount of time in the company of some stranger and assorted smells? It just seemed awkward. Anyway, she really wanted to spend a few hours with *nobody touching her.*

She browsed shops and ate a muffin at the cafe outside Target. It was overly sweet and she could taste the vegetable oil and fake vanilla, but she still ate it all because it was supposed to be her treat. She stayed there until it felt weird. Her plate had been cleared away but she didn't want to order anything more. Eventually, she got up and blundered along until she ended up in a shop that sold nifty stationery and cleaning equipment and kitchen storage solutions, all from Japan. It was when she was inspecting a clip to seal chip bags, shaped like a smiling lobster, that her phone alarm started to chime. It was time to go home.

Fleck decided to buy something for herself, just so that she had something to show for her efforts. She chose a packet of pastel

41

highlighter pens. A little milky rainbow.

She didn't like to admit the relief that she felt now that it was time to go home. It had been uncomfortable to feel adrift, like she didn't even know who she was. Parenting was hard work. It was suffocating. But at least she knew where she stood.

The school gym was loud and echoey, and there was a distinctive tang of rubber in the air. Each class sat on the shiny wooden floor in rows, with a chair for the teacher at the end of each. The little polo shirts and tracksuit pants of the school uniform made a sea of red and blue across the front of the gym.

Fleck had remembered the Button Line money *and* she had even found an envelope to put it in. She hadn't managed to find a pen that worked, not anywhere, but the crayon she used to write 'Sam Flanagan, Button Line money, Class Prep B, $5 encl.' was navy. Navy was a very professional colour for a crayon.

Fleck squinted to make out Sam among the preps. There he was, sitting beside Joseph, talking loudly into his ear and practically climbing into his lap with the excitement of the conversation. When he spotted Fleck, he waved frantically. Fleck waved frantically back.

'I'm so glad you came.' Bev appeared beside Fleck, with Trixie in tow. She deftly steered them both around to the side of the gym, where space was being prepared for the button lines. Each house – Mackillop, Ozanam, Lisieux and Chisholm – was assigned a line of masking tape stretching across the shiny floor. At the end of each line were buckets filled with the buttons each house had collected. This made sense so far.

'What are those other set-ups for?' Fleck gestured across to the trestle tables along the back wall.

'That one is where parents and teachers can buy more buttons for their house. It's amazing how many more donations the Society can get in the heat of competition.' Bev's face broke into a conspiratorial grin.

'What about over there?' Fleck gestured to some stations with labels like *Times Tables Ultimate Challenge* and *Bean Bag Toss to Win*.

'We get donations from local businesses, which buy more buttons that the children can win for their house by doing different tasks. This year it's a mix of carnival-style games and some sporty and educational tasks as well. The teachers have that all organised.'

'Okay. Where do you need us?' Fleck shifted her bag up her shoulder.

'I'm putting you both on the button sales table. Helen will come by in a minute to make sure you're all set up. She's just on the phone.'

Trixie gave Fleck a look. 'If Helen is on the phone, we shouldn't interrupt her. We'll be just fine.'

Pretty soon, the event was underway. Most of the children were gathered around the button lines. Children took it in turns to place a button along the masking-tape guides. Many children were watching the progress and cheering their house. Some were acting as officials, checking for correct button placement and measuring line lengths. Others were attempting to win more buttons at the activity stations or petitioning the adults to purchase more buttons. Sam sat beside Joseph, watching the button lines with interest. They were both in Ozanam, the red team, which looked like it was fluctuating between second and third place.

Helen was striding between stations with the air of a harried wedding planner. She looked like she was quietly fuming. But then, it was hard to tell. Helen had often looked stern when Fleck had met with her. She hadn't figured out what Helen's baseline facial expression was yet. It was possible today that Helen was really angry. It was also possible that this was Helen's everyday face.

Helen approached their table. 'So, it looks like Donna has decided she won't be gracing us with her presence today.' She spat the words out viciously. So, angry, then. Definitely angry.

'Donna is our CEO,' Trixie informed Fleck.

Helen shook her head. 'Donna is too big for her britches. She might call herself the CEO, or the head honcho, or King Canute or whatever she likes, but at the end of the day, she is staff. At the end of the day, we have hired her to do a job. She might think this primary school is small potatoes compared to some of the large corporate donors she has managed to procure, but Our Holy Redeemer Primary is a longstanding supporter of the Society. The school has been in partnership with us for far longer than any bank or insurance company or budget airline. And the school will still be in partnership with the Society when those corporations move on to the next fashionable cause. Donna should be here.'

'I'm sure she has a good reason,' Trixie said.

'Hm.' Helen's short syllable conveyed multitudes. At once it said, 'I highly doubt that' and, 'I do not appreciate *your* opinion' and, 'This topic of conversation is over.' She turned her attention to the sign on the table. Underneath the printed *Buttons $1 each or 6 for $5*, Trixie had written another line in blue texta: *20 for $10! 50 for $20!!*

Helen frowned and pointed. 'What is this?'

Trixie raised a single eyebrow. 'That's a sign, Helen.'

'Why have you altered it?'

Trixie held Helen's steely gaze. 'It is good for sales. It means we don't have to faff about so much getting change.'

'But this is just confusing people. We didn't agree on this. Six for five dollars is enough. You are adding too many variables.'

'I think people are smarter than you give them credit for, Helen.'

'Fifty buttons for twenty dollars? Fifty buttons is ridiculous. You are undermining the whole economy.'

'You do realise the buttons cost us nothing, don't you? I mean, we get them all back at the end, don't we? Technically, this is button rental, not button sales.'

Helen sniffed. 'I am going to find you a replacement sign.' She turned on her heel and strode away.

'Make sure this one says "button rental" on it!' Trixie called after Helen, then she grunted and pulled her crochet work out from her pocket. 'Thanks for the micromanagement, *Helen*.' She began stitching into her work with lime-green thread. 'I swear, Helen can't agree with anything if it isn't her own idea.'

'I like the changes you made,' Fleck offered. 'Lots more people are getting twenty dollars' worth than they otherwise would. It's a good idea.'

'Helen doesn't like ideas. She doesn't like change. Like, I've been saying for ages that I want to run craft workshops in the back room of the shop, on the big table. Don't you think that would be awesome? People could learn how to crochet or learn how to knit, or maybe it could be project-based, like we all make a bag or something.'

'That sounds great!'

'Right? It is great. But do you think I can convince the others? It's all, "Oh, Trixie, you haven't done it before" and, "Oh, you haven't got a program" and Helen – Helen is all, "This is not who we are. This is not our mission." Ugh. Like she would know.'

'I'd love to learn to make stuff. And I'm sure I'm not the only one.'

'They can't handle any sort of change here. But it could be so good.' She moved her crochet work to her lap and started counting off on her fingers. 'It would get people in the shop. It would encourage people to craft, and they might start donating their work to us. It would get people to buy our craft supplies. And we could charge money for the classes as well. It's win-win-win. But Helen says no. Helen can't handle anything that she isn't in charge of. She's such a control freak.'

'What about the others?'

'Oh. Well, Bev backs up Helen, because that's all Bev ever does. Donna says I haven't got a program, and I need a program before they can do anything. Charlie thinks it's a good idea, but I haven't done it before, so he says it might be risky. Douglas wants to know how much it would cost. Dima's happy enough with the idea, I guess, but she's not obsessed with it like I am. Oh, and Jo wants to know about insurance. Whenever somebody wants to say no without actually saying no, they say, "But what about insurance?" That's the official code for "We couldn't be bothered backing you." Overall, the main problem is that I haven't done it before. But how am I supposed to start if I need to wait until I've done it before?'

Trixie huffed and continued stitching. They sat quietly for a while. Fleck watched her progress as the stitches built. 'Is that another budgie?' she asked.

Trixie nodded. 'Yes, this one will be yellow and green. I'm trying out something different with the colour transition this time.'

Fleck ran her hand across the green ball of yarn, which Trixie had placed on the table between them. 'I wish I knew how to crochet. I've tried, but I'm all thumbs. And I can't read a pattern.'

Trixie smiled, then her eyes widened. 'Fleck! What if I run the workshops for *you*? You could be my guinea pig. I could teach you to crochet and do other crafts and we could see what works to put together a program. If I can say I've got a program and I've road-tested it on a human being, they would be much more likely to say yes to me running programs for the shop.'

Fleck hesitated. 'Are you sure? That seems like a lot of work for you to take on.'

Trixie shook her head. 'Are you kidding? You would be doing me a favour. I can't work out what I'm going to do without doing it, and

I need someone to practise on. Plus, we need to find you a hobby, remember? We could try different crafts until we find one that sticks. Maybe we could come back to the shop after the school run on Tuesday mornings? Maybe at ten? I have a shift volunteering after that, so I'll be there anyway.'

Helen reappeared with a piece of paper. She replaced the sign on the table without a word.

Trixie watched Helen's back with a withering expression as she walked away. Then she turned back to Fleck. 'I'm begging you, Fleck. Help me get this started.'

Fleck smiled cautiously. 'Okay. Tuesday mornings. You're on.'

'Brilliant!' Trixie's eyes took on a devious twinkle as she pulled a blue texta from her pocket and uncapped it. 'And now, if you'll excuse me, I have some important modifications to make!'

Tuesday came around quickly. Sam had almost recovered from Red Team's loss at the Button Line, but it was still a sore point. When Fleck arrived at Many Hands for the first workshop, it was Dima behind the counter. 'Hi,' she said, 'I'm here for Trixie's workshop?'

'Oh, hello again! I'm just minding the till while Bev moves her car,' Dima said. 'I wouldn't go back there just yet. Trixie and Helen are having one of their classic battles. Charlie is in there doing his best.'

'Yikes. Sorry, who is Charlie? I think Trixie mentioned him …'

'Charlie is the president of the board of directors. He's one of those men who thinks it's his job to fix things. I know better. I'm staying out of it.'

'Good plan.' Fleck parked the pusher and flipped the brake on. 'We should probably wait here and let the argument run its course.'

'And spy,' Dima added promptly.

'Definitely spy,' Fleck agreed. 'What have I missed so far?'

'Trixie wants to apply for all these grants. She says it was Donna's idea. Helen doesn't believe her. She doesn't want the grants.'

'Why doesn't Helen want grants?'

'I don't know. It's complicated. She wants the Society to retain its independence. She likes the way we've always done things.'

'What does Charlie think?'

'Charlie hasn't had the chance to say anything yet!'

Norah sat on the floor and played with a set of knitted chickens. Fleck and Dima peered across through the doorway to the back room. Helen and Trixie were facing each other with a rather handsome man who must be Charlie standing alongside, like some sort of referee. He seemed vaguely familiar, but Fleck couldn't place him. At first, the two women were speaking over the top of each other, but then Helen's voice won. 'No. No. That's how it starts. I do not feel comfortable with an outside body poking its nose into our affairs. We have our own ways of doing things here and we have managed just fine for almost forty years.'

'But what if we don't want to be just fine? What if we want to be excellent?'

'We do not become excellent by losing sight of who we are. You've been involved in the organisation for all of five minutes and you think you know everything that needs to be done and everything that needs to change. Why don't you spend some of your energy actually pausing to listen? Why don't you take a minute to appreciate how things are before you come in with your bulldozer to change everything?'

Charlie leaned forward. 'I think that—'

Trixie responded to Helen as if Charlie hadn't spoken. 'It's not just me. Donna says it sounds like a good idea. Donna says I should definitely look into it. So that's what I'm going to do.'

'Donna isn't here. Are you the board's president? No. You're not. Charlie is the chair and he agrees with me, don't you, Charlie?'

Charlie raised a placatory hand. 'Look—'

But Helen hadn't finished talking. 'Charlie knows the dangers of grant-chasing. I have seen it far too many times. Organisations end up putting all their energy into ticking boxes and jumping through hoops. Before you know it, they are on a treadmill. I will not have the Society existing for the sake of existing. I will not allow us to lose sight of who we are.'

'But we don't have to change who we are. They just want information. They just want to see that our financial systems are transparent. We can do that, surely. That's not changing who we are.'

'No. I'm not having it. Our finances are our business. We are doing just fine without transforming ourselves into some government bureau.'

'What, so you'll let the Society crash and burn because you're too proud to accept help. Is that it?'

'You are being ridiculous. I don't know why we are having this conversation. If you need me, Charlie, I will be in my car. I have some phone calls to make.'

By now, Bev had joined Fleck and Dima at the counter as they eavesdropped on the argument. Fleck had hardly noticed her arrival. The three of them pretended not to watch as Helen strode through the shop and out the front door. Charlie, meanwhile, disappeared up the stairs. Fleck pushed the stroller with Alice into the back room. Dima followed behind, holding hands with Norah.

Trixie's face was pensive, but broke into a big smile when she saw them. 'The workshop! I almost forgot. Dima, you need to stay and learn as well. Knitting is great and all, but crochet is the best. Come sit at the table.'

The table was set up with balls of yarn and crochet hooks. Trixie talked them through a basic chain and then they started attempting granny squares. Dima split her attention between following the lesson and entertaining Norah, who had Dima thoroughly charmed. Alice dozed in her pusher.

'That was a great argument we walked in on. I still don't get why Helen was so angry.' Fleck was hunting for the right place to insert her hook. Trixie made it look so easy, but it wasn't so straightforward when she tried to do it herself.

'Oh, Helen found out that I was trying to apply for government grants. It was Donna's idea. But Helen says we need to remain independent and that Donna didn't mean we should apply for grants. But she did and the deadline is coming up.'

'Why doesn't Donna sort it out?'

'Oh, she's sick with Covid or something. At least, she had it last week – I don't know if she still has it. And I'd already said I'd look into it. Charlie said I should wait for Donna to get back, but we're going to run out of time!'

'What happens if you run out of time?'

'If we run out of time, we don't get the money. Simple as that. I hope Donna comes back soon.'

'Yeah. It sounds like things are getting confusing without her here.' Fleck held up her work. 'Am I doing this right?'

'Yes. Wait. You've got that twisted back-to-front. Now you've got it. Once you get the hang of granny squares, you can make heaps of things. We can have another workshop later on amigurumi, that Japanese style of crochet, so you can make stuffed toys and things.'

'Slow down! I might be able to manage this when you're sitting next to me, but there's no guarantee I can keep it going when I'm at home by myself!'

When Dima and Fleck had got into a rhythm, Trixie put her own demonstration granny square down. 'Did I tell you I got a new toy?' She dug about in her bag and produced a brightly coloured pouch. She unzipped the pouch and pulled out an electronic device. She held it on her open palm to show Fleck. It was round, flat and navy blue, almost like the lid of a jar of pasta sauce. When Fleck took it into her own hand, it was weighty and smooth.

'It's called a Tapster,' Trixie said, laying the object on the table. 'I bought it for my market stall. It's the coolest little gadget. You can use it for tap-and-go payments. It talks to an app on your phone. Anyway, I think they should get one here for the shop, but nobody wants to spend the money.'

'I think it's a good thing we can't take card payments here,' Dima said as she stitched. 'I already spend too much money here as it is. If I could pay by card, I might go bankrupt!'

By the end of the lesson, they had each constructed a granny square. Fleck's was around the size of a coaster. Dima gave hers to Norah. 'It can be a blanket for your dolls house!'

Norah looked confused for a moment. Fleck crouched down to whisper to her. 'It can be a blanket for your Batcave!'

Norah beamed.

CHAPTER SIX

'I'm giving *The Newsreader* a two. I've heard good things, but I'm not sure if I really want to watch it, or I just want to watch it so I can listen to the companion podcast. I do love a good companion podcast.'

'What did you give *Picard*?' Matthew's fingers poised over his laptop keyboard.

Fleck sipped her latte. 'I gave that one a two as well. I feel like it's jumped the shark. I could cope with it though. I could watch Patrick Stewart read out the user guide for our air fryer. That voice!'

'I gave it a three. You can't go wrong with Star Trek.'

Fleck and Matthew were sitting at the kitchen table drinking coffee and playing TV Tinder. The game was Matthew's initiative. At night, by the time they got the kids to bed, they usually only had time to watch one show together before they fell asleep too. And they only had time enough to *watch*, not to *discuss* what to watch. Hence TV Tinder.

On the spreadsheet Matthew had set up, in the 'candidates' column, there was a place where either of them could submit a TV show for consideration. There was no limit to the suggestions that could be provided. Then each of them assigned each candidate a score from zero to three. A zero was for a show you had no interest in watching, whereas a three was for a show you were very excited to watch. Half-points were also permitted.

The data from this spreadsheet informed an ordered list. This list was labelled *It's a Match!* When it was time to choose a new series to watch, it was merely a matter of reading the name of the candidate ranked most popular at the top of the list.

If the TV show was on a platform they did not subscribe to, it went to a different section. Another table would provide recommendations for which streaming service to trial next according to this data.

'We've still got a few more nights before we get to the end of *Fisk*,' Matthew said. 'I'm out tomorrow, remember?'

'Has it been a month already?' Fleck tried to keep her tone light. She was not resentful. She wasn't. It was really good that Matthew went out and did something for himself. And she didn't mind looking after the kids by herself. It's what she did during the week, anyway.

Matthew had a great love of trains. He was a member of the large volunteer team that ran the nearby miniature railway. Some volunteers sold tickets, some drove the engines, but Matthew loved setting the routes and signals. They often visited the park as a family on Sundays, when the trains ran. Matthew also went to the park on the third Saturday of the month to volunteer with set-up and maintenance.

Did it make Fleck a bad person that she sometimes hated those jolly little engines? Not most of the time. Most of the time she loved them. It wasn't even that she was possessive and wanted Matthew all to herself. Maybe she felt the unfairness that Matthew got to do something fun just for himself, when she had nothing.

It was possible her tone hadn't been as convincing as she had hoped. Matthew looked up. 'There's nothing stopping you from doing something too, you know. I'd be happy to take the kids on a different Saturday if you want to go out.'

Fleck shook her head. 'It's not that simple,' she muttered. Go out? Go out where? At least she knew where she stood with TV. She gave *Scrublands* a three.

Today's workshop was on cross-stitch. Fleck had learned the basics when she was in primary school but had never done it properly, with embroidery floss and aida cloth. Now Fleck and Trixie sat in the back room of the store, each holding an embroidery hoop. Fleck had chosen a pattern with the words *Kindred spirits* above a simple image of two girls side by side. There was enough detail in these small, pixellated figures for an *Anne of Green Gables* tragic to recognise them as Anne Shirley and Diana Barry, the bosom friends of Fleck's favourite book.

She wondered whether she should have started with a simpler pattern, one with only one colour perhaps, but Trixie hadn't seemed to mind. 'It's more important that it's a pattern you like, so you'll be motivated to learn the skills. If it's boring, you'll never finish it,' she'd said.

Dima had started the workshop with the two of them, but before long she'd taken Norah into the shop to look at the buttons. They were in there now. Alice was awake but settled. She eyed Fleck and Trixie solemnly from her pusher.

Fleck had almost finished stitching the letter 'K' when the shop bell jangled. Trixie tilted her head to peer through the gap in the curtains. 'Looks like Douglas Cooper. I swear, he is the crankiest man alive.'

Fleck turned and squinted through the gap as well. She could see an elderly man, wiry and slightly hunched, making his way to the counter.

'He doesn't strike me as someone who's big into crafting.'

'Nah, he does the accounts and stuff.'

It sounded like Douglas was now talking with Bev behind the counter. Fleck peered at her work. 'What do I do once I finish the letter? Do I cut the thread or just move across?'

'You can just move across. The letters are pretty close together.'

Douglas Cooper appeared in the doorway to the back room. 'What's going on?' he barked. 'I need this table.'

'I'm trialling some craft workshops to run in the shop.' Trixie smiled with exaggerated sweetness. 'We need this table too.'

Douglas's frown deepened. 'I need to go over the accounts – the finances for the Society. That's more important than some ladies' crafting circle.'

'I'm not sure if you've noticed, Douglas, but this is a crafting shop. Crafting is what we do.'

'I need the table. I need this space. You can have it back when I'm done.'

'It's fine. You can work up that end. Just move those bags there.'

'That is not enough space. I have a system. I need to spread out. I don't have time for girls playing about making pretty doilies. I have a board meeting tonight.'

'Okay, well, we're not going to be here all day. You can use the table after us or you can work at the other end. It's a big table.'

'What about upstairs? Is there space to work upstairs?' Fleck couldn't help it. She always wanted to be the peacemaker.

Douglas turned his withering expression on Fleck. 'Have you ever been upstairs? It's tiny. Donna's desk and Vanessa's desk and that's it. Unless you are suggesting I do the work on the bathroom bench? No. I'm using this table, like I always do. And I can't have you two sitting around while I'm going over the accounts.'

'That's a pity for you, then. Maybe we can set up a booking system for the table. You could block out the time you need in a calendar or something. Right now, we're using the table.' Trixie made an exaggerated display of pulling her thread through her work.

Douglas glared at Trixie and shook his head. 'Where's Helen?'

Trixie shrugged. Douglas dumped his pile of books on the end of the table and stalked back into the shop.

'Ooh. Here we go,' Trixie said. She put her needlework down and stepped over to the pile of books and folders. There was an accounts ledger with a black cover and red spine, a bottle-green two-ring binder and a few manilla folders in the standard buff colour. 'Watch the door, Fleck. Let me know when he's coming.'

Fleck put her work down and went over to stand by the doorway. She peeked through the curtain. Douglas appeared to be explaining something to Bev. They both bent over the counter, pointing at a piece of paper. Dima was showing Norah a tube of yellow buttons shaped like ladybirds.

Trixie began sorting through the pile of books and papers in front of her. The green ring binder was full of bank statements. Trixie flipped through them. 'Here we go. Account number. Do you remember how I showed you my new toy, the Tapster? I found out you can set up more than one bank account on it. So the Society could use this for the shop when I'm not using it for my stall. We lose so many sales because we're cash only.'

She began copying details from the bank statement into her phone. 'If I show it to them as something that's already set up, I'll have less resistance. But there still will be resistance because all change is bad, apparently.' Trixie snapped a photo of the bank statement and closed the binder. She continued to sort through the pile. 'This is helpful. I need this info for the grant application as well.'

Douglas, meanwhile, had stepped back to glare at a customer who had the audacity to interrupt his conversation with a purchase. Was he going to come back to the kitchen? No. The customer moved on, and Douglas resumed his conversation with Bev.

'Hey, Fleck. Look at this.' Trixie flipped open the manilla folder. A note was taped to the inside cover. It wasn't a sticky note but rather a rectangular card, perhaps the blank back of a business card. It was neatly taped down, with yellowed sticky tape running along each edge. Written on the card, in careful script, was the name, number and password for a bank account. The password was underlined. Trixie beamed. 'High-tech security right here. We're going to need a crack team to infiltrate this system!'

Fleck giggled, then stopped. A woman was coming down the stairs. She was immaculately groomed, with glossy hair and flawless makeup. She darted an anxious glance towards the shop. 'That's not Douglas Cooper out there, is it?'

Trixie gave a start. 'Vanessa! You made me jump out of my skin! Yes. Douglas is here.'

The woman rolled her eyes and stepped into the room. 'Ugh. Douglas Cooper is all I need right now. He's always loading me up with random things to do and it's always ten minutes before I'm supposed to go home.'

Fleck smiled. 'That's the worst. I'm Fleck, by the way.'

Trixie stood clutching Douglas's folders. It was as if she didn't want to keep investigating with Vanessa watching, but didn't want to put them down either. 'Sorry, I should have introduced you. Fleck, this is Vanessa Sparks.'

Vanessa nodded. 'I'm the office manager here. I'm going to the bank to sort out some financial stuff. When he asks, make sure he knows I'm definitely still working.' She slipped out the back door.

Fleck looked back through the curtain. 'Hurry up. It looks like he's about to head back this way.' She stepped back from the doorway and sat down.

Trixie closed the folders and stacked them back in the pile. Then she darted to her seat at the table. 'So, as you can see, Felicity, splitting the embroidery floss allows you to … Oh, hello, Douglas.' But Douglas ignored her and stomped up the stairs. Fleck and Trixie shared a secret smile.

They resumed stitching in silence for a while. Fleck managed to finish the letter 'd' and started on 'r'.

Trixie selected some gold embroidery floss from the set on the table. 'Poor Vanessa. She's so overworked, but some of the older members think we need to justify having someone on the payroll so they're always giving her extra work to do. It's the same with Donna, I suppose, but Donna's more confident and better at saying no. Donna and Vanessa are the only paid people here. Everyone else is a volunteer.'

Trixie's cross-stitch had the words *Per my last email* curling across it. She continued working in the new colour. 'In a way, it's good that the Society is volunteer-run, but it does have its limitations. It can be hard to hold volunteers to account in the same way as staff.'

They could hear Douglas stomping back down the stairs. He stepped into the room and glared at Trixie. 'Did she clock off early?'

Trixie smiled sweetly into her fancywork. 'She's the cat's mother.'

'Vanessa. Our so-called office manager. She hasn't finished her shift, so why isn't she here?'

'I think Vanessa's running errands.'

'She can bloody run errands in her own time, not when she's on the clock. What are we paying her for?'

'It's for the Society. She said she was going to the bank.'

'Gone to the bank? She has work to do here! We never used to need to hire staff to go to the bank. Nobody volunteers anymore. That is the problem with your generation. We shouldn't have to pay people. That money could be spent on more important things.' He looked at the door and huffed. 'Did she say when she'd be back? I have work for her to do.'

Trixie tried, unsuccessfully, to keep the corners of her mouth from turning up. 'I'm sure if you put it in an email, she'll get to it.'

Douglas scowled. 'I don't have time to be writing emails all day long! What is the point of hiring somebody to help us if she's never here? And as for Donna – when was the last time you saw Donna?'

Trixie frowned. 'I'm sure I've seen her. She had Covid a couple of weeks ago. Has she not got better from that yet?'

Douglas shook his head. 'That woman has done a disappearing act on us. Sick leave. Annual leave. Stress leave. *Stress leave?* Let me tell you, in my day, stress leave did not exist. In my day, it was called "Pull your socks up and get on with things"!'

'Sounds healthy,' Fleck muttered under her breath. Douglas seemed to come from Helen's school of antagonistic volunteering.

Trixie frowned. 'I didn't know Donna was on stress leave. Is she okay? Is everything okay?'

'I don't know how she expects us to run things while she is sitting on the couch eating chips and watching television. *Stress leave …*' He shook his head. 'Let me know when Vanessa decides to get back to the job that we are paying her for. I need to talk to her. It's important.'

'But what about Donna?'

'Sure. If Donna decides to turn up, let me know as well.'

'No, I mean is Donna okay?'

'I don't know anything more about it. You'll have to ask somebody else.'

'So you're going to hang around the shop until Vanessa is back?'

'Yes.'

'But you don't have time to write an email?'

Douglas scowled and stalked out of the room.

After the workshop, Trixie unlocked her front door and hung her bike helmet on the hook. She would quickly do the breakfast dishes and hang the washing out, and then she would have several uninterrupted hours for creative work.

In theory, she should get heaps done in that time, but she was still getting used to this routine. In the past, she would need to snatch pockets of time to create where she could. Most of her days had been spent caring for Joseph and when she got a spare twenty minutes, she had be disciplined and put it to good use. It was almost intimidating now to have six hours of Joseph-free time. She was only gradually finding ways to structure things so that she didn't fritter it away. It seemed like a wide expanse of time, but 3.30pm came around really quickly.

Trixie had set up two desks for herself in the study. One was analogue, the other digital. She had read about this idea in a book on creativity. The analogue desk was set up with beautiful pens and textas, thick paper, balls of yarn and reels of embroidery thread. The digital desk had her laptop, lamp and camera equipment on it. By keeping the two separate, her mind could focus on the creative or the analytical without distraction. Today she would be working at the analogue desk, sketching out some new designs. But first, dishes.

Trixie had never been one to enjoy housework. But she didn't mind it so much lately. She gazed out the window as she scrubbed the last bowl and put it on the dish rack to dry. Then she drained the water, dried her hands and went to the laundry. She pulled wet washing out of the machine. It was having her own house – that was what did it. She was grateful to do housework in a house she could call her own.

When Trixie had got the keys to 13A Fleet Avenue, it was like a large, airy room had opened up in her brain. The house was a rental but part of a long-term scheme. Trixie had been told she could renovate and landscape the garden as if it were her own. She could stay here for as long as she wanted and never had to move out.

She pegged Joseph's school uniform on the line. The strain of being in an unstable housing situation had taken up so much of her thinking space. She hadn't realised how much she'd been thinking about a place to live until suddenly she didn't have to. This was more than a house. This was peace.

'I don't know. I told her to wait, but she never listens,' Matthew said. 'Then she'll come back later and complain that it's not working and expect me to fix it. It happens every time. Argh. Let's talk about something else.'

Fleck gazed out of the car window as they approached a large roundabout. 'Are the steam engines going to be out?' It was Sunday and they were on their way to the miniature railway.

Matthew shook his head, his eyes still on the road. 'Nah. They're getting some maintenance done. Just diesels today.'

They drifted into silence as the traffic thickened. Fleck's mind wandered as she gazed out of the window. She picked up George's puzzle in her brain for an idle play. What was that little country in West Africa? She remembered it had four letters. Not Mali, not Niger – Togo! But Togo still had two vowels. Ugh. She mentally travelled some more.

Maybe she should look at Asia. What was the name of that sultanate near Indonesia?

'Felicity? *Felicity!* Can you help me out here?' Matthew was looking harried. Sam and Norah were loudly bickering. Norah had started shrieking at the top of her lungs. Fleck hadn't noticed.

It was a regular point of strain between the two of them that Fleck tuned out backseat tantrums when Matthew was driving, leaving him alone to negotiate heavy traffic and screaming children. It was hard to explain that she genuinely hadn't registered the localised cacophony. She swiftly intervened now, mediating in the dispute over whether Sam was making weird faces at Norah or if that was just his actual real-life face.

The squawking subsided. Fleck blinked and frowned. *Chad. Cyprus. Egypt. Chad. Cyprus. Egypt.*

CHAPTER SEVEN

Fleck arrived at the shop early for the workshop the next week. She spent some time looking at the haberdashery section. Norah was still entranced by the tubes of buttons and the rainbow wall of thread spools. As well as the new buttons in tubes and on cards, there was a large tub filled with assorted second-hand buttons, sold by the scoop. Norah gloried in pushing her arms deep into this tub. Fleck had to stop her, though, when she tried to climb in head-first. Alice was looking sleepy, so Fleck rolled the pusher back and forth as she inspected the stock.

Fleck loved the notions – those extra bits and bobs used in sewing that weren't fabric or thread – best of all. Half the time, she didn't even know what the little devices were used for – she just loved the look of them. She considered purchasing a bobbin. She had no use for one nor did she own a sewing machine, but they were so adorable! Like tiny metal wagon wheels. Maybe she would buy one just to keep in her pocket and play with. It could be her little talisman.

The shop bell rang, and Trixie appeared. 'What are you looking at bobbins for? We're doing knitting today.'

'Why are you *not* looking at bobbins? Bobbins are so good. I'm going to buy this packet.'

'Are they the right sort for your sewing machine?'

'I don't own a sewing machine. You don't need to own a sewing machine to appreciate a decent bobbin.'

Trixie shook her head. 'You're an original.'

Fleck took the small packet to the counter. Bev was already serving a customer there. A woman was purchasing a patchwork quilt. She had grey hair with pearly pink and hot pink streaks and was wearing a brightly patterned shirt dress. Bev held up her hand in response to the woman's proffered card. 'It's cash only, I'm afraid, but there is an ATM just around the corner on Highett Road.'

Trixie looked up. 'Wait. Bev, why aren't you using the Tapster?' Trixie strode over to the counter and turned to reassure the woman who was looking slightly bewildered in her designer-quirky, orange-rimmed spectacles. 'We can take all major cards.' Then she turned back to Bev. 'I programmed it with all the prices. It couldn't be more straightforward.'

Bev shook her head. 'People know this is a cash-only shop. It has always been a cash-only shop. We are only going to confuse people if we introduce things like this.'

'People are still allowed to pay with cash, Bev. We're not stopping them. This is just giving another option.'

Bev huffed and crossed her arms. 'I don't know why we have that thing. It's a waste of money if you ask me.'

'Oh my gosh, Bev. It's not a waste of money. It cost sixty dollars. This blanket costs one hundred and twenty dollars. If the Society had paid for the Tapster, it would have made its money back in one sale. But the Society hasn't paid for the Tapster. It's on loan from me. It costs you nothing. What are you afraid of?'

Fleck, meanwhile, had realised she wasn't carrying any cash. She sidled back to the shelves to return the bobbins.

Bev placed both hands on the counter as if smoothing it. 'It's not unreasonable to just get people to walk to the ATM. It's not far. People are happy to do it.'

Trixie shook her head firmly and gestured to the customer. 'This lady – what's your name?'

'Maureen,' the woman said uncertainly.

'Maureen doesn't want to walk to the ATM. Maureen will say she is happy to do it and then she will leave and then Maureen will never come back. You're losing a sale, Bev. Maureen wants to buy the quilt. She does not want to buy it with cash. Maureen wants to pay with her credit card. We have the facilities right here. You can tap "blanket" and "charge" or you can type in the amount manually if you prefer. Here. The light's green. Tap your card, Maureen. There. Done. Wasn't that easy? And you can even offer to email her a receipt, but nobody ever says yes. Would you like a receipt, Maureen? No? Didn't think so. Thank you for your custom, Maureen. See you next time.'

Bev looked at Trixie levelly. Then, slowly and deliberately, she reached into her bag and pulled out a sign. It was polished wood and shaped like a Toblerone box: a long, triangular log. She placed the sign on the counter with a *thunk*. The lettering curled across the sign in calligraphic capitals: *CASH ONLY PLEASE*.

Trixie narrowed her eyes. She picked up the Tapster. 'I'm going to plug this in and give it a charge,' she said. Her tone said, *This isn't over*.

'Honestly, she's so stubborn. I bet Helen told her not to use it.'

They were sitting at the table, each with a ball of yarn and a set of needles. Fleck knew the basics of knitting, but Trixie was helping her to follow the pattern so that she could make a Trauma Teddy.

Norah was happily playing at the table too. Trixie had given her a large bowl of buttons from the tub and an A3 sheet of white paper. 'You can make a design with the buttons on this, and I'll take a picture with my special camera,' she'd said. Norah had nodded, but for now she seemed happy sorting and re-sorting, sometimes stacking the buttons into little piles.

Fleck was really enjoying these Tuesday morning workshops. None of the crafts she had learned had become her great driving passion, but they were good fun, an enjoyable pastime. It was also great fun spending time with Trixie. It had been too long since she'd spent time with a friend she really clicked with.

The shop bell jangled again. Trixie leaned over to peer through the gap in the curtain. 'It's Charlie. Ha. I wondered why Bev was putting fresh lipstick on. Bev fancies him a bit, I reckon.'

Fleck looked into the shop as well. She recognised Charlie from last week when she'd seen him mediating Helen and Trixie's argument, but she didn't know the other man. 'Hey, I meant to ask you before. Why does Charlie look so familiar? Is he a school dad?'

Trixie shook her head. 'You know him because he's Charlie Marshall.'

'Am I supposed to know who that is?'

'He's famous. He used to play for Carlton back in the nineties.'

'Oh. I don't really follow football.'

'Yeah, but he also owns that hotel chain now. He's sort of famous for being a rich businessman, I guess.' Trixie chose a ball of orange yarn and began to cast on. 'You start with ten stitches, by the way. Legs first.'

Fleck picked up a ball of variegated rainbow yarn and tried to find the end. 'Wait, wasn't he a judge on that TV show where the contestants wanted to be entrepreneurs?' Fleck had seen some ads for this show when she was watching a different reality show in preparation for her next school-gate conversation.

'Um. Yes, I think so. He's often on TV for things.'

'Okay. So he's the president of the board?' Fleck began casting on stitches.

'Yeah. I think he joined a couple of years ago when they were trying to get more members because a few of the old board members died or something. He's one of those people who's on a lot of boards. Most of the directors have been on the board from the start, though. The other guy is John, who's on the board too. He joined at the same time as Charlie. Actually, I think he works for Charlie. I don't know that for sure. I know hardly anything about John Dobson. The man has, like, zero personality.'

The other man was tall with a shaved head. His face, true to Trixie's description, was completely impassive.

Trixie yanked a length of yarn from her ball and started knitting her first row. 'I've been in the Society for six months and I still don't know how he fits in. I think he's Charlie's assistant or security guard or something. He's always around.'

Charlie was chatting to Bev. John was standing slightly apart. He wasn't joining the conversation. He wasn't looking around the shop. He was just standing there, looking serious. Then his eyes shot across to the crack in the curtains. He looked directly at Fleck and Trixie. They both looked quickly back down to their work.

Fleck had almost finished the first leg when Charlie Marshall appeared at the curtained entrance. Trixie gave a welcoming smile. 'Hello, Charlie. This is Fleck – Felicity. We're road-testing the craft workshops today.'

Charlie flashed a charming smile at Fleck. 'A pleasure to meet you.' He turned to Trixie. 'Vanessa upstairs?'

Trixie shook her head. 'I don't know. She might be. I don't think Donna's there, either. Douglas said she's taken stress leave. Is she all right?'

Fleck lowered her knitting to observe the conversation.

Charlie frowned. 'Yeah. She was talking about coming back in, but I convinced her to take some more time. She needs to be careful: I think she's in danger of getting burned out.'

Trixie began casting on for the bear's second leg. 'She didn't seem burned out at all to me. I hope she's okay.'

Charlie smiled. 'She will be. The important thing is she's taking time off. I'm always more worried about the ones who refuse to take measures to look after themselves.'

The back door burst open. Helen Greythorn stepped into the room and made a beeline for Charlie. 'Charlie, what is going on? I need you to tell me what this is all about.' In her hand, she waved a printed sheet of A4 paper.

Charlie shook his head. 'You've lost me, I'm afraid.'

Helen opened her mouth in outrage, but no sound came out. She shook the piece of paper in Charlie's direction again. 'This! Donna has resigned. Just up and left. No notice. Nothing.' She handed him the printout.

'No way. It must be a mistake.' Trixie stood up so that she could read over Charlie's shoulder. 'Oh my gosh, Helen, is this a printout of an email? Someone needs to show you how to use the "forward" button.'

Charlie was shaking his head. 'She never said anything to me about quitting. She did ask if I'd have capacity to take on some of her duties for her while she's on leave, but that was it.'

Trixie continued to read the email over Charlie's shoulder, ignoring Helen's glares. 'Wait. Is she leaving the *country*?'

Helen plucked the paper out of Charlie's hands and folded it over. 'Donna has already left the country. She has moved to Koh Samui indefinitely.'

'Koh Samui?' Trixie said. 'Where is that? Indonesia? Thailand?'

'I do not have time to be giving geography lessons to the wilfully ignorant. Charlie, you're telling me Donna gave you no warning that this was going to happen?'

'None at all. This is completely out of the blue.'

'But she asked you to take on some of her workload? Are you even available to do that?'

'I am. I was just about to head upstairs and sort things out.'

'Hm. Well, I have some phone calls to make. I'll leave you to it.' Helen left through the shop.

Charlie, however, sat down at the table. He stared vaguely at the microwave, shaking his head. 'Maybe I should have seen it coming,' he said. 'This has just thrown me.'

Trixie resumed her seat at the table. 'I know! Why would she ghost us like that? It's not very Donna. She's always been so straight-down-the-line. Why wouldn't she tell us herself? Especially if she was moving overseas.'

Charlie shook his head. 'I mean, I knew she was going through a hard time, but this just seems so drastic.'

Fleck picked up her knitting. 'Why was she going through a hard time?'

Trixie shook her head. 'See, that's the thing: I didn't think she was going through a hard time. When I last spoke to her, she seemed energised. She had all these plans for the Society. Still,' Trixie sighed, 'it's been a while since I spoke with her properly. But to leave the country? It just seems so abrupt.'

Charlie shook his head. 'It isn't like her at all. But I suppose she hasn't been herself these past few weeks. I don't understand it.'

Fleck frowned. 'Do you think there's something going on that you don't know about?'

Trixie pursed her lips. 'It just doesn't sit right with me. None of this sounds like Donna. I mean, she's a hard worker, but she isn't the type to get burned out. She's great at setting boundaries. And she seemed genuinely energised by the job. I don't feel like we're getting the full picture here.'

Charlie looked concerned. 'Really? What do you think we're missing?'

Trixie rubbed her thumb across her stitches. 'I don't know. Something just seems off. I just ... I don't know. Maybe if I could talk to her. Charlie, do you have her contact details? I feel like if I could talk to her, I could get to the bottom of it.'

Charlie shrugged. 'If only it were that simple. But I suppose it doesn't hurt to try.'

Fleck leaned forward. 'What do you think is going on? Do you have any theories?'

Trixie resumed stitching. 'The last time I spoke to Donna, she was planning all these inquiries and audits. She was really enthusiastic about it, but almost everyone else didn't want it. Douglas was deadset against it, and so were Helen and Bev. Charlie and I were the only ones who thought it was a good idea.'

'So, what's your theory?' Fleck was feeling intrigued. Her knitting lay forgotten on the table.

'What if somebody has scared her off? What if there's something going on that they didn't want her to see and they, like, *got* to her?'

'Got to her? That's a bit dramatic, don't you think?' Charlie looked unconvinced.

Trixie was working through a tangle in her yarn. 'I don't know. It just seems weird. She was just starting to look into things. She told me that she thought there might be some errors in the accounts. Next thing you know, she's left the country. No warning. Just left.'

'So somebody thought they'd teach her a lesson by forcing her to move to a tropical island?' Fleck was sceptical.

Trixie huffed. 'I just mean—'

Charlie grinned playfully. 'I wonder if they punished her by making her sit in a deckchair and drink out of a coconut with a little umbrella sticking out of it?'

'Well, it's a standard torture method, isn't it?' Fleck said, 'Waterboarding, cat-o'-nine-tails, sandy beach …'

Trixie rolled her eyes. 'Okay, okay. It's only a theory.'

Charlie nodded. 'We shouldn't tease you. I'm as baffled as you are. And I'm here if you ever want to run theories past someone. The good news is, I'm here to support the Society in whatever way I can. I'll keep on with what Donna started. Maybe, if I'm lucky, I'll be punished and sent to Barbados.'

Fleck had spent the last few months in a fog of breastfeeding hormones. Her strongest urge was always for sleep and more sleep. Matthew was important to her because he could sometimes enable her procurement of sleep. He was her comrade in the trenches, someone to share quips with, to provide solidarity. Anything more than this was beyond her at the moment. So it came as a surprise one morning, as Fleck watched Matthew emerge from their en suite in his boxers, buttoning his shirt, to feel a distinct *zing*. How had she forgotten? Matthew was *hot*.

Matthew grinned his twinkly smile. 'Looks like Madam gave us another full night! When was her last feed?'

Fleck propped Alice up to face him. They were both sitting up in bed, surrounded by cushions. 'Ten pm! She hasn't had another feed since ten!'

'Clever girl!' Matthew clipped his watch onto his wrist. 'I'm in the office today. What do you have on?'

Fleck rubbed her eyes. 'I'm going into the shop. Trixie is going to teach me piecework.'

'Piecework? What is that? It sounds like you're building clocks or something.'

'I think it just means patchwork. Like sewing lots of little bits of fabric together.'

Matthew's mouth curled into a teasing smile. 'Oh no. Please tell me you're not going to take up a new project. Please say it isn't true.'

Fleck pressed her lips together. 'What are you talking about?'

'Our poor wardrobe can't take any more punishment! The wardrobe says no. The wardrobe is putting its foot down.' Matthew said this from within the wardrobe in question. He was getting his pants.

'The wardrobe is *built* for storage. That is its *job*.'

'The wardrobe is built to store clothes. It is not a graveyard for abandoned hobbies.'

Fleck had become still. Her throat burned. Any thought of Matthew being attractive evaporated in the heat of her suppressed anger. 'What are you saying?'

Matthew's voice came from the closet. 'What have we got in here? Let's see. We've got three paint canvases, all unwrapped. One food dehydrator. A leather craft kit. A Japanese pottery-mending kit. A loom. A big pile of fabric. Eleventy million jewellery supplies. This is not a walk-in wardrobe. It's a step-over-the-unfinished-project storage closet.'

Fleck got up out of her bed. She handed Alice to Matthew, who was still smiling. Fleck was not smiling. 'She needs a nappy change. I'm going to get a coffee.'

A crossword. She needed a crossword. Her thoughts were swirling as she walked out of the bedroom. She needed to focus her brain. There on the kitchen bench was the brown letter that had arrived in the mail last week, the address in her mother's familiar loopy hand. The envelope was filled with crosswords and puzzles clipped from Queensland's *The Courier-Mail*. The little note: *Your mother loves you.*

She loved these regular care packages from her mum. But she had done all the tricky ones now. There were only easy ones left. She didn't want an easy puzzle.

Matthew walked in with a freshly changed Alice, still grinning. He clearly still thought this was just teasing. Fleck did not look up from the newspaper clippings. He strapped Alice into her highchair. Fleck could tell from her periphery that he was trying to catch her eye. When he had made himself a coffee, he sat at the table with her. 'Am I in trouble?'

Fleck shook her head without looking up. 'I hate the way you say that.'

'What did I say?'

'*Am I in trouble?* Like the problem is me. Like the problem is that I'm upset with you. Like you have nothing to do with any of it.'

'*Are* you upset with me?'

Fleck stuffed the clippings back into the envelope and folded it closed, stood up and put it back on the shelf, then turned to face Matthew. She worked hard to keep her voice steady. 'The shed, the garage, the study: they are all chock-full of train stuff. And you are complaining about one cupboard. One.'

'I'm not complaining. I'm just—'

'You *are* complaining. Jokes are still complaining.'

'I didn't realise—'

'It's completely different for you. You're a man and you have interests? That is admirable! Everybody, make space for the man and his important interests! It's not the same for me. It's not. I'm not ever allowed to take up space.'

'That's not fair. I'm not saying you can't have interests. But none of these are interests. Half of them haven't even been opened. That's not an interest. That's just hoarding.'

Fleck shook her head. Her nostrils flared. 'Where is Friday's paper?'

Matthew spoke slowly and carefully. 'Given that it is Tuesday, I would say it is in the recycling bin.'

'What? I'm not done with it yet!'

'I'm no expert, but keeping old newspapers is definitely a sign of hoarding.'

Fleck spoke through her teeth as she strode to the recycling bin. 'I only buy one newspaper a week! David Astle is my favourite crossword setter. There is only one Friday crossword all week! The DA is the only one I like. How do you not already know this about me? It is not unreasonable that I hold onto the one newspaper I buy all week for the duration of said week! That does not make me a hoarder!' She extracted the paper from the bin, then extracted the crossword from the paper. She held it up for Matthew to see, then folded it and took it to the table.

Norah called out from her room. Matthew got up and went to her. Fleck sighed and looked at the crossword. A few of the answers jumped out at her and she filled them in. As she felt herself becoming absorbed in the puzzle, her breathing slowed and her thoughts untangled. In this bubble of cogitation, her emotions no longer tripped over each other in a frenzy to be heard. There was only Fleck and the puzzle.

Matthew and Norah emerged. Norah was dressed and out of her night nappy. After he'd set Norah up with a bowl of cereal, Matthew sat back at the table, a little cautiously.

Fleck offered him a small smile. 'I'm still stuck on ten down.'

'Let me hear it.' Matthew was not as obsessed with cryptics as Fleck, but he knew how to work them. And he seemed relieved to have been handed this peace offering of sorts.

'Eight letters. "I wind up putting family first. A golden way to mend something precious." Space-space-N-space-space-space-G-space.'

Matthew frowned. 'What's the definition for that one? Is it "precious"?'

Fleck shrugged. 'I'm completely stumped.'

They both looked at the crossword in silence. Alice chattered happily in her highchair. Norah blinked at her cereal. She had the morning stares. Sam emerged and sat at the table.

'Family could be "kin",' Matthew offered.

'Kintsugi!' Fleck exclaimed. 'A golden way to mend something precious is kintsugi.'

'What is that? I've never heard of it.'

'You know – when you put gold in the cracks and make it beautiful? You make the cracks a feature? No?' Matthew shook his head. Fleck squinted at the grid. 'I can't get all the wordplay. I can see "KIN" and "I" but what's "TSUG"?'

Matthew scratched the side of his nose. 'Why does 'I' come at the end of the word? It's at the start of the clue. Is there some sort of position indicator?'

Fleck muttered to herself. 'Wind-up. Wind-up. I wind up being at the end of the word. I get given the wind-up.'

Matthew pointed at the grid. 'It is a down clue. So "up" could be significant.'

Fleck's eyes widened. 'It's not wind-up! It's not wind – it's wind! Wind as in gust!'

Matthew opened his mouth and nodded. 'I wind. That's "I GUST".

And the "up" tells you to write it backwards up the page.'

'Geez, that's tough!' Fleck wrote the letters into the crossword.

'Hey, I'm sorry about before,' Matthew said. 'I thought I was just teasing. I didn't realise … I'm sorry. I don't really mind if you use the wardrobe. It's a big wardrobe.'

Fleck nodded. 'I know. I think you just hit a nerve. I'm okay.'

'Help me!' Norah had somehow managed to pull the side of her bowl down onto the table. A small flood of cereal and milk spread out, landing on her lap.

'I clean the child, you clean the table?' Fleck smiled like she was inviting Matthew to come on an exciting adventure with her.

Matthew twinkled back. 'You are on!'

CHAPTER EIGHT

'I'm not sure I've mastered it well enough to run a workshop,' Trixie said to Fleck, 'but let's give it a go. My thinking is that I can get everyone set up and run the session, but I can get Bev to come in and help out with the more technical questions.' Trixie had told Fleck that crochet and cross-stitch were her preferred crafts, but she had decided the workshops should have a few other options as well. Hence piecework quilting.

They had taken a while to get set up today: after they'd unpacked the shopping bags of fabric and equipment, they'd searched the store for Trixie's phone. 'It's driving me crazy!' she'd said. 'I thought it was at home somewhere, so I was looking everywhere for it all weekend. But then I remembered that this is the last place I remember having it for sure. I definitely had it here on Friday.' When twenty minutes of looking around the shop and back room brought no results, they'd conceded defeat and begun the lesson.

Dima was back again for this workshop. She and Norah were playing with some scraps of fabric. Dima had used rubber bands to fashion them into little puppets. Alice was watching them play with great interest.

Trixie pinched two triangles of fabric together. 'The thing I like about piecework is that it's all about little steps. Once you've cut your pieces, you're just building up the blocks – that's what you call it when you've sewn a few of these little pieces together – one tiny seam at a time. You don't have to think about the whole quilt. You just need to focus on the little seam. And that's enough for today.'

'It's like a meditation,' said Fleck. Even though there was nothing meditative about the tangle of thread and fabric in front of her. She'd sewn along the wrong edge and there was a snarl of cotton she hadn't pulled through properly. Still. The concept was nice. She could appreciate the concept.

It sounded like the people in the upstairs room were in need of a little contemplative quilting themselves. It was clear they were arguing about something. Maybe Charlie was trying to interfere with Douglas's rigid account-keeping methods? That was one sure-fire way to get him offside. And now it sounded like they were coming downstairs.

Helen and Douglas entered the room, followed by Charlie and Vanessa. Trixie raised her eyebrows at Fleck and they both turned to face the small crowd that had now joined them.

'You need to answer some questions.' Douglas was looking towards Trixie as he spoke. It wasn't always clear to whom his comments were directed. Last week, as they stood waiting for the school bell, Trixie had shown Fleck her list of 'Things Douglas Cooper Never Says'. On it were 'please', 'thank you', 'I was wrong', 'that sounds interesting' and 'your given name'. It was true. He never used names when talking to people. It was up to you to calibrate the specific angle of the tilt of his head when talking in a group to work out if he was actually addressing you. He got impatient if you didn't, but he never deigned to clarify.

Trixie allowed her face to look pleasantly quizzical. Douglas's frown deepened.

Charlie shifted to the side. 'Perhaps I could speak to Trixie upstairs. I think that would be the best way.'

Helen and Douglas both said 'No' in quick succession. First Helen, then Douglas. Then Helen spoke again. 'Definitely not. We need to talk about it here. I want to hear what she's got to say for herself.'

Charlie shook his head. 'I really think this should be done privately.'

'And I don't think she needs to be afforded any such privilege.' There was a tilt to Helen's chin that suggested 'Danger ahead for all who do not comply'.

Trixie looked from Charlie to Helen to Douglas and finally to Vanessa, as if one of them held a clue to the situation in their facial expression. 'What is all this about?'

Charlie stepped aside from the stairway and gestured to it with his arm. 'If you could just come upstairs, we can talk about it in the office.'

Helen shook her head firmly. 'No. I wish to be a party to this. And so does Douglas. I think we've both earned that right.'

Trixie's eyebrows wrinkled in confusion. 'Look, I'm fine to talk down here if it makes it easier.'

Charlie said, 'I—' at the same time as Helen said, 'See?' They both stopped and eyed each other.

'It really is fine to have the conversation here,' said Trixie. 'But please can you just spit it out? You're making me nervous.'

Charlie sighed in resignation. 'It's about the Society's bank account.'

Trixie bit her lip and shot a look at Fleck. 'The bank account?' She affected an innocent tone.

Bev had materialised in the doorway to the shop. She raised an eyebrow at Helen, who frowned in response before speaking. 'Vanessa says she saw you going through the books and looking up the passwords.'

Vanessa had been standing quietly beside the sink up until now. She cleared her throat. 'I didn't know at the time what was going on, but later I realised she must have been getting access to the bank account. She was going through all the paperwork – the passwords, everything. And she was keeping a lookout by the door!' Vanessa was turning pink as she pointed at Fleck, and Fleck could feel her own face warming.

Trixie, however, looked completely unabashed. She gave a reluctant half-smile. 'Okay, yeah, that was a bit sneaky. But I was just trying to set up the Tapster. Excellent security measures, by the way, Douglas. I think maybe ASIO should take up your method of taping the passwords to the inside cover of an unattended manilla folder. Forget retina scans or two-factor authentication. Douglas's methods are watertight!'

Helen gripped the back of one of the chairs at the table. 'There. You see? She admits it. I can't believe this. She *admits* it.'

Douglas, meanwhile, was pacing the room and shaking his head. It seemed like words were beyond him. He paused and opened his mouth. But then he closed it, shook his head and continued pacing. The pent-up rage seemed to radiate from his skin. He was a kettle on the boil.

Dima had been playing on the floor under the table with Norah. She shot Fleck a look of concern through a gap in the tablecloth before returning to her pretend picnic.

Trixie attempted to resume her stitching but succeeded only in picking up her work and fumbling around a bit. 'I needed the details to set up the Tapster account, that's all. I don't see why it's such a big deal.'

'If your motives were so innocent, why did you need to go behind everyone's backs? Why didn't you just say that you needed access to set it up?' Charlie had the face of a school principal who knew in his heart that his student had committed a crime but was sincerely hoping he was mistaken.

Trixie scoffed. 'If I'd said I was thinking of introducing a new system for cashless payments, *she* would say we don't need it, *he* would say we can't afford it and *she* would say the whole process is far too complicated,' she said, pointing to Bev, Douglas and Helen in turn. 'And *you* would probably say we need to think about insurance. But if I come to you with a system already set up and say all you have to do is press this button and it works, you would – well, actually you would still resist if you're Bev – but there would be a much better chance of you taking it on. So I got it all set up. I probably shouldn't have gone through Douglas's things when he was away, but I wasn't trying to do anything dodgy. I just needed access so I could give permission for the payments to go into the account. You can't set it up without access, and if I had to go through one of you, you would have just said no.'

'So you are just openly admitting that you infiltrated our accounts.' Helen peered over the top of her glasses at Trixie.

'What do you mean, "infiltrated"? You're twisting things around. I had to do a bit of snooping, it's true. But it was all for a good cause. Why are you all being so weird about this?'

'Why did you need to go out of your way to set up the system anyway?' Bev said, piping up from her doorway. 'Why do you care so much?'

'What? The same reason you care. The same reason any of us care. I *care*, okay?'

Helen affected a derisive laugh. 'Oh, sure. You care.'

Trixie glared. 'I do. What would you even know about it, *Helen?*' Trixie had a knack of enunciating Helen's name like it was an insult.

Helen shook her head, seething. 'You care about your own ego. You care about exploiting a charity to line your own pockets. You act as if you want to change and improve things, when really you just wanted money.'

Charlie cleared his throat. 'It has come to our attention that you have been using your access to this bank account to steal from the Society.'

The room, full of people as it was, suddenly became very still. Everybody looked at Trixie. Trixie looked at everyone in turn, her evident confusion mounting. Finally, she spoke. 'No, I haven't.' Fleck wasn't sure what tone Trixie was aiming for, but she sounded like a petulant teenager.

Charlie spoke again. 'I've researched some financial counselling organisations that you might want to call. If something like gambling or addiction is an issue for you, I have a list of support agencies. We want you to get the help you need.'

Helen and Trixie exclaimed, 'This is ridiculous!' at the same time. Helen glared at Trixie. 'Why are we treating her like the victim in this situation? She's not the victim. I'm sure she's done very nicely with the spare pocket money she's accumulated from ripping off a charity. I'll tell you who the victims are. The victims are the people we assist who won't be getting as much help from us as they should because somebody has been dipping her hand in the cookie jar.'

'Yes, well, that somebody was not me!' Trixie was almost shouting. 'I've been set up! I would never steal from the Society. Somebody is trying to frame me!'

'Oh, sure. It's not your fault,' Helen said. 'It's never your fault, is it? That's the hallmark of your generation. It's always somebody else's fault.

'Oh, you are loving this, Helen, aren't you? You are *loving* this. You know it wasn't me. You just want to see me go down.' Trixie turned back to Charlie. 'Surely it's just an anomaly? Surely it's just some glitch? I didn't transfer any money. Maybe someone used the Tapster wrong and made the sales go into my account instead. Is that what you're talking about? I can just reverse the transaction if that's what happened. It doesn't mean I stole anything.'

Alice started to grizzle. Fleck unclipped her from the pusher and picked her up. She rocked her against her chest and looked around the room. Everyone was looking at Trixie. Trixie's eyes darted from Charlie to Helen to Douglas to Bev and to Vanessa. She reminded Fleck of a caged animal. Alice gave a loud wail, then put her toy giraffe in her mouth and subsided.

Charlie looked beleaguered. 'It has nothing to do with the Tapster payments. And we're not talking about a single errant transaction. Trixie, this has been a concerted campaign over many days, beginning from when you first accessed the account to set up the Tapster.'

Helen narrowed her eyes at Trixie. 'You tried out small payments at first. Just testing to see if we'd notice, were you? And then you decided to be greedy.'

Douglas, who'd been slowly building up steam as the conversation progressed, finally exploded. '*Twenty thousand dollars!*' he shouted. 'Almost our entire development fund and you took it for yourself. Twenty thousand dollars.'

Trixie shook her head. 'What are you even talking about?'

'It's the same account you set up with us to receive reimbursement payments for the supplies you purchased for the shop.' Charlie spoke slowly and carefully. 'There have been several small deposits made to your account over the past week. Then, over the course of this weekend, you moved twenty thousand dollars from our development account into your own account. I might not have noticed it for a while if I wasn't spending time familiarising myself with the accounts. The thing is …' Charlie hesitated, then continued. 'Your pattern of behaviour matches that of a professional fraudster—'

'It's not *my* pattern of behaviour!' Trixie interrupted. 'It's not me! Somebody else must have put that money into my account!'

'Oh, they did, did they? How nice for you! Who do you think stole the money for you? Your kleptomaniacal fairy godmother?' Helen's eyes flashed with rage.

'Surely you would have seen the money turn up in your account,' Bev said. 'Are we supposed to believe you didn't notice twenty thousand dollars just turning up?'

'My phone has been missing since Friday. I wasn't able to check my balance.'

Bev blew air through her cheeks. 'A little too convenient, if you ask me.'

'Pretty sure nobody did ask you, *Bev*,' Trixie snarled.

'See, Trixie, here's the thing,' Charlie said. 'If you had stolen the money, that's exactly what you would say.' He was clearly trying his best to be the voice of reason in a sea of chaos, but it was getting the better of him. A sheen of sweat coated his forehead.

'It doesn't even make sense,' Trixie said. 'Why would I do something that so obviously points back to me? I would never have got away with it.'

'Don't ask me why you would choose to embezzle twenty thousand dollars from a charity. You're the only one who can answer that question. Or maybe the police can.' Helen's voice was dripping with scorn.

Alice began to fidget again. She was getting agitated, sensing her mother's stress. Fleck felt cold with apprehension. This was serious. What was going on? She tried her best to rock and pat, but Alice was having none of it. She threw her toy to the ground, twisted in Fleck's arms and broke into a loud bout of crying.

Charlie closed his eyes and inhaled through his nose. 'Let's not involve the police just yet. But we are going to insist that you repay the funds that have been stolen. We also ask that you discontinue your volunteering arrangement at this store. Please turn in any keys or other Society property in the next few days. You should leave now.'

'I only have UHT milk, sorry,' Fleck said.

'That's okay,' Trixie replied. 'I drink it black anyway.'

It turned out Fleck had not been carrying a realistic mental image of the mess levels of her house (nor the milk levels in her fridge, for that matter). When she was in the house by herself, she didn't see the mess. It was a little jarring, then, when she invited Trixie over for coffee after the debacle at Many Hands, to suddenly notice the baskets of clothes on the living room floor, the dishes in the sink, the papers across the table and the toys everywhere. The house in Fleck's mind just did not look like that.

Trixie didn't seem to notice the clutter. She didn't seem to notice anything. She lowered herself into a seat at the table, after taking a small train off it. Fleck got to work making the coffee, surreptitiously tidying as she went. Alice was napping in her baby capsule. Norah was watching TV.

Fleck put a cup of coffee and a plate down in front of Trixie and quickly snatched away the surrounding papers to make room for a packet of biscuits.

'So, I guess that's it. I can't volunteer in the shop anymore, the workshops are a non-event and everybody thinks I'm a criminal.' Trixie stared straight ahead. She didn't drink her coffee or eat any of the biscuits.

Fleck sat down in the seat across from her. 'We're going to sort this out. We will get to the bottom of this.'

Trixie looked at Fleck in blank horror. 'What if they evict me? Do you think they'll evict me? I could never afford to rent another home in the area.'

Fleck frowned. 'Wait. Who would evict you? And why? Do you mean like the bank repossessing your home or something?'

Trixie hesitated. She took one of the Scotch Fingers out of the packet and rotated it in her hands.

'Trixie?'

Trixie dropped her gaze. 'My house. I … it's one of their houses. I didn't want you to know.'

'I don't understand.'

Trixie looked at the television. Adam West's Batman was consulting with Robin and Batgirl. She looked back at Fleck. 'I didn't want any of the school parents to know. I didn't want it to come out that I was renting through a program. Through a *charity*.'

'I am one hundred per cent certain that nobody cares about that sort of thing.'

'That's easy for you to say.'

They both paused and sipped their coffees. Fleck studied a spot on the table. 'So, is that how you got involved in Many Hands in the first place? Or was it the crafting thing?'

Trixie drew a deep breath. She looked at the TV again. 'When my husband – Joseph's dad – died, I went through a really rough patch.' She broke her biscuit in half and then began breaking it into smaller pieces. 'I couldn't work. I had all this debt. I had a toddler and no family support.'

Fleck looked at Trixie. 'That sounds awful.'

Trixie nodded. 'My housing situation wasn't settled. I kept having to move. I tried house-sitting a few times, but that doesn't work well when you've got a kid.'

'You were homeless?'

'I mean, sort of. It wasn't easy. We were "of no fixed address" for a while there. And I was … I guess I was in a really bad place emotionally.

'Anyway, we were staying in some emergency accommodation, just for a short while, and I found out about the housing program with Many Hands. There was a woman from the Society who met up with me and helped me to apply for it. It would mean we could have a house. We could treat it like our own home. We could stay there forever if we wanted to. I can't … I can't tell you the difference it made to have a stable place to live. It put me in a better headspace. I was able to find work. It meant Joseph could go to kinder without me worrying about moving him yet again. The crafting – that came later. That came *because* of the other stuff. I taught myself to crochet so that I could make things for the shop. So that I could give back. And I just fell in love with it.'

She shifted two pieces of biscuit on the plate in front of her, gently tapping them against it, as if she were staging a play and the biscuit pieces were her key actors. Eventually she spoke again.

'Crafting is all about being in the moment, just focusing on what's in front of me. And everything is one stitch at a time. There were days that felt endless and full of grief, but I could get through the next minute, the next row of stitches. So, I would focus on that. Crafting brought me hope.'

Trixie dropped the biscuit pieces onto her plate and dusted her fingers. 'Pretty soon, I got to know Donna. She invited me to join the board of directors because she wanted representation from somebody with lived experience. Of course, Helen was super against that idea. If Helen had her way, I wouldn't volunteer in the shop at all. She'll be happy they never got around to inducting me on the board. Anyway, I put a lot of work into teaching myself crochet and embroidery so I could give back to the shop. I got really good at it and now I design and sell patterns.'

Trixie sighed and took a sip from her mug. 'Why would I steal from them? I owe them everything.'

Fleck took a biscuit. 'I didn't know that, about your husband. You've never mentioned him before. I didn't want to ask.'

Trixie smile-grimaced. 'Yeah. I find it easier that way. I'm just a single mum with no baby-daddy in the picture. I don't need people's pity.'

She grew pensive. 'He was supposed to get better. We had a plan. When his visa was denied because of his cancer, he went back to Ghana to get chemo. I wanted to go with him, but he wouldn't let us. Joseph was only small – he'd been prem – and he needed extra care with his asthma. Anyway, it was only supposed to be a temporary fix.

'So then I'm here in Melbourne and he's in the hospital in Accra, only then he isn't in the hospital in Accra. He's dead. He's dead and he isn't supposed to be. And we're not a team anymore. We're not a team with a plan. It's just me and a toddler and I have no idea what I'm doing.'

Batman and Robin were in mortal peril. Norah was on her feet. Fleck watched her, trying to imagine what it must have been like for Trixie to be stranded and grieving with a toddler and no support. She wanted to say something, but no words came.

Trixie looked down at the table. 'He would hate it – me behaving like he just took off and abandoned his child like some deadbeat nobody. He would call it character assassination.' She placed her remaining biscuit pieces carefully in a line. 'But the fact is, he did abandon us.' She swallowed and her voice thickened. 'He left me behind and I'm so angry at him for it. And we can't ever have a big fight where I yell at him and cry and then we end up having really good sex. I'm stuck like this.' Trixie blinked and swatted away tears. 'I'm doomed to remain forever angry and forever horny. It's no fun at all.'

Norah was dancing to the music of the closing credits. She was in her own happy world where the good guys always win. Fleck turned to Trixie. 'What was his name?'

Trixie looked down at her row of biscuit morsels. Then she looked out of the window. For a moment it seemed like she wasn't going to answer at all. 'Isaac,' she said. 'His name was Isaac.'

CHAPTER NINE

Three days later, on Friday, Fleck invited Trixie to her house again, so that they could sit in the mess and drink tea.

'Can I charge my phone?' Trixie held up the battered green device. 'It takes a type-C cable.'

'Sure thing.' Fleck gestured to the corner of the kitchen bench, where there were a few cables and a charging pad set up. 'Oh, hey! So you found your phone?'

Trixie inspected the cables and plugged her phone in. 'Yeah. It was the weirdest thing. It turned up in the little side pocket in my backpack. But it's a pocket I never use. I don't know how it got there.'

Fleck frowned. 'I'm almost certain we checked your backpack when we were searching for it the other day.'

Trixie nodded. 'That's what I thought. But I can't remember if I checked this pocket.'

'And if you never use that pocket, why was the phone there?'

'I've given up on asking myself why I keep losing things. I have a special skill. It's like I'm a monk who has sworn to be detached from possessions, except the possessions I'm constantly detached from are my keys, phone and wallet.'

'And kids' party invitations. And library books. And school forms,' Fleck added.

'Oh my gosh, yes.'

'Yeah. I think I might be a monk, too.'

Fleck made the tea and brought it to the table. 'So have you talked to the police about what has happened? Maybe they can help you.'

Trixie shook her head. 'What could they do to help me? All the evidence points to me having stolen the money. I might as well just turn myself in.'

Fleck sat down. 'Well, what about the bank? Maybe there is someone at the bank who can help you.'

'Maybe. I might call someone this week. But in the meantime I had a look at my bank statement. It turns out there was a series of small payments made into my account from the Society. I didn't notice them when they came through, because they were all for eight dollars seventy.' She wound the string around her tea bag to squeeze it before putting it on the plate beside her.

'Okay, but why does that make a difference?'

'That's the amount I charge for a PDF download of one of my patterns. I'm not going to look twice at a payment for that amount.'

'And what about the twenty thousand?' Fleck had deliberately hidden a packet of chocolate biscuits for them underneath some large brochures advertising guttering companies that were already among the mess on the kitchen table. She had shown them to Trixie, but so far, Norah was happily oblivious of their existence.

Trixie carefully extracted a biscuit from beneath the pile of papers. 'I had a look at my banking app. The money appeared briefly in my account before being moved out again. But I didn't do any of this. And

I didn't see any of it happen at the time because my phone was missing.'

Fleck frowned at the junk mail on the table for a moment. A cartoon seal was gesturing at a tiled roof. Then she blinked and looked up. 'Maybe these transactions were happening *because* your phone was missing.'

Trixie sipped her tea. 'Because my phone was missing?'

Fleck nodded. 'Maybe your phone wasn't missing. Maybe it was stolen and used to access your account.' She rotated her mug in her hands. 'Is there a way to tell what device you were on when you did an online transaction? Like where you were logged in and all that?'

'I'm not sure.' Trixie got up and stepped over to where her phone was charging. She tapped it a few times. 'See, there's been a constant stream of transactions into my account from the Society from Friday when my phone went missing. And there has been a bunch going out of my account into, like, lots of different places. Purchases. Investments. The transactions go on for days. It would be twenty thousand dollars going in and out in small amounts. But I didn't have my phone during that time. None of the twenty thousand is in my account anymore. I'm back to my old balance, which is a bit weird too. Why didn't they clean out the six hundred dollars I had sitting there as well?'

'So, someone could have taken your phone, used it and put it back into your bag again.'

Trixie considered this. 'But there's a PIN and stuff to get into the banking app.'

Fleck frowned. 'Maybe they know some hackers? I don't know. You didn't use something obvious as your PIN, did you? Like one-two-three-four or four zeroes or your birthday or something?'

Fleck noticed the way Trixie went oddly still for a microsecond. 'Oh, no, did you use your birthday?'

Trixie shook her head. 'No, I mean, I didn't use my birthday. I just—'

'You used Joseph's birthday.' As soon as Fleck said it out loud, she knew she had it right.

Trixie blushed. 'I find PINs really hard to remember. I kept getting locked out of my account ...'

Neither of them said anything for a second. Then Fleck spoke. 'I mean, if you're nervous about going to the bank or going to the police I could help you. I could come with you or something?'

Trixie shook her head, first a little, then a lot. She scratched at the back of her neck and looked out of the window. 'It's – I – I don't think I can do that. I don't think ...' She paused, closed her eyes, placed a hand on her chest and took a calming breath. When she opened her eyes, she looked directly at Fleck. 'I need someone to help me figure all this out. I need someone who won't judge me for using obvious passwords for my phone or not being able to drive or have a proper job or being too scared to call the bank. I'm never going to call the bank. I say I am, but it will never happen. I'll keep forgetting and forgetting and then remembering again at three in the morning when I can't do anything about it. I know what I'm like.' Trixie put her hand back on the table and took another breath. 'You're clever. I see how good you are at solving puzzles. And you never make me feel small or stupid. Will you be the one who helps me find out what actually happened?'

Fleck bit her lip. 'Like a detective?'

Trixie gave a small chuckle. 'Like a detective.'

Fleck nodded. 'Right. Let's get started.'

Half an hour later, Fleck and Trixie were sitting beside each other with a packet of textas and a large pad of paper, the sort designed for children's paintings, on the table in front of them. Fleck had written SUSPECTS at the top of the page in block letters and Trixie was idly filling the first letter 'S' with a colourful design.

Fleck watched as Trixie drew swirls and spirals. 'Your phone. Do you think it was charging in the kitchenette at Many Hands?'

'Yes. The last time I remember having it was when I put it on to charge when I was in the shop on Friday.'

Fleck picked up the orange texta and rolled it around in her hand. She was thinking. 'The back door to the shop: is that always locked?'

Trixie nodded. 'Uh, yeah. It's really annoying. If you don't have a key and the back door closes on you, you have to knock for someone to let you in again. Otherwise, you have to walk all the way around to the front.'

'And there's always someone on the counter at the front?'

'Yes, pretty much.'

'So the only people who can access that back room are the staff and volunteers at Many Hands.'

'That's right.'

'So that's our list of suspects.' Fleck uncapped the pen. Before long, she had mapped out nine names across the page and was making little clouds of information around them, mind-map style.

'We can start with Helen,' Fleck said.

'Use red texta, because Helen is evil. Write, "Thinks she is the boss". Helen's not even on the board, but her husband was the chairman, so she thinks she's like the First Lady or something.'

'What's Helen's husband's name? And how long was he the chairman?'

'Like, the whole time almost. He was the founding chairman and remained in that role until he died a couple of years ago. His name was Tony Greythorn. And Douglas Cooper has always been the treasurer. Write that on Douglas's section.'

'Hang on. I need to change textas. Douglas is blue. Okay. So, who's next?'

'Charlie Marshall. He's the chairman and he's also acting CEO until we find someone to replace Donna. Put that down. What colour is Charlie?'

'Green,' Fleck said. 'Okay, I need to put some information on Vanessa. She's purple.'

'Right. Vanessa Sparks. Office manager. She probably does the most work out of anybody.'

'And she avoids Douglas, which shows she's probably the smartest, too.'

'That's right,' Trixie said. 'She's like our admin person. Who do we have left? What colour should we do Donna?'

'Donna is orange, because it's a tropical colour.'

'Write, "Personality change". It just seems very unlike her to have moved away. One minute she's a complete workaholic trying to transform the Society, always up for a chat, then without any warning she's taken off overseas and I can't even contact her.'

'And leaving the country just when twenty thousand dollars goes missing? She's definitely suspicious.' Fleck considered her next texta. 'So if Donna is "Personality change", then John is "Personality not found". I'm putting his one in brown because it's the most boring colour in the set.'

'I met John months ago and I still have no idea what exactly he does. He acts like Charlie's shadow half the time. He always wears a suit. He never chats or does small talk. He just stands about. But he is on the board. You can put that down.'

'Do you know if he's married? Single?'

'He doesn't talk about any of that,' Trixie said. 'You can ask him, if you like. I can't ask a man about his marital status without giving the impression that I'm trying to crack on to him. But I don't think he would tell you anyway.'

'Who else is there?'

'Well, there's Jo and Dima, but I really don't think it would be either of them. They're both too nice. Neither of them are on the board, they're both volunteers.'

'I'll put Jo in dark blue and Dima in gold.'

'I can't think about anything you can put about them.' Trixie furrowed her brow. 'Oh, hang on, there is one thing. It's probably nothing.'

'Well, give it to me anyway. I need to put something on their sections.'

'It was a couple of weeks ago,' Trixie said. 'I'd left the shop but had to dart back in because I'd left something behind. And Jo was handing Dima this fat envelope full of cash. Like, a whole lot of fifties. And they jumped when I came through the curtain. Like, they seemed really furtive.'

'Maybe Jo was ordering a cake?' Fleck offered.

'I mean, maybe. But the vibe was off. And it seemed like a lot of money. Even for a really special cake. And where is this cake? It's weird that Jo would order a big special cake and then not talk about it. Jo wouldn't shut up about it if she ordered a nice cake from Dima. You know what she's like.' Trixie shook her head and took a bite of her biscuit. 'I don't know. It felt like they were in cahoots over something.'

'Cahoots?' Fleck felt the corners of her mouth twitch up.

'I told you it was probably nothing.'

Fleck wrote *Cahoots?* next to Dima's name, with an arrow pointing to Jo. Then she frowned. 'I don't think it could be Dima. She's so lovely.'

'Wait, but we can't rule a suspect out for being lovely. That's not a reason not to investigate someone.'

'Maybe,' Fleck said. 'But it's important. If you feel in your gut that someone is a lovely person, that's as important as evidence.'

'Lovely people can still get into trouble,' Trixie said. 'I would know. You've got to be logical if you want to be a detective.'

'I guess. But my heart says it's not Dima.'

'I tell you what,' Trixie said. 'I'll be the one to chase up Dima and Jo. Then you don't need to feel conflicted.'

'Okay,' Fleck said. 'Last up we have Bev. And our last colour is pink.'

'That works. Bev likes pink. Bev's okay, I guess. She's a devoted disciple of Helen, but she's nice enough when she's on her own. Still, she's always, like, correcting me. Like, I'm a self-taught crafter. I don't know the correct name for things. So, I'll be chatting to her about a project and I'll say, "You can fold the raw edge twice so that it's nice and neat at the hem and you don't have the raw edge showing," and she's like, "Yeah, that's a French seam." Or I say, "You can cut some of the fabric away so it doesn't bunch at the corners," and she goes, "You should just do a mitred corner." I don't know! I don't know what things are called. It drives me crazy.'

Fleck wrote *French seam* in pink next to Bev's name. Then she capped her pen. 'I feel like we should find out all we can about these people and see if anything suspicious comes up.' She couldn't help feeling a bubble of excitement at the thought.

Trixie looked at the clouds of information on the page. 'But will that be enough? It's not like this is a puzzle with a solution just printed upside down at the back of the book.'

'Yes, it is. It is a puzzle, and it has a solution. You didn't put the money into your account, but somebody did. We just need to find out who did it and why.' Fleck took a surreptitious bite of her biscuit. 'If we are to do this properly, we should look at it from all angles. This is like any good puzzle. You have to keep testing different solutions, combine different possibilities until you find the one that sings.'

'Sings?' Trixie's tone was very dry.

'Exactly. The right answer will sing. It will just feel right.'

'How can you be sure?'

'I love a good puzzle.'

Fleck suddenly realised that Norah had been quiet for too long. She found her underneath the table in a sea of floaty white sheets. Norah clutched her stolen Kleenex box and looked up at her mother. 'A tissue, Mummy?'

Lately, the only way to convince Alice to go for an afternoon nap was to take her for a drive in the car. Over the past few days, Fleck had established a new ritual. After lunch on a kinder day, Fleck would bundle Alice into her baby seat and drive to the Peppercorn Street shops. Specifically, she would drive to Many Hands. Sometimes, she would park outside the shop and use the time to read a book or do a crossword. But today, she found Vanessa finishing her shift, pulling out in her little red hatchback. Fleck was ready to tail her.

There were a lot of cars that looked like Fleck's on the road, so it was easy to be inconspicuous. Even so, she was careful to leave a few cars between them as they went. She lost the trail this time at a set of lights, but had still managed to follow her for a few kilometres. She would get better with practice. And Alice was fast asleep.

Black leggings. The school had sent home a notice. All the children needed black leggings and a black t-shirt for their school assembly performance. Sam had a black t-shirt – he could wear his *Star Wars* one turned inside-out – but he did not own any leggings.

Fleck was at Kmart. They had already bought a birthday present for Felix, a boy from school who was having a party at the trampoline place. Sam always insisted on buying balls for his friends. A basketball, a football, a can of tennis balls. It was like he was making investments in his future play experiences.

A brand-new Matildas Soft Touch Soccer Ball Size Five was rolling around in their trolley. But now they needed black leggings. Fleck could see the white space on the shelves where the black leggings were supposed to be. On either side were other plain-coloured leggings. But the stock of black had been completely cleaned out – the other parents had clearly got there first. In the girls' section, there were various leggings emblazoned with characters from various pastel-coloured franchises. Among them Fleck spotted a pair of black ones, the last on the rack, and snatched it up. She held the dangling legs up against Sam.

'Those are girls' leggings, Mum.'

'It's okay. They're just black leggings. Anybody can wear black leggings.'

'No, but they're *girls'* black leggings.'

'They're not really.'

'They have hearts on them.' Sam pointed to the ankle where a small trio of pink glitter hearts were appliquéd. Fleck groaned and pushed the trolley towards the craft section of the store.

'Where are we going, Mum?'

'We are looking for a solution.'

'But why do we still have the leggings? They are girl leggings.'

'We can fix that.'

The craft section was at the back of the store, near the photo-printing kiosks. Fleck scanned the racks. Laundry markers. Where were the laundry markers? If she bought a black fabric marker, perhaps she could colour over the hearts on the leggings. Perhaps she could get away with it. But could she convince Sam?

Fleck was comparing the Sharpie Rub-A-Dub black laundry marker to the Artline 750 Bullet Tip when she caught sight of Douglas Cooper. This man was one of her suspects! If he were the culprit, he certainly looked the part. He was an unpleasant man, with a mouth that turned down at the corners and eyes that darted about, as if he were always looking for something new to be offended by.

He was sitting at one of the photo-print kiosks. He seemed to be getting increasingly aggravated, looking for a staff member to assist him. There was nobody around.

Douglas stood up with a huff and joined the queue behind the customer-service desk. His photos remained on display at his kiosk. Fleck watched him. He had his back to his photo kiosk. Another customer joined the queue behind him. Fleck saw her chance.

Stepping lightly, or as lightly as she could while managing a trolley and three small children, Fleck slipped into the seat at Douglas's kiosk. Norah climbed into the kiosk next to her and started tapping at the screen. Sam frowned. 'I think somebody's using that one, Mummy.'

Fleck responded with a non-committal murmur. Douglas had six photos ready to print. They weren't your usual happy snaps – they looked like the sorts of photos that turned up in your photo reel accidentally. She pulled out her phone and snapped a photo of the screen. There was a photo of an old computer displaying a website for an insurance company; a bottle of gin on the shelves of a shop; a shop window for a superannuation and investment firm; a page from a supermarket catalogue of margarine on special; a real estate sign outside a house; and a close-up of a bottle of toilet cleaner. Some of them seemed like accidental shots, some were carefully lined up. But all had been selected to print.

Douglas still had his back to her. She quickly tapped each photo to enlarge the thumbnail, then took another picture of each. Sam had lost interest and joined Norah at her kiosk. When she had taken a picture of each enlarged photo, she cast another look at Douglas. He was now talking to the teenage boy behind the counter. Fleck quickly navigated back to the screen of the main folder and snapped a photo of that too. This screen displayed a whole bunch of photos. There were pictures of a group of men in matching blue aprons holding tongs and standing beside a barbecue at what looked like a fundraiser event. There were a few blurry attempts to capture some rainbow lorikeets in a tree. There were some photos of old photos. None of these had been selected to print. She tapped forward again. He had chosen to make enlargement prints of just these six seemingly random photos. What—

'Excuse me! I'm working on that computer!' Douglas's voice rang out across the shop. Fleck looked up to see him striding towards her. She quickly slipped away and hid among shelves of photo frames.

It wasn't strange to have random photos of things on your phone, but why did he want to print them? She could hear him instructing the teenage boy. It was clear that there had been no mistake. Those six photos were definitely the ones he wanted to print. The problem was only that he couldn't get the payment screen to work.

Fleck pretended to be looking at a gold 'best friends' frame as the staff member explained the process to Douglas. Then Douglas and the teenager walked back to the counter. The teenager disappeared into a back room and emerged with an envelope of photos for Douglas. Douglas checked each one carefully and then left, satisfied.

'Why do we have the leggings, Mum? I don't want girl leggings.' Sam was becoming insistent.

'I'm going to do a magic trick with them. See those little hearts? I'm going to make them disappear!'

'But what about the back?'

'The back?'

'There's writing on the back. It's girl writing.'

Fleck flipped the leggings over. There, in ornate glittery script, the word *Saucy* curled across the rump of the pants. What? Why?

Fleck sighed. 'We might need to try another shop.'

It had taken a while to find the trampoline place. It was tucked away at the back of an industrial estate. Hippity Hop: The Jump Warehouse smelled of confectionery and old socks. Sam raced over to Felix, brandishing his spherical parcel, while Fleck steered Alice over to the assigned party table and hovered.

Kids' birthday parties were so awkward. Was she supposed to stay and watch? Was she supposed to leave and come back? Felix's mum greeted her, then directed her to a platter with vegetable sticks and three dips. Five other parents stood around the table, also looking uncertain. Fleck said hello. Together they exchanged pleasantries about the excitement of the children, the state of the traffic. They admired the birthday cake, a buttercream tribute to *PJ Masks*. A teenager in a bright-green polo shirt appeared and took their coffee orders, then they lapsed into silence. Except it wasn't silence. That place was many things, but it was not silent.

About fifteen minutes into the party, Fleck was still standing by the snack table, sipping what was supposed to be a strong latte. It wasn't great. It was as if somebody had described coffee to a person who had never before encountered it, using only morse code. And then that latte-virgin was required to recreate the substance with potting mix and the contents of two ashtrays. Fleck sipped again.

Trixie and Joseph arrived. Trixie dumped her bag on the floor and flopped into the chair beside Fleck. 'What is the deal with this place? We got lost *two times* on the way here.' Trixie inspected the dip platter but didn't eat any of it.

Fleck smiled and sat beside her. 'How can you get lost two times? Surely you get lost once and then you're lost. Isn't that how it works?'

Trixie shook her head dismissively. 'No. We got lost two times.' She did not elaborate.

Fleck took a carrot stick and poked it in the hummus. She was itching for a conversation that wasn't about grip socks or royal icing.

Fleck and Trixie watched as Sam ran to greet Joseph then the two of them turned and ran towards the ball pit, stepping into each other's paths and bumping together in that puppy-dog style of small boys.

Fleck looked at Trixie's bag. 'Did you bring your crochet? What are you working on?'

Trixie looked away. 'I've gone off crochet a bit lately. I just … it just … it's making me anxious.'

Fleck frowned. 'What do you mean?'

Trixie paused, then said, 'I can't stop thinking about the money – how everyone thinks I robbed the Society. I can't even look at my crochet work right now without feeling this big brick in my stomach.'

Fleck put her empty coffee cup down. 'We are going to put this right. Don't stop crocheting. You need it. Maybe try making something different, something new.'

Trixie looked out across the field of trampolines. 'I spoke to Charlie yesterday. They aren't going to press charges and they're not going to evict me. They do want me to pay back the money and to get counselling. I tried to explain what happened, that the money moved in and out of my bank account, that I didn't have the twenty thousand dollars.' She shook her head. 'He talked about payment plans and

Gambler's Helpline and what it means to "find your rock bottom". It was horrible. I don't know what I'm going to do.'

Sam and Joseph were in the ball pit together. Joseph was trying to fully immerse himself in colourful plastic balls. Sam was trying to throw the balls out of the enclosure. Trixie scratched her arm. 'I'm not sleeping. I could never find twenty thousand to pay them, and I shouldn't have to! I haven't done anything wrong. I've tried reaching out to Donna, but she's just leaving me on read. I guess she thinks I stole the money too.'

'Cake time, everybody!' Felix's mum called.

Fleck and Trixie allowed themselves to be shepherded over to the cake table, where they dutifully joined in the discordant singing. Even as she cheered and clapped, Fleck's mind was racing. How were they going to fix this?

CHAPTER TEN

It was official: Fleck had nailed the school run. It had only taken half the school term, but things were looking good. Sam's lunch was all packed. It was healthy, it was impressive, it was completely nude. Every item of Sam's school uniform was fresh from the wash. Norah was dressed as well. It was the Batman t-shirt and shorts she had refused to take off the night before and slept in, but that still counted as dressed. Alice had a dry nappy and a clean jumpsuit. Everybody had eaten breakfast. It was library day *and* Fleck had remembered Sam's library bag. She smiled to herself as they all drove to school.

When they arrived, Fleck found a parking spot right next to the entrance. That never happened! She embarked on her routine of unbuckling (you always had to leave Norah's seatbelt until last – you didn't want a loose Norah while you were trying to clip Alice into her stroller) and once they were all out, they walked towards the gate. Fleck's walk was more of a saunter, but her step faltered a little when it dawned on her that things were oddly quiet for a school morning.

A car turned into the driveway for the staff car park up ahead. It paused and the driver waited for Fleck and her children to approach.

'That's Mrs A,' Sam announced. 'Hello, Mrs A!'

'Hello, Sam!' Mrs A replied. 'Did you know it's a student-free day today?'

'I don't know what that means,' said Sam. Fleck groaned loudly.

Fleck gave Mrs A a dejected wave of thanks and trudged back to the car to load the kids back in. The re-buckling routine seemed to take a lot longer than the unbuckling had, even though Fleck made sure to buckle Norah in first. She stood at the boot of the car after she had loaded the stroller, scrolling her phone in search of the notice of the student-free day. How had she missed it?

Fleck subscribed to the school newsletter, but apparently that wasn't enough. You actually had to *read* the thing. She sighed as she flopped into the driver's seat. If only school notifications were presented to her as a five-step puzzle with green and yellow squares to let her know when she was getting close to guessing it. She'd be on top of everything that way.

'What do we do now?' Sam asked from the back seat.

Fleck stared straight ahead. They were in the car now and she really didn't want to go home yet. 'Let's do some detective work!'

Fleck had already worked out where Helen Greythorn's house was a week ago. Helen and Tony were still in the phone book. It had simply been a matter of typing *Greythorn* into the residential section of the online *White Pages*. She felt really proud of this piece of detective work. When she boasted about this to Trixie, Trixie had given her a contact list with the details of everyone who volunteered at the shop. Fleck had felt grateful and a little bit deflated at the same time.

Helen's house wasn't too far from the school. Maybe she could camp out in Helen's street for fifteen minutes or until the kids' patience ran out, whichever came first.

'If a car comes out of that house, we are going to follow it to see where it goes!' Fleck said. Norah and Sam were already tucking into their lunch-box snacks and seemed on board with this new challenge.

As luck would have it, around seven minutes into the stake-out, a silver Mercedes pulled out of the driveway and sailed off down the street. Norah and Sam squealed in excitement as Fleck started the car and they began to follow it.

Fleck tried to stay an inconspicuous distance behind the car while keeping it in sight. They travelled down a few main roads, then started moving south-east on the Princes Highway.

'I can see the big Ikea! Mummy, can we go to the big Ikea?' Sam said.

'Ikea! Ikea!' called Norah.

Why were her children so obsessed with flatpack furniture? True, Sam also had a deep love for the large sporting-goods shop in the same building, but their appreciation of Swedish design was not to be underestimated.

'We're being detectives,' said Fleck. 'We're following the silver car, remember?'

'Oh, yeah,' said Sam.

'Ikea!'

'How about I put on some detective chase music?' Fleck's hand fumbled at the radio buttons.

'Mummy?' Sam piped up from the back seat.

'Yes, Sam?'

'Being a detective is a bit boring.'

'It is a bit sometimes.'

Now they were in Dandenong. They drove past a McDonald's, which set off another round of petitions. Helen's car turned right up ahead. It was a while before Fleck could find a gap in the traffic to turn right after her. By the time she managed it, the silver car had disappeared. Fleck did a little tour of the surrounding streets, but to no avail. She had lost Helen.

Later, Fleck wrote up her findings in her everything book. She included map coordinates for the intersection in Dandenong where she'd seen Helen's car before the trail had gone cold.

'No, I'm the dad and you're the kid,' Sam said. 'And I'm cooking you dinner.' He bustled around the kitchen holding a whisk, while Norah sat at the sleek dining table and inspected her collection of miniature pencils.

'Make sure you stay in this house,' Fleck said, putting her pen down. 'We can go to the one next door when everyone is ready.' Fleck adjusted the 'FRANSALG' lamp and looked across the 'LAGKAPTEN' desk to where Sam and Norah were playing. It looked like they would all be having meatballs for lunch today.

Sometimes, after the school and kinder run and a coffee at George's, Fleck would take Alice for a walk around the neighbourhood surrounding the cafe and shops. The Peppercorn Street shops were situated on the other side of Musbrook Highway. The neighbourhood was prettier over there than the blandly suburban streets around Fleck's house. There, there were leafy avenues of oak and maple, and a mix of charming old homes and architecturally dynamic new ones. This was the difference between Paradise Heights and Paradise South.

But today she wasn't going to wander about gazing at bay windows and Japanese maples. Today she had Alice in the sling. Alice didn't really like the sling (weren't all babies supposed to like slings?) but Fleck hoped the lack of pusher would make it easier for her to get in and out of Many Hands. She wanted to have a stickybeak.

It was possible she was imagining it, but there was something different about the energy in the shop as she pushed open the front door. In the past, the store had seemed infused with a sense of good-humoured bustle. Today, things were quiet and fraught. Even the pair of customers looking through the baby knitwear section seemed reluctant to talk above a whisper.

At first, the counter was unattended. Fleck looked at a rack of earrings shaped like tiny books, milkshakes in glasses, etch-a-sketch toys. There were also enamel pins and brooches of fairy wrens, cabbages, tubas and bundt cakes. Fleck was careful to keep the jewellery out of range of small grabbing hands as Alice grunted and shifted.

Bev emerged from the back room holding a cup of tea and took a seat at the counter. Her face closed over a little when she caught sight of Fleck. It was clear that she recognised Fleck as Trixie's friend.

'Hello, Bev.' Fleck tried to make her voice sound bright and breezy, but it came out a little strangled.

Bev gave a tight smile and nodded.

Fleck approached the counter. She wasn't sure what she wanted to ask. 'How … how have things been, since …?'

Bev made a deep blink and looked back at Fleck without answering. Then she sighed. 'Things have been pretty awful. It just – it feels like a violation, that's what. I can't even talk about it.'

Fleck swallowed and nodded. Bev's large fabric work bag was on the counter. It was a big and sturdy bag, made of patchwork, and it had a striking design of dandelions on the front panel. If Bev had made this herself, she must be very talented. 'Your bag is very beautiful. Did you make it?'

Bev responded as if Fleck hadn't said anything. 'We were already running on the scent of an oily rag, but this might tip us over the edge. Our new refugee outreach projects have been delayed. They were supposed to be launched this year. There was even talk about us cutting back on services. Trixie really threw us under the bus. I don't think I can ever forgive her for this.'

Alice started to grizzle. Fleck patted her back through the sling and started rocking herself side to side, shifting from foot to foot like a human metronome. 'It wasn't Trixie. It was somebody else – she was framed.'

Bev held up her hands as if warding Fleck off. She looked anguished. 'Who else could it be? Look, I don't want it to have been Trixie either, but it doesn't look good for her. I think she's very lucky that the Society isn't going to press charges.'

Alice's grizzles had worked themselves up to a full-blown cry. 'I have to go, but I am going to solve this, Bev,' she half-shouted over the top of Alice's wails as she turned towards the door. 'It wasn't Trixie. I'm going to find out who it really was!'

There was mail sticking out of the letterbox when Fleck got home after kinder pick-up that afternoon. Norah bounced in her seat. There were certain things that were off-limits to Fleck now that she was a parent. If Fleck wanted a peaceful life, she could no longer press the buttons to call lifts or pedestrian crossings, she must never peel the sticker from a 'peel and win' promotion and on no account could she be the one to check the mail. Only Norah could check the mail.

'One, two, three letters!' Norah was admiring the (two) letters in the letterbox but was yet to extract them. Norah's post-retrieval service was not an exercise in efficiency. Fleck idly dead-headed a few roses and gazed up the street. Norah, sensing that she was losing her audience, handed her mother the letters. There was another zip-lock bag with the same cream-coloured paper: a letter from next door.

Esteemed neighbour,

I am receiving a consignment of poultry manure this Saturday afternoon. It will be delivered to my front driveway.

I purchase this in the hope of nourishing my orange tree.

I do apologise for the prognosticated odour.

I remain,

Yours respectfully,

Ranveer D Singh, PhD, CPA

'Look, Mummy!'

Fleck looked up. Trixie was pulling into her driveway on her bicycle. Trixie rode a bright red cargo bike, with an empty bench seat behind it, sturdy enough for Joseph to ride with her when she did the school run. She was wearing her Bakers Delight uniform and there was a bag of finger buns peeking out of the handlebar basket. She jumped off the bike and parked it next to the garage. 'Can I use your printer?' she said. 'I've got some things we need to look at.'

Fleck put the finger buns onto a plate and made the tea. The printer in Matthew's study finished whining as it spat out its last page. Trixie emerged with a stack of papers and sat at the table with Fleck to sift through them. 'I forgot that I still had these files on my computer,' she said. 'Well, no. I didn't *forget*, but I only just realised they could be useful for the case. And then I remembered the information pack I was given when Donna was trying to convince me to join the board, so I brought that along too.'

Fleck pointed to a document with rows of what looked like transactions. 'So, this is their bank statement?' she asked.

'Yeah, I needed to generate a statement to set up the Tapster account, and I downloaded a copy to my computer while I was setting it up using the passwords I got from Douglas's folder. This account is for the office, and this one is for the shop. And these are photos of the balance sheets that Douglas draws up in his black-and-red ledger books.'

'We've got a full-on dossier here!' Fleck exclaimed.

Trixie tore a finger bun away from the others and put it on the plate in front of her. 'I figured it couldn't hurt to have this information.'

Fleck nodded as she pressed the icing and sprinkles evenly across her bun. 'I think this is going to be a vital piece to the puzzle. I know we can solve this. We just need to go through things step by step.'

Together, they carefully read over the pages.

'It would help if we knew what we were supposed to be looking for,' Trixie said at last.

'It would help if we knew what we were doing.' Fleck groaned and paused to stretch.

Trixie drained her cup of tea, then looked pensive. 'Vanessa has started sending me invoices. This payment plan they've been talking about seems to be just that they *plan* that I *pay* them as soon as possible. There's no way I can afford to keep up with their schedule. I can't even look at the invoices. They stress me out. I keep shoving them in a drawer.'

Fleck grimaced. 'That sounds awful.'

Trixie stared out of the window. She spoke in a small voice. 'I've been in bad debt before and I promised myself I'd never let things get that bad again, but it's like I'm getting pulled back into that black hole. I don't know what's going to happen to me.'

Fleck stood up. 'I'll tell you what's going to happen.' She walked to the shelf and returned with a pink zip-up binder. 'What's going to happen is we are going to solve this case. We are going to clear your name. We're going to find out who did this to you and why.' Fleck placed all of the papers into the folder and zipped it closed. 'Somebody knows what happened to that money. We just have to find them out. Plus, now we have a dossier. Everything is better when you have a dossier.'

CHAPTER ELEVEN

The best thing about Rotary Recycle in Paradise Heights was the way the shelves were set up. Unlike the nearby Vinnies, which had the books in a whole different room from the toys, the Rotary op shop had the two sections side by side, so that Fleck could browse the books and supervise Norah at the same time. It was true that the Vinnies had a better selection, but what was the point of that if she couldn't look at it properly without Norah running back into the other room?

That op shop smell. Dusty and sweet. Fleck had moved on from the bookshelves now and was browsing through a plastic tub of dress patterns. She kept one eye on Norah, who was exploring a crate of toy musical instruments, and another on the front counter. Fleck needed to stop buying dress patterns. She didn't even know how to sew. But she *loved* dress patterns. So much potential in a fat paper envelope. She loved the feel of the package in her hands. She loved the power of holding a blueprint, how one good pattern could make several kinds of dresses if you used different fabrics. And she love, love, *loved* the illustrations on the front. She had told herself she wasn't allowed to buy any more patterns until she actually learned how to sew, until she actually *used* one of the fifty-five patterns she already owned.

But this one was special. It had four illustrated women on the front wearing dresses of varying lengths and sleeve styles. They looked so happy admiring each other's clothes. They couldn't get enough of them. *What? You have a collar? That's darling! I don't have a collar but look at my capped sleeves. Yes! I love your capped sleeves!* Fleck placed it in the stroller caddy. It was only fifty cents.

The other good thing about Rotary Recycle was that she could do some detective work here. Fleck needed a win in her detective work. She had spent the last few afternoons with Trixie digging through their dossier, but she didn't feel she had made any progress at all in understanding the spreadsheets and papers. Today would be different. She peered through the racks of clothes: Douglas Cooper was serving a customer at the front of the shop. The front counter doubled as a display case filled with second-hand jewellery and watches. The customer, a rather pudgy man with a beard, was taking a closer look at an antique letter opener. Douglas had put his newspaper sudoku to one side and was watching the man as he looked at the merchandise.

Douglas Cooper, treasurer of Many Hands. Fleck's online investigation of this suspect had uncovered no social media presence of any kind, but when she'd tried filtering out all the other men of the same name by searching 'Douglas Cooper Paradise Heights', she'd discovered the minutes to the latest meeting of the Rotary Club. Attached to the minutes was the volunteering roster for the Highett Road op shop. It was no great surprise that Douglas was not usually rostered on to volunteer at the register. His talents were reserved for the storeroom at the back. Now Douglas Cooper stood trapped behind the counter while Fleck hovered nearby, positioned to strike.

It wasn't time yet. The customer was still turning the letter opener over in his hands, inspecting it from different angles. Douglas was not taking any pains to mask the disgust he felt for this customer interrupting his leisure time. If Fleck had to read his expression, she would guess it said, *Get on with it. Real men don't look at antiques.*

By the time the customer had sauntered off without having made a purchase, Fleck had added an Enid Blyton book and a 1970s Tupperware cake container to her collection on top of Alice's pusher. The store had gone quiet. This was her chance.

Fleck cast an eye at Norah, still immersed in her crate of toys. Leaving her three-year-old to shake a bright-pink maraca experimentally, Fleck pushed Alice, and her items for purchase, to the counter.

'I'm not sure if you remember me.' Fleck used a bright and cheerful tone as Douglas silently tallied up her items. 'I saw you in Many Hands a few times.'

Douglas flipped the Tupperware container over in search of a price tag.

'You were doing the accounts on the big table out the back. You are the treasurer there, aren't you?'

'Nine dollars fifty, please.'

'I – um – sure.' Fleck handed him a $10 note. 'You can keep the change. So. I gather you've been the treasurer there forever, yeah?'

Douglas looked at Fleck and said nothing.

'Is it – like – do you have any procedures in place to keep on top of things? Like, what kind of oversight do you have?'

Douglas raised an eyebrow – a silent query. Norah, meanwhile, had approached the counter to see what was going on.

'I mean, is it just you? Do you have anyone who monitors what you do? How often are you audited?'

Douglas cleared his throat. 'I have been managing the finances of the Society for thirty-seven years. Since the very beginning. There is nobody else who knows as much as I do about how the Society runs, financially speaking, so there is nobody else qualified to … It would be bloody ridiculous to have somebody else supervising me. Nobody else knows the ins and outs – nobody else could possibly understand how it all works.'

'Sure. Sure. But, what about—'

'If those are all of your purchases, I need to get on with it. Goodbye.'

'I was just wondering—'

'No. Bye now.' Douglas buried his head behind his newspaper. Fleck sighed, took Norah's hand and pushed Alice out of the shop.

They'd been putting it off long enough. They had gone through everything else and now they really had to attack the pink zip-up dossier full of financial information.

At the start, the dossier had been fun and exciting. To begin with, Fleck would pull it out and pore over it whenever she had a spare moment. Surely it should just be a matter of reading it from beginning to end. Fleck knew how to read, after all.

But the tables of numbers would swim before her eyes. The whole thing gave her a headache, which was silly. She was great at maths! Wasn't this just another kind of maths? If this had been page after page of logarithmic equations, she would have been rubbing her hands together and sharpening her pencil in glee. But finance was a different language to her. If there was something out of place, Fleck wouldn't know how to look for it.

Plus, and this was embarrassing, but Fleck was put off by how skull-crushingly *dull* the whole process was. It was as if the sight of tables, dates and dollar amounts floated into her head, found the control panel and switched her brain to 'off'. Everything was written in unimaginative shorthand. *Supplies. Donation – Rotary. Neeson Raffle. Hurst Drive. Bequest. Button Line Takings. Rent. Sundries.* What did any of that mean, anyway?

So Fleck had been carrying the finance printouts around with her, even though she'd stopped looking at them. But the dossier was heavy and he straps of the bag cut into her shoulders. She was sick of it. What kind of detective was she if she couldn't even comprehend basic bookkeeping?

It was Trixie who decided they would spend Wednesday, the prep-free day at school, attacking the documents 'once and for all'. She was supposed to have come over around 10.30am, but it was almost 11am and she wasn't here yet. Fleck cleared the table, placing the stack of papers in the middle, and quickly shoved the breakfast dishes in the dishwasher. If Trixie had stopped at the shops on the way over and fallen into conversation with somebody, it could be a while before she got here.

Fleck had just finished cutting carrots and apples into sticks when the front door opened. Sam rushed to greet Joseph and the two of them raced through to the backyard, leaving the sliding door gaping open behind them.

Trixie had someone with her. There was something familiar about him. Late thirties, neatly dressed, dark features – Indian, maybe?

Trixie didn't introduce the man as they came through the door. She carried a shopping bag of food, which she dropped on the kitchen bench. The man followed her inside. He was looking around the room, not in curiosity, but as if assessing danger. Fleck definitely recognised his face. Where did she know him from?

'I brought donuts,' said Trixie. 'They were on special again. Where is the Pink Dossier of Doom? Oh, here we are.' Trixie spotted the documents on the freshly wiped table. She ushered the man over, pulling the chair out for him. 'Ranveer's here to help us out.'

Ranveer. Something shifted into place in Fleck's mind. 'Wait. Aren't you my neighbour?'

Ranveer. The mysterious next-door neighbour. Although Fleck had never spoken to him, she had occasionally caught a glimpse of him pulling into his driveway in his little green car. He wasn't the type to wave back.

Ranveer nodded briefly. He did not sit in the proffered chair. He barely seemed to notice it. 'Is everything okay? Are the children okay?'

Trixie narrowed her eyes at Fleck. 'Don't you *know* he's your neighbour? How can you not know he's your neighbour?'

Fleck felt her face redden. 'I mean, we haven't talked much …'

Trixie raised an eyebrow at Fleck. 'So, wait. If you met him at the shops, you wouldn't recognise him? You wouldn't know he's your neighbour?'

Fleck looked to Ranveer. 'You are really, um, great on bin night. I never know what week it is for, like, recycling? But I can just look at your bins and you always get it right.'

Trixie shook her head. 'I know *all* my neighbours. And I've only lived here for ten months!'

Ranveer looked in confusion from Trixie to Fleck. 'She said you needed help. I thought there was an emergency …'

'There *is* an emergency.' Trixie was emphatic.

Fleck looked at Trixie. 'Wait. How do *you* know Ranveer?'

Trixie shrugged. 'I know he's your neighbour. And I know he's an accountant. That's exactly what we need!'

'How do you know I'm an accountant?' Ranveer looked startled.

'There's a big sign on your front fence: "Ranveer Singh, CPA". That's you, isn't it?'

'Did you just turn up on his doorstep and drag him over here because he has a sign on his fence?' Fleck asked incredulously. 'Do *you* not even know him?'

'I don't need to know him. He's *your neighbour*. And he's an accountant!'

Fleck waited for Ranveer to explain that while, yes, he was a CPA, no, he did not perform random accountancy favours for strangers who turned up on his doorstep. Instead, Ranveer gazed at Trixie uncertainly and said nothing.

Trixie picked up the fat pile of documents that was sitting on the table. 'I really need your help, Ranveer. I'm in trouble. I've been falsely accused of stealing from this organisation. There might be something that clears my name in these documents, but they're so complicated. I don't know what we're going to do!'

Was she putting it on? She was definitely putting it on. Her blue eyes shone. Her lips parted in entreaty. *Screen test for Damsel in Distress*, Fleck thought. *Take one!* She suppressed an eyeroll. Ranveer, however, seemed transfixed.

Trixie passed the bundle of papers to Ranveer. He clutched it with both hands like he'd been handed a life-preserver. As if, finally, here was something that made sense to him. He sat at the table and pulled a pen out of his pocket. Actually, not a pen. A highlighter. It was one of those expensive ones, slim and black with an orange cap on both ends. He held it up. 'Okay for me to annotate?'

Fleck nodded quickly. 'Yes. You can write on it all you want.'

Trixie filled Ranveer in on the situation briefly. Ranveer uncapped the marker and settled down to work. As he read over the tables and figures, highlighting lines and writing questions and notes, he seemed to visibly relax. Fleck stepped back around the counter into the kitchen and put the kettle on. This was surreal.

Trixie seemed unruffled by the whole experience. None of this was strange to her. She stood at the other side of the bench, placing the donuts onto two plates, one small and ceramic, the other large and plastic.

The back door slid open, and Sam and Joseph tumbled inside. 'Donuts!' Sam whooped.

'You can eat these on the outside table,' Trixie said. 'But wash your hands first. And close that door!' She pointed to the gaping doorway, but the boys had already run to the bathroom.

Ranveer thanked Fleck for the tea when it arrived but didn't drink it. He continued to pore over the documents. Sam, Joseph and Norah ate donuts on the outside table, accompanied by an untouched but reassuring plate of fruit and vegetable sticks. Alice began to grizzle. Fleck lifted her out of the highchair.

Sam burst in through the door, followed by Norah. Norah began playing with her toys on the rug. Sam sidled up next to Ranveer.

'Do you play any soccer?' Sam asked.

Ranveer looked up, startled. 'No.'

'Do you want to play basketball?'

'No.'

'Do you want to kick the footy?'

'No.'

'Do you want to play cricket?'

Ranveer blinked. 'It's not cricket season.'

'Okay, but what if it *was* cricket season?'

Ranveer shrugged. 'No.'

Fleck stood at the back door, Alice on her hip. 'Sam! Are you in or are you out?'

Sam cast one baleful look at Ranveer and went outside. Fleck slid the door closed behind him.

Fleck had just set Alice up on a play rug with some toys when the back door opened again. Joseph marched inside and stood next to the chair where Ranveer sat working. He watched him silently for a moment, then spoke. 'Did you know that tawny frogmouth birds are not owls? They are not owls. They are more closely related to nightjars.'

Ranveer looked at the small child with the solemn brown eyes and tangle of dark curls. He capped his marker and drew his eyebrows together in consternation, then spoke. 'Did you know that the main difference between a tawny frogmouth and an owl is their feet? Tawny frogmouths don't have talons like owls do.'

Joseph gazed back at him silently. Then he nodded. 'Interesting,' he said, and ran away. A minute later, Fleck stood up to close the door behind him.

The boys were now bouncing happily on the trampoline. Ranveer was steadily working through the documents. He flipped back and forth between pages to cross-reference. He stopped and frowned at one page for a full two minutes. He did not drink his tea nor eat any of the donuts on the ceramic plate on the table. At one point he pulled some little sticky bookmarks out of his shirt pocket, those little sticky bookmarks people use on contracts to show you where to sign. Fleck wondered what sort of person kept little sticky bookmarks in their shirt pocket. This man was ready. He was completely prepared for any accountancy-based emergency that might come his way.

Fleck had eaten one donut with her tea and now had to pretend the rest weren't there. They were dangerously good. She and Trixie were having the sort of conversation parents had: unfinished ideas punctuated by multiple interruptions from their offspring.

Norah was still sitting on the rug, eyeing Ranveer suspiciously from across the room. She had pulled a tea set out to play with. Alice had crawled over to investigate.

Ranveer closed the cover of the dossier with a sigh and put the cap back on his marker. Trixie and Fleck looked up. He had reached the end of the papers.

Ranveer finally sipped from his mug of tea. If it had gone cold, he didn't seem to notice or mind. He took a donut and began to eat it. Trixie and Fleck waited.

Ranveer swallowed. 'First of all, this document – the one that says "Annual Report". This is not an annual report, not at all. This is just a glossy brochure, an ad for the charity. But there is a lot going on in those spreadsheets,' he said. 'Are you sure they are the accounts of a small not-for-profit?'

Fleck and Trixie nodded.

Ranveer rubbed his chin. 'It doesn't follow the pattern you would expect for an NFP. Usually, if you show me an organisation's accounts book, I could tell you by looking at it what sort of organisation it is. It's like the machinery of a car, like DNA. But this pattern is different.'

'Different how?' Trixie leaned forward.

Norah placed a plastic teacup in front of Fleck. 'I have my cafe. Alice is the chef,' she said. Alice was smashing her rattle against a pile of plastic crockery. 'Ab ab BAB, ab ab ab,' she declared.

Ranveer took another sip of tea and shook his head. 'There is too much going on. It's more like FMCG – that's fast-moving consumer goods – than NFP. And there is an unusual amount being withdrawn for petty cash.'

Norah returned with a plastic plate with a toy train on it. She put it on the table in front of Ranveer. 'Eat it,' she said.

At first, Ranveer didn't notice the culinary offering. He gave Norah a small smile and continued talking.

'Something is not right with those accounts. There seem to be large gaps where parts are missing. It's hard to explain. It's not something I can point at, but it just doesn't hold together. I think—'

'YOU NEED TO EAT YOUR CAKE!' Norah shouted. 'EAT IT! EAT IT!'

Ranveer hesitated. He picked up his half-eaten donut.

Norah stamped her foot. 'NO!' She pushed the plastic plate towards him.

The train belonged to the wooden set. It was Henry the Green Engine, but he was missing his tender.

Ranveer looked at the small locomotive before him and then looked helplessly at Fleck and Trixie. He didn't know what to do. Fleck could tell. It was clear he didn't know many kids.

'Ooh! Can I try some of your cake, Ranveer?' Fleck said. 'That looks delicious!' Fleck picked up the enterprising engine and held it close to her mouth, making eating noises. Ranveer watched her carefully.

'Mummy! That cake is NOT FOR YOU!' Norah looked incensed. She directed her wrath towards Ranveer once more. 'EAT IT. EAT YOUR CAKE.'

Ranveer cautiously picked the train up. He held it an inch from his mouth. 'Delicious,' he said.

Norah's face cleared. She nodded her approval and returned to the pile of toys approximating a kitchen.

CHAPTER TWELVE

Fleck was cheating on George. She was sitting in dangermouse, the large, upmarket cafe next door to Many Hands on Peppercorn Street. She cast a guilty look at George's corner cafe as she slid into her seat by the window. Charlie sat down across from her with a plate of small cannoli and a table number on a metal stand.

'So, you wanted to talk about the missing money?' Charlie asked. 'I got these to share, by the way. Tuck in.'

'Thanks,' Fleck said. She picked up one of the cannoli and looked at it: it had chocolate custard on one side of the fried pastry tube and vanilla on the other. 'Yes. Not just the missing money, but everything around it as well. I think something is going on – something's not right.'

Charlie raised an eyebrow. 'What things do you think are not right?'

Fleck paused as she attempted to bite her pastry. There really was no sophisticated way to attack these, but she managed a small bite without squirting all the custard out the other end. Delicious, but so messy! She put it on the small side plate in front of her, dusted her fingers and swallowed. 'Well, like Donna's resignation. Trixie thought it was really strange that she just up and left. It really came out of nowhere.'

Charlie smiled sadly. 'It was a shock, but I must say it wasn't really a surprise for me.' He hesitated.

Fleck waited. The cafe was fairly busy. A couple sat with their baby next to them in a highchair, feeding her green goo squeezed from a pouch onto a spoon. Two men in their sixties were studying the menu and casting looks across at Charlie. A woman frowned out of the window, her fingers resting idle on a Bluetooth keyboard, her phone propped on the sugar jar.

Eventually Charlie spoke. 'Donna had two speeds. She was either a total force of nature, getting everything done with superhuman capability, or she would crash and burn out. Trixie didn't know her for long enough to realise that.'

'So, what are you saying?'

Charlie cleared his throat. 'It feels disloyal to be talking this way, but I was seeing all the signs. I could see that she was going to burn out soon, but I was surprised that she actually left the country. Donna was impulsive like that, though.'

Fleck frowned, thinking.

One of the men from the nearby table approached them. 'Marsho! I thought it was you! I just wanted to tell you that your goal at the ninety-five grand final was magnificent, mate. Absolutely magnificent!'

Fleck watched Charlie's face transform as he switched on his 1000-watt smile. They discussed statistics together for a while before the man returned to his friend, who had been watching from a distance.

Fleck looked at Charlie curiously. 'Does that happen to you often?'

Charlie shrugged. He looked sheepish. 'A bit. It depends, I guess.'

Their coffees arrived. Fleck sipped her latte. 'What do you think about Trixie's theory: that Donna left because she got too close to what was going on with the finances?'

Charlie nodded. 'There is definitely a need for better transparency with the finances. That's why I organised a consultant to look into things. I was paying him myself, just as my contribution to the Society. I've used him before with other organisations I'm involved in. He's the best in the business. But there ended up being a lot of opposition from a few of the longstanding volunteers and we had to pull the plug. Still, I don't think that's the reason Donna left. I suspect she just got fed up with trying to bring about change. It can be like banging your head against a brick wall sometimes.'

Fleck nodded. 'What can you tell me about the finance situation?'

Charlie sipped his coffee. 'The first thing you need to know about the way Many Hands is run—' He broke off and looked up. A lanky teen with a floppy beanie had stopped by their table.

'Hey, man, can I get a selfie?'

If Charlie felt impatient at this interruption, he didn't show it. Once again, he flipped into charm mode, smiling and chatting. Fleck gazed out the window as Charlie posed and the teenager fiddled with his phone. George was standing out the front of his cafe, adjusting one of the table umbrellas. Fleck sank lower in her seat.

The teen returned to his friends who were standing at the counter, waiting for their takeaway orders. He showed them the photo on his phone. 'Look! It's the dude from the Mortgage Star ads!'

Charlie winced. 'Look, there's a whole heap more I'd like to discuss with you, but I've got to go. But I want to talk to you. I'm beginning to wonder if there is more to this than we first thought.' He handed her a card. 'I can only do so much without proof, but I want to hear more about this, from Trixie's side of things. Maybe next time, you and Trixie could come over to my place and we could talk about things properly? I can't promise better coffee, but we'd probably have fewer interruptions that way.'

'Mummy?' Sam's voice floated out of his bedroom to the corridor where Fleck was sitting.

'It's quiet time now, darling.'

'Yes, but Mummy?'

'Just close your eyes and let your thoughts drift.'

'Norah's jumping on the bed, Mummy.'

Fleck closed her eyes and inhaled through her nostrils. It had been a very long day. She was ready for it to be over. She had *done* all the calming things. She had done the lavender bath and the stories and the lullabies and the hand-delivered sippy cup. Why were her children not tired? *She* was tired! She was bone-achingly tired. She had been sitting on a chair in the space between Alice's room and the bedroom Sam and Norah shared. If she camped out on this chair while the children were settling, she could stop any insurgencies before they developed into a full-blown war against sleep. At least, that was the theory.

Fleck slipped her phone out of sight and stepped into the children's room. Norah was indeed jumping on the bed, her red curls bouncing as she smiled broadly.

'Norah! Lie down – head on the pillow – under the covers – close your eyes!'

Norah smiled and bounced.

Fleck gathered her into a hug and tucked her into bed. She half lay on top of her in what was part cuddle, part restraint. Norah giggled.

'How come Norah gets an extra cuddle? I only got one cuddle. How come Norah gets two?'

Matthew was downstairs doing the dishes and clearing up the

kitchen. He would be finished long before she was. Fleck closed her eyes.

'I'll give you an extra cuddle too, Sam. And then we can play a game.'

'Batman and Robin Save the Day?' This was Norah's favourite game. Her voice was slightly muffled due to the enforced tucking-in.

'No, this game is better. This game is only for night-time. It's called The Quiet Game.'

'That sounds *boring*,' Sam said.

'That's because you don't know how to play it properly, Sam. Maybe you're too young for this game.'

'I am six! I am not too young!'

'Well, let's give it a try.'

Fleck gave Sam his assigned cuddle and then returned to her seat outside the door.

'For this game, you need to see how long you can go without making any sounds. The longer you can go, the more points you can get. I'm going to set a timer so we can see who gets the top score.'

'I think this might be a boring game, Mummy.' Sam's little voice in the darkness sounded unconvinced.

'Let's just give it a try and see how many points you can get.'

The first round lasted only thirty-seven seconds. Norah couldn't resist puncturing the silence with a loud 'BUM BUM!' Sam was awarded a point and the timer was reset.

Eventually, it got to the point where there were stretches of silence long enough for Fleck to get back to what she was working on. She had set up a range of fake social media profiles and was tending to those, getting them to join groups and make comments. It felt just like playing with dolls. She hoped that one of these pretend personalities might be the key to tracking down Donna, the missing CEO.

Donna was fairly active on social media. She regularly cross-posted pictures of her travels on Facebook and Instagram, to the point that her grid looked like a travel brochure. As far as Fleck could tell, there was nobody important travelling with her. Nobody appeared in any of the pictures, not even Donna herself, who seemed to prefer to remain behind the camera, and favoured artistic beach sunset shots over goofy cafe selfies.

Apart from posting pictures, Donna did not seem to be at all active on Facebook. Fleck tried joining some of the larger groups and searching to see if Donna appeared in their memberships, but had no joy. The friendly message Fleck sent from 'Bridget', a young woman seeking mentorship, was read but not responded to.

Fleck rubbed her chin as she pondered another means of attack. She gradually became aware of a quiet, rhythmic squeaking coming from the children's room.

She opened the door. Sam was fast asleep. Norah was silently jumping on the bed.

'Did I win?'

Fleck was sure there was more involved in detective work than watching people and following them in her car, but she was getting pretty good at that part of it. So far, she'd had the most success following Vanessa and Douglas, who had the most predictable routines and were the least aware of their surroundings. Fleck often tailed Vanessa to a nearby shopping centre. She generally found shopping centres bewildering, but it was different when she had a mission. And it was ridiculously easy to blend in and be inconspicuous when you were a lady with a pusher and a toddler.

'Teas, please, Mummy?' Norah had spotted the store with the all the specialty teas and teapots. You could try samples in little paper cups. Norah didn't often like the taste of the tea, but she enjoyed sampling them, just the same.

'We can on the way back. We need to get to our mission first, remember?'

They continued along the row of shops. It was hard to stay focused in this shiny, noisy, exclamation mark of a place. Everything was designed to coax her into distraction: *Stay! Look! Unburden yourself of all that cumbersome income!*

As they approached the bookshop, there was a tall woman with turquoise hair walking out. 'Trixie!' Fleck called. The woman turned around. It *was* Trixie. She smiled at Fleck.

'But this is perfect!' Fleck said. 'Do you have a minute? I want your opinion on something.'

'Sure,' Trixie said. 'I'm done with my shopping now. What's up?'

'We are a *mission*!' Norah assured her.

Trixie fell into step beside them. Fleck gestured ahead. 'It should be just around the corner here.'

They rounded the bend and stopped.

Nail Express was all bright lights and bustle, even though there was only one customer in the store. It was Vanessa Sparks, just as Fleck had predicted. Trixie gave a little gasp of recognition. 'How did you know she would be here?' They stood, ostensibly browsing the racks of personalised magnets at the discount shop opposite, and watched as her hands were delicately towelled off.

Fleck smiled. 'I've been following her. Watch what happens next – I need a second opinion.'

Vanessa gazed straight ahead as the beautician shellacked her fingernails. It was like she was in a trance, except she clearly wasn't relaxed: she was all rigid. It seemed like she wasn't enjoying the manicure but rather enduring it.

Fleck had never got her nails done. From the looks of it, you were required to sit still without the use of your hands and make awkward conversation with a stranger, only to end up with impractical, synthetic talons that would surely make your hands feel claustrophobic. Long, opaque fingernails would not be glamorous when you were changing nappies twelve times a day. And you had to *pay* for it. No. Thank. You.

Fleck and Trixie watched as the nail technician carefully used tweezers to apply gold leaf to her nails. Vanessa turned slightly as the manicurist directed her to put her hand under a nail lamp, and caught sight of Trixie. She gave a start and withdrew her hand, causing a spill of polish and a small commotion.

Trixie kept her mouth fixed in a vague, innocent smile as she muttered under her breath, without moving her lips at all, 'Yes, it's me, Vanessa. Hi there.' She directed a small wave in Vanessa's direction. Vanessa pretended not to see. She turned to Fleck. 'Do you think she thinks if she pulls her hand away, we won't realise she's getting her nails done? Why else would she be sitting there?'

'Perhaps she just came in there with The Book of Mormon and a bunch of pamphlets?' Fleck did not have Trixie's ventriloquist skill. Instead, she rubbed her hand across her mouth as she spoke. 'She was all set to talk about Joseph Smith and Jesus and accidentally got a manicure?'

'Whoops! I just came in here to ask directions to the nearest Muffin Break, and I slipped and some polish fell onto my fingernails. It's not what you think!' Trixie muttered.

Fleck tried to suppress a cackle.

Fleck and Trixie settled themselves and the children on the small oasis of couches outside the salon. They could easily see inside from here. Fleck pulled snacks out from the back of the pusher.

Vanessa's face, meanwhile, had turned bright pink as the beautician and her assistant fussed over her hand, cleaning off the spilled polish. Fleck looked at her closely. She was more than just flustered; she really did look deeply troubled by this upset – shocked, even. Her breathing came out in short puffs and the hand she held out to be cleaned was trembling. She hadn't been caught doing anything wrong. There was nothing criminal about getting a manicure. What was going on?

Vanessa shifted uncomfortably in her chair. It would seem she had decided to maintain the pretence that she'd not noticed Trixie and Fleck in the first place and was now carefully avoiding looking at them. It was a polite fiction that Trixie seemed happy enough to maintain. This was convenient for Fleck as it meant she could watch Vanessa closely without Vanessa noticing her stares.

Vanessa, meanwhile, was looking at her hands with fierce concentration. Her head was tilted to the side, as if she were focusing hard on Trixie, only without using her eyes. Her face was still red to the roots of her hair. There was a sheen of sweat across her forehead. She definitely did not want to be there. The minute she was able to, she stood up, grabbed her bag and strode over to the counter to pay. There was no stopping to admire her hands or chatting with the manicurist. Nope, she wanted to get out of there as soon as possible.

Vanessa turned her back awkwardly to Fleck and Trixie as she prepared to pay. It was almost like she was in a shared changeroom and trying to preserve her modesty. It felt a bit perverted and voyeuristic, then, to watch her instead in the window on the salon wall, but Fleck did it anyway. She knew what was coming and silently gestured for Trixie to watch too. Vanessa was digging in her purse, almost furtively. She had removed her phone and her wallet and was reaching right down into the bottom. When her hand reappeared, it was holding a wad of cash. Her new shiny pink nails matched the new shiny pink $5 notes almost perfectly. She counted them out to pay, then she was gone.

Fleck and Trixie headed back to the bookshop with the cafe to talk over what they had just seen.

'That wasn't the first time I've seen her go out and get a manicure that she seemed to hate and then pay with only five-dollar notes,' Fleck said. 'I've followed her a few times now.'

Trixie sipped her tea. 'How do you manage to do it when you have the kids with you?'

Fleck smiled. 'I have a strategy. It would be too hard to just *follow* Vanessa. There's too much involved. You need to find a park, then you need to unload the pusher and get the kids clipped in. And anyway, it would be too obvious if I was just walking behind her the whole time even if I didn't have to do all that. So instead, as soon as I see Vanessa has pulled into a shopping centre, I stop following her car. I just go into the centre and find a park wherever is easy. It doesn't have to be close to her. Then I sit in the car and pull out my phone and I look up the online centre map of The Glen or Chadstone or Forest Hill Chase or whatever shopping centre it she's parked at and then I pinpoint all the nail salons. Then all I have to do is plan a route around the centre passing these salons and then camp out in a shop opposite to spy. She never notices me.'

'So she always gets her nails done?'

'Nah, it's not always nails. Sometimes she gets a shoulder massage or a blow-wave or does something unusual to her brows or lashes. But each time it is somewhere different and she always, always pays with five-dollar notes.'

'That's really strange. And she really didn't like that we saw her doing it.'

'Why do you think Vanessa looked so freaked out that we were there? Was she supposed to be working?'

'Nah, she doesn't work Thursdays,' Trixie said. 'I don't know what that's about.'

'Hmm.' Fleck thought for a moment. 'And it was more than just embarrassment or awkwardness, you know? She seemed really upset.'

'Like, if she was getting her hair done, I could understand. She might not want people to know it's not her natural hair colour. But nobody has Electric Candyfloss as their natural *nail* colour!'

'Is turquoise your natural hair colour?' Fleck asked, with a tilt of her chin.

'I'll never tell.'

CHAPTER THIRTEEN

'Do you have time for a cup of tea after pick-up? I want to show you something. Also, I have custard scrolls.' Fleck invited Trixie over while they were standing in their usual spot near the prep classrooms, waiting for the bell to ring. Trixie had been working at home all day, which she loved, but still, she was itching for some conversation. Tea at Fleck's house was just what she needed.

As soon as they got there, Sam and Joseph raced through the house, into the backyard and onto the trampoline. Fleck sorted out Alice, Norah and the pastries, flicked the kettle on, and motioned to Trixie to follow her into the laundry.

'Tell me what you think,' she said. Inside was a blaze of colour. Large sheets of butcher's paper marked in coloured textas were taped to the walls and cupboard doors. Coloured sticky notes were peppered about and large sheets of coloured paper corralled information under headings: *SUSPECTS, MOTIVES, ALL ABOUT MANY HANDS* and *TO-DO*.

The laundry had taken on the feel of a primary-school classroom. If Mrs Foster's Grade Two class were to study embezzlement and criminology, this would be the perfect space.

'You motivated me to clean up my laundry,' Fleck said. 'I did, like, five loads of washing yesterday and mopped and everything. You couldn't walk in here before.'

'This is fantastic,' said Trixie, walking around. 'We can look at everything at once this way. I love it!'

Trixie peered at the section of wall dedicated to suspects. Fleck had printed out the photos of each person. 'How did you get photos of everyone?'

Fleck stood beside her, looking at the photos too. 'Most of them are just off the internet, but some of them I took myself when I was lurking outside the shop.'

Trixie inspected the photos more closely. 'John might be boring, but I'll give him this: he has a good head for being bald.'

'What makes a good head for being bald?'

'I don't know, but he's got it. Bruce Willis? Good head. Jason Statham? Good head. It doesn't matter if you don't have a good head of hair so long as you have a good head for being bald. I think it might be, like, if you have a muscular head, then it's a good head for being bald.'

'A muscular head?' Fleck asked.

'Yeah.'

'What do you mean?'

'Like, a muscular head. I don't know.'

'What muscles do you have in your head that need building up to make you look good bald? Do you think Jason Statham does a leg day, a chest day, and then, like, a head day? Like he lifts weights with his eyebrows or something?'

Trixie laughed. 'I don't know what it is, but you can have a good head for being bald and a bad head for being bald.'

'And John has a good head for being bald?'

'Yes, he does. For all his boring qualities, John's head shape is top notch.'

'Good. I'm glad we cleared that up.' Fleck took out her pen and carefully wrote *Good head for being bald* next to John's name.

'Look, it's great that you're being this thorough,' Trixie said, 'but I think it's pretty obvious that Helen is the one behind all of this.'

'Why are you so sure it's Helen?'

'Because she hates me.'

'That doesn't mean she's guilty.'

'Maybe. But it doesn't mean she's not guilty either.'

'I don't know if she'd have time to commit any major crimes,' Fleck said. 'She's too busy hassling call centre employees. I overheard her on the phone at school drop-off this morning telling someone off, asking to speak to their manager. And yesterday I heard her saying to someone else that she was on hold with Telstra.'

'She was often like that at the shop, having a go at the electricity company. Just how many issues can one person have with their service providers?'

'I don't know. But it seems like no day is complete for Helen unless she's voiced her displeasure to some poor lackey on the phone – and also to their manager. That's just how she runs things.'

Trixie pointed at the section of wall beside the door. 'What's this note next to Helen?' she said. 'Dandenong?'

'She goes to Dandenong,' Fleck said. 'Or, at least, she did when I followed her.'

'*Dandenong?*'

'Yup.'

'But don't you think it's a bit ...'

'Far?' Fleck suggested.

'Well, yeah, but – I mean, I'm not being a snob – but don't you think Dandenong's a bit *povvo* for Helen?'

'Povvo?'

'Yeah. Like, she looks like someone who would never travel north of the Yarra.'

'Dandenong's not north of the Yarra,' Fleck said. 'Is it?'

'Well, no,' Trixie agreed, 'but you know what I mean.'

'It's far from her Paradise Heights bubble.'

'Exactly,' Trixie said. 'It's suspicious that Helen is travelling there.'

'You just want to point the finger at Helen.'

'Yes, that too.'

Fleck wrote *Find out what Helen does in Dandenong* on the wall. Then she stepped back. 'Next up is Vanessa. I think Vanessa is super dodgy.'

'Dodgy how?'

'You saw how she's got that manicure and paid with five-dollar notes.'

'Yes,' Trixie said. 'I mean, it's weird, but it's not illegal.'

'Well, I've been following her a lot, and it's happened several times. And it's always five-dollar notes.'

'Still weird. Still not illegal.'

'And there's just something off about the way she behaves there,' Fleck went on. 'It's like she hates it, but she's also desperate for it.'

'Are you not hearing me say weird and not illegal?'

'Yeah, but *something* is going on with Vanessa.'

Trixie gave up and changed the topic: 'So, what do we have on our to-do list?'

Fleck pursed her lips and frowned. 'Find out where Helen goes. Find out what is going on with Vanessa. Follow Douglas and see where he goes. We should also investigate Donna. See if we can get in contact with her. Find out what made her leave in the first place.'

'Good idea. I've been trying to investigate Dima and Jo too, find out what they were in cahoots about. But I haven't got very far.' Trixie wrote on the to-do list. Then she stood back and surveyed the small room. 'I really love what you've done with the place, Fleck.'

'It's all just lists, really,' Fleck said. 'I wanted to put up a map with some red string connecting thumbtacks together, to make it look more authentic, but what would the map be of? And where would the connections go?'

'I still really like it,' Trixie said. 'We don't need a map. We can always add one later if we need it. I need to get a photo of this to-do list. What else do we need here?'

Fleck's eyes widened in shock. 'Kyrgyzstan!' she said.

'What? I don't follow. You want a map of ex-Soviet republics of Central Asia?'

Fleck beamed. She was almost shouting. 'Kyrgyzstan! Kyrgyzstan! Oh! Kyrgyzstan! Oh, my goodness. That feels *so good*.'

Trixie raised an eyebrow. 'Are you okay? Do you need, like, a cigarette or something?'

Fleck shook her head. 'Chad, Egypt, Cyprus, Kyrgyzstan. I can't wait to tell George.'

'Just so we're clear: we are no closer on solving this case, are we?' Trixie asked.

Fleck heaved a happy sigh. 'Yeah, nah. Not a clue. But Kyrgyzstan only has one vowel. I'm pretty happy about that.'

Trixie nodded. 'I'm happy for you. You are a very strange person, but I'm happy for you.'

Fleck sat in her favourite window at George's cafe. She had earned her coffee today. Not because she'd been on time, or at all organised. Because she had lasted the whole morning without committing homicide. That was something.

George was busy with the large table of people in matching sweat-stained t-shirts who had just finished their bootcamp session and were now bantering and drinking coffees. Fleck pulled out her everything book and studied it.

'I'm desperate for a coffee today,' Trixie said as she slipped into the seat opposite her and shrugged off her backpack. 'That school run was horrendous.' She peered across at Fleck's book. 'Anything new since last time?'

The noisy exercise people were starting to leave. There was a scraping of chairs and goodbyes and then the cafe was empty again, except for Fleck, Trixie, Alice and George.

George spoke to them from behind the counter. 'Strong latte, Fleck? What about you, Trixie? Another tea?'

'Nah, it's got to be coffee today, George. Long black, please.'

George's Kitchen had become a regular haunt for Trixie and Fleck. It was such a haven on days when they both needed to get out of the house, and George was now well-versed in all aspects of their investigation. He found it fascinating. Fleck and Trixie, in return, had been fully briefed on Chrisanthe, George's newborn daughter, and her every expression and mood. She was a very clever baby. She was like nothing else. George had fresh photos and videos to show them every visit.

George brought the coffees to their table. 'Any more clues?'

Fleck warmed her hands on the coffee glass. It wasn't far into autumn, but the mornings were getting cooler. 'Nah, we're a bit stuck. Have you seen anything weird from in here?'

George positioned himself to look at the Many Hands shop, next to the double-fronted dangermouse cafe on Peppercorn Street. 'I've never seen anything strange going on there, and I'm often looking that way.

When things are dead here, I look across to Chic to see if they're dead too.'

'Chic?' Fleck peered out the window, trying to follow George's gaze.

'Oh, didn't I tell you? I've named that cafe "Shabby"' – he gestured through the other window to Espresso 312 on Highett Road – 'and I call the other one "Chic".'

'What does that make this cafe?' Trixie asked with a smile.

'George's Kitchen,' George said. 'Haven't you read the sign out the front?'

'Oh, ha ha.' Fleck leaned back in her seat. 'I dunno, I kind of liked when you called dangermouse "Public Health Directive".'

George grinned. 'Danger! Mouse! Yeah, that still makes me smile. They are nice people there – a bit reserved. Still, it makes me happy to see they don't have any customers when I don't either.'

'And what about the other one?' Fleck asked.

George shook his head. 'They get hardly any. Definitely not enough to justify the number of staff they put on. There's something not right about that place: just a weird vibe around it. And there's no way they're making a profit – I've seen the way they operate. I don't know how they stay open.' He squinted at a man across the road who seemed to be the owner as he walked back inside the cafe. 'You know what I think? I think the cafe is a front. I reckon they're using it to launder money.'

'Launder money?' Trixie looked confused.

'You know what I mean. You have some ill-gotten gains – money from drugs or money that's been stolen. It's tainted – you can't use it. You pour the dirty money into a legitimate business, like a cafe, and it comes out clean!'

'Who could be using them? And could it be connected to the Many Hands shop?' Fleck rested her chin on the heel of her hand.

'Hmm, I don't know. You're the detectives. You work it out.'

CHAPTER FOURTEEN

It was Wednesday and Fleck had promised Sam that they would get out of the house and do something fun for his day off school. But 'something fun' for Sam and 'something fun' for Fleck were two different activities. They would do something fun for Fleck first. Just to take the edge off.

She was parked across the street from the Rotary Recycle, waiting for Douglas Cooper's shift to end. 'We'll go to a park soon,' Fleck reassured the three small children in the back seat of her car. 'But first we are going to follow that green car and see where it goes.'

It didn't take too long. When Douglas emerged from the shop and pulled out onto the street in his old BMW, Fleck started the engine and began to tail him, keeping a few cars between them as she did. She followed him as far as Canterbury Road, when he sped through an amber light, leaving Fleck stuck at the intersection. She thought she had lost him but stayed on the major road and caught him a couple of intersections later, where traffic had banked up.

Fleck managed to stay behind him when he travelled up the Eastern Freeway and got off it, two exits later. When he pulled into a parking bay next to a leafy park, Fleck navigated around the block, doubling back, and then parked nearby.

It took her a little while to unload Sam, Alice and Norah from the car. By the time she had set up the stroller and made sure everybody had hats, Douglas was already sitting in a folding camping chair and pouring himself a drink from his thermos.

He had set up on a flat section of the grass with some food and a newspaper, which was normal enough. There was nothing too suspicious about an old man eating his lunch in a park – except for the way he had set up his chair.

Douglas had his back turned to most of the park, with its pretty view of trees sloping down towards the river. Instead, he faced a boring road of mid-sized office buildings that housed a florist and a cafe at street level. There was a Victorian-era rotunda with white metal lacework nearby, but Douglas didn't sit there. His folding chair sat almost at the edge of the park, facing out.

Fleck walked up to the rotunda, which had a set of swings beside it. She couldn't help congratulating herself at this turn of events. She had promised the kids a park. Here was a park and some detective work all rolled into one!

It was a relief to discover that the rotunda did not smell terrible. Norah immediately started climbing on the bench seats for a solo performance of 'Sixteen Going on Seventeen'. Alice laughed and squirmed in her pusher. Fleck settled on one of the seats herself and watched Douglas as Douglas watched the road. It would be easier if she were just that bit closer. She couldn't quite make out what was going on. That's when she saw what was in the basket of Alice's stroller.

To be fair, there were a lot of things in the basket of Alice's stroller. Spare wipes, a bunny-rug, an Aldi Special Buys catalogue, Toby the Tram Engine, Sam's school hat, several hair elastics and an unopened box of teething rusks all nestled together quite companionably. But it was the shiny plastic Bat-noculars that caught Fleck's eye. She snatched them up and trained them on Douglas, then on the building he seemed to be watching. They weren't too bad.

'MUMMY! That's MINE! That's my glasses!' Norah stood in front of her, hands on hips.

'I know, Norah. I'll give them back. I just need to check something.' There was a florist store next to the building Douglas was watching. Was that significant?

'MUMMY! It's MY TURN! I need them!'

'Yup. Yup. One sec.'

He seemed to be waiting for something to happen, but there wasn't much to see. Douglas wasn't reading his newspaper, but he kept checking his watch. ('MUMMY!') On the street, people walked their dogs and visited the florist. Customers and delivery drivers spilled in and out of the cafe. A tram passed.

'MUMMY! YOU'RE NOT SHARING, MUMMY!'

Norah was nearing meltdown. A dog-walker had glanced across at the rotunda. Fleck smiled brightly. 'Your turn, Norah!'

Norah narrowed her eyes at her mother and grabbed the Bat-noculars. Then she turned on her heel and returned to her bench seat balance beams.

Fleck, meanwhile, now had to observe the street without the aid of enhanced bat-vision.

Four people spilled out of an office building and walked in a group along the street. Douglas shifted in his seat. Fleck could tell by looking at him that they had reached the main event. Douglas held the newspaper in front of his face like a shield and peered cautiously over the top of it.

'I want a turn!'

'NO! MINE!'

'You're not sharing. MUM! Norah's not sharing!'

'THEY'RE MINE. I AM BATMAN!'

They were a diverse group. There were two women and two men. One woman was middle-aged and wore a pantsuit with a floaty scarf and pearls, while the other was younger, in her twenties perhaps, her face dotted with piercings and her hair half long and dark, half shaved close to the scalp. The first man was in his thirties, with a thick, light-brown beard and wearing a flannel shirt. The second man was also in his thirties, handsome and well-dressed in an understated style.

'I just want one look. Why won't you even let me have one tiny look?'

They took a table beside the window at the cafe. They were still well within view. Fleck watched them talk, checking back to see what Douglas was doing. He watched them too, his newspaper now at his side.

'NO! NO! NO! NO!' Norah ran around the swing set, holding the Bat-noculars protectively above her head, which, given her diminutive size, did nothing to help the situation. Sam began chasing her.

'Sam. SAM!' It was time to intervene.

Sam reluctantly approached his mother. 'Norah's not sharing, Mum. Why can't I even have one tiny turn?'

Fleck wrapped her arms around him. 'You know those binoculars belong to Norah—'

'But she should be sharing! I only want a turn. Is that even such a bad thing to have one tiny turn?'

His small chest heaved up and down. Fleck gave him a squeeze and made her own breathing slow to try to convince his little lungs to follow suit. When she spoke to him, she kept her voice low and soothing. 'You know that toy is important to Norah right now. She just needs some time with it. Why don't I set my timer for ten minutes and if you can go for ten minutes without pestering Norah, I'll ask her to give you a turn next.'

Sam looked unconvinced, but his body had relaxed slightly. 'Can I help you set the timer?'

'Of course.'

Fleck pulled out her phone while Sam scrolled carefully through the numbers to set the time at ten minutes. Then he tested out the different sounds for the alarm.

The pantsuit lady was talking animatedly, her hands splayed out. She reminded Fleck of the woman who used to do the arts-and-crafts segment on the Friday-night lifestyle TV show from the 90s. Fleck imagined her describing how to decoupage the top of a coffee table or create a fabric cover for a tissue box. The bearded man was nodding. He looked like a Canadian lumberjack.

The other woman was doodling in a notebook. Fleck decided she wouldn't look out of place in a dystopian sci-fi movie, with one of her tattooed arms replaced with a bazooka and a watch that projected talking holograms. The clean-shaven man turned his laptop around to show the others. He looked like a fashion designer on his day off: Weekend Marc Jacobs. What was he showing them? Floral prints from his summer line?

Their coffees had arrived. Were they having a meeting at the cafe? It was a pity she couldn't get a closer look. Norah was still traipsing around with her Bat-noculars firmly attached to her face. Bat-noculars were a hot commodity at the moment. Fleck wasn't going to get her hands on them any time soon. Then she had another great idea. She pulled out her phone and opened the camera app. Training the lens on the cafe group across the street, she increased the magnification to 5x. Not bad. And less conspicuous too. Anybody passing by would assume she was a doting mother taking photos of her children as they played.

She shifted her attention to Douglas. He was definitely watching the four people at the cafe. She couldn't decipher his facial expression.

'MUM! Can you push me?' Norah had climbed into the swing. She was still clasping the Bat-noculars tightly with one hand while she held the chain of the swing with the other.

'I – um – ah – yes. Just a minute.'

'MUMMY!'

'Yep. Yep. Yep.'

Douglas was unwrapping a sandwich, but his attention was still on the cafe. Fleck clipped the little safety belt across Norah's lap. Her phone sang out a twinkly tune.

'Mum! Mum! That's ten minutes! That's the alarm I chose! Mum! It's my turn! It's my turn!'

'NOOO! MINE!'

Fleck kept one eye on the meeting across the street as she walked to Norah's swing and negotiated terms for Sam's lease of the Bat-noculars. Norah looked unconvinced as she watched Fleck set the timer and warily handed Sam the toy.

These days, Fleck only administered twenty pushes at a time, ever since the afternoon when Sam was three and he stayed on the swing so long he ended up depositing his lunch all over the tanbark. She positioned herself to look like she was scrolling mindlessly through her phone as she began to push Norah. In reality she was using her phone to try to magnify her view of the people in the cafe. What was this meeting about?

As she reached twenty pushes, the four people were leaving the cafe. Douglas had put his newspaper shield back in place to watch as they walked back to the office building and disappeared inside. Douglas, seemingly satisfied, folded his newspaper and his camping chair, packed up and left.

Fleck squinted after him. What was the deal with that?

Fleck and Trixie stepped through the gate of Charlie's large Canterbury property, an ornate period home, all in white. The front garden was well tended, with large European trees.

'I mean, I knew he was rich, but …' Trixie blew out a breath as she gazed up at the house.

'I know, right?' Fleck grinned as she walked up the steps leading to the front door. 'I could definitely cope with living in a house like this.'

'I don't think it's fair that one person gets to be famous *and* good-looking *and* gets to live in a house like this.'

'Do you have a thing for him? A little crush?'

'I said "good-looking". I did not say "attractive". There's a big difference.'

'Sure, sure. You keep telling yourself that.'

There were pretty stained-glass windows set in the doorframe. Trixie's hand paused over the doorbell. 'So Charlie thinks I'm innocent?'

Fleck bit her lip. 'Charlie is willing to be convinced. I really think he's starting to doubt that you stole the money. That's why he invited us over. He wants to help. But he needs to be careful about it.'

Nobody had rung the doorbell, but Charlie opened the front door with a broad smile. It was strange to see him in a t-shirt and jeans instead of his usual suit. His hair was slightly tousled, and a shadow of stubble clarified his jawline. Trixie shot Fleck a look as they followed him down the hallway.

'Excuse the mess.' Charlie picked up a pair of soccer shoes, a skateboard and an AFL football. 'Kids, eh? Would you get that door for me, Fleck?'

Fleck slid open what turned out to be a cupboard door and Charlie tossed the clutter inside.

The kitchen was a beautiful sight to behold, gleaming and fully appointed. Fleck could smell recent baking. She and Trixie hovered by the table, while Charlie moved to close the oven door. 'The kettle's just boiled,' he said. 'Take a seat while I make the tea. Trixie, would you butter the scones in that basket?'

Fleck raised an eyebrow at Trixie. 'He wants you to butter his scones,' she muttered with the faintest gleeful undertone.

Trixie shot a mirth-suppressing frown at her and pulled the tea towel off the basket, snapping it in Fleck's direction as she did so.

Charlie brought another plate of food to the table, which Fleck immediately recognised with a pang of nostalgia. 'Is that raspberry coconut slice?' she said. 'I haven't had that in ages.'

Charlie smiled. 'My mum used to call them Louise cakes. I'll just get the tea.'

Trixie had lined the buttered scones up on the plate beside the basket. She was avoiding Fleck's gaze, which was a pity, because Fleck was definitely trying to make a face at her.

Charlie returned with a tray loaded with milk, sugar and a large ceramic teapot. He set to work pouring out the tea. 'My mum taught me to bake, and now I do it to relax. It's good to have someone over to eat it, now that my boys are back at their mum's house. Milk?'

Fleck nodded. 'Are you separated?'

Charlie handed her a steaming cup. 'Divorced. But we're making it work. It's been two years now. Milk for you, Trixie?'

Fleck took one of the squares and put it on her plate. It had a biscuity base, a jam centre and a baked coconut meringue topping, exactly how she remembered them. 'Two years. That must have been around the same time you joined the board?'

Charlie finished pouring the tea and sat down. 'That's right. Some men get a motorbike. Some men dye their hair. I sign myself up to boards of directors. At Many Hands, I started out with the role of membership officer. It was a thankless job a lot of the time. I'm on a lot of boards, and I can tell you, Many Hands is particularly resistant to change.'

'You don't have to tell me!' Trixie sliced one of the buttered scone halves in half again and put this smaller piece on her plate.

'What sorts of things do they need to change?' Fleck asked.

'All sorts of things. They can't get away from the idea of "the way things have always been done". I mean, I can cope with their resistance to certain knitting patterns or needlework designs—'

'I can't,' Trixie interjected.

'—but when it comes to things like correct policies and accountability and compliance and transparency …' He sighed and sipped his tea. 'I've tried getting consultants in to overhaul the accounts system or to introduce some basic OHS policies for the shop, but it's just a series of constant roadblocks.'

Fleck nodded. She took a bite of the coconut slice and was immediately transported to Aunty Janice's kitchen, with its laminex tabletop and the cabinets with push-button latches. It even had the chewy jam like she remembered. 'This is really good,' she said.

Charlie took a square for himself and put it next to his cup. 'They were always my favourite growing up.'

'So, when did you become chair?' Fleck asked.

'That was only supposed to be a temporary thing. Tony had been the chairman since the beginning. When he got sick, I took over his duties until he could get better, and when he didn't get better, I stayed on until we could find another chairman. But nobody came forward. Three men actually dropped off the board when Tony died. They were getting into their eighties, and it was just time. There was just nobody around willing to take on the roles. We barely had enough members to form a proper quorum, so I got John inducted.'

Fleck blinked and frowned. 'What's John's connection to everything? He works for you, is that right? What does he do?'

Charlie smiled broadly. 'It would be quicker, perhaps, to tell you what he doesn't do. That man is invaluable. But more importantly, I would like to hear Trixie's side of things. That's why we're here, after all.'

Fleck noticed how neatly Charlie seemed to dodge the question, but she said nothing and allowed Charlie to refill her cup as Trixie told him about the missing phone and the money in her bank account.

Charlie rubbed his jaw. 'It's a complicated business. I'm really glad you're looking into this, Fleck. It's not an easy job. I've always thought the Society needed better practices and transparency. They've needed it for a long time. Donna knew it. I just wish she'd hung around to help us sort it out.'

'Have you heard from her?' Trixie said.

Charlie sighed deeply. 'I spoke to her on FaceTime.'

'What did she say?' Trixie leaned forward.

'Not much. She said she needed a clean break. She wanted to reinvent herself and needed space. It was all a bit strange. She looked healthy, though, tanned. I thought maybe I could convince her to come to the next board meeting on Zoom and just tell us what was going on.'

'And what did she say to that?' Fleck asked.

'That was a big no. She didn't even want to be talking to me. At any rate, the internet is too bad over there to cope with a video meeting.' Charlie sighed again. 'I think maybe she just burned out. I can only hope she'll come back again after she's had some space, but it feels like she's dropping off the map. I'll try her again in a few weeks maybe.'

Fleck paused and sipped her tea. 'You said you tried to get a consultant in to investigate the Society's finances. Do you have any of their findings?'

Charlie grinned and left the room. When he returned, he was holding a large folder.

'They never got to finish their inquiry, but I have their working notes here. You can take them. I could never get very far with them. Wait, here …' He ducked out of the room again and reappeared with a cream backpack with a corporate logo on it and zipped the folder into it. 'You can keep the bag – I get them all the time. Just make sure you keep me posted on what you find out. I really want to get to the bottom of what's going on. I wish you luck.'

Charlie walked them to the front door. Fleck and Trixie thanked him for the cakes and walked down the front steps as Charlie went back inside.

'Who gives away a brand-new backpack?' Trixie said as they walked back out the front gate. 'I mean, I know it's got a logo on it, but still, that's expensive-looking. Look how sturdy it is!'

'It needs to be sturdy,' Fleck said. 'This folder weighs a ton!'

Trixie was sailing down Highett Road on her bicycle towards the Peppercorn Street shops. She wanted to grab some things from the IGA before school pick-up. As she was nearing the intersection, she saw a couple of women step out from George's Kitchen: it was Dima and Jo. Of course, they might just have been having coffee together, but she thought about the word *Cahoots?* written on Fleck's laundry wall. Here was a chance for her to do some investigating. She quickly parked and ducked inside.

'Hi George!' Trixie said brightly. The cafe was otherwise empty.

George smiled broadly. 'Long black?'

'Make it a pot of tea,' she said. 'Too late in the day for coffee.'

Trixie sat at the table closest to the counter. It was easy to continue chatting to George from here, though the cafe was so small, this was true of any of the tables. The cafe's name was apt. It really did feel like you were sitting in George's kitchen, having a chat as he made you a hot drink. And he did tea properly. Trixie appreciated this. There was nothing worse than a cafe that fussed over carefully crafting their coffee, with perfectly textured milk and beautiful latte art, but then charged the same amount for a cup of hot water with a tea bag indifferently thrown in it.

George brought the tray across to her table. A teapot of loose-leaf tea (Darjeeling) with a metal jug of hot water to adjust the strength. A cup. A teaspoon. A jug of milk. Trixie smiled in satisfaction. Other cafes should take note!

She set to work pouring herself a cup. 'Hey, George, you know those two women who were just in here? Did you hear any of their conversation?'

George laughed. 'You need to know this about me. If you are here and the cafe is empty, I'm going to be listening in to your conversation. What else am I gonna do? But people forget that I'm here. They talk about all sorts of stuff around me.'

Trixie smiled. 'I knew you'd come up with the goods. So, were they talking about anything interesting?'

George paused to move a tray of muffins into the display fridge. 'They weren't talking about much, really. It sounded like business talk. Ingoings and outgoings, profit and loss. And they were talking about a man. They were expressing concern about him. Saying his behaviour has been more erratic than usual lately.'

'Did the man have a name?'

'No. They were just talking about "him".'

'Weird.'

'It wasn't too weird. It was just obvious to the two of them who they were talking about. I think this must be a regular topic of conversation for them.'

'Something is going on with those two. I need to work out what it is.'

Another customer came into the cafe and ordered a takeaway. Trixie sipped her tea and looked out of the window. Did Dima and Jo have a business together? But Jo worked full-time already. Did it have to do with Dima's cakes? Then who was the man they were discussing?

'It's a mystery,' Trixie said to George fifteen minutes later, as she paid for her tea.

'Sorry I couldn't be more help.' George shut the till drawer. 'I did wonder why they came in here, though.'

'What do you mean?'

'I wondered why they came in here.'

'I got that part. But why did you wonder?'

'Because they're both from the shabby cafe across the street. I mean, I get it. Sometimes you need a break from the office and all that, but – wait, didn't you know that?'

'No! What do you mean?'

'I think the younger one works there sometimes. And she delivers cakes and slices. The other one just hangs about a lot. Oh, actually, I saw the older one digging through the bins there once. I just remembered that. Weird, yeah?'

'She was digging through the bins?'

'Yup.'

'What, like she lost something?'

'No, it was definitely more sneaky than that. She kept looking around, like she was worried she'd get caught.'

'And you're sure it was her?'

'Absolutely. I'm in here every day except Sunday. If you're a local, I know about you. There's plenty of people-watching to do when things get quiet. And Tuesdays are dead.'

'You saw her on a Tuesday?'

'Yes. And the other one, she works there on Mondays.'

Trixie frowned. 'Hmm. I did not know that. That's definitely weird. I can add it to Fleck's laundry wall for sure. But I don't know what it means.'

'Haha. So long as that laundry wall gets some love,' George said. 'That's better than nothing!'

CHAPTER FIFTEEN

Fleck arrived at the Many Hands shop a little early only to discover that Vanessa was already driving off. Fleck cruised along, following her at a distance. It looked like she might just be going home. But the car sailed past Vanessa's street and continued down Station Street towards Box Hill Central.

Vanessa obviously knew her way around as she managed to find free two-hour on-street parking not too far from the shopping centre. Fleck managed to find another spot a little further up the street from her.

Fleck waited for Vanessa to be almost out of sight, then unpacked the stroller and eased Alice into it. She was still asleep.

Norah was revelling in her unfettered screen time and did not appreciate being interrupted. 'C'mon Norah!' Fleck said. 'It's time for an adventure! Don't you want to be a detective like Batman?' Norah narrowed her eyes at her mother but allowed herself to be unstrapped from her seat.

The three of them trundled along, Fleck keeping Vanessa in her sights up ahead. Norah chattered about something that had happened at kinder the day before. It became trickier once they got inside the shopping centre. Usually, Fleck would try to predict Vanessa's moves, but today was different. Fleck was almost certain that Vanessa wasn't getting her nails done this time. She wasn't sure how she knew this, but it seemed as if Vanessa was still in work mode. Something about the way she moved, plus the fact that it was earlier than the time she usually finished.

Fleck kept catching glimpses of Vanessa through the small crowd, which kept her on the trail. They moved through the north precinct building and stepped out into the arcade. Fleck managed to catch a glimpse of her just as she slipped into one of the Main Street banks. Fleck took a deep breath and followed her inside.

Fleck could not remember the last time she had been inside an actual bank. She did all of her banking online (and, to be fair, Matthew did most of it) and she hardly even used ATMs anymore, getting cash out at the supermarket when she needed it.

This bank had people in suits hovering at the entrance. According to their name tags, they were 'banking concierges'. Their main job seemed to involve sending people off to the ATMs. Vanessa, however, was pointed towards the single teller at the back of the room. Fleck could just hear what was going on. Vanessa produced a cash bag and was handing over a card.

'How can I help you today?' One of the banking concierges approached Fleck. His name tag said *Lawrence* and he had impossibly white teeth.

Vanessa was talking to the teller about 'petty cash'. Fleck's eyes flicked from Vanessa to Lawrence. She had to think fast. 'I, uh, I want to open a bank account for Norah here!'

She really didn't want to open a bank account for Norah. She had opened a bank account for Sam a few years ago and it had been a disaster. There was *admin* involved: passwords and PINs and identity verification. Sam now had a bank account with fifty dollars in it, but Fleck had completely forgotten how to access it. Nothing ever went in and nothing ever came out. There was probably some important information to it that she had lost. She was sure there was some way she could sort it all out, but it would involve too many steps and she was too embarrassed to ask for help. Now, every few months, a bank statement arrived in the mail like a folded paper reproach. If she opened an account for Norah, there would be *two* reproachful envelopes in the letterbox.

Lawrence smiled broadly. The effect was dazzling. 'So, you're looking to open a juvenile account. Right this way, ma'am.' He was gesturing towards one of the little cubicles with a desk and computer. That wouldn't do. She wouldn't be able to monitor Vanessa at all from in there.

'Oh, um, actually, I have some other, um, bank business that I need to complete!' Fleck would need something that would require a teller. 'I have a foreign cheque that I need to cash. I'd like to sort that out first, please.'

Vanessa, meanwhile, was enunciating Many Hands' name for the teller. So, she was withdrawing money for the office's petty cash supplies.

'Well, you might need to see our teller for that, but I can get you started. What currency is the cheque in?'

'Lira! It's Italian. No! No! Not lira! Um, euro. It's in euros.'

The teller was asking Vanessa something. Did she want a mix of notes and coins? Vanessa answered. No. She only wanted $5 notes: $500 in $5 notes. This was getting interesting.

Fleck turned to the concierge. 'The cheque. It's in my bag somewhere. I just need a minute to find it. Can I get back to you?' Lawrence nodded with another flash of teeth and Fleck crept to the corner to dig through her bag in search of an imaginary foreign cheque. Norah began to complain.

Vanessa was fidgeting as she waited, like a caffeine addict before her morning espresso. When the teller returned with the packets of notes,

Vanessa zipped them carefully into the petty cash bag and then put that into her shoulder bag. She thanked the teller, straightened her jacket and left.

Norah was getting louder. 'Mummy, this is *boring*!'

Fleck packed up her bag and smiled apologetically at Lawrence. 'I think I, um, I think I left it in the car,' she announced.

Lawrence only gave her a distracted smile in return. He was busy teaching an octogenarian how to make a deposit using the ATM.

Fleck had promised Norah that they would be detectives, so they spent the next ten minutes wandering vaguely around the shopping centre looking for 'clues'. As they walked, Fleck thought.

Was it just a coincidence that the petty cash stores at the office consisted of $5 notes and Vanessa's pamper missions were completely funded by $5 notes? Perhaps it was just that Vanessa had an odd fascination for that denomination? And yet, now that Fleck thought about it, she had occasionally seen Vanessa pay for other things on her excursions out. When she wasn't getting her hair and nails done, Vanessa would pay using tap-and-go.

There was no way the office funds of a charity extended to using petty cash for manicures and massages. But was that what was happening? Fleck had no actual proof that Vanessa had been stealing money from the charity. But her behaviour had certainly been odd.

There was another thing. It was itching at the back of Fleck's brain as they wheeled through the fresh food market. It was something to do with the way Vanessa moved.

They stopped at the little bakery to buy a couple of Hong Kong egg tarts. 'Let's go eat these in the park,' she told Norah.

Fleck thought of the way Vanessa had fidgeted as she'd waited for the petty cash, and yet when she walked out of the bank, she was calm and relieved. Surely most people would be more agitated once they were carrying $500 worth of cash. Come to think of it, $500 seemed a lot for a small office to need for petty cash. Was that a lot? Fleck didn't really know.

Box Hill Gardens had its usual daytime crowd of preschoolers and their parents, retirees gathering for picnics and hardcore athletes training for their triathlons, half marathons or CrossFit ultimate challenges. The egg tart was lovely – flaky and not too sweet. Norah ate hers quickly and ran to the slide. Fleck ate hers slowly and mused.

Vanessa's body language had been strange when she had gone on her nail excursions too. Grim and compulsive. There was no gleeful anticipation about her, even though you'd think getting your nails done would be a fun thing to do. Was that because she knew she was doing something wrong?

Alice was now awake, and Fleck gave her a quick breastfeed on the bench seat while Norah played. She had no real evidence that Vanessa had done anything wrong. Everything she had was circumstantial. Still, even if she had rock-solid proof, the question remained: *How could she confront her with it?*

The next time she tried to follow Helen on a Thursday, Fleck managed to get the whole way to Dandenong without getting stuck at a single traffic light. At one point, they reached a mid-sized roundabout with a tree on it. Helen circled it twice before taking the second exit. Was she lost? Fleck felt ridiculous following her. The roundabout was big enough for two cars to circle around it twice, but not so big that they could do this inconspicuously. After a couple more kilometres, Helen pulled into the car park of a McDonald's. Fleck looped around the block and then parked there as well. She couldn't see inside from where she'd parked.

Should she wait and see what Helen did next? But what if Helen was meeting someone here?

Meanwhile, the fact that they were currently parked in such close proximity to Happy Meals and cheap soft-serve cones was not lost on Norah. She began her campaign. 'Playground! You can get a coffee, Mummy? You can get a coffee, please?' This child was a marketing genius. She had figured out the chief selling points of her proposed venture and was working hard at promoting them.

Fleck sighed. 'Maybe a quick play. But when Mummy says it's time to go, it's time to go, okay?'

Norah raced through to the McPlayPlace as Fleck manoeuvred Alice's stroller through the heavy door. The air was alive with bleeps and chirps. Fleck found a table next to the playground and parked the stroller. Helen was at the counter collecting her order ('one-nine-five – senior's coffee!'). Fleck had only finished setting the brake and tucking her bag into the basket underneath Alice's pram when somebody sat at her table opposite her. It was Helen, her face white with fury.

'I do not know what you think you are doing, but you need to stop right now,' she hissed.

Fleck stared back at her open-mouthed. 'I—'

'Do *not* follow me again. Do you understand?'

'Helen, I—'

'You could compromise an entire operation with your thoughtless meddling. Do *not* follow me. I will know if you try.'

'But—'

'You are playing a dangerous game. A very dangerous game. I need you to back right off. Stop asking questions. I am going to leave now. You are not going to follow me. Never again.'

Helen stood up, holding her coffee. She turned on her heel and was gone.

CHAPTER SIXTEEN

Trixie had an hour before pick-up, so she rode her bike to Fleck's house, swinging by the Asian grocery, the one with the cheap bubble tea, on the way. She loved going to Fleck's house, with its bright colours and welcoming chaos.

Fleck smiled with her finger to her lips as she opened the door.

Trixie grinned back. 'I brought treats!' she whispered, pulling two sealed plastic cups and two fat straws from the basket at the front of her bike.

They crept inside past Alice's door and made their way to the laundry. Fleck had set up two camping chairs in there. They settled down, fitted their drinks into the armrest drink holders and looked at the walls.

Trixie sipped her drink. It was quite possible grapefruit with lychee jelly was a new favourite. She gazed at the walls. They were a perfect balance of colour and form – it was lovely to behold. Fleck had added to the display since Trixie last saw it. *Known routines* were now listed beside some of the suspects. Other scraps of information surrounded each section in a cloud of colourful sticky notes.

Trixie fitted her cup back into the armrest cup holder. 'So, tell me what happened with Helen.'

'Oh my gosh, it was the weirdest thing. I followed her and we got to Dandenong again, but this time she parked at Macca's and went inside.'

'Why does she drive all the way to Dandenong just to go to McDonald's?' Trixie mused. 'We have McDonald's here.'

'I'm pretty sure she wasn't planning on going there,' Fleck said. 'That's just where she stopped when she realised I was following her. I don't think she's driving twenty-five kilometres just for that special Big Mac flavour.'

'And she confronted you?'

'Yes! She told me to stop following her and said I was "compromising her operation".'

'Is she a crime boss? I think she might be a crime boss.'

'I definitely think we need to find out more about Helen.'

Trixie swirled her drink. 'I have a bit more to put on Jo's section as well – and also Dima's.' Trixie told Fleck what she had learned from George about Jo and Dima's connection to the cafe on Highett Road.

'The dodgy cafe!' Fleck exclaimed. She wrote this new information onto a sticky note and pressed it to the wall.

'I'm going to try to visit there on a Monday when Dima's supposed to be working and see what I can find out,' Trixie said.

'We also need to find a time to go through the stuff Charlie gave us.'

Trixie pursed her lips. 'Yeah. Or we could get Ranveer to help us again.' The cream backpack with the bottle-green logo hung on a hook next to the ironing board. Trixie eyed it appraisingly and then fished the shiny piece of fabric she'd brought out of her pocket. It looked like it would be exactly the right size.

'I've been saving this patch up for something important,' Trixie said. She unhooked the bag and held the patch against the logo on the front.

It covered it completely. She took her sewing kit out from her other pocket to sew it on. Trixie had bought the patch online. It had stylised, curling letters spelling *NEUROSPARKLY* on a pearlescent rainbow backdrop.

'It looks gorgeous!' Fleck said. 'It gives the whole thing a My Little Pony aesthetic. What is "neurosparkly", though?'

'Oh, you haven't heard of it? Um, basically it means "not neurotypical", so that could mean a bunch of things: autism, dyslexia, ADHD …'

Fleck scrunched her face up and nodded cautiously. 'So, like, do you mean if a person is neurodiverse?'

'Fun fact: one person by themselves can't be neurodiverse. Only a group of people can. The word you're thinking of is "neurodivergent". A neurodiverse group might be made up of neurodivergent and neurotypical people. You hear people say "neurodiverse" when they actually mean "neurodivergent" all the time.'

Trixie didn't like correcting people. Well, she didn't like correcting *Fleck*, but this one was such a useful distinction, she couldn't help herself. Anyway, Fleck didn't look offended or upset. She looked like she was carefully filing the word away in her brain. Fleck was like her: she liked to be precise with her language. They were quiet for a minute. Trixie sewed the patch onto the bag. Once she tied off the thread, she gazed at the wall again. 'Those pictures are new. What are those?'

'I told you about Douglas's random photos,' Fleck said. 'I printed them off and added them to the display.'

'Toilet cleaner, margarine, gin and – what are these last three?'

'Real estate agent, insurance company and a super fund.'

'Okay, sure. That's weird, but what does it have to do with anything?'

'Well, the other day I followed him.'

'Really? And?'

'Well, he's spying on this guy in his lunch break.'

'That sounds weird, but what does it have to do with anything?'

'It sounds like: "further research required".'

'If you say so,' Trixie said. She stretched and looked at her watch. 'I've got to walk up to get the boys soon.'

Fleck nodded. 'If they get stuck playing in the climby tree, tell them I have Weet-Bix slice.'

Trixie stood, looking at the picture of Charlie. 'Geez, talk about a glamour photo. Was this one of the ones you got off the internet?'

Fleck smiled. 'What? Do you like it? I can give you a spare printout, if you'd like?'

'Yeah, 'cos that wouldn't be creepy at all.'

'He's not that much older than you, you know,' Fleck said. 'And you're both single ...'

Trixie rolled her eyes. 'I am not interested. Why would I be interested in a good-looking, wealthy man who looks like he should be selling Nespresso pods in a high-budget ad? Why would I want to marry someone with a beautiful home in Canterbury who can bake delicious scones and make charming conversation?'

Fleck poked her straw about in her drink. 'So, this isn't one of those Jane Austen situations where you see what a nice house he has and decide he's actually really hot after all?'

'No, it is not. A man is not a financial plan. Plus, I'm actually not interested. I don't know why. He ticks so many boxes, but there's still something missing.'

Fleck nodded. 'I think I know what you mean. He's so attractive *in theory*. He's attractive on paper. What is it? Is it that he's too perfect?'

Trixie wrinkled her nose. 'You know what it's like? You know those video games and movies that have like the absolute best computer animation? Like, it's such high quality and it looks so close to real. Or when you see one of those AI pictures. And you know you ought to feel impressed, but it just feels like something is missing.'

Fleck nodded. 'The uncanny valley.'

'Exactly! Charlie is Mr Uncanny Valley. He's the *Polar Express* of good-looking men. That's what it is. I like my men just that little bit ugly. Though that's all pretty much an academic question these days.' She sighed. 'Still. Can you imagine how much yarn I could buy if I was his sugar baby?'

Fleck sipped the last of her drink with a rattling sound. 'You know what else is weird, now that you mention it? The mess at his house. A skateboard, a football and a pair of sneakers. It was bothering me, and I couldn't work out why.'

'You were bothered by his mess?'

'No. Well, yes. It was too perfect.'

'His mess was too perfect?' Trixie said, incredulously.

'Yes.'

'I'm not following you.'

'Like, if you had to choose mess, you would choose his mess. It's perfect. It's the perfect mess. It's almost a cliché.'

Trixie stared at her blankly.

Fleck tried again. 'If you were dressing a set for a TV show and you wanted to show that the house belonged to a dad with school-aged boys, how would you show it?'

Trixie chewed slowly on a tapioca pearl, then she got it. She looked at Fleck. 'A skateboard, a football, a pair of sneakers.'

'Exactly! It wasn't mess – it was exposition. Real mess isn't like that. Real mess is much more random. Where were the loose Connect Four tokens? Where were the stupid collector figurines the supermarket keeps handing out? Where were the endless art projects and scrunched-up worksheets? Everything else was immaculate.'

Trixie frowned. 'But what does that mean?'

Fleck shook her head. 'I don't know. Maybe I'm overthinking this.' Fleck gestured to the corner of the room, where a toy truck was parked beside a sample tube of nappy cream and an old lanyard cord. 'Maybe it's just me who has random mess?'

Trixie felt like a tea, but she would order a coffee. She had no way of telling whether this cafe did a good job of tea or not. Actually, she did, and all signs pointed to 'not'.

Trixie stood hovering in coffee-scented limbo inside Espresso 312, the Highett Road cafe George called 'Shabby'. It was a strange place. It had all the trappings of a cafe but it also sold a random assortment of oddly specific homewares and gardening supplies. To the left of the counter was a tall stack of vitamin-shake powder for sale. A table to the right held tubs of miracle cleaner, as well as some books with glossy covers.

She was still waiting to order. She had thought she might see Dima here today, but there was no sign of her. There was a man in his late sixties, whom Trixie took to be the owner, moving about the cafe with a proprietary air, buzzing with energy. He talked to a table of customers, all men his age, in a different language as he wiped an adjacent table with a cloth. But he didn't seem to notice Trixie waiting. At any rate, he didn't take her order. Maybe that was Dima's job?

Perhaps Dima was in the kitchen? Trixie edged closer to the side of the cafe and peered through the rectangular servery. It didn't look like there was anyone in the kitchen right now. There was a sound from what looked to be a courtyard at the back. Trixie crept into the courtyard and peeked around the corner to the bin area beside the cafe.

Jo and Dima were standing beside the bins, deep in conversation. They hadn't heard Trixie slip through the door.

Dima was wearing an apron and holding a stack of empty cardboard trays. Trixie presumed she had been taking them out to the bins when she'd encountered Jo. Jo was standing next to the bin in her stylish cream suit with a large pair of tongs. Had she been sifting through the rubbish again?

Their conversation seemed intense. They stood close together. At one point, Jo's hand clutched Dima's upper arm and she spoke to her imploringly. They were talking too quietly for Trixie to catch the words. Jo seemed really agitated: her hand raked through her hair, her eyes darted about.

Trixie crept closer, crouching behind a stack of highchairs beside the fence to keep hidden. She could almost hear what they were saying from here. She just caught the end of Jo's hushed but impassioned statement.

'—drugs again.'

'Are you sure?'

'I need you to access the secret account. I need to—'

The cafe door opened. It was the owner. Dima greeted him, a little too brightly, but Jo had very quickly leaped out of sight. She must have hidden among the bins. The man was telling Dima that she was needed in the cafe. Dima dumped the boxes and the two of them disappeared inside. Trixie waited.

After a moment, Jo emerged, looking a little shaken. She brushed herself off and escaped out the back gate. After waiting for a beat, Trixie stood up and moved towards the back gate as well.

There was a car park behind the small nature reserve that ran alongside the cafe, but it was mostly empty. Trixie looked at the cars parked on the street, but she couldn't see Jo there either. Eventually, she worked out that Jo must have gone through the reserve.

Trixie darted down the bike path that led into the reserve. She ran down the hill and crossed the little bridge over the creek. Up ahead, past the grassy hill and ancient scout hall, she could see Jo getting into her car, parked on the suburban street alongside the park. She drove away.

Trixie stood by the bridge, panting and staring. Drugs? Secret bank accounts? What was going on?

CHAPTER SEVENTEEN

Fleck and Trixie had developed a habit of sending voice memos to each other. Talking on the phone was hard when interruption could strike at any moment, and composing a text message could be mentally taxing, but these little recorded telegrams were the perfect way of microdosing conversation.

This morning Fleck was at the Little Blue Car playground, waiting for an opportunity to listen to Trixie's latest voice memo. To the untrained observer, this playground might seem a little dull – only a few pieces of equipment, nothing too challenging or high off the ground – but to Fleck, this playground was perfect. There was enough to engage Norah without it being so attractive that it was overrun with other kids. As well as the eponymous blue car, there were a couple of spring-based motorbikes and a little slide-fort with a toy telescope at the top. Best of all, there was a park bench right next to the playground, and it was within a five-minute walk from their house. It was perfect for when they needed a break and wanted to get outside.

Today was one of those days. Fleck spent a bit of time as Norah's passenger in the back of the blue car, but then, as Norah ran off to be a pirate on the slide-fort 'pirate ship', Fleck slipped onto the bench and played Trixie's message.

As Fleck pressed play, Trixie's voice sang out from her phone. 'Fleck, Fleck, I'm telling you, it's Jo. I'm convinced now. And Dima is mixed up in it too. It's all to do with that dodgy cafe. And there's drugs. And a secret bank account.'

Fleck smiled and held the phone to her mouth to record a response. 'Come on. That's a bit of a stretch.' She pressed send.

'Ahoy, Mummy! AHOY!' Norah shouted from the top of the fort.

'Ahoy, Norah!' Fleck called back.

'NO! YOU DON'T SAY AHOY!'

'Oh. What do I say?'

'You don't say anything. I say, "Ahoy". You don't say, "Ahoy".'

'Okay, then.'

Trixie had replied with another voice memo: 'Nope, I'm obsessed with this idea now. Some drug operation using that cafe – and they stole money from the Society too and framed me and it's all part of some major conspiracy.'

Fleck recorded her own voice again. 'I thought you were convinced it was Helen. I thought you said Helen was a crime boss.'

The response pinged back within seconds. 'Maybe they're in cahoots with Helen!'

'Wait, so Dima is in cahoots with Jo, and then both Dima and Jo are in cahoots with Helen?'

Fleck smiled as she listened to Trixie's response. 'Yes! Triple cahoots!'

'Triple cahoots. Remind me to get some red string for my laundry wall.' She pressed send.

'AHOY!' Norah had the telescope pointed at Fleck.

'Aye, matey!' Fleck called back.

Norah narrowed her eyes but seemed to permit this response.

Fleck recorded another message. 'I probably should investigate Dull John more, but he's so boring. I know boring people can still be criminals, but I can't be bothered.'

She sent it, then immediately recorded another. 'It would actually be a handy defence mechanism for a criminal if they were so boring nobody wanted to investigate them. Can you imagine a heist with a weapons expert, a locksmith, a contortionist and a getaway driver – and then you have John. What talents does he bring to our squad? Well, sir, John is proficient at being intensely dull. He will shield us from scrutiny because nobody will want to focus on him for too long. The boredom he induces is at a Stage Five – or Centrelink application form – level of intensity. It can cause physical pain. Boring John is our secret weapon.'

A woman had approached Fleck as she sent her message. She made a face at Fleck. 'It breaks my heart to see mothers at a park on their phone ignoring their children. You should be playing with your daughter.' For the record, this woman did not look heartbroken – not in the slightest. Her eyes gleamed avidly as she stood looking down at Fleck. She jabbed a finger at Norah. 'What if she fell? What if a stranger snatched her and took her in his van? Are you even supervising her at all? And anyway, it won't be long before she's all grown up and you're missing it! You should be soaking this in.'

Ugh, the pressure to cherish. Fleck had not experienced a moment all morning when somebody hadn't needed her. And they had been needing her since 5am. She *was* soaking it up. She was soaked through. She was just trying to claw back a moment of sanity in the middle of a difficult day. Did this make her a bad person?

The woman raised her eyebrows at Fleck: pious and just that little bit self-impressed. Fleck could try to convince this woman, but she knew already that this would be a waste of her energy. Norah would only be distracted by the playground for a little bit of time. She didn't want to spend all of it arguing with a stranger.

Fleck affixed a bright smile to her face. 'Thank you for the advice.'

The woman nodded and moved to sit beside Fleck. No! Was she planning to have a conversation with her? Did she consider attacks on a person's ability to parent to be a standard icebreaker? Fleck had to act fast. She held her hand up in a 'wait' signal.

'You need to soak it up too,' Fleck said firmly. 'Don't stop now! You're missing out on life! What is it that you like to do best? Impress people with your own moral superiority? Well, go on, get out there! Don't sit. Find someone else to lecture. You're missing it. You must not miss a single moment.'

The woman scrunched her nose in confusion, reconsidering her plans. Then she hitched her bag on her shoulder and continued walking down the path.

'Next time, pick a dad to lecture!' Fleck said the words under her breath and out of earshot, but it still gave her some measure of satisfaction.

Fleck had a basket on her hip as she fished under Sam's bed. Another uniform top for the wash. From among Norah's bedclothes, she untangled two pairs of leggings and the long-sleeved ladybird t-shirt. There was a garden of dirty socks around the couch and a pile of used onesies next to the change table. By the time Fleck made it to the laundry, the basket was almost full.

When Matthew put a wash on, he did a load of the clothes that were already in the laundry. While Fleck was sure that this method made sense to Matthew's way of thinking, it wasn't the most helpful way to do laundry. The most important clothes, the clothes that needed to be washed most urgently, were never in the laundry. They *never* were. The basket in the laundry was the place where boring clothes went to die. It wasn't logical, but it was the truth.

Fleck programmed the machine and set it off. Then she turned around and gazed at her walls. She read over each fact and allowed her brain to tick over contentedly.

Of course, it was terrible that Trixie had been falsely accused. It was awful that she had been slandered and she could no longer volunteer at Many Hands. But on another level, Fleck love-love-*loved* investigating it. It was her absolute favourite thing. When she wasn't spending time on the case, she was planning ways to steal more time for detective work. She was certain the answer to everything was available – it was just out of reach. It was up to her to methodically untangle the clues. This was how they would clear Trixie's name.

Her eyes fell on the backpack. The pearly rainbow *NEUROSPARKLY* patch matched the cream of the backpack perfectly and looked so much better than the ugly green logo had. It transformed the look of the whole bag, really.

Just quietly, Fleck thought she might be neurodivergent. She had done lots of online tests, including one that said that if you were obsessed with doing online tests, that was probably enough evidence that you had ADHD and you didn't need to do this one. She had never had an official assessment done. It was very expensive and there were so many steps involved. The whole idea was overwhelming. But she had been reading up on ADHD just the same. It looked different in girls than it did in boys: girls with ADHD were more likely to present as well behaved and high achieving, even though they might be desperately disorganised. So many things were falling into place with this possible understanding of her brain. Did Trixie think Fleck had ADHD too? Was that why she'd chosen that patch? Fleck sighed and looked at the empty washing basket. There was one thing to be said for detective work: her newfound love of the laundry room meant that Fleck was definitely staying on top of the washing.

Fleck decided there was probably a limit to the amount of time a person could stand and admire an arrangement of native perennials without testing the patience of the florist inside the shop. She had smiled and said, 'Just browsing, thanks!' twice now. Further up the road, the same four workmates had walked out of the office building and made their way to the cafe next door. Across the road, Douglas again sat in his folding chair, ostensibly reading the newspaper.

Fleck had examined every leaf spike and gumnut spray in the outdoor bouquets. She had considered setting up in the cafe itself but decided against it. She wouldn't be able to leave the cafe in a hurry – she'd need to pay or wait for her coffee or something.

The four workers were now sitting at an outdoor table on the street. That was considerate of them. It was much easier to spy this way. If she moved closer, she might be able to overhear their names. Fleck had tried to research Canadian Lumberjack, Off-duty Fashion Designer, Female Cyborg and Lifestyle Crafts Presenter during the week, but it was difficult without their names or the name of their company. Still, her research hadn't all been in vain. She *had* figured out the name of the lady Ms Pantsuit reminded her of: Tonia Todman. That had been driving her crazy.

Fleck wandered past their table and then stood in the street, within earshot but just out of view. She feigned playing with her phone.

It sounded like they were having a team meeting of some sort. A lot of it was jargon that she didn't understand: 'Upload the CMYK format', 'in line with PMS colour' and some other things about 'vectors' and 'knolling'. She did, however, manage to find out their names. The Lumberjack had an accent that sounded more Boronia than British Columbia, and his name was Finn. Weekend Marc Jacobs was actually named Martin. Dystopian Sci-fi Hero was not Rivet or Sprocket of DS-147 but Jane. *Jane!* Fleck didn't manage to catch the older lady's name, but to Fleck she would always be Tonia. Martin stood up and told the others he was heading back early. Fleck watched Douglas as Martin left. As soon as Martin was in the building next door, Douglas packed up and left.

Fleck walked slowly down the road, thinking. If Douglas was leaving now, did that mean that this urbane man – Martin – was the one he'd been watching? Did this have anything to do with the random photos Douglas had printed?

The others were now getting up to pay for their lunches. Fleck hurried towards the office building. The whole thing would be a lot easier if she knew the name of the company they worked for.

The directory at the side of the lifts was extensive. There were two floors dedicated to a company called Designworx, plus a number of medical specialists, some lawyers and a children's psychologist named Leanne Tran.

The door to the building opened, and Vancouver Finn and Last-Hope-For-Our-Planet Jane walked in, alongside the woman who looked like she could itemise every possible way you could repurpose rinsed-out jam jars. Fleck had planned to let them get in the lift and then watch to see what floor it stopped at. That had been the plan. Instead, she was seized by an impulse to step onto the lift with the others. Sure, it might have made more sense to go home and quietly research, but she was here now. And child-free time was so difficult to orchestrate. She needed to make the most of this opportunity while

Marian had the kids. The Lumberjack swiped his keycard and pressed the button for level four. Fleck gave a brief 'Oh, that's what I was going to do' nod. She reached into her over-the-shoulder everything bag and pulled out a blue insulated cooler bag. She smiled wryly. 'My husband left his lunch on the kitchen bench.'

Jane eyed Fleck's lunch bag and grimaced. 'You're a good wife. My girlfriend would have just let me starve.'

Fleck smiled briefly. 'I was in the area.'

Finn looked at her. 'You must be Dave's wife,' he said.

Fleck smiled vaguely in response, trying to make the face a person gives when they haven't quite heard what the other person has said but are too polite to ask for clarification. Then she turned back to watch the lift doors until they opened.

The offices of Designworx looked like those of a dotcom startup. Spacious and airy, the central part of the room sported table tennis, foosball and air hockey tables. None of them were in use. Beanbags sat next to gaming consoles, and a kitchenette held a gleaming coffee machine and a glass-fronted fridge full of energy drinks.

Finn placed large headphones on and walked off. Jane turned towards Fleck. 'Who were you looking for again?'

Fleck swallowed. 'Um, Martin?' She really hoped she wouldn't be asked for his last name.

Jane narrowed her eyes. 'Martin *Zhang*? That's so weird. I could have sworn he was gay. He's in there.' She gestured to a door behind Fleck, shrugged a pair of noise-cancelling headphones on and loped away.

Fleck was about to exhale in relief when Tonia Todman swivelled around. She studied Fleck. 'Martin *is* gay. I've met Kenneth.' Her frown deepened. 'You're not his wife. Who are you? Wait right here. This needs sorting out.' She briskly disappeared, no doubt in search of the Office Police.

Fleck immediately stepped into Martin's office and closed the door.

'Oh, great,' Martin said, looking up in annoyance. 'Great. Super fantastic. This is exactly what I need right now. Honestly, what's the point? What is the *point* of getting the one office in this entire building that has an actual *door* if people keep coming inside? I'm trying to get into a state of flow. Do you even know what "flow" is? It's very important to the creative process. Flow is essential. I cannot handle all these interruptions. No, I do not want to sign Sandra's card. No, I am not interested in coming out for the special afternoon tea. No, I do not want to join the fun run in October. I want to do my work. I just want to get my work done. Is that really too much to ask?'

There was something about the way he ranted, the tone and the cadence. Fleck peered at him, then eyed a photo on his desk. Martin in a dinner suit, smiling broadly and holding a glass of champagne. A young Asian man, also in a suit, wrapping both arms around him in a comically clumsy embrace, his head resting on his shoulder. 'Zhang is your *married* name,' she said.

Martin's face scrunched up in confusion 'What? What has that got to do with anything?'

Fleck stared. 'Martin Cooper. You are Martin Cooper. He's your *dad*. That's what it is: he is your *dad*.'

Martin's confusion was giving way to mild alarm. 'Did you even sign in downstairs? Who are you? Hello? Are you even listening to me?'

Fleck was definitely not listening to Martin – not anymore. She had suddenly caught sight of the pictures in frames around the walls of the office. She stared at them.

Spritz toilet cleaner. Clarion life insurance. Barrington 0% gin. JPW Superannuation. Morning Gold margarine. Kennedy & Scott Property. They were professional shots – there were no grainy pictures of computer screens or covert shots of buildings – but still, they were the same.

'The logos,' she breathed. She looked at Martin, recognition dawning. 'You're a graphic *designer*,' she said, 'These logos are all your work. And look – they've all won awards!'

She beamed at Martin, who gazed back in beleaguered bewilderment. Fleck's brain was buzzing with the significance of what she'd just seen. The door burst open again.

The security guard wore an outfit that looked like the public-domain version of the Victoria Police uniform. 'Ma'am, I'm going to ask you to please open that lunch bag and present the contents clearly for display.'

Fleck looked uneasily at the security guard, a young man standing poised for action, a walkie-talkie strapped against the front of his left shoulder, and at Tonia Todman standing beside him.

She opened the bag and carefully extracted two teething rusks and a squeeze pouch of Rafferty's Garden peas and apple, laying them on Martin's desk.

'I can let myself out,' she murmured.

CHAPTER EIGHTEEN

Fleck had composed a text message for Matthew: *What's ur eta?* Her thumb paused over the send button. The last three text messages she had sent her husband were shopping lists, and before that had been a question about their joint calendar. Is this what they had become? Housemates with a shared childcare business? She added a string of heart emojis to her message for good measure and sent it.

There was nothing wrong with them. They weren't in trouble or anything. They had a relationship full of laughter and affection. But, Fleck mused, they seemed to have forgotten how to be a couple. Everything they did and every conversation they had was somehow related to the kids.

There was still romance of a kind, she supposed, if you knew where to look. Fleck had got up one Friday morning to discover a crisp newspaper on the kitchen table, with a single red rose acting as a bookmark for the pages containing the DA crossword. Matthew had gone out early to buy it for her. And while it was probably an apology for having almost thrown out the previous week's crossword prematurely, it had still been kind of romantic. Sometimes he bought her chocolate. Occasionally he'd bring home a bunch of flowers from the supermarket. (Matthew didn't understand the point of fresh flowers; he just knew it was a rule he should follow.) And Fleck? Well, Fleck *had* just sent him a bunch of heart emojis. So, there was that.

Magic and romance had never been a problem at the start. It had been Matthew's sister who'd introduced them. Not Aggie, the eldest sister who married young and had lots of kids; not Ruth, the baby who had only been a little girl when they'd got together. It was Therese, the cool middle sister.

Therese had been a temp at Fleck's office at the time. This was when Fleck was working in HR, before she'd realised that HR wasn't at all what she wanted to do for a job. Therese had orchestrated for Fleck and her brother to beta-test an escape room together. Looking back, Fleck realised that Therese might have had other motivations beyond gathering feedback for her puzzle designer friend when she'd locked her single brother and her single workmate in a room together on a Friday night.

Fleck was used to solving problems in a social setting. When she joined in with trivia nights and break room crosswords, she was always careful to temper her intellect. It spoilt the fun for the others if the same person kept getting the answers. Nobody liked a show-off. That swallowed 'Aha!' That split-second glance around the room to gauge others' dawning comprehension before confessing that her penny had dropped. This was second nature to her. Waiting for somebody else to shout, 'I GOT IT!' before saying, 'I think I might have it too' was basic social housekeeping to ensure nobody's ego was getting bruised. Nobody's feelings were being hurt. After all, she wanted to be invited back to play again.

It hadn't taken Fleck long to realise that it would be different with Matthew. Not only could he hold his own admirably, but it was also clear from the start he delighted in Fleck's deft cognition. For the first time in a long time, Fleck had had the freedom to allow her brain to run in top gear without upsetting or intimidating anyone, and it had been exhilarating.

When Therese had first locked them in the room, Matthew had awkwardly avoided eye contact. But as Fleck had raced to solve the puzzles, it was like he couldn't help looking at her, like he couldn't believe she was real. Fleck had blushed and tried to look back at him. She'd wanted to find out what would happen when she held his gaze. But it was almost like trying to grasp a hot oven tray with her bare hands. Her eyes darted away the moment they met his. They had only been in the room for fifteen minutes, but Fleck had fallen, and she had fallen hard.

Fleck looked at Matthew now, as he clattered in through the front door. He hadn't become any less attractive. There were men who had that annoying quality of becoming more attractive with each grey hair and wrinkle, and Matthew was one of them. Of course, it didn't hurt that he was currently wearing a crisp white shirt, casually unbuttoned at the neck (was there anything more sexy on a man than a Crisp White Shirt, Casually Unbuttoned at the Neck?). It wasn't that she had stopped finding him attractive, it was just that this spark had become slowly buried under piles of family admin and small resentments and relentless children and sleep deprivation. Plus, there was that niggling fear, fuelled mostly by mass media and a cruel advertising industry: did he still find *her* attractive?

Maybe she should organise for them to go on a date. But that was an overwhelming idea. Too many things to coordinate. Too many favours to call in. And, the idea whispered at the back of her mind, what if a date only confirmed what she feared? That the magic and the romance were gone? What then?

Fleck had decided what she was going to do. She didn't know enough to accuse Vanessa of stealing the money, but there was enough unusual behaviour to warrant a quiet conversation with Charlie Marshall and to seek his advice. He seemed like a reasonable enough man, and he might be able to shed some insight on the whole situation. At the very least, it might be enough to throw Trixie's accusation into doubt.

There was nobody at the counter when Fleck, with Alice strapped to her back, entered the shop on Monday morning. They sailed on through to the back room. With any luck, Charlie would be in the office upstairs.

The back room was not empty. Sitting at the table, reading a thick Peter FitzSimons book, was John Dobson. He ignored Fleck until she made for the staircase. 'You can't go up there.' His voice was deep and gruff.

'Says who? And what are you doing here?' Fleck placed a hand on her hip and tried to act like an assertive person, pretending she didn't recognise him. She met John's stare. 'Do you even work here?'

John just gazed levelly back. It was as if she hadn't asked him anything. The back door opened and Bev walked into the room carrying bags and boxes. She deposited them in the corner of the room and then went through to the shop, shooting Fleck a suspicious glance as she passed.

There was somebody shouting in the upstairs room. It sounded like Douglas. 'This is bureaucracy gone mad! It is woke nonsense! We have managed just fine for thirty-seven years—'

Another man's voice interrupted. Was it Charlie Marshall? This voice was lower and Fleck couldn't make out the words, but she could hear his insistent tone and caught a few phrases: 'duty of care', 'policies and procedures' and 'what you need to understand'.

Then Douglas's voice interrupted, loud and clear as a bell. 'You are drowning us in red tape. We are going to lose our volunteers over this. Do you know how hard—'

Fleck took another step towards the staircase.

'I'm going to ask you to remain downstairs.' John wasn't shouting, but his volume had climbed up one notch.

'I need to talk to Charlie Marshall.' Fleck jutted out her chin.

'Charlie Marshall is not available.'

'It's important.'

'He's not available.'

Douglas's voice sounded again. Fleck and John stared each other down as the belligerent voice rang clearly down the stairs. 'What sort of crime do you expect a seventy-five-year-old woman might have committed in the three years since her last police check? It is insulting. It is a complete and total insult.'

Fleck shifted towards the stairs again. John stood up and shook his head firmly. Suddenly, the upstairs door opened. Douglas stomped downstairs and busied himself with the kettle. He shook his head at the tea bags and muttered.

'What's going on down here?' Charlie appeared on the stairs and looked from Fleck to John. John looked exasperated. Fleck smiled.

'Charlie! I was hoping I could talk to you. Can I speak with you in private?'

'Uh. Sure. Come on upstairs.'

Fleck couldn't resist shooting John an innocent smile as she sailed up the steps towards Charlie.

It didn't take long to fill Charlie in on her suspicions about Vanessa: the stealthy manicures, the use of cash – specifically $5 notes – and the way the petty cash for the office was also withdrawn as $5 notes.

Charlie rubbed his hand over his chin as he listened. Then he stood up and walked downstairs. Fleck followed at a distance. Had she upset him?

John was no longer sitting at the table downstairs. Perhaps he had found a quiet place to sulk. But Charlie wasn't looking for John – he stood at the curtained doorway and called through to the shop. 'Douglas! Can I have a word?'

Douglas stalked into the room, mug of tea in hand, and raised his eyebrows at Charlie.

'The petty cash. You reconcile the petty cash every month, don't you? Have you noticed anything unusual?'

Douglas frowned. 'I make the financial reports every fortnight. The balance sheets, the bank reconciliation, the general ledger. Every fortnight. Not every month.'

Charlie put his hands on the table and leaned forward. 'Yes, but I'm asking about the petty cash specifically. You reconcile it, yes?'

Douglas sighed. 'No, that's Vanessa's job. I don't have time to be doing that sort of menial stuff.'

'Vanessa does the petty cash?'

'Yes. I assigned it to her. What do we have a staff member for if we still have to be the ones fiddling around with receipts? Vanessa manages all of that.'

Charlie rubbed a hand across his face. 'Just so we're clear: the person who spends the petty cash is also the person who keeps track of how it is spent?'

Douglas glared at Charlie. 'I can't be doing everything around here. Do you expect me to account for every tea bag? Every black lead pencil?' Spittle flew from his mouth on the 't' of 'tea bag' and the 'p' of 'pencil'. A rosy hue was blooming across the old man's forehead as it contracted.

Charlie rubbed a finger alongside the bridge of his nose. 'Right. We are going to need to investigate this.' He looked at his watch, then turned to Fleck. 'Vanessa should be back soon. Do you think you could—'

The back door opened and Vanessa stepped in. She frowned at the party collected around the table staring at her, then walked up the narrow staircase to her office.

Charlie watched her progress, then turned back to Fleck. 'Shall we?'

When Charlie and Fleck entered the office upstairs, Vanessa was already hard at work at her desk. She looked surprised when Charlie asked to have 'a quick word', then sat down in front of her desk with Fleck.

'Petty cash? It's just in the drawer here. Why? Do you need it for something?'

'No, I'm not looking for the cash itself. I just wanted to have a look at the reconciliation statements.'

'Oh. I can't help you with that, I'm afraid. I got super behind with things and petty cash reconciliations is just one of those things that got dropped. But leave it with me. I'll put it together for you soon.'

Charlie smiled. 'It's okay – just give me the money and the receipts. I'm sure I can figure it out.'

'Oh, no, no, I can sort it,' Vanessa said.

'Really, it's no bother. Just hand it over so I can have a look at it.'

'I'll get it to you on Monday,' Vanessa insisted. 'Just let me get it organised.'

'I need it now. Is there a problem?'

'Yes, there is. It's ... it's such a mess.'

'I don't mind, really,' Charlie said. 'I just need to get a sense of it.'

'What is *she* doing here?' Vanessa frowned at Fleck.

Charlie sighed. 'We need to talk about the petty cash, Vanessa.'

Vanessa's eyes darted from Fleck to Charlie. She shook her head in tiny increments, an oscillation of minimal amplitude. She opened her

185

mouth to speak, then closed it and shook her head more determinedly. 'I don't know what you're talking about. I told you I was behind. I can't be expected to be on top of everything.'

'But you're telling me that if I were to look in the petty cash drawer, the receipts would more or less add up to the amount withdrawn?'

'I haven't put all the receipts in there yet. You'd need to give me some time to get it all together. I mean, some might be in my car, in the bottom of my bag – you know how it is.' Vanessa gave a little laugh that had no humour in it.

Fleck looked at Vanessa intently. 'But that isn't you.' Both Charlie and Vanessa turned to look at her. 'If it were me, sure. There would be receipts on the floor of my car, receipts through the washing machine. I'd probably forget to even *ask* for a receipt half the time. But that doesn't seem like you.' Fleck gestured to Vanessa's desk. The neatly printed labels. The colour-coded drawers. 'You're meticulous. A loose receipt would itch at you until you had it properly filed. The only reason you wouldn't have filed a legitimate receipt' – she locked eyes with Vanessa – 'is if there were no receipt in the first place.'

Fleck allowed the silence to hang in the air. Vanessa's eyes flashed with defiance, but then, as if somebody had switched the power off on a jumping castle, Fleck watched her slowly deflate. Vanessa placed her head in her beautiful hands. She stayed quiet for a moment. Then said, 'You don't know what it's like to be me.' Her voice was small, almost like a child's.

Charlie looked from Vanessa to Fleck and back again. A moment passed, then he said, 'Why don't you start at the beginning?' He kept his tone neutral. A crease of worry contracted his brow.

Vanessa shook her head, but didn't lift it from her hands. 'I've got a bad habit,' she mumbled.

Fleck leaned back in her chair to regard Vanessa. After a pause, she spoke. 'Tell us about your habit, Vanessa.'

Vanessa looked from Fleck to Charlie, her eyes pleading. Once she started talking, it all came out in a rush. It was as if she had been waiting to unburden herself for a long time.

'I thought that working for a charity would be, like, a really good job. I thought that people working in a charity would be – I don't know – caring and respectful or something.'

Fleck shot a glance at Charlie, who was watching Vanessa steadily. They waited.

Vanessa swallowed. 'But it's hard. Nobody notices how much work I do.' She was slowly rolling a pen along the table and back again. A tiny rolling pin. 'And the workload was getting to me. Do you know that nobody has ever thanked me for all the extra hours I put in? Not once! I was finding it really hard to come into work. The pressure would build until I almost couldn't stand it. Then I would take a shiny pink note out of the petty cash bag and put it into my own bag and the pressure would go away. I deserve a treat sometimes.'

'But you were stealing.' Charlie's expression was earnest.

'I never took more than five dollars.'

'At a time,' Fleck prompted.

'Yes. But never more than five dollars.' This seemed important to Vanessa.

'So you would take the money and spend it on something for yourself?' Fleck thought of the times she'd seen Vanessa getting manicures, how little she appeared to be enjoying it.

Vanessa paused. When she answered, she chose her words carefully. 'There are certain standards I have to maintain in this job,' she said. She held the pen upright, testing the button on the end against the surface of the table, without fully compressing it. 'I am the front of house. I'm, like, the face of the organisation. My face, my hair, my nails – they all need to be maintained. It's part of my job.' She dropped the pen with a clatter. 'But they don't pay me enough to maintain this image. They have no idea. They're men. They aren't expected to have the same level of grooming as me. They don't even have to think about it. They can walk straight into a board meeting without even glancing in the mirror. They're completely oblivious.'

Fleck didn't answer. She continued to watch Vanessa. Vanessa rushed to fill the silence. 'And, look, I know. I know it's the wrong thing to do. I'm not trying to justify myself. I just … I don't know. It became like a compulsion. Like I had to do it. It was just my way of dealing with it when things got too much. A pressure-release valve. I was going to stop. I was always going to stop.'

Vanessa shook her head. She raked her hands through her hair. 'What am I going to do?' Her voice was barely discernible.

'Do you have an idea of how much you have stolen from the Society over this time?' Charlie spoke in a gentle voice. It was if he was worried that Vanessa might shatter into pieces if he showed any anger.

Vanessa swallowed. 'It's not exactly like that. I didn't just keep stealing and stealing.' She held both hands flat in front of her, like she was demonstrating a set of scales. 'The stress would get to me, and it would just build and build.' She moved her left hand slowly higher, while keeping her right hand steady. 'And stealing the money was like scratching an itch – it would make the pressure go away.' She slowly lowered her hands, her eyes pleading for understanding. 'But then I'd spend the money, and I would just hate myself. And the guilt would grow and grow.' Now she slowly raised her right hand. 'And when it got too much, I'd make a big anonymous donation to the Society, so everything would be all right again. But before long, the resentment and stress would grow, and the cycle would start all over again. Binge and purge.'

Vanessa reached into her handbag and pulled out a tiny notebook. She opened it up to consult the latest page. 'I started to keep track of what I had taken. Just because I couldn't stand not knowing if I'd covered it all when I paid it back. Right now, since the last time I donated money back, I've taken fifteen dollars.' She put the notebook back into her bag.

Charlie shifted in his seat. He looked at a loss for words. 'I'm going to need some time to digest all of this, I think.' He looked at Fleck. 'This is ...' He shook his head and blinked. Then he looked at Vanessa. 'Why don't you go home for the day? I'll be in touch about where we go from here.'

CHAPTER NINETEEN

'It turns out Vanessa kept meticulous records of all of her transactions,' Fleck said to Trixie. 'She's going to pay it all back with interest. It came to around six hundred dollars in the end. But not really, because she kept paying it back. Still, she wants to make amends. Not up there, Sam! Stick to the main path!'

They were walking the path along Gardiners Creek with Sam, Joseph, Norah and Alice. Trixie pushed an overhanging branch aside as they continued towards the bridge. 'That's a lot of five-dollar notes. But it's not twenty thousand dollars. Does this mean Vanessa is off our list of suspects?'

'Technically, no,' Fleck said. 'I mean, maybe she also stole other money in a different way. But my gut says no. At any rate, she's provided us with a whole lot of information on the Society's finances. I put it in the backpack with the other stuff.'

Trixie nodded. 'We'll need to invite Ranveer over again.'

'I'll make a nice cake.'

They walked quietly along the sandy gravel track. On the other side of the creek, Fleck could see two labradors chasing each other down the path.

'What's Charlie going to do about Vanessa?' Trixie asked.

'He's arranged for her to have counselling, and he says that she's on "probation". I'm not sure what that means and I don't think Charlie knows what that means either. I think he just wanted to feel like he was doing something. He didn't want to let her off the hook, but he definitely didn't want to sack her.'

'I can see that. She did the wrong thing, but the Society wouldn't function without her. It'd be hard enough with Donna gone.'

'I still haven't had any real success getting in contact with Donna either,' Fleck said. 'Ducks! Ducks! Norah! Can you see the ducks over here?'

'I wanted to get Donna's contact information from Charlie and talk to her myself,' Trixie said. 'I was going to. Charlie was going to check with her if it was okay to share her number, but then everything happened, and I never got it. I wonder if he would share it now, or if he thinks a criminal like me shouldn't talk to her.'

'He might,' Fleck said. 'I get the feeling Charlie is starting to doubt that you did it, but that he doesn't know who did, so his hands are tied. I think that's why he never pressed charges or anything.'

When they got to the footbridge, they walked onto it and stopped in the middle.

'They should be just around here,' Trixie said.

'They will look like wood,' Joseph said. 'They will actually look just like wood, because of camouflage. They will be camouflaged. We might not see them. They might look just like wood.' He was bouncing on the spot.

At first, Fleck couldn't see them, even when Trixie was pointing right at them. It took a while for her eyes to adjust and see that the odd growth of wood coming off the branch of the gum tree reaching across the creek was, in fact, a nesting pair of tawny frogmouths with their chick sitting beside them. Joseph jumped up and down and flapped his hands with glee.

Eventually, they turned around to go back to the oval so that the kids could kick a ball around for a bit. Joseph was talking nonstop about tawny frogmouths. When they got to the second footbridge, Norah began complaining that her legs were tired, so Trixie gave her a piggyback ride.

Fleck watched Sam and Joseph as they ran ahead together. 'Hey, you know the patch you put on the backpack? The one that says *neurosparkly?*'

The patch had been weighing on her mind. Fleck tended to swing between two extremes. In one, she was boring and normal and pretending to have ADHD because ADHD was trendy. It was all in her mind. She was a fake and an imposter. On the other, she was obviously different and everyone else could tell. She was the only one who was oblivious to how weird she had always been. Other people could see clear as day that there was something wrong with her. Could Trixie tell? Was that why she'd used that patch?

'Yeah, sure. The shiny one. I got it online.'

'Is that … was that because you think I have ADHD or something? Is it that obvious?'

'Are you ADHD too? I thought you might be. Nah, the patch isn't for you. I bought the patch for Joseph and me. Joseph is Autistic, I'm ADHD. We're both neurosparkly.'

'Sorry, did you say Joseph is Autistic?'

'Yup. I was really lucky to get the assessment done without too much fuss. I know it can be really hard to do. Some parents find it impossible to find a psych because the waiting lists are a mile long. But he's part of this longitudinal study and they organised it all. That's how I got my diagnosis too.'

Fleck pulled a leaf off an overhanging branch and started to shred it. 'I don't think you need to worry. I think Joseph is fine. He's, like, barely Autistic at all, super high-functioning.'

'He's developed some good coping strategies to get by in a neurotypical-centred world,' Trixie said, 'but please don't say he's barely Autistic. I know you're trying to say something kind, but that isn't kind.'

Fleck hesitated. She had thought she had been saying something reassuring and helpful. She still didn't really understand what was wrong about it. She tried again. 'I mean, we're all a little bit Autistic, aren't we? All a little bit ADHD?'

Trixie covered her face in her hands and groaned out through her fingers. 'Argh. No. Stop. Please stop. It's … No.' Trixie frowned, searching for the right words. 'It's like – you know how Joseph is West African?'

Fleck nodded.

'So, if you were to say, "Joseph hardly seems West African at all," or "Don't worry, you can't even tell he's West African," or "Everybody is a little bit West African and it's not a big deal," you can see why that might be offensive, yeah? It's like you're saying it's a bad thing.'

Fleck swallowed. 'I think I see what you mean.'

Trixie nodded. 'I know the world seems to act like it's a bad thing, a "disorder", like we should be ashamed about being neurodivergent, but I think it's a matter of pride. I'm proud to be ADHD and I'm proud that Joseph is Autistic. I won't have anybody try to minimise that for any reason. And neither should you.'

'I'm sorry I got it wrong.' Fleck put her hand on Trixie's arm and slowed her walking pace a little.

Trixie gave Fleck's hand a reassuring double-pat. 'Don't worry. The whole world gets it wrong most of the time. But we're slowly changing things.'

'I don't know for sure that I'm actually ADHD,' Fleck said. 'I haven't been tested or anything.'

'Yeah, but I see self-diagnosis as valid. There are that many barriers to receiving a diagnosis. It's almost impossible to sort out adult ADHD diagnosis without wheelbarrows full of cash and the ability to, like, not be ADHD and organise everything. If you think you are ADHD, I say you are, for sure.'

'But is that allowed?'

Trixie grinned and shrugged. 'There are no rules. Oh, finally, the oval. My back is killing me!'

Maybe Fleck's rule about not buying dress patterns until she actually made one of the dresses was too strict. These ones were gorgeous. Fleck pictured herself looking like one of these serene, willowy illustrated women. What if she became the sort of woman who wore cute dresses? And people would compliment her and ask where she bought it. And she would say, 'This? I made it!'

And what if she made a *miniature version for Norah*? And a baby version for Alice? Imagine her stepping out in a cute dress with two little girls in *even cuter dresses*. What if she could be that sort of mother?

Of course, she probably wouldn't be able to convince Norah to take her Batman-pyjamas-as-daywear off. And if she were really honest, she wasn't sure she would want Norah to transform into the sort of child who was easily convinced to humour her mother's fabric-inspired whims. Still. Matching handmade dresses. Surely that was the pinnacle of domestic aspiration?

'Stop it,' Fleck muttered aloud. 'You're a detective, remember?' And this made her smile. But she chose three patterns anyway, because she was not quite ready to let go of this ridiculous uber-capable image of herself. She could still be a detective who aspired to be a textile wizard.

She was getting sidetracked. She was not in the op shop to buy dress patterns. She glanced around: there were still a couple of customers lingering by the door. Fleck waited for them to leave before she approached the counter.

She handed the three patterns to Douglas Cooper and offered a winning smile. 'Lovely weather outside today.'

Douglas grunted, somewhat impatiently.

'Are you going to spy on your son again after this?'

Douglas looked up sharply but said nothing.

Fleck softened her tone. 'You know, you could probably go talk to him. You're obviously proud of him, and you should be. He's doing so well.'

Douglas was now looking determinedly away, as if Fleck had suddenly turned invisible.

'Why don't you have a relationship anymore? Is it because he's gay? That's not a reason to disown your son, you know.'

Douglas rang up the purchases. 'That will be one dollar fifty and it is cash only.' His tone was a warning.

Fleck opened her mouth to say something else, and then closed it again. She paid for the patterns, then picked them up and turned to leave.

Trixie had stayed with Alice and Norah at the playground across the road. Fleck plonked down on the bench beside her.

'No joy?' Trixie wore a brightly coloured crocheted jacket over her bakery uniform.

Fleck huffed out a sigh. 'I don't know what I hoped to achieve.'

Trixie leaned sideways to give Fleck a friendly shoulder-bump. 'Ah, you can only do what you can do, especially when dealing with emotionally stunted men who only know how to be angry. I'm about to head off, but if you want to stick your head in towards the end of my shift, I can probably fix you up with some free pull-aparts and maybe some bread. Are you still good to pick up Joseph?'

'All good. I'll see you later.'

Fleck stretched and watched Norah play. When she felt someone sit beside her on the bench, Fleck assumed that Trixie was back, that she had forgotten something. But it wasn't Trixie.

It was Douglas.

'It's not because he's gay.' He barked out the words aggressively, staring straight ahead.

Fleck looked ahead, too. Norah was attempting to climb up the slide. His words hung in the air between them. Fleck didn't know what to say.

'It was never that.' The words were wrenched from him. Then he added in a quieter voice, 'Joan and I – we always knew. He was always that way. Sensitive.'

Fleck could see the effort it took him to speak. His face was contorted as he continued to look straight ahead. A grey miner bird was harassing a pair of magpies, swooping and pecking. A man sat with his golden retriever outside George's Kitchen. Fleck could see him feeding the dog pieces of toast from his plate. Douglas drew a breath. 'Martin was always Joan's boy. Damian was my boy. But now Damian is in America. And it's all … it's all too hard.'

Norah had managed to climb halfway up the slide before slipping back down again. She tried again, her gumboot seeking purchase on the side of the slide.

Douglas made a grunting sound, then continued. 'When Joan died … When … She was the one who knew how to talk. It was her who … Without her we …' He couldn't finish a sentence. He still wasn't looking at her. 'We're not fighting. We just, just don't know …' He lifted a hand in defeat.

Fleck looked at Douglas as he struggled to talk. 'Did you go to his wedding?'

Douglas shook his head. 'It was a lockdown wedding. They eloped. Nobody went to his wedding.' He paused, then said in a quieter voice, 'I've never even met the bloke.'

'I think you should talk to him.'

The old man shook his head more firmly this time.

'Or you could write to him. But you need to do something. You know what Joan would want you to do.'

The magpies had turned on the noisy miner. They chased it out of sight. The golden retriever on the other side of Highett Road barked once.

Douglas looked at her. 'I can't do it. I'd sound like a bloody idiot.'

Fleck blinked and swallowed. 'He's your son. It's worth making a fool of yourself about it.'

CHAPTER TWENTY

Fleck had the packet of milky highlighter pens she had bought from the cute Japanese shop, ages ago now. Cute stationery helped when the job was boring. She and Trixie sat beside each other on the couch in the library. A table would have been better, they could have spread their papers out, but there wasn't a table close enough to the children's section.

Fleck pulled out a pink highlighter for herself and passed the packet to Trixie. 'Okay. Let's go through it line by line. For each entry, tell me if you can definitely identify what it is or if it's a bit weird-sounding. Actually not weird-sounding, because nothing here is weird-sounding. Everything here is boring-sounding. But if it's boring-sounding, but you can't tell me what boring thing the entry is for, we have to highlight it.'

Norah was inspecting a child-sized table-shelf full of board books. Joseph was sitting on the brightly coloured rug, poring over a large, illustrated fact book. Sam was lying on his back on the long ottoman seat, his head hanging upside down over the edge, talking to Joseph. Fleck made faces at Alice while Trixie examined each entry.

'So we've got the occasional corporate sponsor or social club donation. There's no government funding at all. And there are these little fundraisers and raffles that bring in bits of money throughout the year.' Trixie pointed at the page in front of her. 'It's all a bit hodgepodge. It's like the Society is a wonky old car that still manages to get down the road despite being held together with duct tape and cable ties. If you ask me, nobody really knows what's keeping it going. Not even Douglas.'

Trixie picked the papers up. 'The Neeson Raffle is that one you see set up outside Kmart every year with the quilts and baby clothes. OHR Cakes is the cake stall they set up once a month after ten thirty Mass at Our Holy Redeemer.'

Fleck took the papers from Trixie's hands and squinted at them. 'Have you had any more thoughts as to what the Hurst Drive is?'

Trixie shook her head. 'Nah. I haven't heard of that one. None of the old vollies are named Hurst. Unless it's someone who died before I joined and it's named in their honour?'

'You can't have that many books! That is too many books!' Sam was off the ottoman and now faced Norah with his hands on his hips.

Norah stood beside a large pile of board books, almost as tall as her, to which she had also added several adult novels. She looked incensed. 'No! This is my books! This is my BOOKS!'

'But that one isn't even a kids' book. That's a grown-up book.'

Norah's face was turning red. Her small body tensed as she picked up a fat Rachael Johns novel and shook it in Sam's face. 'NO. This is my book! This is my book for Mummy!'

Fleck looked at Trixie. 'I get the sense things are about to go badly wrong. Should we move this to my house?'

Trixie nodded. 'Time to bail!'

'There's something about the Hurst Drive that is itching at my brain. Something about it is not right.' Fleck set the papers up on the kitchen table as Trixie made them both tea.

Things were quieter now. The drive had worked its magic and now Alice was asleep in the study. Fleck didn't want to risk waking her by taking her upstairs to her room. Joseph, Norah and Sam were all looking over their library books.

Fleck frowned at the spreadsheet. 'All of these Hurst entries are for payments going out. Surely at some point the drive would provide income for the Society? But look: every one of them is for expenses.'

'Why does that one have a number next to it?' Trixie sat beside her and pointed to an earlier entry.

Fleck stared for a moment. *150 Hurst Drive.* Then she looked up at Trixie. 'What if it's not a fundraising drive? What if it's an address?'

Trixie pulled out her phone, then frowned. 'I'm not sure how to find a list of Hurst drives in Melbourne. Even when I look up "Hurst Drive Melbourne", it just comes up with a random street in some real estate listing – how would we know it's the one we're looking for?'

'Google is useless for this. What we really need is the back of the Melways.'

A few minutes later, Fleck and Trixie were sitting inside Fleck's car in the garage. With the door through to the house open, they could still catch glimpses of the kids sitting around the table with their books.

'Why are we in the car?' asked Trixie.

'This is the only Melways I can get to. Matthew buys a new one every year—'

'Wait, Matthew buys a new Melways *every year?*'

'What can I say? It makes him happy. He's got a stack of them, but they're in the study and I don't want to wake Alice.'

'Do you know that this street directory is actually named "Melway", not "Melways"?' Trixie asked.

'I *know* that, but I can't *say* that.'

'Yeah, me either. It's like it has an anti–silent letter. Hey, why don't we just take this one inside and look at it there?'

'I don't want to take it out of the car,' Fleck said. 'I know if I do, I'll get distracted and forget to ever put it back. And then in a couple of weeks I'll be trying to get somewhere and my phone will be dead and I won't have the Melways in the car and I'll be completely stuffed. You have no idea how many times I get lost with a dead phone and the Melways saves me. Actually, "lost with a dead phone" describes my constant state of being, I think.'

'It could be the title of your memoir.'

'*Lost, with a Dead Phone: The Fleck Parker Story.*'

Fleck opened the large street directory to the back pages, which contained an index of all the street names. 'Okay, let's see. Harkaway … Harold … Hooper … Hunter … Hurst! Here it is. Oh, wait. You are not going to believe this.'

'What is it?'

'There's a bunch of Hurst streets, some Hurst roads, a few Hurst avenues. But there is only one Hurst Drive in Greater Melbourne. And it's in Dandenong.'

The address was for an industrial lot, 150–160 Hurst Drive. When Fleck and Trixie looked at it in satellite view on Google Maps, they could see cars parked in the centre of a horseshoe-shaped group of buildings, probably small warehouses. There was an outlet centre for carpets, a party supplies company, an alarm systems company, a school uniform supplier and a screen-printing business. There was one building, Unit 5, that was unlabelled. Neither Fleck nor Trixie could find a name online for the business that rented the site, but they also couldn't find any evidence that the unit was vacant and available for lease. Fleck used Google Street View to get a picture of the property, then printed it off for their wall.

Fleck and Trixie both sat gazing at the photo. 'You can't tell me Helen is not the villain of this story when she spends regular time in an actual abandoned warehouse,' Trixie said. 'I mean, what more evidence do you need?' She was crocheting as she spoke, another budgerigar forming under her rapidly moving fingers. 'What's the bet that the entire premises is decked out with mediaeval torture equipment that she's using on defenceless kittens?'

Fleck pursed her lips. 'I mean, we don't know for sure that this is where she goes. And none of her behaviour is illegal, but it definitely is strange. It would help if we could find out what that building is actually for. Why isn't it listed anywhere?'

'Because it's Helen's criminal lair, that's why!'

'Hmmm, further investigation is required,' Fleck said. 'But we mustn't forget we have other suspects.'

'Yes. Just because we now know why Douglas printed those photos, doesn't mean he can't still be Helen's minion in her secret murder factory!'

A few hours later, when Trixie had gone home, Fleck came back into the living room with a freshly changed Alice. Matthew had been playing the Tickle Monster with Norah and Sam. This was a game where he lay on the couch pretending to be asleep. Norah and Sam would creep up and climb on him. This monster would grumble and sleep through all manner of prodding and clambering until that magic moment when somebody tapped his nose three times. This was what woke up the Tickle Monster. Said monster then growled and lurched and, yes, tickled its assailants until it suddenly became overcome with exhaustion and fell asleep again. Fleck suspected Matthew liked to play this game when he got home from work because it involved him spending most of his time lying on the couch feigning sleep.

It looked like the game, which had been in full force when Fleck had left the room to change Alice, had now lapsed somewhat. Sam and Norah had become involved in a Duplo city on the carpet while the Tickle Monster rested unencumbered.

Fleck strapped Alice into her highchair and slipped onto the couch beside Matthew. It was just deep enough for them to lie alongside each other. Matthew wrapped his arms around her and they spooned, watching Sam and Norah negotiate their imaginary world.

'Let's make it that this one can fly,' Sam said 'No, wait. Let's make it this is his aeroplane and he flies it to work.' He manipulated a brightly smiling plastic figure and a Duplo construction around in the air above the plastic village.

'This is the mummy,' Norah declared, brandishing a smiling plastic figure that had eyelashes and a hair ribbon.

'Okay. What does she do?' Sam pulled his brick plane in for a gentle landing.

'She's a tectiffwork!'

Matthew and Fleck stifled giggles from their vantage point on the couch. Fleck rolled over to face her husband and they pressed their foreheads together, silently shaking with laughter.

'Because that's what mummies do, you know?' Matthew murmured into the little space between them. 'Mummies do tectivework.'

Matthew's skin was warm, his jaw was rough with whiskers and he smelled deliciously of Matthew. His hand rested on her hip.

Fleck smiled a little ruefully. 'Maybe that's a sign that I've been doing it too much. Detective work, that is. I have been a little obsessed lately.'

'Well, there was that time I came home from work and you were so wrapped up in what you were doing that you hadn't even realised it was getting dark, and the kids were getting into the Milo on the pantry floor.'

'Oh, yeah. And you boiled up hot dogs for dinner because I forgot to put anything on.'

'Well, when raw Milo is served as a starter, it should always be paired with white-bread hot dogs for mains. That's just the rule.'

'Oh, boy, I'd forgotten about that. And I was really surprised when you turned the light on. I thought it was still four o'clock or something. I was just so absorbed in what I was doing.'

'I don't think you're capable of lukewarm interests. Or lukewarm anything. But I've always loved that about you.'

'Oh, yeah? What else do you love?'

'No! You can't have lots!' Sam said, his voice sharp and loud. 'You can only have one. He is the one!'

'NOOO! I want a chief suspeck! MY chief suspeck!'

'But we already *said* that *he* is the chief suspect!'

Fleck rolled over to see what was going on. Sam was holding a Duplo man in his hand. Norah had gathered three figurines: two Duplo and one from the Little People set.

'Mu-um. Norah says they're all chief suspects, but you can only have one and I already said my one was the chief suspect. I said it ages ago.'

'NO! MINE! My chief suspeck!'

'You're not playing it right!' Sam shouted at his sister.

'It's okay. It's okay,' Fleck reassured them. 'Norah, don't worry. You can have a lot of suspects. You can have a whole line-up. Why don't you put them in a line-up? And Sam.' Fleck lowered her voice to beneath a whisper and mouthed, 'Your one is the chief!'

Sam nodded, a little suspiciously, then he and Norah resumed their game in relative peace. Fleck and Matthew shuffled on the couch so that Matthew was lying on his back with Fleck's head on his chest.

Matthew yawned. 'I mean, hot dog dinners aside, I like that you've found something you love so much.' Alice made a squawking noise from her highchair. She banged her water cup on the tray. Matthew continued. 'It lights you up from the inside. That can only be good, right? And it's not just that you're happier when you're doing detective work. It's made you more happy all the time.'

Fleck gave a little nod. 'You're right. It has made me happier.'

There was a thump. Alice had dropped her water cup. But it had a lid on. It would be fine. Fleck closed her eyes. 'It's like I've finally found my rhythm.'

There was a comfortable pause. Then Matthew spoke again. 'I do worry, though. It could get dangerous. I need to know that you'll be safe doing this. I need to know the kids will be safe.'

Fleck huffed a little laugh. 'I don't think I'm good enough at this for that to be a problem. I'm nowhere near the centre of this mystery. It's not like I'm a threat to anyone.' She sighed deeply. After a moment, she continued. 'Sometimes I think this is something I really enjoy. I like looking at a mystery from all angles and finding loose threads. I like the research and the speculation and working out connections.' She picked at a crisp fragment of tissue on Matthew's t-shirt, a gift from the washing machine. 'But then I remember that this isn't some fun exercise for me to play with. This is someone's life. This is someone else's pain. Who am I to have fun with a person's problems?'

Matthew shifted and pulled Fleck in closer. 'Well, you're not hurting Trixie by doing this. She asked you to do it, remember? It's not like you're taking the place of some other investigator who knows exactly what they're doing. I mean, surely a flawed effort is better than no effort at all. And you are allowed to enjoy what you do.'

Fleck rolled the piece of tissue between her fingers. 'Maybe.' Her voice was small.

'I think sometimes you overthink things. You go looking for reasons to beat yourself up. You're allowed to enjoy things, you know. Enough of what you do is hard work. You're allowed to have something that you enjoy without looking for a reason to be guilty about it.'

Fleck gave Matthew a squeeze. 'Okay.' After a moment, she groaned. 'I need to get up, but I don't want to get up. Can I just stay here for the rest of the night?

Matthew kissed the top of her head. 'Suits me fine.'

Norah and Sam had resumed bickering. Alice started to grizzle. The oven timer beeped insistently.

'You get the plates, I'll serve up?' Matthew gave her shoulder a squeeze.

Fleck groaned into his chest in response. Then they both stumbled to their feet.

'Is that all the tea sorted?' Fleck asked. 'I'm going to put the thermos away. Okay. Now you all need to admire my cake.'

Ranveer sat with Fleck and Trixie at an outdoor picnic table. They were at the local reserve near his house, the one he heard Fleck call the Little Blue Car park. Norah, Sam and Joseph climbed on the equipment. Alice was in her stroller. Fleck pulled the lid off her vintage Tupperware cake container. The most delicious smell wafted out.

'Oh, yes! I love your half-eaten apple teacake! The buttery cinnamon on the top is the best part. I could literally eat a whole plate just of the buttery cinnamon on the top.' Trixie was bouncing on the bench seat in anticipation, her face alight.

Fleck had levered the cake out onto a plate and was handing out slices. It was still warm.

Ranveer inspected his slice. It was a golden wedge with sliced apple baked into the top. It was still warm in his hand. He frowned dubiously. 'Why is it called "half-eaten" when it's a whole cake? How is the cake half-eaten?'

Fleck laughed. 'Oh, don't worry. The cake isn't half-eaten ...'

Ranveer smiled in relief and took a large bite.

'... the apples are!'

Ranveer made a choking noise.

'It's okay! She cuts the bad bits off!' Trixie reassured him.

'It's just that I have all these apples all over the house with one bite taken out of them. It's such a waste. So I use them to make half-eaten apple cake. It's perfectly fine.'

Ranveer was supremely unconvinced, but he chewed slowly. As he swallowed, he shrugged the cream-coloured backpack off his shoulders and passed it to Fleck.

'So, I finished looking at the inquiry reports that Charlie Marshall gave you.'

'What did you find out?'

'You don't have to feel bad if you found them hard to understand,' he said. 'It looks like somebody has gone to a lot of trouble to make them that way. This is not the sort of mess you get when an amateur works the accounts either. This is professionally obscure.'

'But wasn't the consultant hired to make things more transparent?' Trixie spoke with her mouth half-full of half-eaten apple cake.

Ranveer shook his head. 'It's almost as if he has hired this consultant to obscure things, not make them clearer. And that's another thing.

You said Charlie says this consultant is best in the business? I have never heard of him. He only seems to have done this work for Charlie. He's not well known in the industry at all. And everybody has been talking about how the Society has been struggling financially, but they are consistently breaking even. Almost too consistently. It is almost unnatural how little fluctuation there is.'

Fleck wrote this down in her exercise book. Ranveer ate more of his cake. He hated to admit it, but this cake made of discarded apples was quite delicious. He ended up eating three slices of it. These strange women were becoming a bad influence on him.

CHAPTER TWENTY-ONE

Trixie was a little early for her shift at the bakery. The Paradise Heights Bakers Delight was on Peppercorn Street, at the edge of the shopping strip on the opposite end from George's Kitchen. Trixie checked her watch as she walked down Highett Road. George was standing on the corner, clearing one of his outdoor tables. 'Hey, Trixie! Do you have a minute?' he said.

'Sure,' Trixie said, 'I've got time.' She stepped into the cafe with him.

George dumped the plates in the sink and pulled out his phone. 'Chrisanthe has started talking!'

Trixie opened her mouth and then closed it. Chrisanthe was still just a newborn. George handed her his phone, on which a video was playing: a close-up of a baby lying in a bassinet. Very new. Very squishy. Trixie would never tell George this, but all newborn babies looked like cantankerous old men to her.

This particular tiny grandfather frowned and blinked and looked bewildered. 'You need to wait a minute, but then she talks!' George was bouncing on the balls of his feet as Trixie peered dutifully at the video.

Little Chrisanthe seemed to consider the world in front of her, then she paused and opened her mouth. 'Ooooohaaaa,' she declared.

'Did you hear that? Did you hear it?'

George looked like he was on the brink of replaying it just to be sure, so Trixie nodded hard. 'She's going to be a child genius. She's so clever.'

They enthused over the many wonders of this miraculous child for a few more minutes, then George pocketed his phone. 'Have you got any further on the case? Have you talked to those two women yet – Dima and Jo?'

'No, it's tricky,' Trixie replied. 'They think I stole from the Society, so it's hard to tee up a heart-to-heart, if you know what I mean.'

'Well, the reason I ask is because it looks like one of them is on her way over.' George gestured out the window. Jo was crossing Highett Road at the intersection. When she reached the other side, she pressed the button to cross Peppercorn Street and waited, her eyes on her phone.

George looked at Trixie. 'What if you hide in the bathroom? I could talk to her and you could listen in. Nobody else will go in there – it has an out-of-order sign on the door.'

The cafe toilet was in the back corner of the shop, tucked behind some shelving. It was clean and fresh, if incredibly poky. Trixie knew it wasn't really out of order. George used the sign to discourage people on the street from using the cafe as a public convenience. Trixie ducked behind the door and opened it a crack. It sounded like Jo was stepping into the cafe. Trixie heard her ordering her coffee.

'Busy day?' George was rolling out his standard banter.

'Yes. Busy. Look, can I ask you – was the cafe across the road open yesterday?'

'The one on Highett Road? It was closed yesterday, open the day before that.'

'Oh. I know it was open the day before that. I made sure of it. I shouldn't have to babysit him every day. I do enough.'

'Is that your cafe?'

'No, it's my dad's cafe. I just pay for everything. It's an investment. It's not an investment that makes me any income, but it's money well spent.'

George left a curious pause in the air while he rang up the purchase. People tended to open up to George.

Jo took the bait. 'I mean, the cafe is an investment in my own mental health. My dad … he needs to be kept busy. If I wasn't putting money into propping up this cafe, I would be spending it on rehab or gambling debts or extracting him from yet another creepy cult. He's better when he has a project. Sorry. You don't need to hear all of this.'

'It's fine. I love a chat. So, the cafe runs at a loss? And you cover it?'

'Pretty much. It's not so bad. The rent is pretty reasonable. The landlord is an old mate of Dad's, I think. Dad makes friends all the time; he's very charming.'

'But not a businessman?'

'Noooo. That he is not. He needs to stop letting his cronies eat there for free. We're not running a soup kitchen. And he needs to stop cluttering up the place with stock from his failed business ventures. But he won't listen to me. I mean, what could I possibly know about running a business? I could be five times as successful as I am right now and he would *still* treat me like some five-year-old playing shops.'

'But what about Dima?' Trixie said, bursting out of the bathroom. 'How does she fit into all of this? What about the drugs? The secret account? And why are you paying Dima off?' She couldn't help herself.

Jo stared at her, mouth agape. '*Trixie?* Where did you come from? What is going on?'

'There's something dodgy going on with you and Dima. Admit it.

You're in cahoots. Something is up. There's something going on. There has to be. There *has* to be.'

Jo didn't say anything. She just looked at Trixie. George had put down Jo's coffee carefully on the counter. He was looking at Trixie too.

Trixie had started and she wasn't going to stop. She planted a fist on her hip. 'I didn't steal that money. I didn't. But somebody did. Somebody knows something. And you're acting incredibly suss and so is that cafe and so is Dima. I know there's something up with you and I know it has to do with the stolen money. And also drugs.'

Jo looked uncertainly from Trixie to George and back again. 'Okay. I'm really confused right now—'

'Hey, what's going on?' It was Dima, who'd just stepped into the cafe. She turned to Jo. 'I got your text and came straight over. I was home today anyway so it was no biggie.'

Jo turned cautiously away from Trixie and addressed Dima. 'Dad hasn't turned up. Can you open the shop? I need to track him down.'

Dima nodded and, shooting Trixie a strange look, stepped back out of the cafe.

This was too much for Trixie. 'That. That is what I am talking about. What was that?'

Jo shook her head wearily and expelled a sigh. 'Dima helps me with Dad's cafe. I pay her to open on a Monday when he won't get out of bed. And she's on hand to cover gaps when Dad doesn't turn up, like today. And …' Jo paused and drew a breath. 'And I pay her extra to spy on him. There's a limit to how much meddling he'll tolerate from me, so I pay Dima to give me the inside word.' Her face slackened and she rubbed her elbow. 'I know I'm controlling. I know. But I just feel safer when I know everything. I just need to know.'

Trixie felt like everything was draining out of her. 'But what about the drugs? The secret account?' Her voice had lost all of its conviction.

Jo blinked and reddened. 'I don't know how you know about that.' She paused and looked out the window to where Dima was waiting to cross Peppercorn Street. Then she looked back at Trixie and spoke in a low tone. 'I was worried that Dad had started using again. As it turns out, I was wrong. But I have trust issues, I guess. And that's why I have a secret expense account for the business. I'm still scared that Dad will see a bunch of money and use it to go on a bender. It's not fair, maybe, but it's what I do.'

The two women looked at each other for a beat. Then Trixie nodded once. It was all she could manage.

Jo hesitated before she spoke again. 'I never ... It never rang true for me.' She drew a breath. 'I mean, maybe you're just a master manipulator, but it doesn't make sense that you stole the money. I hope you find out who did.'

Trixie blinked a couple of times and nodded. She felt a lump swelling in her throat and swallowed hard.

'Oh. Look who has finally decided to turn up!' Jo snatched up her coffee and strode out of the shop. Across the road, a man in his sixties was unlocking the front door of the other cafe. Trixie watched as Jo jaywalked across the road, outstripping Dima who was using the pedestrian crossings. The man smiled broadly and waved, but his smile faltered as he caught sight of his daughter's face.

As Trixie watched Jo, George said, 'Are you okay?'

She could feel it coming. Not here. She hadn't realised how much she had hoped that Jo and Dima would be connected to some conspiracy that would explain everything. That if she could just uncover what was going on, she could be exonerated. She could go back to how things were. She wouldn't have to pay a massive debt. Her name would be cleared. And now ... and now ...

'Here, sit down. Just breathe. Let's take things slowly.' George was looking alarmed. He led her to a table. She sat in the chair and looked up at him, bewildered.

I needed for it to be her. That was the sentence she wanted to get out. But her lungs wouldn't let her. 'I – need – I – I – need – I—' Her gasps were deep and ragged. She could feel her eyes bulging as she gulped at empty air.

'You don't need to talk. Just breathe. Let's breathe slowly.'

Breathe. Remember your comfort cues. She placed a shaking hand on her chest. *It's different this time. You have friends in your corner.* Her chest convulsed. This was ridiculous. She was ridiculous.

'Just take it slowly,' George said. 'Don't worry about work. I'll call Jodie. I'm sure she can get it covered.'

No! I need the shift! 'No – I – I – I – No—' The gasps kept coming. The words just wouldn't come out.

'You can sit here for as long as you need. Just take your time. You're safe.'

But she wasn't. She wasn't safe. She wouldn't be safe. She was in a deep pit. She was in a deep pit, and she could never climb out.

George and Fleck had an instant messaging thread where they shared Wordle results and the occasional meme. Fleck had been surprised by the message she had received fifteen minutes ago. *Can you come by the cafe? Trixie needs you.*

When she arrived, Trixie was sitting at a table with a pot of tea in front of her. She looked pale and drawn. Norah immediately ran over to press her face against the display fridge while Fleck parked the pusher and sat down opposite Trixie.

Trixie looked at her without smiling. Then she looked back down.

'I'm scared we're not going to solve this.' Her voice hitched oddly on 'solve'. Then she told Fleck what she had discovered about Jo and Dima's situation.

George quietly placed food and drinks in front of them as Trixie spoke, occasionally chiming in with extra information.

Fleck frowned. 'Wait: how did Dima get here so quickly?'

George shrugged. 'She lives behind the fish and chip shop. Didn't you know?'

'What? Really?'

'Yup. There's a fully contained two-bedroom apartment back there. It's very nice. I saw it when Stav was getting it fixed up.'

Fleck peered across the road. Paradise Fish and Chips was on Peppercorn Street, four doors down from Many Hands. 'And how do you know Dima lives there?'

'Are you kidding? I know everything that goes on in this street!'

A pair of customers entered the cafe, and George turned his attention to them.

Trixie shook her head. 'I didn't realise how much I was counting on this leading somewhere.'

Fleck poked at some brownie crumbs with her finger. 'If you think about it another way, we've actually made progress. We can rule out that line of investigation.'

Trixie looked up. 'But what happens when we run out of lines of investigation?'

Fleck shook her head firmly. 'We won't. Because somebody stole that money. We just need to find out who it is.' She stood up. 'But first, I need to change Alice's nappy.'

It was a bit of a blowout, but thankfully Fleck still had a clean onesie in the glove box. Norah insisted on helping, so Fleck installed her in the back seat of the car while she had Alice laid out on a bunny-rug on the front passenger seat, and asked her to pass wipes. So many wipes.

As soon as everyone was clean and fresh and sanitised again, they walked back to the cafe.

Fleck had been so engrossed in the task of getting Alice clean – always keeping one hand firmly on her chest so that she didn't roll over and crawl away, while also chatting brightly to Norah so that she stayed engaged in her role as Wipe Dispensing Assistant and didn't get bored and start investigating the function of the parking brake – that she hadn't noticed Helen walking past.

As Fleck approached George's Kitchen, she saw Helen looking into the cafe window. Fleck didn't need to guess at Helen's facial expression this time. She looked incensed. Utterly furious. Then, as if renewed with sudden purpose, she strode off to her car.

Fleck watched Helen slam herself into the silver Mercedes parked on Highett Road. Then, with Alice on her hip and holding hands with Norah, she pressed her way through the plastic strips into the cafe. Trixie didn't look up. Fleck suspected she hadn't even noticed Helen giving her the evil eye. Trixie sat behind the large teapot and plates of cake, looking forlorn. She had gone inside herself.

CHAPTER TWENTY-TWO

'Helen is staring at us.' Fleck was standing with Trixie under their usual tree the next day at school pick-up.

'No, she isn't,' Trixie said, looking around. 'Where even is she?'

'There. On the other side of the playground. She is definitely staring at us.'

'Oh, gee! She really is. What is her—' Trixie paused mid-sentence.

A police car pulled into the teachers' car park and two uniformed officers stepped out. Fleck noticed that Helen was looking from the police striding towards the playground to Trixie, and then back again. Fear curdled in the pit of her stomach.

The police officers approached them. They were both quite tall. 'Beatrix Anne McAuley?' The male officer spoke in a pleasant voice but with a firm undertone. Trixie nodded, her face white. The policeman continued, 'Ms McAuley, I am Senior Constable Barnes from the Paradise South police station, and this is Constable Shaw. We are here to place you under arrest for the theft of twenty thousand dollars from Many Hands Society. You do not have to say anything if you don't want to, but anything you say or do will be recorded and can be used in court. Do you understand?'

Trixie opened her mouth slightly and shook her head. 'There's been a mistake. I didn't do it.' Her eyes darted around the playground at the staring parents, as if hoping to find a solution. Helen was watching the proceedings with great interest. Trixie's eyes narrowed. 'You!' she hissed.

Helen continued to watch, an eyebrow raised in defiance. Trixie scrambled towards her. 'YOU DID THIS!' she roared.

The policewoman, Officer Shaw, ran in step beside her. 'Beatrix, you need to stop and come with us. Let's make things easy.'

Trixie continued hurtling towards Helen as if she hadn't heard the constable. Helen stood her ground. Fleck hurried along in their wake. Constable Shaw deftly restrained Trixie and spoke to her in a calm, firm voice, but Trixie wasn't listening. She struggled against the police officer and shouted at Helen. 'They weren't going to press charges! They weren't going to involve the police! It was you! It was you! You vindictive MONSTER!'

The school bell rang. Officer Shaw continued to issue directions to Trixie, her voice louder than before. Trixie continued to struggle and hurl abuse at Helen. Shaw nodded at SC Barnes as he approached, who put handcuffs on Trixie.

Children were pouring out of the classrooms, jostling down the path with their backpacks. Some carried art projects in their hands, some bounced balls or chased each other. The noise of their chatter intensified as more and more children spotted the police. The teacher on yard duty emerged from the building, pulling on a hi-vis vest. She quickly hurried over when she saw what was happening. 'Okay, everybody off the tanbark. The playground is out of bounds right now. Let's give the police some room. Off the tanbark. Jason Mayne, that means you too! Off!'

Fleck scanned the crowd. She could see Sam and Joseph emerging from their classroom door. The backpacks always looked so big on the prep kids. Joseph didn't need to see his mum in handcuffs. Fleck pushed her way through the crowd of excited children and intercepted the two little boys. Sam beamed. 'Can we have a play on the playground, Mum?'

'Let's just stop here a minute, Sam. How was school? Did you have library today?'

'It was good. Can I go on the monkey bars?'

'Guess what? Joseph's coming to our place for a play after school!'

Joseph looked carefully at Fleck and then at the mass of children not flowing out of the school gates, then stopped, watching something. 'What's going on? Where's my mum?'

Fleck swallowed. Two Grade Four girls came running towards them from the crowd. Their eyes were alight with the drama of the situation. They shouted over the top of each other with all the self-importance that comes from being nine years old.

'Joseph McAuley-Musah! Guess what?'

'Your mum is a criminal!'

'I think she's going to jail!'

'She's under arrest. Your mum is under arrest!'

'Why is she going to jail, Joseph McAuley-Musah?'

Joseph's eyes widened. Then he bolted off towards the playground. The girls scurried away, eager to discuss this shocking new development with their friends. Fleck and Sam tried to follow Joseph, elbowing their way through chattering schoolkids. They reached the front of the crowd in time to see Joseph dart across the forbidden tanbark to where his mum was being led away. Fleck followed him as he stood watching his mother, a small, uncertain smile on his face, his eyes filled with fear. Fleck remembered Trixie telling her how Joseph sometimes smiled when he was feeling anxious.

Trixie looked deflated. She gazed back at her son. Shaw seemed to have worked out what was going on and paused to wait. Fleck put her hand on Joseph's shoulder. 'Joseph can stay at our house for a bit until you come back,' she said.

Trixie nodded. 'I've got to go away, but I'm coming back,' she said to Joseph. Fleck could hear her striving to keep her voice from wavering. She felt a large lump building in her own throat.

Joseph was rocking from foot to foot. He gazed at his mother. 'Did you know that tawny frogmouths produce mucus in their mouths and this mucus helps them when they breathe? It helps them to cool down in summer. It can cool their whole body,' he said in a small voice.

Trixie blinked away tears and took a shuddering breath. 'I love you too, baby boy.' Then she walked to the police car with Officer Shaw and was gone.

Matthew left work early when Fleck told him what had happened. As soon as he got home and the kids were settled, Fleck took off for the police station.

When she arrived, Trixie was standing out the front. She looked pale and bewildered. Fleck ran up to her. 'What happened? Did they let you go?'

Trixie shook her head. 'I haven't – I – they gave me a mention date – I – I can go home but – I have to come back to court – I could still go to jail.'

Fleck wrapped her in a hug. Trixie patted her back vaguely. 'I still don't understand how you're out here.' Fleck said. 'Did you have to pay bail? Was it expensive? Can I help cover it?'

Trixie still looked dazed. 'No. It's – I didn't—'

The door swung open, and Charlie Marshall stepped out with another man. He looked tired and a little rumpled. He said goodbye to the other man, and then turned to them. 'All sorted,' he said to Trixie. 'Oh, hello, Fleck.'

Trixie turned to Fleck. 'They didn't set bail. Charlie came here with his lawyer. I think he's a QC. Or is it KC? Is that what they're called now? Charlie wants to pay my legal fees. It's too much.'

'It really isn't,' Charlie said. 'I already told you I don't think involving the police is necessary, but it's a bit late for that now. I don't want this to be any more painful than it has to be. I'm happy to be the one to cover expenses. Now, it's cold out here and I'm starving. Have you had dinner, Fleck? I was thinking the three of us could go to the pizza place near here. My treat.'

Trixie shook her head. Colour was slowly returning to her face. 'At least let me pay for the pizzas. I owe you so much.'

Charlie grinned. He touched Trixie's shoulder briefly. 'That's a nope, I'm afraid. Please let me do this. It's easy for me. And we have so much to discuss.'

Trixie blushed and shrugged. Fleck looked at Trixie, then at Charlie and gave a tentative nod.

'Yes? Good? Thank you! I could murder a meatlovers!'

They had begun walking to the cars when Trixie stopped. 'Actually, I'm sorry, Charlie. You're very generous, but I can't do this. I really need to go home and hug my boy right now. Fleck, do you mind driving me?'

A shadow crossed Charlie's face for the briefest of moments, but then he brightened and nodded. 'Of course! We can touch base another time.'

Trixie spent most of the drive in silence. When she did speak, it was to praise Charlie's extravagant generosity. Fleck remained quiet. Charlie *had* been generous. So why couldn't she stop thinking of that dark shadow of displeasure that crossed his face when he didn't get his own way?

221

CHAPTER TWENTY-THREE

Fleck sat in the car watching 5/150–160 Hurst Drive, the building that may or may not have been Helen Greythorn's murder factory. She saw two women approach the industrial lot on foot from the driveway, speak into an intercom and get buzzed in. Fleck got out of her car.

It was impossible to see inside the building. The door had mirrored glass and all the other windows were set high in the walls. Fleck checked her reflection, pulling a stray curl out of her face before she pressed the intercom button. Fleck leaned towards it. 'I'm here to see Helen Greythorn?'

A scratchy voice responded with a query. Fleck couldn't make out the words. The audio was very muddy. Fleck repeated her request.

The door clicked open. Fleck pushed her way through. There was a young woman sitting at a desk behind a protective glass screen. 'I'm sorry, I couldn't hear what you were saying. We really need to fix that intercom. Were you here for Legal Aid? Centre Against Trafficking? Family violence support? English class?'

Fleck summoned a confident smile. 'I'm here to see Helen Greythorn.'

The woman nodded. 'Of course. We have a few different agencies sharing this space. It can get a little confusing. Helen's with Many Hands, is that right? She's in room eight today. Just follow the corridor along to the left until it opens into the main room, and then it's the third cubicle on the right.'

Fleck walked down the corridor, but before she got to the main door, somebody darted out of one of the side rooms and accosted her. The woman was rather tiny and wore a cream blouse, long brown skirt, socks with sandals, a silver brooch. 'You're late,' she said to Fleck. Then she hooked her elbow through Fleck's and pulled her into the room she had just emerged from.

It was an office strewn with files and boxes. Fleck was about to correct this small dynamo, then reconsidered. Spending time in this room with the fierce old woman might help Fleck to investigate the situation. And, after all, wasn't that what she was here for?

Five minutes later and Fleck was still baffled. She had worked out that the woman's name was Ben. Small and angular, Ben (*Ben?*) had short grey hair, a mouth set in a straight line and sharp, intelligent eyes that were more glare than twinkle.

'Those go in the shred pile. We're done with that. No not *those*. They go in the pile for the tutoring program. Put them there.' Fleck's new boss pointed a sharp finger at the pile on the corner of the table. Fleck meekly complied.

Fleck read from a set of papers. '"Six signs of slavery: Identifying instances of Human Trafficking". Where do these go?'

'Oh, that goes with the ACRATH stuff.'

'ACRATH?'

'Australian Catholic Religious Against Trafficking of Humans'

'Does that go with overseas aid?' Fleck asked.

'No. That's local.'

'No, the stuff on slavery, I mean.'

'Yes. Local. We have slavery in Australia too, you know.'

Fleck did not know. She felt herself blushing.

Ben passed her a sheaf of papers. 'Here's some outdated stuff from the Food and Friendship Van. That can be shredded.'

Fleck took the pile and started feeding pages through the shredder. 'I didn't know that,' she said, 'about Australia and slavery. I mean, slavery has been illegal for centuries.'

'Yes, well, almost two centuries, if we are talking about the *Abolition Act*. But many countries have continued to enslave people despite the law enacted in Britain. And Australia's past isn't squeaky clean in this regard. Have you heard of "blackbirding"? No? You should look it up. As for today, slavery might be illegal, sure. But the drug trade is also illegal. Theft is illegal. That doesn't mean these things don't happen. Human trafficking is big business. Quite literally.'

'Literally how?'

'It's like – well, it's like confectionery. You know how there used to be all different manufacturers of sweets and chocolates? Small local companies producing small amounts and selling to a small market? But gradually things have changed. Companies merge and before you know it all these products are sold by a large faceless corporation working with ruthless efficiency.

'We are seeing the same thing happen with human trafficking. Except we're not talking about chocolate bars, we're talking about humans. Once upon a time, these were one-off situations, small operators. One person enslaving one other person. A car-load of women here and there. But things aren't like that anymore. Now it's large syndicates providing people to work as slaves for domestic servitude, forced marriages, farm work, factory work and sex work. It's happening in our suburbs, only just out of sight.'

'So, what does the action group do?'

'We commission research to help provide patterns and insights. We work with survivors and document their stories. We cooperate and collaborate with the Federal Police. We consult with our international partners to share resources and information. We also help the survivors to integrate into the community.'

Fleck inspected the information sheets in her hands. 'These people who have been enslaved – are they locked up? Why don't they just escape?'

Ben huffed a sigh. 'It's never that simple. That's a bit like asking why women don't leave abusive relationships. Often these people have nowhere to go. They're vulnerable. Our strict immigration laws make it easy for traffickers to threaten deportation if they don't comply. They're scared of the police and they often don't know the language. And the traffickers confiscate their passports, promising to give them back only when they've paid off their debt. Confiscated passports are a dead giveaway that the people involved are traffickers.'

A woman poked her head in the door. 'Sister Benedicta, you've got your meeting starting in five. The UN subcommittee?'

Ben winced. 'Oh, blast. I almost forgot.' She turned to Fleck. 'Thanks for your help. I've got to go. I've double booked myself, I'm afraid. Can you see yourself out?'

Once Ben disappeared, Fleck left the office and continued down the corridor towards room eight. She paused when she got to the door. From here, she could see inside. It was a large room, with freestanding dividers in place to make smaller meeting areas. Fleck slipped behind the partitions to walk quietly on the closed side of the cubicles, along the narrow corridor formed between the divider walls and the actual wall of the room. The dividers were low enough that a tall person might be able to peek over the top of them. Fleck was not a tall person.

While she couldn't see into the little 'rooms', Fleck could imagine cheap plastic chairs set up around a chipboard desk. The decor of the place was all very 1980s primary school. Helen was not in the first cubicle. She could hear a woman talking in a loud, hearty voice with a broad Australian accent. 'This one is for groceries, and I've got another one here for furniture. Here's a gift card for the op shop. Do you know how to use these? If you don't, the person at the register will be able to help you …'

The next cubicle also emitted a woman's voice, but it wasn't Helen's either. She spoke in a quieter voice that Fleck could only just make out. '—and this might not seem important, but you need to try to set a small amount aside each month for treats. I like to think of it as "no questions asked" money. When you have that built into the budget, you're more likely to stick with it and not fall off the wagon. Now if you look over here …'

At the next cubicle, she could hear a woman speaking in a foreign language. Then another woman translated for her. Something about an electricity bill? Then Helen's voice responded. 'Well, no, that's not right. I spoke to them about that a few weeks ago. Let me check. Yes. The twenty-sixth. I spoke to them about that on the twenty-sixth. There is absolutely no reason that charge should still be appearing on your bill. Do you have the bill here?' Helen waited for her words to be translated. There was a rustle of paper. 'Honestly. These people are hopeless. I spoke to them for an hour on the phone. You would think they could sort a simple thing like hardship assistance easily enough. It's like they make it deliberately difficult so that nobody applies for it. That's okay. You don't need to translate that part. I'm just having a rant. All right. Maryam? Don't pay this bill yet. All right? Don't pay. I will call the electricity company and talk to them. Now, what other bills have you brought along?'

Fleck pressed her face against the crack between the two dividers. She could see the three women sitting around a table. Helen was copying details from an electricity bill into her leather-bound day-to-a-page diary. 'I will let you know when I've sorted things out with these people. Now, show me your water bill. It should have the relief grant – here. Yes. Good. That's gone through.'

Fleck heard a sound directly behind her. In the dark corridor between the room divider and wall, a large black rat raced along the skirting board towards her. Fleck yelped and jumped backwards into the screens. The boards teetered forwards, bounced on their footings and then tipped back, toppling in two directions and exposing Fleck standing in the middle. She stared at Helen, her heart racing. 'There was … a rat …' She faltered.

Helen closed her diary with a snap and checked her watch. She addressed one of the women sitting across from her, even though both women were staring at Fleck. 'I will make sure the power bill gets sorted out, Maryam. And thank you for translating, Haneen.' She stood up and fixed Fleck with a steely glare. 'You. Come with me.'

Helen marched Fleck through the cubicle city, out of the main room and into a tearoom. She closed the door and pulled a curtain across the window. 'Who knows you are here? Who have you told?'

Fleck frowned. 'I … What? It's just me. Why are you being so secretive?'

Helen narrowed her eyes. 'Just you. Are you sure? You haven't told a friend? A family member?'

Fleck shook her head. 'I told Trixie that I was going to follow you today, but that's all. And I met a lady named Ben just before and did some filing for her. What's this about?'

'What were you talking to Ben about? Did you see any of the sensitive files?'

'I dunno. There was some stuff about a tutoring program?'

'What are you doing here? Were you digging up addresses? Have you taken on a missing persons case? I will not allow you to poke your nose around here. You are not welcome.'

'Missing persons? What are you on about? What's going on here? I'm not looking for a missing person. I'm trying to clear Trixie's name.'

Helen's face relaxed a fraction. She turned her back and began making tea. 'We've got a good set-up here. I do *not* want to move again.'

Helen began making two cups of tea. She did not ask Fleck how she took her tea. It would be a standard issue white-with-none and Fleck would shut up and be grateful for it. Helen put the mug into Fleck's hands and sat on the couch opposite her. Helen peered into her face. 'So, you are not acting as a private detective for some rich businessman?'

Fleck stared back at Helen. For somebody so dismissive of Fleck's credentials, Helen seemed to have grossly overestimated Fleck's success as a detective. Rich, paying clients? In what universe was that happening? She shook her head. 'Why are you asking about missing persons? Do you have missing persons here?'

Helen put her mug firmly on the coffee table between them and stood up. 'I think I need to show you to your car. You can't be here. I will not compromise the safety of this facility. How did you even get in here?'

Fleck shook her head. 'I'm here because I'm investigating *you*. I'm not interested in any missing persons. Well, I am, but only because you brought it up – and because missing persons are interesting.'

Helen hesitated. 'Why are you investigating me?'

Fleck peered up at Helen. 'I wanted to know what you were being so secretive about. I thought it had something to do with the missing money.'

Helen lowered herself back into her seat. 'The missing money? That's not really a mystery, Felicity. I know she's your friend, but you might need to accept that Trixie stole the money. Perhaps you don't know her as well as you might think.'

Fleck shook her head. 'It's not Trixie. I know it's not. But it is somebody. I'm going to find out who that is.' Fleck inspected her mug. It had the logo of a software company on the side of it. The tea itself was still too hot to drink. 'Why didn't you want me to find out about this place?'

Helen watched Fleck. She seemed to be weighing something up in her mind. Finally, she spoke. 'We help all sorts of women here. Many are escaping family violence; some are survivors of human-trafficking rings. It is imperative for the safety of our volunteers and for the women we assist that our location remains a secret. We have had problems in the past with violent men turning up on our doorstep. I don't want to go through that again.'

Something shifted into place in Fleck's mind. 'Those other times … when I've seen you arguing on the phone. Were you making calls on behalf of these women?'

Helen sipped her tea and looked out the window. 'We have a lot of talented people working here. I am not a social worker. I am not qualified as a drug and alcohol counsellor. I can't give free legal advice. But I can badger utilities companies and government bureaucrats until the cows come home. So that's what I do to help.'

Fleck blew over the top of her tea. So now she knew where Helen secretly spent her Thursdays. But she was no closer at all to discovering who had set Trixie up. What if this mystery couldn't be solved?

CHAPTER TWENTY-FOUR

Fleck rested her chin on Norah's rusty curls. 'All clear!' The guard on the platform whistled and they were off.

It was Sunday, and they were visiting the miniature railway park. Straddling a padded bench inside a carriage painted to look like *The Ghan*, Fleck wrapped her arms around Norah, who was sitting in front of her, as they pulled away from the station. Matthew was with Sam and Alice in another train ('a steamie!'), so that they could wave when they crossed paths. Matthew, having designed the course, already knew the points where this would happen, the most exciting being when one passed over a bridge above the other. Fleck hoped it would all run smoothly. She knew how hard Matthew had worked on it.

The first train they passed was not Matthew's, but they waved anyway. It was what you did. How much nicer the world would be, Fleck mused, if everyone always behaved the way they did on the little trains. If cars on Warrigal Road in peak hour had drivers who gave each other sunny smiles and waved complacently at each other as they passed. It would make for a more altruistic society.

Thinking of altruism made Fleck think of Charlie Marshall and the way he had paid for Trixie's bail. He hadn't had to do that. It was very good of him.

Fleck gazed out over the valley with its creek and flowering wattle, thinking. A kookaburra sat on the branch of a nearby gum tree. She really couldn't fault Charlie. She couldn't.

Charlie was charming and generous, good-looking and famous. He was on their side. He was intelligent. She should like him a whole lot more than she actually did. By rights she should even be harbouring a small crush on him. But she didn't. Not at all. It wasn't that she *disliked* him but – what? What was it?

The little steam engine pulling Matthew's train was approaching. Matthew was sitting in the second carriage with Alice strapped to his chest. Sam bounced on the seat in front of him. Fleck and Norah waved and shouted like they hadn't seen these people in years, until the train disappeared around a bend.

Trixie had called Charlie 'The *Polar Express* of Good-Looking Men'. He *looked* like an attractive man. He looked like he *definitely should* be attractive without actually being so. Some invisible key ingredient was missing. But it was more than that. It was almost like his *personality* was high-quality CGI as well. He had all the features of a good character, but it was somehow artificial. Highly rendered, but ultimately synthetic.

But this was nonsense. This was not evidence-based. And Charlie had just been incredibly generous. Why would she want to investigate Charlie more because he had done something good? She couldn't even explain her thoughts to herself properly. He'd done absolutely nothing wrong.

The train entered the first tunnel, and they were plunged into darkness. All the passengers immediately began shrieking and hooting. How did they know to do this? There was no sign at the entrance of the tunnel that said, 'Everybody shriek now'. There was no pre-tunnel meeting at which this behaviour was decided upon. Yet it happened without fail every time.

As they emerged from the tunnel, the shrieking subsided as quickly as it had started. Norah took her hands from her ears and settled them in her lap.

If Fleck were to look for some *actual* dirt on Charlie, instead of an uneasy gut feeling, she could maybe have a conversation with somebody who knew him, like his ex-wife. But how would she even go about setting something like that up? Fleck chewed her lip and stared out across the park.

'Daddy! Daddy!' Norah bounced on the seat in front of her. Fleck looked up, startled, just in time to see Matthew's train run under the bridge they were crossing. It was a good thing Norah had been paying attention, or Fleck might have completely missed an opportunity to wave and blow kisses frantically, before the train disappeared into its own tunnel. They could hear the faint echo of hoots as they passed. What if all the cars were to hoot and squeal the next time they drove through the Burnley Tunnel? What then?

As it turned out, tracking down Charlie's ex-wife wasn't nearly as difficult as Fleck had thought it would be. As Charlie was a public figure, there was plenty out there on Bethany, from *Women's Weekly* puff pieces to shots of her in an emerald-green shift dress at the AFL Brownlow Medal ceremony (this was from Charlie's short stint coaching for Carlton – she was too young to have been his girlfriend when he was a player).

It wasn't hard at all for Fleck to find out Bethany's maiden name and discover her personal profile on Facebook. It was a private profile, of course, but the publicly available information included the names of some groups that she was a member of. Fleck used one of her fake accounts to join these groups as well. She searched them for posts by Bethany and used some of this information to extrapolate other groups she may be a part of. The Frankenstein profiles she'd invented to investigate Donna came in handy here. They were already involved in so many private groups. She trawled all of these for Bethany and joined a few more for good measure.

It wasn't long before she had built up a little profile of Charlie's ex-wife. Bethany was in 'Yoga Mums Australia' and a few other yoga groups, 'Heidelberg and Ivanhoe local community group', 'Mums who clean' and some local sports clubs, including a Banyule under-14s boys' water polo group.

There was a comment Bethany had made in one of the cleaning groups that captured Fleck's interest. The original post was about an argument a woman was having with her boyfriend about towels, in which the boyfriend 'played tricks' by re-folding the towels in the way she didn't like. Bethany's response was deep in the comments. She provided a string of 'red flag' emojis, then wrote, *Get out while you still can! This sounds like classic narcissist behaviour.*

Fleck used her 'Brenda Stephens' account to join a whole lot of secret narcissist support groups on Facebook and searched through each one. It turned out Bethany was a member of 'Narcissistic Abuse Survivors Australia' and 'Narcissist Recovery and Healing'. Fleck paused. This really didn't feel right. She could probably find out a lot about Charlie and Bethany's relationship if she trawled through the posts Bethany had made in these groups, but that felt somehow invasive and voyeuristic. She logged out of the 'Brenda Stephens' profile and logged in to her own account. Then she sent Bethany a direct message.

Bethany's kitchen in leafy Eaglemont gleamed with those sorts of expensive appliances that have their own cult status and need to be bought from skilled consultants. Bethany grinned at Fleck as she pulled a bottle of chardonnay out of the fridge. 'It's mummy wine time!' she cackled.

Fleck snuck a glance at the clock. It was 10.47am. 'Oh, I shouldn't. I'm still breastfeeding …' she said, casting an eye at Alice, who sat in her pusher, gazing around the room inquisitively as she gabbled.

Bethany twisted the screw-top open with a snap and poured two glasses regardless. 'You can have *one*, babe.' She snorted. 'I'm going to need a wine if you expect me to talk about Charlie.'

Fleck had been honest in her message to Bethany, telling her that she had wanted to find out more about Charlie Marshall, that she didn't trust his charming exterior. That she suspected he might be a narcissist. Could Bethany help?

Bethany had been surprisingly gracious and helpful. She'd invited Fleck to her house after the morning school run. It felt a little odd, but Fleck got the sense that Bethany was lonely and didn't like to leave her house.

Fleck twisted the wine stem in her fingers, then placed the glass back on its coaster. 'It sounds like it didn't end well?' she ventured.

Bethany scoffed. 'It didn't *anything* well. That relationship was doomed from the start. It just took me a while to work it out and then several more years to do anything about it.' She took a fortifying sip of wine. 'The thing is, when you're with a person who is so charming, so socially deft, you become convinced the problem must be you. I didn't know anything back then about narcissists or how they operate. I didn't understand how he was manipulating me. How he was manipulating everyone he ever met.'

Alice interjected with nonsense words, keen to have her part in the conversation. Both women paused to coo at her. She held a toy giraffe in her hand and used it to gesticulate. 'Ab aaa bub da MUM.' She waved the toy about and then tossed it on the ground.

Bethany immediately scooped up the toy and took it to the sink, washing it in hot water and soap and then drying it. She gave it back to Alice, and then returned to the conversation.

'He didn't hit me. I like to think that if he'd hit me, I would have known that he'd crossed a line and I could leave. It would be clear, something I could point to. Then again, by the end I was so broken down, so dependent on his approval, that I might not have. He didn't hit me, but he hurt me in other ways.'

Fleck looked at Bethany. 'What do you mean?'

Bethany sipped and then paused. 'Nothing I could really point to,' she said at last. 'He just seemed to be constantly undermining me, making me question my own memory, even on stupid things that didn't matter. He'd insult me, kind of, but he'd disguise the insults. He might ask pointed questions or give pretend compliments that put the idea in my head that I was stupid or worthless, without him having to actually say it. It took me so long to realise how bad things had got. I was like a little fish who didn't know that she was swimming in toxic water.'

Fleck waited. Bethany swirled the wine in her glass and looked out at the ornamental grapevine through the large glass doors that opened onto the deck. She seemed to disappear inside herself for a moment. Then she spoke again. 'I used to say, "It wasn't always like that"?' Her intonation made the statement sound like a question. 'Like, to begin with he was so loving ... No, that's not it.' She sipped and tried again. 'To begin with, he was so *attentive*. Flowers – so many flowers; front-row tickets to stage shows when stage shows are, like, my favourite thing ever; jewellery; surprise gifts. And he'd call me all the time and tell me how wonderful I was, you know?'

Fleck nodded, even though most of the time Matthew's idea of a grand romantic gesture was a shared trip to Ikea to look at outdoor settings followed by hot chocolate for two in the food hall. Alice, meanwhile, had thrown her toy on the floor again. Bethany stood up to wash it, but Fleck scooped the giraffe up and tucked it into her bag before Bethany could get to it. 'I think that toy needs to go on holiday for a bit,' she said. Now Alice was pulling on her straps and wriggling. She had taken it all in and was keen to explore this gleaming new wonderland. She grunted and looked appealingly at her mum. Fleck smiled vaguely at her. She knew what Alice wanted, but having a nine-month-old baby on the loose in an unknown house would be just too complicated.

Bethany sipped her wine. 'And he'd act like everything I said was just so *fascinating*. I got addicted to the attention. But then he would switch off, go completely cold. And it would drive me *crazy*. Sometimes we would go out and he would be so sparkling and witty and lovely to everyone, and then we'd get home and he'd treat me like dirt, like *nothing*.' She put her glass down and looked at Fleck. 'I used to think there were all these different Charlies. That you never knew which one you were going to get. I used to think that the extravagant, love-bombing Charlie was the good one. And I always was striving to unlock the good Charlie. But now I can see that this was all part of the same toxic behaviour. It was all just manipulation and control. Charlie is a chameleon. He is whatever you want him to be. And he doesn't have any real friends. He only has disciples of the Cult of Charlie. Hah. Can you tell I'm bitter?' She drained her glass and immediately refilled it.

Fleck shook her head at the proffered bottle and rotated her full glass on its coaster. 'I don't think you're bitter. It sounds like you've been through hell. I'm so sorry you had to go through that.'

Bethany shrugged. 'It's not your fault. So what else do you want to know?'

Fleck paused to think. 'So, when you said Charlie is a chameleon …?'

Bethany nodded emphatically. 'Different personalities carefully designed for the person he's trying to charm. He has it down to a fine art.'

'So what would he do if he wanted to charm me, for example?'

Bethany peered at Fleck, her lips pursed. 'That depends. Does he want to seduce you or just impress you?'

Fleck shook her head. 'Nah. Just platonic.'

Bethany nodded, frowning. She looked at Fleck like a dressmaker sizing up a model. 'For you, I think he'd play the "Involved Domestic Dad" role. He'll talk to you about how it's a good day to get the washing done and how he's going to the school working bee on Saturday. But I don't know how he'd do that now he doesn't have the boys. Hah! But he would definitely still use the Benjamin Franklin effect. He was always going on about that one.'

'The Benjamin Franklin effect?'

'He used to talk about it. I have no idea why it's named after Benjamin Franklin. But it's this thing where you get people to warm to you by asking them to do little favours for you. I don't know. It makes you seem humble. It makes them feel like you're in their debt and they like that about you.'

Fleck thought about the way Charlie had asked her to hold the door open, had asked Trixie to butter the scones. 'So, it's all calculated?'

'He was always reading stuff about it. And his other big thing was food. He'd go on about food evoking an emotional response, and he'd always get Rosa, our chef, to cook these different things. Not, like, impressive food; more like, I don't know, comfort food? He'd spend ages researching it. It had to be unusual yet familiar. Oh, wow. I'd forgotten about how he used to do that. And different food for different people. Like, I dunno, like depending on their age and sort of demographic and everything. And sometimes he'd pretend he'd cooked it. He never cooked it.'

Fleck tried not to stare at Bethany as she talked. Fleck had been completely won over by Charlie's old-school raspberry slice. What if this had been carefully calibrated? What if he had researched and chosen it as a long-forgotten lunch-box treat of white, middle-class 90s kids?

Alice had managed to work one chubby arm out from its restraint. She arched her back and began to grizzle. Fleck shook her head and cast her eyes around the immaculate family room. Perhaps she could let Alice out for a little wander. There was nothing within reach that she could break. No choking hazards. There were no stray toys or shoes. No mess of any description. 'Hey, Bethany,' Fleck said suddenly. 'Do either of your boys play football? Or skateboard?'

Bethany shook her head. She didn't seem surprised by this abrupt change in conversation. 'Crispin is really into his water polo. That takes up most of his time. And Ralph isn't sporty at all. He plays the cello and does coding. He's actually very advanced. I'm not just saying that. He really is.'

Alice strained against her five-point harness and made complaining noises. Fleck moved over to unclip her. 'What about when they go to their dad's house? Do either of them play football when they stay there?' There had definitely been a football in Charlie's hallway. She hadn't imagined it.

'They don't ever stay at their dad's house. Like, ever. Their dad has virtually zero contact with them. He is very all-or-nothing. He knew he wasn't going to get full custody, so he decided not to have any.'

Fleck gaped. 'They never go to see him?'

Bethany shook her head. 'At the start, I tried to convince him to take them every second weekend – to give me some time off once in a while – but he wasn't interested. He couldn't deal with their schedules, he said. I realise now that it was probably for the best. He's pretty toxic. It's better that he doesn't influence the boys with that.'

Fleck watched Alice as she crawled over to a white leather couch. Her mind whirled. Charlie's too-perfect mess? The mess that had looked staged? That was because it *was* staged. Charlie had carefully scattered the clichéd detritus of a school-aged boy down his own hallway to give the appearance of being an involved dad so that Trixie and Fleck would warm to him – would trust him. What else was Charlie lying about?

'Did Charlie ever have any money problems?'

'Charles has many problems. But money isn't one of them. I guess having no moral compass can give you a real edge financially.'

'Did you ever get the sense that he was involved in some shady dealings? Like something illegal, maybe?

Bethany shook her head. 'Nah. But then, I never really took much interest in his work. I wish he did. I would report him *so hard.*'

Fleck watched as Bethany refilled her glass again. She bit her lip. 'So, do you have to do the school run later?' She tried her best to keep her voice neutral. She didn't want Bethany to think she was judging her. On the other hand, the thought of allowing children to be driven around by someone who had drunk the better part of a bottle of wine pricked at her conscience.

Bethany took a sip and cast a defiant look at Fleck, but when she spoke her tone was also neutral.

'The boys' school has a bus service that drops them home. Then Anja is taking them to their activities.' She took another sip, then placed her glass down rather firmly on its coaster.

Alice, having inspected the room, returned to Fleck and pulled at her leg. 'Up, up,' she declared.

Fleck lifted Alice to her lap, and she immediately lunged for Fleck's wine glass and knocked it over. Bethany sprang into action, catching the spill with a cloth before it ran off onto the floor. She quickly wiped the gleaming benchtop clean again and polished it dry. She tossed the cleaning cloths into a bucket under the sink and washed her hands. Then she picked up the wine bottle. 'Let's get you topped up.'

'Oh, no, I should head off. I need to get Alice home for her nap. I'm sorry about the spill. And thank you so much for sharing all of that with me.' She stood up, Alice on her hip, and began steering the empty pusher towards the front door.

Bethany stood at the end of the hallway, wineglass in hand, watching her retreat. 'Keep in touch, Fleck. And be careful. Charlie's a lot more dangerous than he looks.'

CHAPTER TWENTY-FIVE

Fleck unlocked the front door and welcomed Helen inside. It had seemed straightforward at the time. Helen had seen Fleck at school drop-off and asked if they could talk. Alice had needed a feed, so Fleck invited Helen to her house. But now, as Fleck opened her front door, she immediately felt awkward as the sight of the mess piles that had become invisible to her over the past few weeks suddenly sharpened into full focus. She darted to shift items while Helen continued down the hall. Helen seemed completely relaxed and unaware of the Mess Situation.

'I'm so sorry, the house is a tip.' Fleck faltered. It was actually tidier than usual, but Helen didn't need to know that.

Helen shook her head. 'That's one thing I cannot understand,' she said. 'Your generation of women all seem to think they need to have these pristine showrooms for houses. Heaven forbid a house looks like a family lives in it. I don't understand it. I blame social media.' She spun on her heel, turning to face Fleck. 'You invited me into your home.' She spoke slowly, enunciating each word. Her finger pointed squarely at Fleck's face. 'You do *not* apologise for that.' She punctuated her pronouncement with a stern nod, then continued down the hall.

Alice had been fussing in the car, but now that they were inside, her grizzling became wailing. 'I'm going to need to feed her,' Fleck announced, a little apologetically. She carried Alice to the couch and pulled the feeding pillow onto her lap. It wasn't until she had lifted her t-shirt up and got Alice latched on that she realised Helen had abruptly left the room. What? Did Helen feel awkward around breastfeeding women? Was this a generational thing? Fleck felt strongly that mothers should be allowed to breastfeed in all public places, of course, but she preferred to advocate for *other mothers* to do this than to be the poster girl herself. Sometimes she didn't want to make a statement. Sometimes she just wanted to feed a hungry baby. She could feel her cheeks blazing. She had tried to do it discreetly, not that it should matter. And these days, Alice didn't make it easy, pulling her head away to look around the room mid-feed whenever she heard something interesting going on. But this was her own home, for heaven's sake! What was Helen's problem?

Helen returned to the room holding a tall glass of water. She handed it to Fleck and sat down. 'You mustn't forget to drink water every time you feed your baby,' she said in a stern voice. 'You'll give yourself a headache if you don't watch out.'

Fleck sipped gratefully at the water. She hadn't realised how thirsty she was. Helen sat on the couch opposite her. Norah was carrying her Batman bucket around. This was a regular red laundry bucket with a handle. Inside was a variety of Batman toys. There was a small vinyl Batman with black button eyes, several plush Batmen, some Batmobiles, a variety of villains and many Robins. Norah emptied the contents over the rug and extracted a Robin figurine from the tangle of plastic limbs. She toddled over to Helen and presented it to her. Helen accepted the plastic Boy Wonder graciously. She looked around the room. 'Your home reminds me of Joan's in the early days. So much going on.'

Fleck looked around the room. The main thing that was 'going on' in this room was the washing, and it wasn't 'going on'. That was the problem. It was getting stuck on the 'fold and put away' stage. That was why it was piling up. 'Joan was Douglas's wife, is that right?'

Helen watched Norah as she sorted her Batmen. 'Joan was my best friend. And she was unstoppable. Her kitchen table was our control centre. She had an extension landline that took all the calls of women who needed assistance. We'd take it in shifts to answer the phone. Sometimes we'd all sit around the table knitting and sewing, babies at our feet. There was no shop back then, but we'd set up little stalls on card tables at the school and after mass on Sunday. Sometimes we'd do a fundraising drive with the tennis club. And cooking – we'd do cakes and jams and chocolate crackles and sell those as well. It didn't used to be all boardrooms and real estate and balance sheets. Forty years ago, it was a bunch of young mums around a kitchen table. We didn't agonise over a bit of clutter back then. We just got on with it.'

Fleck placed the glass of water on the arm of the couch and adjusted Alice and the cushion on her lap. 'So, to begin with, the Society was – what? – a helpline? And fundraising?'

'I suppose so. We saw a need and did something about it. And then there were the women who used to stay at Joan's house. We hosted a couple at ours once or twice, but it was mostly Joan. Often, they were pregnant with nowhere else to go. We would give them a place to stay while we helped them to get set up. The girls would often help us with our crafts and cakes for the stalls. Back then, lavender bags, frilly hangers and toilet roll covers were our top sellers!'

Fleck smiled. 'How did Douglas cope with having these young women stay at his house? Was there even enough room?'

Helen frowned. 'I never really thought about how Doug felt about it. Everybody just got on with it. He was just devoted to Joan, in his

243

own way. He and the boys always followed her lead. And Doug's always had a strong sense of duty. I doubt he ever stopped to think whether he was happy with the situation. That just didn't come into it. Anyway, it was only ever emergency accommodation. Just short-term while they sorted something else out. Gosh, times were innocent back then. You could never do any of that now. These days we "outsource" all of that to shelters and other crisis accommodation services, even though they're scandalously underfunded.'

'So, to begin with it was just you and Joan?'

'To begin with, yes. And Bev would help out sometimes too. She's Joan's little sister, did you know? Gradually, other school mums or ladies from the parish or the tennis club would join us to help out in various ways. Some would answer the phone. Some would help with the fundraising or donate their old prams and cots for the young mums staying with Joan.

'After a while, we got better organised. We learned to coordinate our efforts with other local organisations and we worked on specialising our services. We did less of the phone service and moved towards providing stable, long-term accommodation for single mothers, as well as the drop-in centre for women in crisis situations. That's what we do best. That's our niche.

'We became a formal not-for-profit organisation and formed a board. Many of our husbands became directors. We hired some administration staff. But the *spirit* remained. In everything we do, we try to keep the spirit of Joan's kitchen table. Women helping women. That's what it is at its heart.' Helen's face grew animated as she talked.

'One thing I don't understand,' said Fleck, 'is that if you and Joan were the founders of this organisation, why weren't you on the board?'

Helen sniffed. Her face lost some of its animation. 'Board meetings were at seven o'clock on a Wednesday evening. You know how hard that time of night is with small children. We were busy with dinner, bath and bed. It was much easier to send Tony and Doug along. And they were better at that sort of thing anyway. I've always been much more interested in doing the thing than sitting around in boardrooms talking about it.'

There was a clatter at the front door. Trixie's voice sang down the hallway. 'Oh my *gosh*, we were so late today! Joseph couldn't find his bumper book of birds and he got all stressed out about it. He'd said he was going to bring it and he wouldn't get dressed or eat until we found it. And there was no fruit for his lunch box. Not a single piece of fruit in the house. What a nightmare!' She pulled up short when she saw Helen sitting on the couch. 'What is *she* doing here?'

Fleck felt a jolt of apprehension. Helen gazed back at Trixie levelly. Fleck cleared her throat. 'Helen was just telling me a little about the history of Many Hands.'

'*Helen* is the woman who got me arrested,' said Trixie. 'Did you forget that detail about her?'

'It's not that, I didn't forget, I—' Fleck's words were tripping over each other.

Helen made a scoffing noise. 'You got *yourself* arrested, thank you very much. It is not possible to "get" another person arrested. Police won't go after a person without due evidence. You do know that, don't you?' Helen had returned to her usual haughty demeanour.

Trixie didn't even acknowledge that Helen was talking. She continued to address Fleck. 'What even is this? Doesn't this count as fraternising with the enemy? This woman has it in for me! She has been trying to take me out of the picture from the very start!'

Helen rolled her eyes. 'Oh, please. Having you arrested was simply the right thing to do at the time. It was not personal.'

'Oh, it wasn't personal? Really? Getting arrested in the schoolyard in front of my six-year-old son felt pretty personal to me! Having my son watch the police take me away in a divvy van was the very definition of "personal"!'

'I wasn't coming after you to punish you,' Helen said. 'That wasn't what this was about. It's … I refuse to work for organisations that say they can deal with crime and wrongdoing "in-house". There has been far too much of that in the past in just about every institution in this country, and it is toxic. All the men on the board wanted to deal with this quietly, but I disagree. If a crime has been committed, it should be dealt with by the police, not swept under the rug. Transparency. It was about transparency.'

Trixie made a scoffing sound. 'Transparency? Oh, I'm glad to see you're willing to embrace transparency when it suits you.'

'What are you talking about?'

'You're happy to be transparent when it means sending me to jail. But when have you ever been open about anything else? What about the finances of Many Hands? When have you made that clear and shown that it's above board?'

'That is not the same thing.'

'It is exactly the same thing,' Trixie said. 'You run such a closed shop. Nobody knows what's going on. If you'd been transparent about accounting practices in the first place, it wouldn't have been possible for someone to play with the books.'

Helen set her mug firmly on the coffee table. 'Someone? Who is this "someone"? *You* are the one who played with the books. You are unbelievable. Why can't you just admit it? Even now?'

'Why can't you accept that I didn't do it?' Trixie retorted. 'It wasn't me, Helen. Somebody is setting me up. But I suppose you know all about that already.'

Alice had pulled away from her mother and was watching the

argument with interest. Norah continued playing, undisturbed. Fleck re-clipped her bra cup and pulled her t-shirt back down. She sat Alice upright on her lap. 'Helen, if someone was to closely scrutinise the accounts, what would they find? What are you worried about?'

Helen opened her mouth, then closed it again and looked out the window.

Trixie stood up. 'Stop right there. If we're talking accounts, I'm going to get Ranveer.' She walked out of the front door. Fleck and Helen sat in silence for a moment.

Helen sighed. 'I know that Trixie and I bring out the worst in each other. I just wanted the police to investigate the theft properly. I didn't want them to traumatise her little boy. It wasn't personal.' She paused and hesitated. Then she spoke again. 'I had just come from a meeting at the shop, discussing how we were going to need to cut back on some of our services because of a lack of funds. Then I walked past the cafe and saw Trixie sitting there. Trixie who never paid a cent back of what she stole, crying poor. She was enjoying an elaborate high tea right after she'd told us she could never pay back the money. She was sitting there with cakes and slices when we can hardly afford to pay our staff anymore. I ... I snapped. I drove straight to the police office and reported her. It was impulsive. But I don't regret what I did.'

'It wasn't an elaborate high tea, you know. That food was a gift from George.'

Helen sniffed. 'Hmm. Well, you can see what it looked like from my point of view. Lady Muck having a tea party.'

They sat quietly for a few moments. Norah retrieved Robin from Helen and delivered the Joker to Fleck. Fleck fed Alice on the other side. After a minute, she tried again. 'What is it you don't want us to know about Many Hands' finances?'

Helen sighed. 'It's not ... I'm not *hiding* things. It's just ...' She huffed again. 'Not everything about the running of the organisation is everybody's business. Some of those things are private.'

Fleck raised an eyebrow. 'That *kind* of sounds like you're hiding things.'

Helen scowled. 'I want to make things clear and public. Just not yet.'

'Not yet? Someone has been embezzling funds – what on earth are you waiting for?'

Helen sighed again. 'There are just some parts of how we run things that I would rather were not public knowledge. I ... I wanted to fix them before we put it all out in the open.'

'You do realise how dodgy that sounds?'

'It's not that. It's just ... Many Hands is not a self-sufficient organisation. I'm fairly certain it has been running at a loss for years.'

'How can you be fairly certain? And isn't it okay that you're not making a profit? I thought that's the way not-for-profits were supposed to be?'

Helen hesitated. 'There's a difference between "not-for-profit" and "not sustainable", "not viable".'

Fleck frowned. There was something tickling at the back of her brain. What Helen was saying didn't match with what they'd seen in the backpack paperwork. Ranveer had explained that the charity was breaking even, sometimes even running into a modest surplus.

'I don't think the finances are as bad as you think they are, Helen. They're not unhealthy.'

Helen sighed. 'Tony and I have been quietly propping the charity up with our own money for many years. I don't want people to know. I want people to think it's a successful venture all on its own. And it was on its way to that state, but it was just harder than I thought it would be. It was awful when Tony died, but it was also a reality check.

We couldn't pour money in forever. What will happen when I die too? We need Many Hands to be self-sufficient. I couldn't bear for people to know that the charity was underperforming. If people knew … That's why I didn't want financial transparency. Not until I had things running independently.

'And then I found out that Trixie had been helping herself to the funds. I found out she had been eroding Joan's legacy, ruining the very thing I had been pouring every effort into making strong. Can you blame me for taking it badly?'

Fleck shook her head. 'But it wasn't Trixie. It was someone else. Trixie is innocent!'

Helen smiled sadly. 'Who else could it possibly be?'

The front door banged open again. 'I'm back!' Trixie called. 'And I've brought reinforcements.'

Ranveer followed Trixie down the hall. He held the backpack and a tin of Danish shortbread in front of him like a shield.

Fleck's eyes fell on the biscuit tin. 'Morning tea!' she exclaimed. 'Oh, Helen, I should have offered you something!'

Trixie rolled her eyes and made a high-pitched noise that sounded like '*Oh, Helen! I should have offered you something!*' She stalked into the kitchen and flipped the kettle on.

'Morning tea time!' Norah sang. She raced to the table. Alice had finished feeding, so Fleck put her in the highchair. Ranveer placed the biscuit tin on the table and Helen shifted some of the clutter to the side to make space. After a bit of fussing with plates and mugs, they were all sitting around the table. There was an awkwardness shared by everyone except Norah, who happily collected the paper dividers from the biscuit tin, the sort that look like miniature patty-pans, and stacked them on the table in front of her.

Fleck cleared her throat. She put her mug down on the table. 'Helen,

I think you need to tell Trixie and Ranveer what you just told me.'

Helen looked around the table. 'Fine. When I found out that Trixie had been stealing money from the organisation I had worked so hard to build, it destroyed me.' She sipped her tea, glaring at Trixie over the rim as she did so. Trixie narrowed her eyes in a withering expression and glared right back.

Fleck tried again. 'That's not what I meant. I want you to tell them about how you think that Many Hands won't survive without your support.'

Trixie scoffed. 'That's no secret! Geez, speak to Helen for five minutes if you want to know about how everyone depends on her and how important she is to the organisation. Tell me something I *don't* know.'

'Are you sure you need me here?' This was Ranveer. 'I have a meeting with clients this afternoon, so—'

'Stay here.' Trixie was firm. 'We want to hear about finances and we need you to translate.'

'It doesn't seem like you want to hear about anything except for your own self-important pontificating,' Helen said coolly. 'Frankly, I'm not sure I have the stomach to be your audience for much longer.'

Trixie bristled, but Fleck cut across her. 'We are talking about finances,' she said. 'Helen is concerned that Many Hands would not be able to survive without her financial support. That's why she has kept everything so quiet.'

Ranveer smoothed his hands over the binder. 'From what I've found in here, your contributions are generous, but they are not entirely indispensable. Are you talking about the monthly donations, or some other form of support?'

Helen shook her head. 'It's complicated. I'm not talking about donations at all. It's all in the real estate. We've always covered the

Dandenong building and the shop with the upstairs office space.'

Fleck cocked her head. 'What do you mean by that? What does "cover" mean?'

Helen gave an elegant shrug. 'It is just our contribution. We look after the rent, any maintenance or repairs. And we cover the utilities bills. That sort of thing.'

'When you say "we", do you mean you and Tony?'

'Well, yes. I suppose I should say "I", but old habits …'

Trixie stared at Helen. 'You pay the rent, utilities and maintenance for both these properties? That must cost you a fortune.'

Helen coloured. 'It was never supposed to be public knowledge. We are comfortable in our situation and are fortunate to be in a position where we can give back.'

'I had no idea. That is a huge financial commitment.'

'It's my life's work,' she said. 'It's Joan's legacy.'

Ranveer was frowning. He had opened the binder and was looking through it. 'Did you say you pay the rent and the maintenance fees on the shop and the building in Dandenong?'

'Yes, although I was hoping we could restructure things so that—'

'Here.' Ranveer turned the binder to show Helen. 'Also here, here and here.' With his pen, he showed different entries in the ledger: *Rent – shop*, *Hurst Drive*, *Plumber – shop*. 'If you're paying these bills separately, what are these payments? Where is this money actually going?'

CHAPTER TWENTY-SIX

The thing they didn't tell you about babies – the thing that Fleck should have learned by now but somehow kept forgetting – was that 'sleeping through the night' was not a finish line. It wasn't like it happened once and then you had yourself a baby who'd sleep from that point onwards. Sleeping through the night was more like a ceasefire. It was a fragile peace that could be breached at any moment, for any length of time and for any reason.

Alice had stopped sleeping through the night. Maybe it was a tooth, maybe it was a wonder week, maybe Alice had just decided that sleep was for squares. At any rate, Alice was waking throughout the night and fractious all through the day.

After a morning of grizzling and fretting and shrieking any time Fleck put her down, Alice was finally asleep. Fleck texted Trixie to see if she could bring Sam home from school. She didn't want to wake Alice from her nap. Or should she try to stop her from sleeping too much during the day so she'd sleep at night? But then, sleep begets sleep. Was that the rule? But some people said you shouldn't let them sleep too long during the day, that they needed to do their sleeping at night. This was her third child. She should be an expert by now. She had no clue. Norah had also fallen asleep on the couch, which was both bad news and a welcome relief. Fleck knew she would pay for this brief reprieve later, when bedtime came along and Norah was wide awake.

But she would make the most of this bonus solitude. Time for some detective work. This was what she needed. She sat at the table with her everything book and flipped from page to page. Nothing. She had nothing. Ideas floated around her head, but she couldn't catch any of them. She couldn't complete a single thought. Focus. Why couldn't she *focus*?

The whole problem was so big. How could she ever get her head around it? She wasn't clever enough. Suburban mums weren't detectives. The whole idea was ridiculous. She gazed at the colourful writing until it swam in front of her. What if she couldn't do it? What if the answer just wasn't there to be found? What would happen to Trixie?

Fleck stood up and walked to the laundry. It was no longer the gleaming control centre it had once been. Dirty clothes littered the floor and random objects that belonged nowhere were now everywhere. You could no longer sit on the two camp chairs. They were fully laden, providing a skeleton for the lumpy, hulking clutter monster in the corner of the room. The floor was strewn with sticky notes. The purple-coloured sticky notes had been of the cheaper, off-brand variety. Fleck knew she was supposed to buy the quality sticky notes, but they didn't have quality sticky notes in purple and she needed to have purple to make the colours balanced. Now the purple sticky notes were scattered over the floor, festooning the laundry piles and discarded toys and obsolete DVDs and, look there, yes, *actual rubbish*.

This was a joke. She was a joke.

What was she even doing? Why did she think she was even good at this? She had no more clues, she had no idea how to solve the case and she was delusional for even thinking she could in the first place. A detective? Really? How about trying to be a mother who can keep a tidy house? How about being a mother who knows anything at all about sleep schedules? Who on earth was she trying to kid?

Fleck looked blankly at the purple notes strewn across the floor. There were so many of them, heavy with the weight of expectation. Laced with the sting of thwarted ambition. Slowly she shook her head. 'I can't. I can't.' Fresh tears filled her eyes and her shoulders shook.

Fleck began to cry, with great heaving sobs. She felt the weight of overwhelm descend on her and she sank to the floor.

Trixie always let Joseph play on the school playground for ten minutes before they went home. She sat on the bench, pulled her work out of her trench-coat pocket and her crochet hook from behind her ear and continued working on her green budgerigar. She was a little obsessed with these birds, it must be said. She wanted to try a gold cockatiel next.

The boys raced ahead as they made their way to Fleck's house. When they arrived, Sam and Joseph dropped their school bags on the front lawn and ran through the side gate to the backyard. Trixie picked the bags up and opened the front door.

Fleck was sitting at the table. She didn't look like herself. In front of her was a book of puzzles. She worked methodically and did not look up when Trixie came inside.

Trixie sat down at the table. 'What are you working on?'

Fleck gave a small sniff. 'They're acrostic puzzles, or sometimes they're called anacrostics. They are the best sort of puzzle. But you can't buy a whole book of them. You can only get them in the variety puzzle books.' Her voice was dull and subdued. 'You solve the crossword clues, and that puts letters in the quote. And then you solve words in the quote, and that puts letters in the crossword clues. And then when you solve all of them, you get to read what the quote is. They're very satisfying.'

She didn't sound like a person who was enjoying a satisfying pastime. She sounded like a person who was trying to numb her brain.

Fleck's detective book was also on the table. There were a lot of things on the table. Trixie picked it up. 'How are things with the case? What's our next angle?'

Fleck was staring straight ahead. She gave a small shake of the head. 'I can't.'

Trixie flipped through the pages of handwritten notes, maps and charts. 'What do you need? Coffee? A nap? Something to eat?'

Fleck blinked and then looked directly at Trixie. 'No, I mean I can't do it. I can't do any of this. I'm not a detective. I can't even function as a basic person.' She shook her head. 'I'm done.'

Trixie felt a chill descend into her bones. 'You don't mean that. You're just tired. I need you, Fleck. We need to keep doing this.'

Fleck did not look up. She just blinked and shook her head.

Trixie swallowed. 'You're a good detective. You're just having a bad day.'

Fleck picked up her pen and carefully wrote an answer into her puzzle. 'I'm sorry I made you think I'm something that I'm obviously not.'

Trixie snatched at the puzzle book and tossed it aside. It hit the window with a snap. 'What? So, things get hard and then you stop – is that it? What? You're so clever you've never had to struggle before? I need you. You're the only one who believes me. You're the only one in my corner.'

Trixie had hoped that Fleck would get fired up. She had hoped to provoke her into a healthy argument. Instead, Fleck seemed to dissolve. Her eyes brimmed over with ready tears. Her face crumpled. Her arms clutched at herself. Fleck had always been short, but she had never seemed *small* like this before. She convulsed with sobs. 'I can't, I can't,' she gasped.

Trixie watched her silently until the bout of panic subsided. Then she stood up and retrieved the puzzle magazine. She placed it on the bookshelf. She found Fleck's everything book in a pile on the bench. She put it carefully on the table and sat beside Fleck. 'First of all, I'm not buying any of this "I'm not a good detective" crap. Those are just imposter thoughts. You are a good detective. You're smart. You see things other people don't. Second of all, even if you weren't a good detective – which you are – but even if you weren't, it's not about that. It's never been about what kind of detective you are. You've been in my corner from the start. You are the only one who believed I was innocent. That's not nothing. That is massive.' She smoothed her hand over the cover of the notebook, and they sat beside each other in silence for a minute before Trixie spoke again. 'What's the smallest first step?'

Fleck stared straight ahead. 'I don't know.'

Trixie stood up. 'Let's just go stand in the laundry. We don't need to do anything else. Let's just go stand there.'

Trixie steered Fleck to the laundry. The door dragged on a few items, but she managed to get it open most of the way. They both looked inside. Fleck's shoulders slumped. 'The purple notes don't stick,' she muttered.

Trixie pulled out her phone. 'Let's do five minutes. We'll do five minutes, then we'll have a cup of tea.' She set the timer.

Fleck looked at her blankly.

'Pick up the purple notes,' Trixie said.

Fleck's facial muscles contracted, making her chin look like a red peach stone. Her eyes filled with tears again. 'I can't,' she whispered.

Trixie held her gaze. 'Pick up *one* purple note,' she said.

Trixie, meanwhile, decided she should put a wash on. She stepped over the piles of washing and opened the machine. It had a wet load inside it already. She set the machine for another rinse cycle and gathered the floor clothes into the basket, which turned out to be empty underneath a pile of things. Fleck was slowly picking up the notes.

Trixie was still pulling clothes off the chairs and tossing them in the basket when the timer went off. It wasn't perfect, but the laundry was a lot more functional than it had been before. 'I'm putting the kettle on,' she announced.

Fleck carried the purple notes to the table and cleared a space.

When Trixie brought the two steaming cups across, Fleck was gazing vacantly at the table. She looked up at Trixie as she took her mug. 'I'm sorry you had to see me like that,' she said.

Trixie sat down with her own mug. 'What, so it's fine for me to fall to pieces all the time, but you can't? You're supposed to be the perfect one and I'm the mess? That's not fair. Why can't you let me be capable for a change? I need this.'

Fleck managed a small smile. She looked like a wrung-out dishcloth.

The purple notes were in a crumpled pile on the table. Trixie looked at them. 'Which ones were these notes, anyway?'

Fleck smoothed them out in front of her. 'The purple notes were for Jo and Dima. The dodgy cafe.'

Trixie pointed to one of the notes. In capitals, Fleck had scrawled *LAUNDERING OPERATION?* 'Was that to do with the case, or were you just reminding yourself to put a wash on?'

Fleck managed a small chuckle and picked up the note. 'At one point, I was running with the theory that the cafe across the road from George was laundering money. It didn't make sense that they were still afloat when so much was going wrong with the business. George thought that maybe some organised-crime outfit was running money through the business to launder it. You know – to turn dirty money into clean.'

'Oh, yeah. I remember that conversation. Money laundering is one of those things that I've heard of, and I know it's a thing, but I don't really know what it is. Like, if I had to describe it to someone else, I'd be lost.'

'Yeah. I know what you mean,' Fleck said. 'I bet Ranveer could explain it. I just know that it's what you do when you want to turn crime money into money you can actually use. Like, the money from a crime is a pile of t-shirts with obvious stains on them. The washing machine is a legitimate business supported by the criminals. When they run money through the business, it comes out the other end as something clean that they can use.'

'Even though the washing machine chews up a few t-shirts.'

'Exactly.'

Fleck rotated the purple note in her hand. Then she suddenly stood up. She looked at Trixie in shock. 'Wait!' she said. She disappeared into another room and reappeared with the binder from the cream backpack. She didn't open it but stared at its cover, thinking. Then she looked up at Trixie again. 'What if we've been thinking about this the wrong way?' She paused and looked away. Trixie could almost see the wheels in her brain turning. Then she looked back. 'What if we're not looking for a thief? What if somebody has been using the Society to launder money?'

CHAPTER TWENTY-SEVEN

'Don't climb on that, Sam!' Fleck sat at a white laminex table looking across at a plastic tangle of play equipment. Everything smelled vaguely of earth. She held the store's free homemaker magazine in front of her, but she wasn't reading it. Her mind was racing.

They were at the Bunnings playground cafe. Sam was attempting to shimmy up the outside of the tube slide while Norah parked herself at the top of the other slide, enjoying her moment of power as the children behind her waited patiently for her to go down. She did not budge.

Fleck scanned the shelves of pots and outdoor furniture displays. No sign yet. Should she order her coffee now or wait? She flipped through the pages of the magazine. There were a lot of ads. Fleck was just getting absorbed in 'Quick Fixes and Clever Hacks to Transform Your Space' when someone sat in the chair opposite her. It was Bethany Marshall.

Charlie's ex-wife had called her yesterday and asked to meet. She'd refused to elaborate on the phone as to what it was about, only stating that she had a present for Fleck. As Bethany settled herself in her chair, she put her handbag on the table and a zip-up supermarket freezer bag on the floor between them.

They ordered their drinks and Fleck waited for Bethany to start talking. Bethany rotated the sugar dispenser on the table in front of her and began. 'Charlie had some weird habits. He was obsessed with the latest tech, always wanted the best gadgets. Everything was all about the Shared Calendar and the Cloud and the Online Shopping List. But at the same time, he had these old-fashioned notebooks. You know, the sort with the black leather cover? He would spend heaps of time writing in them, but he would also be really, I don't know, cagey about it.'

'Norah! Slide down or move away. You can't camp there!' Fleck shouted. Then she turned back to Bethany. 'Sorry. I *am* listening. Please go on.'

'He never really went through them in front of me, but you don't live with someone for ten years without picking up on this sort of thing. He never left them out, though. I wanted to know what he wrote in there, but at the same time I had so much going on that I didn't press him about it. All I knew was that he kept them in his study in a locked cupboard.

'Anyway, a while after we separated, it was arranged for me to come to his house and clear out my stuff. He wasn't home for this. He kept his study door locked, but he didn't know that I'd made copies of the keys back when we were still married. I had this plan. I know it was kind of petty, but I guess I had a lot of anger to work through. I got into the study and into the cupboard. I had a whole bunch of replica notebooks, but they were filled with all these abusive messages to him.

'So, I swapped them around. I arranged the fake books so that they looked exactly the same and I put the originals in my bag. Then I locked the cupboard and the study and took his notebooks home. I don't know if he's even noticed yet, since he doesn't check them super often, but when he does, I want him to know he's not the only one who can play power games.'

Their food and drinks arrived. Norah and Sam came running over from the playground. Fleck broke the oversized oat biscuit in two, removing a small 'Alice tax' from each side. Then she set Norah and Sam up at the children's table and returned to the conversation.

'Did you find anything interesting in the notebooks?' she asked.

'I don't really know what I expected to find. I thought maybe there might be some proof that he was having an affair or that he was working on his great novel or something, but none of it really made sense to me. It was all a bit of an anticlimax. Then, when you were asking questions and doing all this detective work, I thought maybe they might be useful to you.'

She looked around, casually but cautiously, then nudged the cooler bag forward with her foot. Fleck went to reach for the bag, but Bethany stopped her. 'Not here. Wait until you get home. I never know if someone might be watching.'

Fleck looked around. There were people everywhere, pushing trolleys and inspecting citronella lamps. Could it be possible that Charlie was keeping tabs on his ex-wife? If someone was watching, it would be easy for them to blend in.

Sam and Norah sat at the children's table across from them, each munching on their half of the oat biscuit. Bethany stood up. 'It was good to see you!' she said loudly. And then she was gone, leaving the heavy bag at Fleck's feet.

'Why's it called Go Fish when they're dogs, Mummy? Why isn't it called Go Dog?' Sam inspected his fistful of large *Bluey*-themed playing cards.

'Well, that's a very good question, Sam. Do you want to call it Go Dog? We can call it Go Dog if you like.'

'No, we can't! You can't do that, Mummy! That's not the *name*.' Norah didn't hold her cards in her hands but laid them on the table in front of her. She shot her mother a warning look.

'But we could make it the name,' Fleck said.

'NO! That's not the name. That's not what it's called!'

'Maybe we could call it Dog Fish?' Fleck was pushing her luck, she could tell. Norah wasn't enjoying this thought exercise. Her brow furrowed and her breath came out in little puffs.

'It's called FISH, Mummy! That is its NAME!'

'Okay, okay. Do you have a Bandit?'

'NO, GO FISH.'

Fleck often kept a crossword or something by her elbow when she played games like this with her kids. She needed something to alleviate the skull-crushing boredom of Uno and Spotto and Sight Word Bingo. The constant 'Whose turn is it?' 'It's not your turn yet, Norah' and 'Hurry up and take your turn, Sam' was enough to make her brain implode.

But Fleck didn't have a crossword today. In between her turns making pairs of Bluey and Bingo, Fleck snuck glances at one of Charlie's notebooks.

There appeared to be different kinds. Some books held columns of figures and totals. Some were like dossiers of people, their ages, nationalities, professions. Today's notebook had a map in it.

Fleck's Year Seven geography teacher would not approve of this map. It did not include BOLTSS. There was zero Border, no Orientation or Legend. There was no Scale and no Source. It did, however, have a Title: *Location of PPs*.

The map underneath looked like a sketch of a couple of city blocks.

Squares, presumably houses or buildings, lined up in rows along two un-named streets. It might have been a gated community, because a square enclosed the whole thing, with a section missing at the bottom, like a gate. This square was labelled *RFR2: 1032*. Only one of the square buildings inside was labelled. An arrow pointed to the second from the back on the right-hand side: *Sunshine Valley PB*.

Did he mean 'PP'? Or was the title wrong and it was 'PB' location? Or were they meant to be different?

'Mu-um!' Sam whined. 'I said did you have a Chilli?'

'Um, no. I mean, yes, I do! Here you go.'

Sam took the card with a satisfied smile and added the pair to his stack.

Fleck asked Sam if he had a Mackenzie. She knew that he didn't. But she also knew that Norah did, and she wanted to give Norah a chance.

Norah immediately asked Fleck for her Mackenzie card. Sam narrowed his eyes suspiciously at his mother then turned his attention to his cards. He often took a while to make his selection. Fleck looked back at the notebook.

'Sunshine Valley PB' … This seemed to be the point of the map, the place you were getting directions to. None of the other buildings were labelled. Why was this one important? Fleck pulled out her phone and googled *Sunshine Valley PB*. Her search returned images of peanut-butter jars and labels. Of course. Now that she saw the logo, it made sense. She was vaguely aware of Sunshine Valley being a minor brand of peanut butter and other spreads. Could this be a map to a peanut-butter factory?

Fleck's brain, most unhelpfully, unearthed footage from the *Sesame Street* of her childhood and played the song about all the nuts that make a jar of peanut butter on repeat.

Could *RFR2: 1032* be the name of a business park or factory lot? And why would a peanut-butter factory be important or relevant?

'We're not allowed to *see* them, Norah!' Sam leaned over and flipped Norah's cards so that they were face down.

'SAM! They are MY CARDS!'

'OW! She pushed me, Mum! MUM! She PUSHED ME!'

'Norah, we don't ever push,' Fleck said. 'Sam is trying to help you play the game, that's all.'

'They are MY CARDS!'

'Norah, do you have a Lucky?'

Norah glared at Fleck, small chest heaving. Summoning all of her dignity, she picked her cards off the table and inspected them one by one. 'No. Go fish,' she mumbled.

It took a few more rounds before Fleck felt brave enough to return to her research. It wasn't hard to discover that Sunshine Valley Peanut Butter was not manufactured in Australia but imported from Thailand. There were no Sunshine Valley corporate offices in Victoria, but the parent company, McMahon Bolling Foods, had a regional office in Clayton.

The pile of cards was fast diminishing. The game would be over soon. This way, at the end of the day, Fleck could tell herself that she took time out to play a game with them today. She was a good mum who did good mum things. Ugh.

Fleck looked up maps of the business park in Clayton as well as the address of the manufacturing plant in Samut Prakan, Thailand. Neither of these resembled the configuration of the hand-drawn map in the notebook. The corporate offices were situated on a horseshoe-shaped drive, while the factory was its own large complex and not a single building at all. There was no building situated on one of two parallel streets like the map in the notebook showed. Fleck narrowed her eyes at the page in front of her. She needed to spend some quality time with her exercise book and pens. She didn't have any answers, but she did have a fresh load of questions to write down.

The last 'fish' card had been drawn and they played the cards out of their hands until the game ended. 'Time to count our pairs!' Sam was gleeful. 'I already know! I already counted mine! I have TEN!'

Norah spread her paired cards on the table in front of her with a self-important lift of the chin. She pointed at the cards and rattled off numbers. 'One – two – three – four – five – six – seven – eight – nine – ten!'

Sam looked outraged. 'You don't have ten, Norah! You have six. I have ten. I win!'

Norah's lower lip wobbled. Fleck swooped in. 'Guess what, Norah? I only have three pairs! Only three! You beat me!'

'Oh, yeah! You beat Mummy, Norah!' Sam said, and Fleck's heart squeezed at the sight of his encouraging smile. 'We both beat Mummy!'

Norah beamed. Fleck beamed back with a smile that only faltered when Norah said, 'Fish again?'

Later, Fleck decided to clear the table. To *really* clear the table, not just shove everything to the side like she'd been doing lately. There was an impressive collection of stuff here. Some large paintings from kinder. A notice about the school's upcoming fun run. A magnet from a local real estate agent. Matthew's *Rail Enthusiast* magazine, still in its plastic sleeve. A scattering of crayons. A handful of brochures. The Friday crossword. Two library books.

Fleck made a start at clearing. What was she supposed to do with all of Norah's artwork? Surely she shouldn't keep every piece? If Norah caught her chucking it out she'd be in big trouble. But she was drowning in the stuff! She made a mental note to buy a large envelope when she was next at the shops. Maybe she could post a bunch of them to her parents in Queensland.

Under Norah's masterpieces were the accounts papers from the original dossier. She looked at them, spread out across the table. In the past they had stared back at her blankly, giving nothing away. But now … she began to feel a whirring in her brain.

Once, when Fleck was small, her family went to an outdoor market by the sea. Fleck's nanna, entranced by the beautiful, handmade toys, had bought them each a present. Fleck got a doll that switched from Little Red Riding Hood to the Big Bad Wolf when you pulled the skirt over her head. Her two older brothers got presents as well. She can't remember what Michael was given, but Steven got a wooden car that was actually a brainteaser puzzle. It didn't come with instructions, but pieces would twist and swivel out from each other as you manipulated it. The smooth wood hid latches and seams. Steven fast became impatient with it, tossing the tangle of wooden shapes and hidden mechanisms aside. 'It's for babies!'

It wasn't long before Fleck adopted Steven's toy. She fidgeted with the pieces and coaxed them into place. It was frustrating at times but she couldn't let it go. Steven didn't seem to mind. It was a while before she finally solved it. With a click, the critical piece moved into place and the pieces all fitted together neatly – into a smooth, almost seamless, brown duck.

Fleck couldn't count the hours she must have spent worrying the puzzle pieces into a car, into a duck and back into a car again. She became quite good at it. Her favourite part came just before she solved it. She could always tell when she was close. She would move a wooden arm a particular way and there would be a neat shift where something clicked into place and then all the pieces started moving at the same time, like the tumblers in a lock.

Fleck stared at the mess of papers on the table. She felt like she was so close, like any minute things were going to shift into place. She picked up one of the original spreadsheet printouts, the one she had felt so intimidated by. She looked at Ranveer's neat annotations and occasional highlighted entry. She gazed at it for a moment, then slowly sat down at the table. Placing the papers from the dossier to the left side, she opened one of Charlie's notebooks alongside them on the right. She tried out three of the notebooks before she found the one that fit.

The records in Charlie's notebook matched up with the discrepancies in the Many Hands accounts that Ranveer had flagged. Fleck could suddenly see with clarity how it all fit together. Fake and inflated invoices, unexplained deposits, false expenses: it was all there. Fleck cast her eyes greedily over the documents. How had she thought those spreadsheets dull? This was perfect!

CHAPTER TWENTY-EIGHT

Fleck sat in her car, watching the glass automatic doors. She had arrived here in such a rush, but now that she had parked, she couldn't figure out her next steps.

It was the Many Hands annual retreat and planning day. Everybody who worked for the Society would be there. This was the perfect place to clear Trixie's name.

Fleck knew the date and location of the planning day from the email newsletter she still received – not exactly brilliant detective work, but it did the job. So now she sat in the car, watching the front doors of Stonecrest Apartment Hotel Whitehorse.

The hotel itself was one from the group that Charlie owned. Not the big one in the city – this was in the suburbs, but it was still large enough to host a sizeable conference centre and restaurant. Fleck had spotted Helen and Bev bustling to the side door with grocery bags hanging off each arm. Fleck would need to be careful that they didn't see her before she – before she what?

She had tried to call Trixie but hadn't been able to reach her. She would try her again later. Maybe Trixie could meet her there? Or maybe she could call Trixie later and tell her it had all been solved? It would be like giving her the best present ever!

In a detective novel, the detective stands at the head of the table and explains the case to everybody in the room, including the culprit. Everybody watches on in stunned wonderment as the detective talks them through her reasoning. She knew what to say. Everybody was going to be inside. So what was stopping her?

Trixie considered the wood-grain pattern of her ceiling. It was their lazy Saturday, and she had been asleep. But now something was not right. What was it?

Joseph was still asleep beside her, his dark lashes curled against his little-boy cheeks.

She looked back at the ceiling and squinted. The door! Someone was knocking at the door!

The woman on Trixie's doorstep was also wearing a jumper pulled over pyjamas. Her blonde hair was half-sticking up and last night's mascara formed dark smudges around her eyes. But while, like Trixie, this woman looked like she had come straight from bed, unlike Trixie, she was wide awake.

'Are you Trixie?' she said. 'Do you know how to get in contact with Fleck Parker? Are you that Trixie? Fleck's friend? Do you know Fleck?'

This was far too much to deal with before coffee. Trixie just *looked* at the woman.

'It's okay,' the woman said. 'You don't have to worry. Well, you do have to worry. You definitely have to worry. But you don't have to worry about *me*. I'm not – it's – it's Charlie.'

Trixie blinked and squinted. 'Charlie Marshall?' Her voice was a dry croak.

The woman looked momentarily relieved. 'Charlie Marshall. Yes. I'm his ex. I'm Bethany.'

Trixie peered at Bethany. 'You'd better come in.'

Bethany talked rapidly while Trixie cleaned her teeth and threw clothes on.

'Charlie was at my house this morning. He knows he's not supposed to just turn up, but he was at my house. I was still in bed. And he was so mad. He grabbed me by the shoulders and was shaking me and yelling right into my face. He found the fake notebooks. Someone tipped him off, maybe that creepy bodyguard. Did Fleck tell you about the notebooks? Yes? Well, I was trying to show him that he didn't have any power over me anymore. I didn't want him to think he could scare me. Even though he was being, like, really scary. So, I yelled right back at him. Right back in his face. I said I didn't have the notebooks anymore and what a pity. I said I'd given them to a detective, and she was going to use them to bring him down. And the moment I said that, he said, "Right." Then he let go of me walked to his car and drove off. Just like that. And he drove off really fast. Like, he wrecked the gravel in the drive.

'I couldn't get in contact with Fleck. She's not answering her phone at all. I tried her heaps. And then I remembered there was a contact list for the volunteers and you're on it and I knew that you were Fleck's friend and so … and so I came here …' Bethany petered out with a ragged breath.

Trixie finished tying her shoes and put her hand on Bethany's arm. 'Joseph is asleep upstairs. I'm going to call his babysitter, but can you cover the gap until she gets here?'

Bethany nodded and kept nodding. 'Trixie, I'm really scared for

Fleck. He knows she has the notebooks. He's going to go after her. Trixie, I'm scared. You don't know how bad he can get when he's angry. I keep trying to call Fleck, but she's not answering. If he does something to her, I'll never forgive myself.'

Trixie bit her lip. She pulled her bike helmet off the hook and unclipped her phone from the charger. She gasped as she saw the screen. *Missed call (12) Fleck Parker.*

Fleck quietly made her way to the front of the hotel. The automatic doors slid open. The front desk was unattended. Fleck grabbed one of the pamphlets off the desk and stepped into a quiet corner.

She cast her eye over the map on the back of the pamphlet. She already had a vague idea of where the conference room would be, because she'd seen it from outside. The hotel restaurant was not too far from there. She made her way down the corridor in the direction of these two places.

Fleck could hear voices coming from the kitchen of the restaurant as she walked past. As she had suspected, Helen and Bev had taken over this space, using the broad metal benchtops to make up trays of sandwiches and to prepare platters of scones with jam and cream.

Fleck quickly stepped behind a tall plant when Helen swung through the kitchen doors, holding a commercial-sized tub of margarine. 'It was just a tiny bit. They won't miss it,' she was saying to Bev as she strode down the corridor, away from Fleck. Soon she arrived back empty-handed.

The door to the conference room was closed, but clearly labelled: *CONFERENCE ROOM: CR 1029.* Fleck decided to set herself up in a little armchair at the end of the corridor. She could listen in to what was going on in the planning meeting and figure out the best time to burst in. She took out her everything book and pen and settled in.

But it was no use – she couldn't hear a thing. Maybe she should get herself a stethoscope for listening through the walls. Of course, it would be impossible to listen to a wall with a stethoscope without attracting suspicion, and there were no stethoscope salespeople within the vicinity, so the whole thing was a moot point, really.

Fleck sighed. This was boring. She opened her everything book and studied it. She had made notes about the dirty money, about the use of the Society as an unsuspecting participant in a laundering scheme. She had worked out that those extra notebooks – the ones that didn't match up with the Society's accounts records – were for other charities and sporting clubs with poor bookkeeping practices that were being exploited in a similar way.

She studied the map. RFR2: 1032 ... The map still wasn't explained. What did *peanut butter* have to do with any of this?

She was tempted to start playing on her phone, but then she realised she didn't have it with her. Had she left it in the car? Should she go back and get it? *You're not here to play on your phone, Fleck*, she chided herself.

She had got herself a whole morning of babysitting. She didn't want to come home empty-handed. She took a deep breath and pushed open the door of the conference room.

CHAPTER TWENTY-NINE

Ranveer stood in his front yard. It was time to look at his Washington Navel. His mum and dad were visiting from Sydney this week, and he knew his dad would comment on the state of the garden. 'That orange tree needs pruning, Ranveer. Can't you see the dead wood there? How long has it been since you have given this tree a good prune? They like it, you know? The trees love a good pruning.' The tree had needed a prune for a while now.

He had been squinting at the glossy leaves early that morning, trying to figure out what branches to cut and where to cut them, when Fleck had looked over the fence and asked for his help deciphering some accounts books to do with her case. He was over there in a flash. Account books he could understand. But that work was done now and so he was back in his front yard, navel-gazing.

Should he even be pruning it when it had fruit growing? Or was that the time when you were supposed to prune it? His dad would know, of course. But he wasn't going to ask his dad how to prune a Washington Navel. His mum and dad were going to visit and they were going to see a neat and thriving orange tree. And they would see his lovely house and successful business and they would stop telling him that he should move to Sydney to be closer to them and his brother. They would be happy for him, and they would be happy for his life in Melbourne.

He had the wrong secateurs. He needed the other ones. And gloves. He would need gloves to get around those thorns. Did he have gardening gloves? He was sure he did somewhere.

It was a while later when Ranveer emerged from his garage carrying a bucket, secateurs and gloves. Time to get to work.

There was another car in Fleck's driveway next door. It was a sleek black Mercedes-Benz S-Class. This was not Marian's car. Ranveer had met Marian when she had arrived to babysit Fleck's children. She was lovely. Very easy to talk to, mostly because she did all the talking.

A man was walking from the house to the car. His face was set like flint. It was Charlie Marshall. He got into the car and drove away at speed. Ranveer stood staring at the driveway. He knew from talking with Fleck that Charlie Marshall was involved with criminal undertakings. Was Marian okay? Were the children? Should he go over there? Should he call the police? But what would he tell the police? He saw somebody visit his neighbour? He was still standing with his hand on the gate, trying to work out what to do, when a bike sped past and pulled into Fleck's driveway. Trixie!

Ranveer rushed over as Trixie parked her bike and took off her helmet. She was panting.

'Charlie Marshall,' Ranveer said. 'He was just here. I saw him!'

Trixie's eyes widened in horror. She shook her head as she continued to gulp for air. Together they ran to Fleck's front door in a panic.

Fleck pushed open the door to the conference room. A large table took up most of the room and a whiteboard had words like *Mission* and *Core principles* on it. There was a woman wearing a blue floral blouse at the table with a laptop open in front of her. She smiled expansively at Fleck as she entered. It was a very facilitator-like smile.

'Everybody has gone to the breakout rooms for their reflection groups at the moment,' the woman said, 'but if you'd like, I can help you find where to go. What's your name?'

'Uh ... hold that thought!' Fleck said. 'I just remembered I need to get something ... I just realised I left something ... I'll go get it and then ... I'll come back when I get it!'

Smooth, Felicity, so smooth, she thought to herself once she was standing back in the corridor. What now?

She could hear voices coming down the corridor. She quickly darted out of sight before John Dobson walked past. He seemed to catch sight of her movement, because he abruptly changed direction, turning around to look. This caused him to run headlong into Helen, who had just stepped out of the kitchen, carrying a tray of devilled eggs.

In the confusion, while Helen insisted on taking John's suit jacket straight away so that she could deal with the stains and John insisted that it was fine, Fleck escaped around the corner. She needed to find a quiet place to camp out. She rounded another corner and found herself face-to-face with John Dobson again. He strode towards her with purpose.

Without his suit jacket, John looked a lot more intimidating. Had he always been this tall? And bulky? A black t-shirt hugged his biceps, which were patterned with tattoos. Tattoos! He crossed his arms in a way that emphasised his menacing bulk and glared at Fleck.

'I don't know what you're doing here.' His voice was gravelly and low. 'But you need to leave right now.' The way he said it, he could have been a standover man, a hired thug, sent to collect her overdue loan payments.

Fleck smiled nervously. 'I was just delivering some margarine to the kitchen. Helen called me. They forgot the margarine.'

John narrowed his eyes. 'You need to stop poking your nose into this operation.'

'What operation?' Fleck lied. 'I don't know what you're talking about.'

'Don't waste my time with that,' John said, seeing right through her. 'You are playing with fire.'

'Are you *threatening* me?'

'I'm warning you,' he said. 'If you're smart, you'll back away now. Don't get involved – it will not work out well for you.'

'But—' Fleck protested.

'Do you hear me? Get out now while it's still safe. This is not—'

There was the sound of a door opening somewhere around the corner. John glanced over his shoulder and then turned back to Fleck.

'Get out of here.' he said. 'NOW.'

He turned on his heel and walked away. Fleck watched him leave. Then she hitched her backpack up on her shoulders and continued on her way.

CHAPTER THIRTY

Marian beamed at them as she opened the door. 'I tell you, it has been like Bourke Street Mall in here today. You will never guess who was just here. Come in, I'll put the kettle on.'

Trixie had finally caught her breath, but her heart was still hammering. She pushed ahead through to the kitchen. Norah and Sam were playing happily at the table. Alice was in the highchair. All safe. All unharmed.

'Is everything okay, Trixie?' Marian asked.

'Was Charlie Marshall in here?' Trixie demanded.

'Ah, yes. That's what I was going to tell you. How did you know? Charlie Marshall! He's quite handsome in real life, I must say. He was looking for Felicity. I suppose he couldn't get in contact because she left her phone behind. She had made a breakthrough in her case, you see, and she was so excited she ran off with her phone still in the charger.'

'And you were talking about all of this to Charlie? The case and the breakthrough and all of that?' Trixie felt a creeping sense of dread descend.

'Yes. He's very personable, did you know? An excellent conversationalist. So, I said, it was a pity, but I supposed if I really needed to reach her, I could just call the hotel. And he was interested when I said the hotel – well, I suppose he is in the hotel business – but he was interested when I said the hotel and I said it was the one near Mont Albert – I said it was one of his ones. Well, he was very interested to hear that, and he said – it's the funniest thing – but he said he was planning to go there next. They are having a planning day or something there. It was such a coincidence – although I suppose not really because Felicity must have been going there for the same reason, but still, it was a handy coincidence because it meant that Charlie could take the phone and deliver it to her. He said he would track her down. Those were his words. *Track her down*. Anyway, speaking of tracking things down, I've been called into service this morning because Matthew is at work on the trains. Have you ever been to the little train park?'

'You gave Fleck's phone to Charlie?'

'Yes – well – yes. Don't look at me like that! He's a very respectable man. He isn't likely to steal it. It's old and it has scratches on it. He's very wealthy. He doesn't need to be stealing phones. And even if he did, he wouldn't because I already know who he is. Wait – where are you going?'

But Trixie and Ranveer were already running out the front door.

Fleck was lost. She had no plans to leave, as John had suggested, but it would be nice to at least know where she was. All the rooms and corridors looked the same. She pulled the brochure out of her pocket and studied the map. It was a pity she didn't have her phone with her. She could have used the GPS.

There was a coolroom around the corner at the end of a corridor. It looked like a large but otherwise ordinary commercial fridge. Printed across the door were the words:

REFRIGERATED STORAGE ROOM 2
RFR2: 1032

Fleck froze. She stared at the letters. Was it a coincidence? She pulled out her everything book and opened it to the page where she had carefully copied the notebook map. There it was. *RFR2: 1032.*

She stole a look up and down the corridor, then opened the door and stepped in.

'It's seventy along here. You can go faster, Ranveer.'

'I'm allowing for a safe stopping distance.'

'This is an emergency! We need to be there already!'

'Why don't you crochet something? You might feel better.'

'Crochet doesn't make the car go faster. You need to speed up!'

Trixie and Ranveer were in Ranveer's dark green Volvo sedan travelling towards the hotel at a safe and legal speed.

'Why do we need to go so fast anyway? Do you have a plan for when we get there? What is our plan?'

'Our plan is to get there as soon as possible.'

'And then? What is our actual plan when we get there? We park the car and then what?'

'Oh, I am not waiting for you to park the car. You can let me out at the front. We don't have any time to waste.'

'But what is your plan then? What are you going to do then? If you could just tell me what the plan is, I could ascertain whether risking our lives to save five minutes is warranted.'

'The plan is to work out what to do next when we get there. But I can't *do* that if it takes six to nine working days to get ourselves down Elgar Road!'

The coolroom was crowded. Metal shelving ran around the walls and through the middle of the room, creating two narrow aisles of shelves filled with boxes and tubs. Two aisles. Fleck looked at the map again. Then she looked up at the room. She had been going about this all wrong. The map was not of roads and buildings. The map was a guide to the coolroom in which she was currently standing. The 'gate' or 'entrance' was the door to the room. Which meant …

Fleck walked down the aisle on the right-hand side, scanning the shelves. There were boxes of cheese slices, pallets of drink bottles, large containers of mayonnaise and mustard. On the bottom shelf, almost at the end of the aisle, there was a large drum. On its label was the logo for Sunshine Valley Peanut Butter.

'Here. Here. Here. Here,' Trixie said as they approached the front entrance of the hotel.

'I think it would be a better idea if we were to approach the situation together,' Ranveer said. 'A united front. Just give me a minute to find an appropriate parking space and—'

'Nope. Nope. Let me out here. I need to get out.'

'But—'

'I need to GET OUT, Ranveer! Stop right here.'

'Okay. Look, I still think—'

'Okay, bye.'

Ranveer blinked and watched Trixie race up the path.

CHAPTER THIRTY-ONE

Fleck's breath came out in little puffs of vapour. It was too cold to sit on the floor, so she sat on a box of 'Masterfoods Squeeze-on Tomato Sauce 300 × 14g Portions' that she'd pulled out from the shelf. She wasn't digging with her hands anymore, either. She had found some empty containers in the corner. Now she scooped out the little packets with an empty, rinsed-out hummus bucket and emptied them into a clear storage tub. She was making good progress.

Sitting on a coolroom floor digging through a commercial drum full of breakfast-spread packets hadn't been her plan when she arrived at the hotel today, but she was exactly where she needed to be. She dipped her little bucket into the well of single-serve peanut butter portions and emptied it into the plastic box beside her. This was good.

Fleck was almost halfway through the drum. The clear plastic crate beside her was filling up with little peanut butter packets. It was kind of satisfying the way they all slid over each other to fill the space. She was really in the zone. She almost jumped out of her skin when one of the chocolate chip packets fell off the shelf behind her. Her task was so mesmerising, she had almost forgotten where she was. She held her breath, waiting for another noise. Silence. Fleck waited a few minutes to be sure, then got back to work. The drum was still too heavy to lift. She had to keep on scooping.

That was when she hit the bottom of the drum. Except it couldn't be the bottom. The drum only looked halfway empty. Its floor couldn't have been more than two-thirds of the way down. Could it be a false bottom? This was exactly what she had been hoping for!

Working with renewed vigour, Fleck scrambled to clear the last of the packets.

It really did look like the bottom of the drum. Fleck inspected the smooth white base with edges that curved up to meet the walls seamlessly. She ran her fingers along the edges of the false bottom, feeling for a gap to lever her fingers into. It was smooth. She searched for a switch or a seam, a button or a latch. Nothing. She turned her attention to the outside of the drum. Maybe there was a hidden door at the side or underneath? Nothing obvious.

Her gut told her that the false floor of the container was designed to lift out somehow. She looked at it again. She stood up so that she could reach all the way in. She pressed down on the base. It compressed in, like a button, then clicked up, as if on a spring. The entire floor of the drum was now an inch higher, and loose. Fleck pulled it out and placed it to the side. She peered into the cavity underneath. The entire lower part of the drum was filled with passports: black and red, navy and green. Fleck reached in and pulled a few out. They weren't Australian passports. She opened one of them. A woman with an angular face and serious expression gazed back at her from the photo.

And that's when someone directly behind her cleared his throat.

'Oh, well done. You really are a clever little sleuth after all.'

Fleck jumped. He was standing in the doorway, a small smile playing on his mouth. He wore an expensive-looking suit, perfectly tailored. He stepped into the aisle, blocking the narrow space with his broad frame.

'Charlie,' she breathed.

'The one and only.' The way he stood, the way he talked, he could be at a cocktail party, regaling her with his wit, not standing in an industrial refrigeration unit, confronting her over her intrusion.

Fleck looked at the passports in front of her, then at Charlie with his faintly mocking smile. She thought of the laundered money, the names and nationalities recorded in the notebooks. It wasn't drugs. It wasn't weapons.

'People.' Fleck peered up at Charlie. 'That's what you're trafficking. That's why you have to launder your profits through charities. You're running a human-trafficking operation.'

Charlie pursed his lips. 'I run a supply-and-demand business. That's all. People require cheap, unskilled labour. I provide this on a scale that could not be met with a local workforce. I am merely meeting the market where it's at.'

'So, it was you who framed Trixie for stealing money from the Society.'

'Miss McAuley was asking far too many questions, applying for grants that invited government scrutiny. The money in her account created the necessary distance for us to continue our operations unencumbered.'

'She was arrested!' Fleck said. 'She could go to jail because of you!'

'Yes, that tiresome Greythorn woman saw to that. That was never part of the plan. It would have been much easier for everyone if she had been ousted from the organisation but not arrested. I wasn't expecting Helen to go rogue like that.'

'Is Helen involved in any of this? Or is it just you and John?'

Charlie shook his head in amusement. 'Helen was very helpful, of course, the way she would cling to outdated practices and avoid proper oversight, but no, she has no idea about any of this. Neither do any of those other dinosaurs. John is involved, though. You are quite clever to pick up on that.'

Fleck felt a chill run through her bloodstream that had nothing to do with the refrigerated air that surrounded her. Why was Charlie admitting to all of this in such a relaxed way? She was not safe. She needed to get out of here.

Her eyes darted at the narrow spaces between Charlie and the shelves. Could she rush him and squeeze past and through the door? What if she made use of a weapon of some sort? Surprised him with a stab in the thigh?

'There's no need to look for an escape. You will be staying here from now on. I recommend that you make yourself comfortable.'

'What do you mean?' She had to keep him talking. She had to keep him from leaving the coolroom. She wasn't sure what his next steps were, but she was certain they would not be good for her.

'You know altogether too much about our operation. You have become a complication that needs to be cleared up.'

'Are you planning to kill me?' Suddenly, Fleck felt oddly detached. None of this seemed real.

'We do have contingency plans in place for a situation such as this. It is unfortunate, but it is, of course, impossible to run an operation of this size and scope without some collateral damage.' He smiled reassuringly at Fleck. 'It's all very straightforward. The workers we use are reliable and swift. You will be no more. Clean and done.'

Fleck shook her head. 'There's no such thing. You could never get away with it. I have friends and family. Even if you leave zero physical evidence, you can't just kill me and expect nobody to notice when I disappear without a trace.' She was babbling. She couldn't help it.

Charlie's smile broadened with genuine pleasure. When he spoke, his voice was gentle. 'Oh, but that is the beauty of this methodology. There *will* be traces. Lots and lots of pretty little traces.'

Fleck tensed her legs. 'What do you mean?'

'We have many friends, you see. All sorts of international connections in law enforcement and various government departments. They'll be able to provide confirmed reports of sightings of a woman of your description at a remote overseas location. We can also leak evidence of a false passport using your photo. You will be disappeared, yes, but never dead. That won't be the story.'

'The story?' Fleck gripped the sides of her box seat.

'It's all about the story. We have become very skilled at managing the narrative. Our friends in the press will promote reports and studies about maternal burnout and cite your case as an illustration. The mother who'd had too much. The mother who snapped and ran away. You will be the cautionary tale – or perhaps not. Perhaps you will be a hero to all who wish to escape their mundane lives, to leave it all behind and live the high life in some exotic location.'

Fleck drew in a breath. 'Like Koh Samui,' she whispered.

'Like Koh Samui. Or we could provide some other locations in Eastern Europe or South America, if you prefer. But I think some time in South-East Asia might work best for you.'

Fleck blinked. 'You've done this before.'

Charlie nodded in encouragement. 'Ah, yes. Donna. Such a waste. She was just too inquisitive, I'm afraid. That was just one of those things. It couldn't be helped.'

'So you killed her? Donna is dead?'

'Personally, I prefer to believe what everybody else does: that Donna is taking some much-needed time off overseas. The truth is much more mundane. Donna has become involved in construction. She has become an integral part of my new South Melbourne tower. A foundational member, you might say.'

He regarded her with a slight tilt to his head. 'A job like you would be a little more complicated than an unconnected woman like Donna. Still, that's why we hire the best. And they do love a challenge.'

Fleck began to scream loudly. 'Help! Help! Oh no! It's a fire! FIRE! FIRE! Oh! It's going everywhere! FIRE!'

Charlie watched her, a small smile playing on his lips. He waited until she stopped shouting. It took a while. When she finally paused to rest her voice, Charlie spoke again. 'Admirable effort, but I think you'll find these walls are very thick and practically soundproof. You can scream if it makes you feel better. Me? All I need is to make a phone call and you become a myth, nothing more.'

How had she ever thought him good-looking? Those twinkly ice-blue eyes now seemed cold and glinting. The charming half-smile was now a snarl.

He pulled a phone from his pocket and held it to her face. It took her a second to realise it was her own phone. Face ID activated and unlocked the screen. 'Ah, there we are. Excellent. Thank you for that. It always makes things easier when we have access to the phone and social media accounts.' He held the phone up again and Face ID unlocked another barrier. 'Ah, and now NetBank. We're all set.'

She needed to keep him talking. If he left the room, she would be stuck. So long as he remained with her, there was an exit. He seemed to enjoy talking. He probably didn't get many chances to explain his criminal genius at length to others.

There was a noise in the coolroom behind Charlie. A footstep? As he glanced over his shoulder, Fleck seized her chance. Springing off her box seat and keeping low, she sped to the space between Charlie and the wall, below his elbow. She had almost managed to push past him to the door when his hand gripped her arm and he flung her into a pile of boxes, grazing her elbow on a metal shelf. When she righted herself, she saw that they were no longer alone in the room. John Dobson was standing by the doorway. Had Charlie summoned him somehow? Was he actually Charlie's hitman? Was he here to kill her? Had that been his job this whole time?

Fleck blinked and swallowed. John was holding a gun. That was definitely a gun in his hands. They looked somehow more solid in real life than they did in the movies, like they were dense with the gravity of their potential. Fleck stared at the ultra-solid gun. It took her another moment to register that the gun was not trained on her.

CHAPTER THIRTY-TWO

John Dobson stood by the door, his back to the metal shelves, pointing his gun at Charlie.

'Charles Marshall, I need you to put both hands in the air, turn and place them on the wall in front of you. I am placing you under arrest for the suspected murder of—'

Charlie lunged and everything was suddenly black. There was a heavy thump and a yell, some shuffling, then the sound of the large door clunking shut. Fleck stood up cautiously and felt her way to the door. She couldn't get it to open. She felt along the wall to the light switch and turned it on.

John was sprawled under a collapsed metal shelf and a pile of white potatoes. He had a small gash at the side of his head. As he picked himself up, he felt his pockets. 'He's taken my gun and my phone.' His voice was hoarse. He touched the side of his head and swore.

'Did he pull the whole shelf down on you?' Fleck looked at the debris surrounding him.

'Bloody light switch! How could I have missed that?' John said as he picked himself up. Potatoes rolled off him and he kicked them aside.

The switch on the wall would have been just behind where Charlie was standing.

'So, he switched the lights off, then knocked you out with the shelf, then nicked your gun and phone, then left.' Fleck walked through each step methodically, pointing to the light switch, the shelf, John, the door. 'He was very quick.'

'Is the door locked?' John strode over to the door, tested the handle and inspected the seals.

'Are you with the police?' Fleck asked. 'And do you want a bandaid? I think I have a Batman bandaid in my bag.'

'Do you have an angle grinder in your bag too? This place is a fortress.'

Fleck walked back down the aisle to the shelf where she had stowed her backpack while John continued to look for a weakness in the door. She unzipped the front pocket and retrieved a small first-aid pouch. When John had finished prodding at the door, she handed him a bandaid.

'Thanks.' He tore the bandage open. 'You're going to need one of those for your arm as well.'

Fleck pulled another one out of the bag and affected a bright smile. 'Sure. We've got to be all nice and healthy when they bury us both under the new hotel.'

'None of that talk. That's not what's going to happen.'

Fleck looked at John, whose face was set in a stubborn frown. 'How do you know?'

'Because I know. That sort of talk is useless. We're not beaten yet. Aren't these places supposed to have an emergency release thing? Can you see a lever or anything anywhere?'

'Charlie doesn't strike me as a person who would miss a detail like that. I don't think there's an emergency release.'

'We should look for it anyway. There should be a lever.'

'I can see where it's supposed to be.'

Fleck pointed. In place of an emergency-release lever was a sawn-off stump of metal.

The woman in the blue floral blouse smiled at Trixie. 'Can I help you? Everyone is in their share groups at the moment, but they'll be meeting back here soon.'

'I'm looking for my friend. She's short, brown eyes, lots of curly red hair.'

'Oh, yes, I remember. She was another latecomer. I lost track of her, I'm afraid. She was going to come back, but I haven't seen her. Popular lady.'

'What's that?'

'Popular lady, your friend. Charlie Marshall was in here just before. He was looking for her too.'

'Who keeps potatoes in the fridge?' Fleck said as she watched as John picked up the scattered potatoes and returned them to their sack.

'It stops them from sprouting,' John said.

'Yes, but you should never keep potatoes in the fridge,' Fleck insisted.

'Aren't you supposed to keep them in a cool, dark place?' John said. 'That's what the fridge is!'

'It turns the starches into sugars!' Fleck said. 'These potatoes are going to go dark and taste awful.'

'Really?' John said. 'I guess I never really eat potatoes.'

'How can you not eat potatoes? A potato is a meal in and of itself, John. You need to rethink some of your life choices, John.'

John pulled the potato sack closed and set it neatly beside the shelf. 'Max,' he said.

'What?'

'You might as well call me Max. John was my cover name.'

'Max? What – is it short for Maxwell or Maximillian?'

'Just Max. My birth certificate says "Max".'

'Okay, so you're Max. And you're – what? CIA? Police?'

'I am not CIA, given that I am not American and we are not living in the United States of America right now.'

'Well, what's the Australian version of the CIA?' Fleck asked. 'ASIO?'

'Technically ASIO would be the Australian FBI, given that they deal with internal investigations. The Australian CIA would be ASIS. But neither of those is a direct match and neither of those have anything to do with me. I'm an undercover operative with the AFP, part of Operation Dragonfly. We've been investigating Charlie Marshall and his schemes for quite some time now.'

'Wait, so you knew he was dodgy this whole time?'

'We knew there was a human-trafficking ring operating in the eastern suburbs of Melbourne. We suspected the money was being laundered through a network of charities and sports clubs. We had reason to believe that Charles Marshall was a person of interest, but we had very little evidence.'

'So that's why you have been working so closely with him undercover.'

'Yup. And the more I worked with him, the more certain I became. But unfortunately "Detective Max Roberts has a really strong feeling" isn't admissible evidence in court.' Max walked into the aisle with the peanut-butter-drum passports. 'The thing I really want to know is, how on earth did you know where to find these? I've been looking for months, and you just swooped in and dug these out from their hiding place.'

'The passports? How did you know about those?'

'I was in here too,' Max said, picking up a few passports and checking the photo pages.

'You were what?'

'I was in here with you. I followed you in. I was hiding in that other aisle.'

'I had no idea,' Fleck said. 'Some detective that makes me.'

'I don't know about that – you found the passports. How did you know where they were?'

Fleck opened her backpack again and produced the notebooks. She found the one with the map and handed it to Max. 'I got these from Charlie's ex-wife. Apparently, he kept them locked in his study.'

Max was silent for a while as he pored over each notebook. 'This is everything,' he said at last. 'Names, contacts, accounts. It's the missing piece of the puzzle.' He sighed heavily, his breath coming out in a little white cloud. 'This would have been perfect. We have everything we need here to bring down this entire operation – if only we could get out of this room.'

CHAPTER THIRTY-THREE

Fleck jumped as the handle turned on the freezer door. Max did not jump but began issuing directions to Fleck, his voice low and urgent. 'He is going to want to take you to a different location. You need to resist. Do not go with him. Do not make it easy for him. Stall, keep him talking, whatever it takes. The important thing is—'

Max broke off as the door swung open to reveal Charlie, his broad frame filling the doorway. He held a gun. It was not the pistol he had taken from Max earlier. This one was sleeker, less chunky.

And it was pointed directly at Fleck.

'Me again!' Charlie affected a cheerful tone. 'Felicity, let's get you out of this cold room. You must be freezing in here. John, you'll need to wait, I'm afraid. I can only manage one at a time. In any case …' He paused for a menacing fraction of a second, running his eyes over the other man shivering in his t-shirt. 'I'm going to want to take my time with you.'

'I'm good, thanks.' Fleck couldn't manage to keep her voice from wavering, but she held her eyes on Charlie's cool blue gaze.

Charlie smirked. 'Forgive me for the misunderstanding. This is not a request. Your attendance in this case is compulsory.'

Fleck wished she could engage in some sort of witty banter, like James Bond or Adam West's Batman. Instead, she pressed her lips together and shook her head. Max, meanwhile, had become incredibly still. He was watching their interaction with intense focus.

Charlie sighed heavily. 'Let's not make this more difficult than it needs to be.' He raised the pistol, extending his arm to point it directly at Fleck's head. She gasped and stepped backwards. Charlie's gaze hardened with purpose, holding the pistol ahead of him with both hands, and moved his finger to the trigger. Fleck looked back at him. His eyes had turned dark, his pupils dilated in a shark-like glare. *He's going to do it*, she realised. *He's already made the decision.*

Suddenly, there was a loud *thunk*. Charlie's eyes slid out of focus and he stumbled forward. Max leaped across and slammed Charlie into the floor. Above him, Trixie stood, eyes wide, chest heaving. In her hands was a full-size non-stick Tefal crepe pan.

Max had disabled Charlie's handgun and slid the weapon out of reach. He was now kneeling on Charlie's back and pulling a set of cable ties out of his back pocket as he informed Charlie that he was under arrest. Fleck didn't know too much about police work, but it looked like Max was opting for the maximum end of the scale when it came to using 'reasonable force'.

Fleck stumbled out of the coolroom and she and Trixie fell on each other in a wobbly embrace.

Fleck followed Max and Trixie down the corridor. Max asked Trixie for her phone. She looked back at Fleck for confirmation, then unlocked it for him and handed it over, her hands shaking a little. The conference room was empty. Even the facilitator lady was missing. 'They must be still in the breakout rooms,' said Trixie. Max led Charlie into the room as he quietly spoke into Trixie's phone. Then he hung up and secured Charlie to a metal bracket in the dividing wall with another cable tie. He pulled one of the large boardroom chairs alongside him and flopped into it.

'You should probably eat something,' Trixie said. 'Do you want an egg sandwich, Fleck? John? They're pretty good. I've had them before.'

Fleck gazed blankly back at Trixie, but when Trixie put a sandwich into her hands, she automatically started eating it. She was starving. Max ate his too, though his eyes never left Charlie.

'What on *earth* is going on in here? Those are *not* for you!'

Helen stood in the doorway holding a large platter of scones. Bev was behind her with a tray of jam, butter and cream.

Fleck hesitated. Trixie shoved the rest of her sandwich into her mouth and glared at Helen as she munched. Max stared. Now that Fleck looked at him properly, he was looking pale and woozy. Charlie seized his chance.

'Helen! They've tied me up! Do you have scissors? We need to stop them. They're out of control!'

Helen placed the tray of scones on the food table beside a tall cake decorated with cascading nasturtiums and turned to face them. Bev followed suit. Charlie kept pleading and Fleck talked over the top of him. Trixie had her mouth full of sandwiches, but she made insistent noises until she swallowed and then joined the chorus.

'You need to help me. Something is very wrong. She's going on a rampage!'

'What? No! That's not true! He's a murderer! Charlie's a murderer!'

'The cable ties are cutting into my skin.'

'Don't untie him! Do not untie him!'

Bev pulled out her set of keys. She unclipped a small pair of folded scissors and handed them to Helen. They both turned to look at Charlie.

'Oh, thank goodness we've got some sanity in the room at last,' Charlie said. 'Thank you, Helen. Thank you, Bev.' His tone was the perfect blend of weary and authoritative.

Trixie and Fleck both exclaimed in protest. Max, meanwhile, had picked up a nearby wastepaper bin and vomited neatly into it. Helen looked on in horror. 'What have you done to them? What on earth is going on here?'

The room began to fill as others returned from their breakout sessions. Fleck saw familiar faces, like Douglas, Jo and Dima, and others she recognised as volunteers from the drop-in centre in Dandenong.

Max tried to protest as the room filled. He held up a hand to stop them coming in, but then was overcome with another wave of nausea.

It took the various participants a while to adjust to the changes in the room. Some noticed the food first ('Look at that cake! Dima, you've outdone yourself!'). Others noticed Trixie and Fleck ('What are they doing here?'). They milled around in some confusion.

The door burst open once more and Ranveer rushed inside. His mouth fell open when he saw Trixie and Fleck.

Charlie wrestled against his restraints and gave Helen a look of appeal. Helen picked up the scissors and moved towards him. Trixie and Fleck stood to block Helen from getting to him. Max croaked, 'No!'

Helen stopped and put her hands on her hips. 'Somebody needs to tell me what is going on right now.'

'If you would untie me, Helen, I'll tell you everything.' Charlie was so *compelling*. Even Fleck was almost convinced that he was in charge of the situation.

'No! You need to listen!' Fleck said. 'It's him! It's been him all along! He's dangerous! He's a murderer!'

'I'm afraid the poor woman is unwell, as you can see,' Charlie said. 'I believe she's having some sort of episode. But I really need to get out of these ties. They're starting to affect my circulation.'

'Is Charlie *tied to the wall*? What is this?' This was Jo, who had a bit of catching up to do.

'Why, in the name of all that is good and holy, are we listening to these ridiculous women?' Douglas looked around the room in outrage.

'Pardon me,' Ranveer jumped in. 'We need to show some proper respect to these ridiculous women.'

'Who are you?'

'I am Ranveer Singh. I am a certified practising accountant.'

'Okay, let's all just everyone stop,' Fleck said. 'Have a sandwich. They're very good. And let's not untie Charlie just yet. Trixie and I will explain everything.'

Trixie looked at Fleck. 'Where do we start?'

'I don't know.'

'Okay, we have been pandering to these women's delusions for far too long,' Charlie said. He strained against his restraints. 'Enough is enough. I would like to go home now. *Please untie my hands.*'

'We will once the police get here. Sit tight till then.' Trixie could have been giving cheerful crochet instructions.

'The *police*?' Helen exclaimed. 'What is going on? Will somebody please tell me what is going on?'

'We're getting there, Helen,' Fleck said. 'How about you take a seat?'

'I don't even understand why you are here in the first place,' Helen retorted. '*She* is no longer a volunteer and *you* never were!'

'Would somebody *please* untie me and put a stop to this nonsense?'

'No …' This was Max, his voice barely a croak now.

'What have you done to John?' Helen asked. 'He really does not look well.'

'I think he might be concussed,' Fleck said. 'He suffered a head injury about half an hour ago.'

'You see?' Charlie said. 'She's violent! She's unhinged! Please let me go! I need to get away from her!'

'I'm calling the police,' Helen said, taking charge.

'The police have already been called,' Fleck assured her. 'They're already on their way. Max *is* the police.'

'Who on earth is Max?' Helen said.

'Sorry, I meant John. John is Max and Max is the police.' Max confirmed this with a weak thumbs-up.

Helen narrowed her eyes and looked from Fleck to Trixie to Max and Charlie. Everybody else – the people from the drop-in centre, Bev, Douglas, Jo, Dima, the facilitator lady – they all watched Helen. Slowly, Helen pulled a chair out from the table and sat down, facing Fleck. 'All right,' she said. 'I'm listening.'

Speaking quickly and dodging interruptions from an increasingly desperate Charlie, Fleck told everyone about the laundered money, about how Trixie had been framed, about the trafficking ring, about Donna's murder. As she spoke, the others gradually found seats, all listening carefully to her explanation.

Helen had turned quite pale. When Fleck finished, she stood and walked deliberately to stand opposite Charlie. She stepped right in his space and spoke quietly and viciously, enunciating her fricatives so that small flecks of spittle landed in his face.

'You stole from us. You used our organisation to exploit vulnerable women. You treat human beings like they are some sort of commodity. You murdered an innocent person. Death is too good for you.'

She turned on her heel and walked to a large, quilted dandelion bag at the side of the room. She looked almost deranged in her determination as she rummaged, throwing scraps of fabric and spools of thread aside.

'What are you doing, Helen?' asked Bev nervously. It was Bev's bag, after all.

Helen stood up. She was holding a very large pair of fabric scissors. 'I plan to emasculate Charlie with these.' She was quite matter of fact.

'Stop!' Bev looked properly alarmed.

'What?' Helen raised a single eyebrow at Bev, as Charlie squealed and scrabbled desperately at his bonds.

'Not with the *good* scissors!'

And then the uniformed police were in the room, and everything started moving very quickly.

The paramedics, who arrived at the same time, moved in as soon as Charlie was apprehended to tend to Max and to check everybody else for shock. It was possible Charlie needed them most of all. His face had turned lily-white, and his wary eyes did not leave Helen until he was safely led away.

EPILOGUE

'Helen can't do her shift today,' Trixie said. 'Douglas is going to cover it, but he's running late. I might have to duck out to cover the register if customers come in.'

Fleck and Trixie sat at the back-room table in Many Hands. They were working on their cross-stitches. Norah sat at their feet, digging through a box of felt scraps.

'No worries,' Fleck said. 'By the way, do you know how to make orange cake?' She was studying the back of her work, pulling at threads.

'Orange cake?'

'Ranveer gave me a big bag of navel oranges from his tree.'

'I think you use almond meal and you boil the oranges whole,' Trixie said. 'Dima would know. She's coming in after lunch.'

'Oh, good idea. I'll ask her. I was going to use them make a "get well" cake for Max, but I didn't have a recipe, so I still need to use them.'

'Max?' Trixie asked.

'Dull John.'

'Oh, yeah.'

'Then I thought I'd make him Chatters' Crack, but I burned it and didn't have any more Saladas. In the end, I made him blonde brownies – you know, the ones that are like one hundred per cent brown sugar?'

'I know the ones.'

'But by the time I got organised, they weren't a "get well" present. They were a "welcome back to work" present. Anyway, he told me all about the case. I took notes.' Fleck put her cross-stitch down and opened up her everything book.

'So Max said they've made five new arrests, which brings the total up to twenty-seven. And he's not really supposed to say anything about an ongoing investigation, but he called it a "major sting". And he did say the interviews are going really well. With Charlie out of the picture, it's a bit of a race for who can be the first to dob on the others. He also hinted that the backpack full of notebooks has been really important evidence.'

'He hasn't taken the backpack, has he? That's a good backpack!'

'Nah. Just the notebooks. The backpack's in the laundry.'

'What about all of the victims in this?'

'Well, it's looking like they will be able to have a funeral for Donna next week. Once they found her body, it was a straightforward homicide investigation.'

Trixie gulped and nodded. They were quiet for a moment, each thinking her own thoughts. Then Fleck continued. 'As for the victims of the trafficking operation, they are now receiving care from the Red Cross.'

'That's good to hear,' Trixie said.

'So you're back on after this? You've got your Tuesday morning shift back volunteering after the workshop?'

Trixie smiled and leaned back in her seat. 'That's right. I'm volunteering again, all the charges have been dropped and I get to stay in my beautiful little house. Everything has come good.' She paused as she pulled the embroidery thread through her work. 'Hey, did Max like the brownies?'

'Well, he put them in the break room because he doesn't eat sugar.'

Trixie shook her head. 'So, what you're telling me is that he's just as boring as Max as he was as John.'

'It doesn't make you a boring person to not eat sugar,' Fleck said. 'It only makes you a boring person if you make your sugar-free lifestyle the cornerstone of your entire personality and believe everyone is aching to hear you talk about it. Max wasn't like that. He was nice about the brownies. He said it would get him into everybody's good books.'

'It would give him brownie points?' Trixie said, smiling impishly.

'I'm going to pretend you didn't just say that,' Fleck replied.

The bell rang as some customers entered the shop. Trixie started to put her work away. They could hear the subdued voices of two men talking. Then one of the voices exclaimed more audibly: 'Oh my gosh! They've got Baby Yoda here! Oh my *gosh*! We need to buy it!'

Trixie stood up quickly to look through the curtain. Fleck stood beside her and looked too.

'I know that man!' Fleck said. 'Not the one talking – the quiet one. That's Douglas's son!'

Fleck and Trixie stepped into the shop and went to stand behind the counter. The man who'd been talking, who must be Kenneth, approached them both. 'Hello, we're looking for Douglas Cooper. We were told he'd be here?'

Trixie smiled. 'Yes. Douglas is running a little late, but he'll be here soon. If you'd like—'

'You're looking for Douglas Cooper?' Fleck's voice came out breathless and squeaky.

'Yeah. He's Martin's dad, my father-in-law,' Kenneth said. 'I only got to meet him for the first time a month ago. We've caught up a couple of times since then. Anyway, I've decided it's *my* job to make sure they *keep* catching up because they are both emotionally constipated white men.'

'Kenneth …' Martin was frowning.

'Well, am I *wrong*?' Kenneth leaned towards Trixie and Fleck. 'Oversharing is my special skill. Anyway, we thought we'd surprise him today and take him out.'

Martin was looking at Fleck. 'Do I know you from somewhere?'

Fleck could feel her cheeks reddening. 'I think I just have one of those faces.'

The door of the shop opened, and Douglas walked in. Fleck had never seen Douglas Cooper smile – it was simply not a facial expression the man made. Douglas did not smile now, but the frown lines softened momentarily around his face. In another person, Fleck thought, this would be the equivalent of a beam.

'We are here to take you out, old man,' Kenneth sang. 'We are going somewhere delicious for lunch. Our treat.'

'Nowhere spicy,' said Martin.

'Nowhere spicy,' conceded Kenneth. 'Honestly, you two are impossible.'

'I can't come,' Douglas said. 'I need to man the shop …'

The door opened and Helen walked in. 'So, it turns out I can work my shift after all. Thanks anyway, Doug.' Her face broke into a genuine smile. 'It's so good to see you, Marty.'

As Helen, Douglas, Kenneth and Martin fell into conversation, Fleck and Trixie returned to the back room and resumed their cross-stitching. Norah was still absorbed in her little felt village under the table.

'Helen's looking good,' Fleck commented.

'Did I tell you she joined the board?' Trixie said. 'And she's nominating for chair. I think she'd be perfect for it.' She looked like she meant it.

Fleck peered at her. 'You've really changed your mind on her, haven't you?'

Trixie shrugged. 'We still clash, but I think we just understand each other better these days. Helen said they're going to advertise to hire a paid manager for the shop and she asked if I would consider the role. I'm definitely thinking about it.'

'That's great!' Fleck said. 'You'd be an excellent manager.' She put the last few stitches into her cross-stitch design and held it up for Trixie to inspect. *Kindred spirits.* Fleck had followed the pattern faithfully. Two girls stood side by side in dresses with boots and aprons. The only difference was that the Diana figure, the one who stood beside Anne with her red braids and flat straw hat, had hair stitched with turquoise-coloured thread.

'That's a perfect design,' Trixie said. 'There's just one problem with it.'

'I made a mistake?' Fleck said, looking over her work.

'Yes,' Trixie said matter-of-factly. 'You see, I'm Anne. You're Diana.'

Fleck made an affronted gasp. 'I think you'll find that I am Anne. I have the right hair for it.'

'Being Anne is about more than hair!'

'Maybe we can both be Anne?' Fleck offered. 'Only you're Anne with different hair?'

'Okay, deal.'

Trixie gave Fleck a sideways hug and planted a kiss on the top of her head. They sat quietly for a bit.

Eventually, Fleck spoke. 'I think I finally know what I want to do for my hobby, but it's a bit weird.'

'You're talking to someone who makes birds out of yarn,' Trixie said. 'How weird can it be?'

'Matthew has the kids all day this Saturday,' Fleck said. 'I want to spend it solving a mystery.'

'What mystery?'

'I don't know yet. I know it's silly. I just get so curious about things. I just want to solve real-life puzzles. It feels like the thing that lights me up inside.'

'Well, what's stopping you?' Trixie asked.

'Because it's not a thing. *It's not a thing.* Who does that?'

'Is that a reason?'

'What do you mean?'

'That doesn't sound like a reason not to do it.'

'Well, it kind of is …'

'Nope!'

'But people are going to say—'

'That also doesn't sound like a reason.'

'What?'

'People will say stuff anyway. Let them say stuff. It's none of your business.'

'But I can't just—'

'Are you waiting for somebody to give you permission to do the thing? 'Cos that can be me.' Trixie snatched a flyer advertising an upcoming crafting workshop off the table and flipped it to its blank side. She fished a pen out of her bag. As she wrote, she read the words aloud: 'I hereby give Felicity Parker permission to do the thing that gives her joy.' She wrote the date on the form and signed it with a flourish. She grinned as she handed the piece of paper to Fleck. 'Now you can be a detective. May all your problems be perfect. May all your solutions sing.'

Marian had texted, incorporating an impressive string of emojis, to say that she was running a little late. Fleck had put everything she needed for her Thursday me-time by the front door in a little backpack. Norah bounced by the window in anticipation. 'Grandma! It's Grandma! I saw Grandma! It's Grandma!'

Marian's arms were full of bags and baskets. Fleck thought she saw an economy-sized tin of Milo peeking out of one of them. 'You would not believe the traffic on Station Street! You would think it was peak hour, but it wasn't. It was backed right back. All the way back to – now what's the name of that street? You know the one I mean? Oh, it's on the tip of my tongue, but it was backed right back. Right, right back. I should have taken a *rat run*. Matthew is so good with his rat runs – oh, well, I don't need to tell you that! But he has always been good at finding those little shortcuts. I'm always worried I'll get lost or go backwards by mistake. I don't have Matthew's internal compass. But what are you still doing here?' She looked accusingly at Fleck. 'You need to get out of here and have your time. We're fine here, aren't we, Norah? We're going to have a lovely time. Just let me put my things down and hand me that beautiful baby. You head off right now, Felicity. Off you go! I'm sure you have plenty of things to be getting on with.'

Fleck beamed and picked up her bag. 'I do. I really do.'

When Fleck arrived at George's cafe, he was out the front with a cloth and a can of WD-40. The white bricks of the cafe had been defaced by a large graffiti tag. *TACO* was scrawled across the wall in jagged purple writing beside some sort of stylised picture – a taco, perhaps? It was hard to tell.

'So, this is the graffiti,' Fleck said. 'When did it happen?'

'Just yesterday. Usually I'd get my landlord to deal with it, but he's on holiday so I thought I'd try to attack it now. That's the thing with graffiti. You have to get on it right away, otherwise more will come.'

Nip it in the butt, thought Fleck. She squinted at the wall. 'Weird. It doesn't look like graffiti. You know what I mean? Usually, you can't clearly read the words in a tag, but these ones you can. It looks like the sort of graffiti you'd do if you've never done it before.'

George shook the cloth out and folded it. 'Amateurs, I guess. And there's something funny about the paint they used. Look at it. It doesn't seem the same as regular spray-paint. It doesn't clean the same either.'

It was true. The paint was metallic and glossy. It seemed off, somehow. And it wasn't violently bright, like most spray paints. The colour was deep and muted.

Felicity frowned at the wall. 'Do you often get graffiti?'

George shrugged. 'That's the funny thing. I used to get it every now and then, maybe once a month or once every two months. But lately, it's happening all the time. I don't know who it is. It's driving me nuts!'

'Is it the same person each time, do you think?'

George put the lid back on the aerosol can and nodded. 'Definitely the same person. Come on, I'll make you a coffee.'

He walked into the cafe. Fleck began to follow him, then paused. She took a photo of the graffiti, one from a distance, another close up. Then she pocketed a pebble on the ground that was covered in the shiny purple paint and followed him inside.

It was the midmorning lull. Fleck was the only customer in the small cafe. She gazed out of the window as she sipped her coffee. 'It's all down the street as well,' she said.

George squinted across the street. 'Yup. All down Highett Road. But none on Peppercorn Street. Whoever it is always seems to target that strip of shops across the road. I went to the council about it last week. It was getting to be too much, and the landlord hadn't fixed it. Plus, there's that broken window in the empty shop. It just looks bad.'

Fleck frowned and tapped her pencil. 'If I were a vandal, I wouldn't work on a main road with cars driving past all night. I'd do it on Peppercorn Street. More privacy, but still, lots of people would see it the next day.'

George shook his head. 'Nah, see, that's the other thing,' he said. 'The graffiti on my wall? It didn't happen at night. Whoever did this did it in broad daylight.'

'How do you know?'

George leaned forward. 'Yesterday I shut up the cafe at two thirty. Since it was Wednesday I had my catering job for the retirement place up the road. Forty-three orders for corned beef with white sauce, with chocolate pudding for dessert. Beautiful. The oldies love it. I come back after and the graffiti's all over the wall.' He leaned back, raising his eyebrows significantly.

'What time was that?' Fleck asked.

'It would have been no later than seven.'

She squinted out the window. 'Why are they targeting that strip? Why are they using strange paint? Why now? And it's not like they're a seasoned professional. Why would an amateur start out on a public road? And in broad daylight?' She looked at George. 'What is the deal with this graffiti?'

George grinned. 'So, what do you think? Do you want to take on the case?'

Fleck's pencil oscillated between her thumb and index finger.

She was still thinking. Then she blinked and smiled. 'It's a delicious mystery.'

George fired up the coffee machine as he spotted one of his regulars approaching from across the street. Fleck turned to a fresh page in her everything book. Her mind was still turning over the facts of the case. At the top of the page she wrote, *The Mystery of the Purple Tags*.

ACKNOWLEDGEMENTS

I always feel a little daunted when it comes to writing acknowledgements. I never feel like I can thank people hard enough. I'm terrified I'll forget someone important. And when you see just how many people have been involved in the putting-together of this book, you'll wonder if I did anything at all. The jig will be up.

From an early age, sitting at the dinner table, my family has listened to me and encouraged me to tell entertaining stories. When I write, they are the ones I imagine reading it. Mum, Dad and Ma Ma, Daniel, Emily, James, Michael and Felicity. They continue to help me in so many ways, only now they come with bonus features. Dani, Luke, Kathy, Sarah and Hatchy, I'm so glad you're sitting around the table now too.

My sisters, Emily Walter and Felicity Neeson, are my first readers. Thank you for all of your work as sounding boards for my plot problems.

Many Hands is inspired by some real-life charities I have had the privilege of being involved with. At least, the good and inspiring parts are! Both of these organisations are scrupulously transparent, and I made Many Hands the opposite in this respect. Many thanks to the Caroline Chisholm Society and the St Vincent de Paul Society for providing me with the inspiration of decent, hardworking people who see a need and seek to do something about it.

ACRATH (Australian Catholic Religious Against Trafficking in

Humans) is a real organisation. I am immensely grateful to Sister Joan Kennedy, who shared morning tea and discussed suburban slavery with me. Any errors here are my own.

Not long after my first book was published, it seemed to make friends with a couple of other books on the 'New Releases' shelf. I am grateful every day that Kerryn Mayne, Emma Grey and I decided to become friends too. Thank you for your constant support.

Look, Julian Sargeant isn't George. And Julian's Kitchen isn't George's Kitchen. BUT I'm grateful that I have a lovely little corner cafe in which to write and chat and do the quiz. Julian has also been an invaluable font of knowledge for all of my cafe-related questions.

The 'countries' puzzle that has Fleck so preoccupied at the start of the novel was presented to me as a delicious morsel by my then eleven-year-old son, who knows I relish such things. When I told him I wanted to thank him in the acknowledgements, he let me know he'd found the puzzle in the newspaper. It was one of David Astle's Wordwits. So thank you to DA for providing the brainteaser, and thank you to James for knowing I would like it.

Michael Walter loaned me his laptop for many months. Bob and Nola Solly allowed me to write in their beautiful quiet house. I stole the idea of TV Tinder from fellow writer Averil Robertson and her husband, Wayne. Thank you!

Julian Roberts is my friend at the school gate. He loaned me his favourite crime novels and patiently taught me how to defraud a charity, drawing flowcharts of dummy companies as our children climbed over the playground at pick-up time. While I'm at it, I want to put it in writing that I love the parents at my children's primary school. They are a beautiful and supportive community, and I've never once heard them discuss reality television. Fleck's experiences are not my own!

The bookish community is a wonderful space. I have met so many warm, supportive and incredibly generous writers, readers, librarians, bookshop owners and bookstagrammers since I published my first book. I want to thank the established writers who held my hand and explained things to me, especially Lisa Ireland, Kylie Orr, Sandie Docker, Cate Kennedy, Toni Jordan, Jack Heath, Rachael Johns, Josephine Moon and Kate Mildenhall. Thank you also to the writers who read an early copy of my book for endorsements.

For Andy Hamilton and the beautiful group of writers and creatives who meet at his house on the occasional Sunday afternoon. For Tara Marlow and the Type-In Tuesday crew, Jodi Gibson and Thursday's Write Squad, and Sandie Docker and the Friday Morning Scribblers. Thank you for your writerly support.

Leanne Tran purchased the right to name a character in a silent auction for charity, as a gift for her friend Chelle Griffin. They didn't ask me to say this, but I think you should really check out their excellent podcast *Between the Lines*. It's a great listen.

To Sergeant Peter Northey, for once again assisting me with policing questions (and being so lovely about it). To Lisa Johnson, who prayed a novena to Mary, Undoer of Knots (yes, that's a thing), when I was desperately trying to fix plot issues. It brought me such peace. And I'd like to send a grateful prayer for Saint Therese of Lisieux. Her philosophy helped me through the hardest times.

There are some people I want to thank who gave me inspiration from afar. I pictured Dima's gorgeous cakes as being just like the cakes that Kate Pritchett (of Chat 10 Looks 3 fame) displays on her Instagram page (@ rarerollingobject). When I was developing Trixie's personality as an avid crafter, I imagined her as being a bit like Adele from @cro_with_the_flo. Adele also crochets budgies. Trixie's analogue desk was an idea I got from Holly Ringland's *The House That Joy Built* (a most excellent read).

I would also like to thank Kerryn Mayne for taking the time to read an early version of this and for giving feedback and reassurance.

This might sound strange, but I want to thank a Facebook group. The Chat 10 Looks 3 Community has done so much to support and encourage me. Thank you to all Chatters, and especially the tireless Brendalings!

To everyone at Affirm Press, but especially Kelly Doust, Zoe Sorenson, Armelle Davies, Dana Anderson, Alistair Trapnell, Susie Kennewell and Kevin O'Brien. You really helped me through this.

For my beautiful children, thank you for your patience and constant encouragement.

For David Solly, the love of my life, for slipping a block of chocolate into my laptop bag when I was going through some gruelling edits, lavishing attention upon our younger children when Mummy kept having to go off writing at night, and pressing me to dig deeper when I insisted on too-easy solutions for my plot problems. (I know I sulked and didn't express appreciation for your blunt observations at the time, but they really were helpful!)

Writing a second book to be published is a privilege, it's true. But it's also rather terrifying. There were many (*many*) times I worried I didn't have it in me. When I thank people for 'encouraging me', that isn't a small thing. That's huge. And now you, beautiful reader, are taking a chance on me and reading the book I was scared I couldn't create. It means the world. Thank you. Thank you.

BOOK CLUB QUESTIONS

1. Do you like puzzles such as Wordle or cryptic crosswords? Which do you most enjoy? Why do you think Fleck is so attracted to solving puzzles?

2. Are Fleck and Trixie well suited as friends? Did this portrayal of female friendship resonate with you?

3. Are you a crafter? Do you have any hobbies? How do they enrich your life? And you can't say hobbies are stupid. That's the patriarchy talking.

4. Why do you think Helen and Trixie argue so much? Do you think their ceasefire will last?

5. Were there any surprises for you when reading the book? Which twists did you pick? Which ones came out of nowhere?

6. 'Fleck had become used to the facial expression people made when she told them her job was being a stay-at-home mum' – have you experienced a sense of being invisible in your own life?

7. Who was your favourite minor character? Was there a character who you simply couldn't stand?

8. Why do you think that cosy mysteries are gaining in popularity right now? What other writers do you enjoy in this genre?

9. Unlike Kate Solly's first novel, where neurodivergence is suggested but not named, many of the Autistic and ADHD characters in this novel are openly identified. Why do you think the author chose to do this? What is your response to the discussions around neurodiversity in this book?

10. At the beginning of the novel, Fleck doesn't know what to do with her free time. Have you ever experienced a loss of identity due to an intense caring role?